THE SEA

JOHN BANVILLE

THE SEA

PICADOR

First published 2005 by Picador
an imprint of Pan Macmillan Ltd
Pan Macmillan, 20 New Wharf Road, London NI 9RR
Basingstoke and Oxford
Associated companies throughout the world
www.panmacmillan.com

ISBN 0 330 48328 5 HB
ISBN 0 330 43625 2 TPB

Copyright © John Banville 2005

9 8

A CIP catalogue record for this book is available from
the British Library.

Typeset by SetSystems Ltd, Saffron Walden, Essex
Printed and bound in Great Britain by
Mackays of Chatham plc, Chatham, Kent

To Colm, Douglas, Ellen, Alice

I

THEY DEPARTED, the gods, on the day of the strange tide. All morning under a milky sky the waters in the bay had swelled and swelled, rising to unheard-of heights, the small waves creeping over parched sand that for years had known no wetting save for rain and lapping the very bases of the dunes. The rusted hulk of the freighter that had run aground at the far end of the bay longer ago than any of us could remember must have thought it was being granted a relaunch. I would not swim again, after that day. The seabirds mewled and swooped, unnerved, it seemed, by the spectacle of that vast bowl of water bulging like a blister, lead-blue and malignantly agleam. They looked unnaturally white, that day, those birds. The waves were depositing a fringe of soiled yellow foam along the waterline. No sail marred the high horizon. I would not swim, no, not ever again.

Someone has just walked over my grave. Someone.

The name of the house is the Cedars, as of old. A bristling clump of those trees, monkey-brown with a tarry reek, their trunks nightmarishly tangled, still grows at the left side, facing across an untidy lawn to the big curved window of what used to be the living room but which Miss Vavasour prefers to call, in landladyese, the lounge. The front door is at the opposite side, opening on to a square of oil-stained gravel behind the iron gate that is still painted green, though rust has reduced its struts to a tremulous filigree. I am amazed at how little has changed in the more than fifty years that have gone by since I was last here. Amazed, and disappointed, I would go so far as to say appalled, for reasons that are obscure to me, since why should I desire change, I who have come back to live amidst the rubble of the past? I wonder why the house was built like that, sideways-on, turning a pebble-dashed windowless white end-wall to the road; perhaps in former times, before the railway, the road ran in a different orientation altogether, passing directly in front of the front door, anything is possible. Miss V. is vague on dates but thinks a cottage was first put up here early in the last century, I mean the century before last, I am losing track of the millennia, and then was added on to haphazardly over the years. That would account for the jumbled look of the place, with small rooms giving on to bigger ones, and windows facing blank walls, and low ceilings throughout. The pitchpine floors sound a nautical note, as does my spindle-backed swivel chair. I imagine an old seafarer dozing by the fire, landlubbered at last, and the winter gale rattling the window frames. Oh, to be him. To have been him.

When I was here all those years ago, in the time of the gods, the Cedars was a summer house, for rent by the fortnight or the month. During all of June each year a rich doctor and his large, raucous family infested it – we did not like the doctor's loud-voiced children, they laughed at us and threw stones from behind the unbreachable barrier of the gate – and after them a mysterious middle-aged couple came, who spoke to no one, and grimly walked their sausage dog in silence at the same time every morning down Station Road to the strand. August was the most interesting month at the Cedars, for us. The tenants then were different each year, people from England or the Continent, the odd pair of honeymooners whom we would try to spy on, and once even a fit-up troupe of itinerant theatre people who were putting on an afternoon show in the village's galvanised-tin cinema. And then, that year, came the family Grace.

The first thing I saw of them was their motor car, parked on the gravel inside the gate. It was a low-slung, scarred and battered black model with beige leather seats and a big spoked polished wood steering wheel. Books with bleached and dog-eared covers were thrown carelessly on the shelf under the sportily raked back window, and there was a touring map of France, much used. The front door of the house stood wide open, and I could hear voices inside, downstairs, and from upstairs the sound of bare feet running on floorboards and a girl laughing. I had paused by the gate, frankly eavesdropping, and now suddenly a man with a drink in his hand came out of the house. He was short and top-heavy, all shoulders and chest and big round head, with close-cut, crinkled, glittering-black hair with flecks of premature grey in it and a pointed black beard likewise flecked. He wore a loose green shirt unbuttoned and khaki shorts and was barefoot. His skin was so deeply tanned by the sun it had a purplish sheen. Even his feet, I noticed, were brown on the insteps; the majority of fathers in my experience were fish-belly white below the collar-line. He set his tumbler – ice-blue gin and ice cubes and a lemon slice – at a perilous angle on the roof of the car and opened the passenger door and leaned inside to rummage for something under the dashboard. In the unseen upstairs of the house the girl laughed again and gave a wild, warbling cry of mock-panic, and again there was the sound of scampering feet. They were playing chase, she and the voiceless other. The man straightened and took his glass of gin from the roof and slammed the car door. Whatever it was he had been searching for he had not found. As he turned back to the house his eye caught mine and he winked. He did not do it in the way that adults usually did, at once arch and ingratiating. No, this was a comradely, a conspiratorial wink, masonic, almost, as if this moment that we, two strangers, adult and boy, had shared, although outwardly without significance, without content, even, nevertheless had meaning. His eyes were an extraordinary pale transparent shade of blue. He went back inside then, already talking before he was through the door. 'Damned thing,' he said, 'seems to be . . .' and was gone. I lingered a moment, scanning the upstairs windows. No face appeared there.

That, then, was my first encounter with the Graces: the girl's voice coming down from on high, the running footsteps, and the man here below with the blue eyes giving me that wink, jaunty, intimate and faintly satanic.

Just now I caught myself at it again, that thin, wintry whistling through the front teeth that I have begun to do recently. *Deedle deedle deedle*, it goes, like a dentist's drill. My father used to whistle like that, am I turning into him? In the room across the corridor Colonel Blunden is playing the wireless. He favours the afternoon talk programmes, the ones in which irate members of the public call up to complain about villainous politicians and the price of drink and other perennial irritants. 'Company,' he says shortly, and clears his throat, looking a little abashed, his protuberant, parboiled eyes avoiding mine, even though I have issued no challenge. Does he lie on the bed while he listens? Hard to picture him there in his thick grey woollen socks, twiddling his toes, his tie off and shirt collar agape and hands clasped behind that stringy old neck of his. Out of his room he is vertical man itself, from the soles of his much-mended glossy brown brogues to the tip of his conical skull. He has his hair cut every Saturday morning by the village barber, short-back-and-sides, no quarter given, only a hawkish stiff grey crest left on top. His long-lobed leathery ears stick out, they look as if they had been dried and smoked; the whites of his eyes too have a smoky yellow tinge. I can hear the buzz of voices on his wireless but cannot make out what they say. I may go mad here. *Deedle deedle.*

Later that day, the day the Graces came, or the following one, or the one following that, I saw the black car again, recognised it at once as it went bounding over the little humpbacked bridge that spanned the railway line. It is still there, that bridge, just beyond the station. Yes, things endure, while the living lapse. The car was heading out of the village in the direction of the town, I shall call it Ballymore, a dozen miles away. The town is Ballymore, this village is Ballyless, ridiculously, perhaps, but I do not care. The man with the beard who had winked at me was at the wheel, saying something and laughing, his head thrown back. Beside him a woman sat with an elbow out of the rolled-down window, her head back too, pale hair shaking in the gusts from the window, but she was not laughing only smiling, that smile she reserved for him, sceptical, tolerant, languidly amused. She wore a white blouse and sunglasses with white plastic rims and was smoking a cigarette. Where am I, lurking in what place of vantage? I do not see myself. They were gone in a moment, the car's sashaying back-end scooting around a bend in the road with a spurt of exhaust smoke. Tall grasses in the ditch, blond like the woman's hair, shivered briefly and returned to their former dreaming stillness.

I walked down Station Road in the sunlit emptiness of afternoon. The beach at the foot of the hill was a fawn shimmer under indigo. At the seaside all is narrow horizontals, the world reduced to a few long straight lines pressed between earth and sky. I approached the Cedars circumspectly. How is it that in childhood everything new that caught my interest had an aura of the uncanny, since according to all the authorities the uncanny is not some new thing but a thing known returning in a different form, become a revenant? So many unanswerables, this the least of them. As I approached I heard a regular rusty screeching sound. A boy of my age was draped on the green gate, his arms hanging limply down from the top bar, propelling himself with one foot slowly back and forth in a quarter circle over the gravel. He had the same straw-pale hair as the woman in the car and the man's unmistakable azure eyes. As I walked slowly past, and indeed I may even have paused, or faltered, rather, he stuck the toe of his plimsoll into the gravel to stop the swinging gate and looked at me with an expression of hostile enquiry. It was the way we all looked at each other, we children, on first encounter. Behind him I could see all the way down the narrow garden at the back of the house to the diagonal row of trees skirting the railway line – they are gone now, those trees, cut down to make way for a row of pastel-coloured bungalows like dolls' houses – and beyond, even, inland, to where the fields rose and there were cows, and tiny bright bursts of yellow that were gorse bushes, and a solitary distant spire, and then the sky, with scrolled white clouds. Suddenly, startlingly, the boy pulled a grotesque face at me, crossing his eyes and letting his tongue loll on his lower lip. I walked on, conscious of his mocking eye following me.

Plimsoll. Now, there is a word one does not hear any more, or rarely, very rarely. Originally sailors' footwear, from someone's name, if I recall, and something to do with ships. The Colonel is off to the lavatory again. Prostate trouble, I bet. Going past my door he softens his tread, creaking on tiptoe, out of respect for the bereaved. A stickler for the observances, our gallant Colonel.

I am walking down Station Road.

So much of life was stillness then, when we were young, or so it seems now; a biding stillness; a vigilance. We were waiting in our as yet unfashioned world, scanning the future as the boy and I had scanned each other, like soldiers in the field, watching for what was to come. At the bottom of the hill I stopped and stood and looked three ways, along Strand Road, and back up Station Road, and the other way, toward the tin cinema and the public tennis courts. No one. The road beyond the tennis courts was called the Cliff Walk, although whatever cliffs there may once have been the sea had long ago eroded. It was said there was a church submerged in the sandy sea bed down there, intact, with bell tower and bell, that once had stood on a headland that was gone too, brought toppling into the roiling waves one immemorial night of tempest and awful flood. Those were the stories the locals told, such as Duignan the dairyman and deaf Colfer who earned his living selling salvaged golf balls, to make us transients think their tame little seaside village had been of old a place of terrors. The sign over the Strand Café, advertising cigarettes, Navy Cut, with a picture of a bearded sailor inside a lifebuoy, or a ring of rope – was it? – creaked in the sea breeze on its salt-rusted hinges, an echo of the gate at the Cedars on which for all I knew the boy was swinging yet. They creak, this present gate, that past sign, to this day, to this night, in my dreams. I set off along Strand Road. Houses, shops, two hotels – the Golf, the Beach – a granite church, Myler's grocery-cum-post-office-cum-pub, and then the field – the Field – of wooden chalets one of which was our holiday home, my father's, my mother's, and mine.

If the people in the car were his parents had they left the boy on his own in the house? And where was the girl, the girl who had laughed?

The past beats inside me like a second heart.

The consultant's name was Mr Todd. This can only be considered a joke in bad taste on the part of polyglot fate. It could have been worse. There is a name De'Ath, with that fancy medial capital and apotropaic apostrophe which fool no one. This Todd addressed Anna as Mrs Morden but called me Max. I was not at all sure I liked the distinction thus made, or the gruff familiarity of his tone. His office, no, his rooms, one says rooms, as one calls him Mister not

Doctor, seemed at first sight an eyrie, although they were only on the third floor. The building was a new one, all glass and steel – there was even a glass-and-steel tubular lift shaft, aptly suggestive of the barrel of a syringe, through which the lift rose and fell hummingly like a giant plunger being alternately pulled and pressed – and two walls of his main consulting room were sheets of plate glass from floor to ceiling. When Anna and I were shown in my eyes were dazzled by a blaze of early-autumn sunlight falling down through those vast panes. The receptionist, a blonde blur in a nurse's coat and sensible shoes that squeaked – on such an occasion who would really notice the receptionist? – laid Anna's file on Mr Todd's desk and squeakingly withdrew. Mr Todd bade us sit. I could not tolerate the thought of settling myself on a chair and went instead and stood at the glass wall, looking out. Directly below me there was an oak, or perhaps it was a beech, I am never sure of those big deciduous trees, certainly not an elm since they are all dead, but a noble thing, anyway, the summer's green of its broad canopy hardly silvered yet with autumn's hoar. Car roofs glared. A young woman in a dark suit was walking away swiftly across the car park, even at that distance I fancied I could hear her high heels tinnily clicking on the tarmac.

Anna was palely reflected in the glass before me, sitting very straight on the metal chair in three-quarters profile, being the model patient, with one knee crossed on the other and her joined hands resting on her thigh. Mr Todd sat sideways at his desk riffling through the documents in her file; the pale-pink cardboard of the folder made me think of those shivery first mornings back at school after the summer holidays, the feel of brand-new schoolbooks and the somehow bodeful smell of ink and pared pencils. How the mind wanders, even on the most concentrated of occasions.

I turned from the glass, the outside become intolerable now.

Mr Todd was a burly man, not tall or heavy but very broad: one had an impression of square-ness. He cultivated a reassuringly old-fashioned manner. He wore a tweed suit with a waistcoat and watch chain, and chestnut-brown brogues that Colonel Blunden would have approved. His hair was oiled in the style of an earlier time, brushed back sternly from his forehead, and he had a moustache, short and bristly, that gave him a dogged look. I realised with a mild shock that despite these calculatedly venerable effects he could not be much more than fifty. Since when did doctors start being younger than I am? On he wrote, playing for time; I did not blame him, I would have done the same, in his place. At last he put down his pen but still was disinclined to speak, giving the earnest impression of not knowing where to begin or how. There was something studied about this hesitancy, something theatrical. Again, I understand. A doctor must be as good an actor as physician. Anna shifted on her chair impatiently.

'Well, Doctor,' she said, a little too loudly, putting on the bright, tough tone of one of those film stars of the Forties, 'is it the death sentence, or do I get life?'

The room was still. Her sally of wit, surely rehearsed, had fallen flat. I had an urge to rush forward and snatch her up in my arms, fireman-fashion, and carry her bodily out of there. I did not stir. Mr Todd looked at her in mild, hare-eyed panic, his eyebrows hovering halfway up his forehead.

'Oh, we won't let you go quite yet, Mrs Morden,' he said, showing big grey teeth in an awful smile. 'No, indeed we will not.'

Another beat of silence followed that. Anna's hands were in her lap, she looked at them, frowning, as if she had not noticed them before. My right knee took fright and set to twitching.

Mr Todd launched into a forceful disquisition, polished from repeated use, on promising treatments, new drugs, the mighty arsenal of chemical weapons he had at his command; he might have been speaking of magic potions, the alchemist's physic. Anna continued frowning at her hands; she was not listening. At last he stopped and sat gazing at her with the same desperate, leporine look as before, audibly breathing, his lips drawn back in a sort of leer and those teeth on show again.

'Thank you,' she said politely in a voice that seemed now to come from very far off. She nodded to herself. 'Yes,' more remotely still, 'thank you.'

At that, as if released, Mr Todd gave his knees a quick smack with two flat palms and jumped to his feet and fairly bustled us to the door. When Anna had gone through he turned to me and gave me a gritty, man-to-man smile, and the handshake, dry, brisk, unflinching, which I am sure he reserves for the spouses at moments such as this.

The carpeted corridor absorbed our footsteps.

The lift, pressed, plunged.

We walked out into the day as if we were stepping on to a new planet, one where no one lived but us.

*

Arrived home, we sat outside the house in the car for a long time, loath of venturing in upon the known, saying nothing, strangers to ourselves and each other as we suddenly were. Anna looked out across the bay where the furled yachts bristled in the glistening sunlight. Her belly was swollen, a round hard lump pressing against the waistband of her skirt. She had said people would think she was pregnant – 'At my age!' – and we had laughed, not looking at each other. The gulls that nested in our chimneys had all gone back to sea by now, or migrated, or whatever it is they do. Throughout that drear summer they had wheeled above the rooftops all day long, jeering at our attempts to pretend that all was well, nothing amiss, the world continuous. But there it was, squatting in her lap, the bulge that was big baby De'Ath, burgeoning inside her, biding its time.

At last we went inside, having nowhere else to go. Bright light of midday streamed in at the kitchen window and everything had a glassy, hard-edged radiance as if I were scanning the room through a camera lens. There was an impression of general, tight-lipped awkwardness, of all these homely things – jars on the shelves, saucepans on the stove, that breadboard with its jagged knife – averting their gaze from our all at once unfamiliar, afflicted presence in their midst. This, I realised miserably, this is how it would be from now on, wherever she goes the soundless clapping of the leper's bell preceding her. *How well you look!* they would exclaim, *why, we've never seen you better!* And she with her brilliant smile, putting on a brave face, poor Mrs Bones.

She stood in the middle of the floor in her coat and scarf, hands on her hips, casting about her with a vexed expression. She was still handsome then, high of cheekbone, her skin translucent, paper-fine. I always admired in particular her Attic profile, the nose a line of carven ivory falling sheer from the brow.

'Do you know what it is?' she said with bitter vehemence. 'It's inappropriate, that's what it is.'

I looked aside quickly for fear my eyes would give me away; one's eyes are always those of someone else, the mad and desperate dwarf crouched within. I knew what she meant. This was not supposed to have befallen her. It was not supposed to have befallen us, we were not that kind of people. Misfortune, illness, untimely death, these things happen to good folk, the humble ones, the salt of the earth, not to Anna, not to me. In the midst of the imperial progress that was our life together a grinning losel had stepped out of the cheering crowd and sketching a parody of a bow had handed my tragic queen the warrant of impeachment.

She put on a kettle of water to boil and fished in a pocket of her coat and brought out her spectacles and put them on, looping the string behind her neck. She began to weep, absent-mindedly, it might be, making no sound. I moved clumsily to embrace her but she drew back sharply.

'For heaven's sake don't fuss!' she snapped. 'I'm only dying, after all.'

The kettle came to the boil and switched itself off and the seething water inside it settled down grumpily. I marvelled, not for the first time, at the cruel complacency of ordinary things. But no, not cruel, not complacent, only indifferent, as how could they be otherwise? Henceforth I would have to address things as they are, not as I might imagine them, for this was a new version of reality. I took up the teapot and the tea, making them rattle – my hands were shaking – but she said no, she had changed her mind, it was brandy she wanted, brandy, and a cigarette, she who did not smoke, and rarely drank. She gave me the dull glare of a defiant child, standing there by the table in her coat. Her tears had stopped. She took off her glasses and dropped them to hang below her throat on their string and rubbed at her eyes with the heels of her hands. I found the brandy bottle and tremblingly poured a measure into a tumbler, the bottle-neck and the rim of the glass chattering against each other like teeth. There were no cigarettes in the house, where was I to get cigarettes? She said it was no matter, she did not really want to smoke. The steel kettle shone, a slow furl of steam at its spout, vaguely suggestive of genie and lamp. Oh, grant me a wish, just the one.

'Take off your coat, at least,' I said.

But why at least? What a business it is, the human discourse.

I gave her the glass of brandy and she stood holding it but did not drink. Light from the window behind me shone on the lenses of her spectacles where they hung at her collar bone, giving the eerie effect of another, miniature she standing close in front of her under her chin with eyes cast down. Abruptly she went slack and sat down heavily, extending her arms before her along the table in a strange, desperate-seeming gesture, as if in supplication to some unseen other seated opposite her in judgment. The tumbler in her hand knocked on the wood and splashed out half its contents. Helplessly I contemplated her. For a giddy second the notion seized me that I would never again be able to think of another word to say to her, that we would go on like this, in agonised inarticulacy, to the end. I bent and kissed the pale patch on the crown of her head the size of a sixpence where her dark hair whorled. She turned her face up to me briefly with a black look.

'You smell of hospitals,' she said. 'That should be me.'

I took the tumbler from her hand and put it to my lips and drank at a draught what remained of the scorching brandy. I realised what the feeling was that had been besetting me since I had stepped that morning into the glassy glare of Mr Todd's consulting rooms. It was embarrassment. Anna felt it as well, I was sure of it. Embarrassment, yes, a panic-stricken sense of not knowing what to say, where to look, how to behave, and something else, too, that was not quite anger but a sort of surly annoyance, a surly resentment at the predicament in which we grimly found ourselves. It was as if a secret had been imparted to us so dirty, so nasty, that we could hardly bear to remain in one another's company yet were unable to break free, each knowing the foul thing that the other knew and bound together by that very knowledge. From this day forward all would be dissembling. There would be no other way to live with death.

Still Anna sat erect there at the table, facing away from me, her arms extended and hands lying inert with palms upturned as if for something to be dropped into them.

'Well?' she said without turning. 'What now?'

There goes the Colonel, creeping back to his room. That was a long session in the lav. Strangury, nice word. Mine is the one bedroom in the house which is, as Miss Vavasour puts it with a demure little moue, *en suite*. Also I have a view, or would have were it not for those blasted bungalows at the bottom of the garden. My bed is daunting, a stately, high-built, Italianate affair fit for a Doge, the headboard scrolled and polished like a Stradivarius. I must enquire of Miss V. as to its provenance. This would have been the master bedroom when the Graces were here. In those days I never got further than the downstairs, except in my dreams.

I have just noticed today's date. It is a year exactly since that first visit Anna and I were forced to pay to Mr Todd in his rooms. What a coincidence. Or not, perhaps; are there coincidences in Pluto's realm, amidst the trackless wastes of which I wander lost, a lyreless Orpheus? Twelve months, though! I should have kept a diary. My journal of the plague year.

A dream it was that drew me here. In it, I was walking along a country road, that was all. It was in winter, at dusk, or else it was a strange sort of dimly radiant night, the sort of night that there is only in dreams, and a wet snow was falling. I was determinedly on my way somewhere, going home, it seemed, although I did not know what or where exactly home might be. There was open land to my right, flat and undistinguished with not a house or hovel in sight, and to my left a deep line of darkly louring trees bordering the road. The branches were not bare despite the season, and the thick, almost black leaves drooped in masses, laden with snow that had turned to soft, translucent ice. Something had broken down, a car, no, a bicycle, a boy's bicycle, for as well as being the age I am now I was a boy as well, a big awkward boy, yes, and on my way home, it must have been home, or somewhere that had been home, once, and that I would recognise again, when I got there. I had hours of walking to do but I did not mind that, for this was a journey of surpassing but inexplicable importance, one that I must make and was bound to complete. I was calm in myself, quite calm, and confident, too, despite not knowing rightly where I was going except that I was going home. I was alone on the road. The snow which had been slowly drifting down all day was unmarked by tracks of any kind, tyre, boot or hoof, for no one had passed this way and no one would. There was something the matter with my foot, the left one, I must have injured it, but long ago, for it was not painful, though at every step I had to throw it out awkwardly in a sort of half-circle, and this hindered me, not seriously but seriously enough. I felt compassion for myself, that is to say the dreamer that I was felt compassion for the self being dreamed, this poor lummox going along dauntlessly in the snow at fall of day with only the road ahead of him and no promise of homecoming.

That was all there was in the dream. The journey did not end, I arrived nowhere, and nothing happened. I was just walking there, bereft and stalwart, endlessly trudging through the snow and the wintry gloaming. But I woke into the murk of dawn not as I usually do these days, with the sense of having been flayed of yet another layer of protective skin during the night, but with the conviction that something had been achieved, or at least initiated. Immediately then, and for the first time in I do not know how long, I thought of Ballyless and the house there on Station Road, and the Graces, and Chloe Grace, I cannot think why, and it was as if I had stepped suddenly out of the dark into a splash of pale, salt-washed sunlight. It endured only a minute, less than a minute, that happy lightsomeness, but it told me what to do, and where I must go.

I first saw her, Chloe Grace, on the beach. It was a bright, wind-worried day and the Graces were settled in a shallow recess scooped into the dunes by wind and tides to which their somewhat raffish presence lent a suggestion of the proscenium. They were impressively equipped, with a faded length of striped canvas strung between poles to keep chill breezes off, and folding chairs and a little folding table, and a straw hamper as big as a small suitcase containing bottles and vacuum flasks and tins of sandwiches and biscuits; they even had real tea cups, with saucers. This was a part of the beach that was tacitly reserved for residents of the Golf Hotel, the lawn of which ended just behind the dunes, and indignant stares were being directed at these heedlessly interloping villa people with their smart beach furniture and their bottles of wine, stares which the Graces if they noticed them ignored. Mr Grace, Carlo Grace, Daddy, was wearing shorts again, and a candy-striped blazer over a chest that was bare save for two big tufts of tight curls in the shape of a miniature pair of widespread fuzzy wings. I had never before encountered nor, I think, have I encountered since, anyone so fascinatingly hairy. On his head was clamped a canvas hat like a child's upturned sand bucket. He was sitting on one of the folding chairs, holding a newspaper open before him and at the same time managing to smoke a cigarette, despite the stiff wafts of wind coming in from the sea. The blond boy, the swinger on the gate – it was Myles, I may as well give him his name – was crouched at his father's feet, pouting moodily and delving in the sand with a jagged piece of sea-polished driftwood. Some way behind them, in the shelter of the dune wall, a girl, or young woman, was kneeling on the sand, wrapped in a big red towel, under the cover of which she was trying vexedly to wriggle herself free of what would turn out to be a wet bathing suit. She was markedly pale and soulful of expression, with a long, slender face and very black, heavy hair. I noticed that she kept glancing, resentfully, as it seemed, at the back of

Carlo Grace's head. I noticed too that the boy Myles was keeping sidelong watch, in the evident hope, which I shared, that the girl's protective towel would slip. She could hardly be his sister, then.

Mrs Grace came up the beach. She had been in the sea and was wearing a black swimsuit, tight and darkly lustrous as sealskin, and over it a sort of wraparound skirt made of some diaphanous stuff, held at the waist with a single button and billowing open with each step she took to reveal her bare, tanned, rather thick but shapely legs. She stopped in front of her husband and pushed her white-rimmed sunglasses up into her hair and waited through the beat that he allowed to pass before he lowered the newspaper and looked up at her, lifting his hand that held the cigarette and shading his eyes against the salt-sharpened light. She said something and he put his head on one side and shrugged, and smiled, showing numerous small white even teeth. Behind him the girl, still under the towel, discarded her bathing suit that she had freed herself of at last and, turning her back, sat down on the sand with her legs flexed and made the towel into a tent around herself and rested her forehead on her knees, and Myles drove his stick into the sand with disappointed force.

So there they were, the Graces: Carlo Grace and his wife Constance, their son Myles, the girl or young woman who I was sure was not the girl I had heard laughing in the house that first day, with all their things around them, their folding chairs and tea cups and tumblers of white wine, and Connie Grace's revealing skirt and her husband's funny hat and newspaper and cigarette, and Myles's stick, and the girl's swimsuit, lying where she had tossed it, limply wadded and stuck along one wet edge with a fringe of sand, like something thrown up drowned out of the sea.

I do not know for how long Chloe had been standing on the dune before she jumped. She may have been there all that time, watching me watching the others. She was first a silhouette, with the sun behind her making a shining helmet of her short-cropped hair. Then she lifted her arms and with her knees pressed together launched herself off the dune wall. The air made the legs of her shorts balloon briefly. She was barefoot, and landed on her heels, sending up a shower of sand. The girl under the towel – Rose, give her a name too, poor Rosie – uttered a little shriek of fright. Chloe wobbled, her arms still lifted and her heels in the sand, and it seemed she would fall over or at least sit down hard, but instead she kept her balance, and smiled sideways spitefully at Rose who had sand in her eyes and was making a fish face and shaking her head and blinking. '*Chlo*-e!' Mrs Grace said, a reproving wail, but Chloe ignored her and came forward and knelt in the sand beside her brother and tried to wrest the stick from him. I was lying on my stomach on a towel with my cheeks propped on my hands, pretending to read a book. Chloe knew I was looking at her and seemed not to care. What age were we, ten, eleven? Say eleven, it will do. Her chest was as flat as Myles's, her hips were no wider than mine. She wore a white singlet over her shorts. Her sun-bleached hair was almost white. Myles, who had been battling to keep his stick, snatched it free of her grasp at last and hit her with it on the knuckles and she said 'Ow!' and struck him in the breastbone with a small, pointed fist.

'Listen to this advertisement,' her father said to no one in particular, and read aloud, laughing, from the newspaper. '*Live ferrets required as venetian blind salesmen. Must be car drivers. Apply box twenty-three.*' He laughed again, and coughed, and, coughing, laughed. 'Live ferrets!' he cried. 'Oh, my.'

How flat all sounds are at the seaside, flat and yet emphatic, like the sound of gunshots heard at a distance. It must be the muffling effect of so much sand. Although I cannot say when I have had occasion to hear a gun or guns being fired.

Mrs Grace poured wine for herself, tasted it, grimaced, and sat down in a folding chair and crossed one firm leg on the other, her beach shoe dangling. Rose was getting dressed fumblingly under her towel. Now it was Chloe's turn to draw her knees up to her chest – is it a thing all girls do, or did, at least, sitting that way in the shape of a zed fallen over on its front? – and hold her feet in her hands. Myles poked her in the side with his stick. 'Daddy,' she said with listless irritation, 'tell him to stop.' Her father went on reading. Connie Grace's dangling shoe was jiggling in time to some rhythm in her head. The sand around me with the sun strong on it gave off its mysterious, catty smell. Out on the bay a white sail shivered and flipped to leeward and for a second the world tilted. Someone away down the beach was calling to someone else. Children. Bathers. A wire-haired ginger dog. The sail turned to windward again and I heard distinctly from across the water the ruffle and snap of the canvas. Then the breeze dropped and for a moment all went still.

They played a game, Chloe and Myles and Mrs Grace, the children lobbing a ball to each other over their mother's head and she running and leaping to try to catch it, mostly in vain. When she runs her skirt billows behind her and I cannot take my eyes off the tight black bulge at the upside-down apex of her lap. She jumps, grasping air and giving breathless cries and laughing. Her breasts bounce. The sight of her is almost alarming. A creature with so many mounds and scoops of flesh to carry should not cavort like this, she will damage something inside her, some tender arrangement of adipose tissue and pearly cartilage. Her husband has lowered his newspaper and is watching her too, combing his fingers through his beard under his chin and coldly smiling, his lips drawn back a little from those fine small teeth and his nostrils flared wolfishly as if he is trying to catch her scent. His look is one of arousal, amusement and faint contempt; he seems to want to see her fall down in the sand and hurt herself; I imagine hitting him, punching him in the exact centre of his hairy chest as Chloe had punched her brother. Already I know these people, am one of them. And I have fallen in love with Mrs Grace.

Rose comes out of the towel, in red shirt and black slacks, like a magician's assistant appearing from under the magician's scarlet-lined cape, and busies herself in not looking at anything, especially the woman and her children at play.

Abruptly Chloe loses interest in the game and turns aside and flops down in the sand. How well I will come to know these sudden shifts of mood of hers, these sudden sulks. Her mother calls to her to come back and play but she does not respond. She is lying propped on an elbow on her side with her ankles crossed, looking past me narrow-eyed out to sea. Myles does a chimp dance in front of her, flapping his hands under his armpits and gibbering. She pretends to be able to see through him. 'Brat,' her mother says of her spoilsport daughter, almost complacently, and goes back and sits down on her chair. She is out of breath, and the smooth, sand-coloured slope of her bosom heaves. She lifts a hand up high to brush a clinging strand of hair from her damp forehead and I fix on the secret shadow under her armpit, plum-blue, the tint of my humid fantasies for nights to come. Chloe sulks. Myles goes back to delving violently in the sand with his stick. Their father folds his newspaper and squints at the sky. Rose is examining a loose button on her shirt. The little waves rise and plash, the ginger dog barks. And my life is changed forever.

But then, at what moment, of all our moments,

is life not utterly, utterly changed, until the final, most momentous change of all?

We holidayed here every summer, my father and mother and I. We would not have put it that way. *We came here for our holidays*, that is what we would have said. How difficult now it is to speak as I spoke then. We came for our holidays here every summer, for many years, many years, until my father ran off to England, as fathers sometimes did, in those days, and do still, for that matter. The chalet that we rented was a slightly less than life-sized wooden model of a house. It had three rooms, a living room at the front that was also a kitchen and two tiny bedrooms at the back. There were no ceilings, only the sloped undersides of the tarpapered roof. The walls were panelled with unintentionally elegant, narrow, bevelled boards that on sunny days smelled of paint and pine-sap. My mother cooked on a paraffin stove, the tiny fuel-hole of which afforded me an obscurely furtive pleasure when I was called on to clean it, employing for the task a delicate instrument made of a strip of pliant tin with a stiff filament of wire protruding at a right angle from its tip. I wonder where it is now, that little Primus stove, so sturdy and steadfast? There was no electricity and at night we lived by the light of an oil lamp. My father worked in Ballymore and came down in the evenings on the train, in a wordless fury, bearing the frustrations of his day like so much luggage clutched in his clenched fists. What did my mother do with her time when he was gone and I was not there? I picture her sitting at the oilcloth-covered table in that little wooden house, a hand under her head, nursing her disaffections as the long day wanes. She was still young then, they both were, my father and my mother, younger certainly than I am now. How strange a thing that is to think of. Everybody seems to be younger than I am, even the dead. I see them there, my poor parents, rancorously playing at house in the childhood of the world. Their unhappiness was one of the constants of my earliest years, a high, unceasing buzz just beyond hearing. I did not hate them. I loved them, probably. Only they were in my way, obscuring my view of the future. In time I would be able to see right through them, my transparent parents.

My mother would only bathe far up the beach, away from the eyes of the hotel crowds and the noisy encampments of day trippers. Up there, past where the golf course began, there was a permanent sandbank a little way out from shore that enclosed a shallow lagoon when the tide was right. In those soupy waters she would wallow with small, mistrustful pleasure, not swimming, for she could not swim, but stretched out full-length on the surface and walking along the sea-floor on her hands, straining to keep her mouth above the lapping wavelets. She wore a crimplene swimsuit, mouse-pink, with a coy little hem stretched across tight just below the crotch. Her face looked bare and defenceless, pinched in the tight rubber seal of her bathing cap. My father was a fair swimmer, going at a sort of hindered, horizontal scramble with mechanical strokes and a gasping sideways grimace and one starting eye. At the end of a length he would rise up, panting and spitting, his hair plastered down and ears sticking out and black trunks abulge, and stand with hands on hips and watch my mother's clumsy efforts with a faint, sardonic grin, a muscle in his jaw twitching. He splashed water in her face and seized her wrists and wading backwards hauled her through the water. She shut her eyes tight and shrieked at him furiously to stop. I watched these edgy larks in a paroxysm of disgust. At last he let her go and turned on me, upending me and grasping me by the ankles and pushing me forward wheelbarrow-fashion off the edge of the sandbank and laughing. How strong his hands were, like manacles of cold, pliant iron, I feel even yet their violent grip. He was a violent man, a man of violent gestures, violent jokes, but timid, too, no wonder he left us, had to leave us. I swallowed water, and twisted out of his grasp in a panic and jumped to my feet and stood in the surf, retching.

Chloe Grace and her brother were standing on the hard sand at the water's edge, looking on.

They wore shorts as usual and were barefoot. I saw how strikingly alike they were. They had been collecting seashells, which Chloe was carrying in a handkerchief knotted corner-to-corner to make a pouch. They stood regarding us without expression, as if we were a show, a comic turn that had been laid on for them but which they found not very interesting, or funny, but peculiar only. I am sure I blushed, grey and goosepimpled though I was, and I had an acute awareness of the thin stream of seawater pouring in an unstoppable arc out of the sagging front of my swimming-trunks. Had it been in my power I would have cancelled my shaming parents on the spot, would have popped them like bubbles of sea spray, my fat little bare-faced mother and my father whose body might have been made of lard. A breeze smacked down on the beach and swarmed across it slantwise under a skim of dry sand, then came on over the water, chopping the surface into sharp little metallic shards. I shivered, not from the cold now but as if something had passed through me, silent, swift, irresistible. The pair on the shore turned and trailed off in the direction of the wrecked freighter.

Was it that day that I noticed Myles's toes were webbed?

Miss Vavasour downstairs is playing the piano. She maintains a delicate touch on the keys, trying not to be heard. She worries that she will disturb me, engaged as I am up here in my immense and unimaginably important labours. She plays Chopin very nicely. I hope she does not start on John Field, I could not bear that. Early on I tried to interest her in Fauré, the late nocturnes in particular, which I greatly admire. I even bought the scores for her, ordered them from London, at considerable expense. I was too ambitious. She says she cannot get her fingers around the notes. *Your mind*, more like, I do not reply. Recreant, recreant thoughts. I wonder that she never married. She was beautiful, once, in her soulful way. Nowadays she wears her long grey hair, that formerly was so black, gathered into a tight loop behind her head and transpierced by two crossed pins as big as knitting needles, a style that is to my mind suggestive, wholly inappropriately, of the geisha-house. The Japanese note is continued in the kimono-like belted silk dressing-gown that she wears of a morning, the silk printed with a motif of brightly coloured birds and bamboo fronds. At other times of the day she favours sensible tweeds, but at dinner-time she may surprise us, the Colonel and me, coming rustling to the table in a calf-length confection of lime-green with a sash, or in Spanish-style scarlet bolero jacket and tapered black slacks and neat little shiny black slippers. She is quite the elegant old lady, and registers with a muted flutter my approving glance.

The Cedars has retained hardly anything of the past, of the part of the past that I knew here. I had hoped for something definite of the Graces, no matter how small or seemingly insignificant, a faded photo, say, forgotten in a drawer, a lock of hair, or even a hair-pin, lodged between the floorboards, but there was nothing, nothing like that. No remembered atmosphere, either, to speak of. I suppose so many of the living passing through – it is a lodging house, after all – have worn away all traces of the dead.

How wildly the wind blows today, thumping its

big soft ineffectual fists on the window panes. This is just the kind of autumn weather, tempestuous and clear, that I have always loved. I find the autumn stimulating, as spring is supposed to be for others. Autumn is the time to work, I am at one with Pushkin on that. Oh, yes, Alexandr and I, Octobrists both. A general costiveness has set in, however, most unPushkinian, and I cannot work. But I keep to my table, pushing the paragraphs about like the counters in a game I no longer know how to play. The table is a small spindly affair with an undependable flap, which Miss V. carried up here herself and presented to me with a certain shy intentionality. *Creak, little wood thing, creak.* There is my sea-captain's swivel chair too, just like the one I used to have in some rented place where we lived years ago, Anna and I, it even groans in the same way when I lean back in it. The work I am supposed to be engaged in is a monograph on Bonnard, a modest project in which I have been mired for more years than I care to compute. A very great painter, in my estimation, about whom, as I long ago came to realise, I have nothing of any originality to say. Brides-in-the-Bath, Anna used to call him, with a cackle. *Bonnard, Bonn'art, Bon'nargue.* No, I cannot work, only doodle like this.

Anyway, work is not the word I would apply to what I do. Work is too large a term, too serious. Workers work. The great ones work. As for us middling men, there is no word sufficiently modest that yet will be adequate to describe what we do and how we do it. Dabble I do not accept. It is amateurs who dabble, while we, the class or genus of which I speak, are nothing if not professional. Wallpaper manufacturers such as Vuillard and Maurice Denis were every bit as diligent – there is another key word – as their friend Bonnard, but diligence is not, is never, enough. We are not skivers, we are not lazy. In fact, we are frenetically energetic, in spasms, but we are free, fatally free, of what might be called the curse of perpetuance. We finish things, while for the real worker, as the poet Valéry, I believe it was, pronounced, there is no finishing a work, only the abandoning of it. A nice vignette has Bonnard at the Musée du Luxembourg with a friend, it was Vuillard, indeed, if I am not mistaken, whom he sets to distracting the museum guard while he whips out his paint-box and reworks a patch of a picture of his own that had been hanging there for years. The true workers all die in a fidget of frustration. So much to do, and so much left undone!

Ouch. There is that pricking sensation again. I

cannot help wondering if it might presage something serious. Anna's first signs were of the subtlest. I have become quite the expert in matters medical this past year, not surprisingly. For instance I know that pins-and-needles in the extremities is one of the early symptoms of multiple sclerosis. This sensation I have is like pins-and-needles only more so. It is a burning jab, or series of jabs, in my arm, or in the back of my neck, or once, even, memorably, on the upper side of the knuckle of my right big toe, which sent me hopping on one leg about the room uttering piteous moos of distress. The pain, or smart, though brief, is often severe. It is as if I were being tested for vital signs; for signs of feeling; for signs of life.

Anna used to laugh at me for my hypochondriacal ways. *Doctor Max*, she would call me. *How is Doctor Max today, is he feeling poorly?* She was right, of course, I have always been a moaner, fussing over every slightest twinge or ache.

There is that robin, it flies down from somewhere every afternoon and perches on the holly bush beside the garden shed. I notice it favours doing things by threes, hopping from a top twig to a lower and then a lower again where it stops and whistles thrice its sharp, assertive note. All creatures have their habits. Now from the other side of the garden a neighbour's piebald cat comes creeping, soft-stepping pard. Watch out, birdie. That grass needs cutting, once more will suffice, for this year. I should offer to do it. The thought occurs and at once there I am, in shirt-sleeves and concertina trousers, stumbling sweat-stained behind the mower, grass-haulms in my mouth and the flies buzzing about my head. Odd, how often I see myself like this these days, at a distance, being someone else and doing things that only someone else would do. Mow the lawn, indeed. The shed, although tumbledown, is really rather handsome when looked at with a sympathetic eye, the wood of it weathered to a silky, silvery grey, like the handle of a well-worn implement, a spade, say, or a trusty axe. Old Brides-in-the-Bath would have caught that texture exactly, the quiet sheen and shimmer of it. *Doodle deedle dee.*

Claire, my daughter, has written to ask how I am faring. Not well, I regret to say, bright Clarinda, not well at all. She does not telephone because I have warned her I will take no calls, even from her. Not that there are any calls, since I told no one save her where I was going. What age is she now, twenty-something, I am not sure. She is very bright, quite the bluestocking. Not beautiful, however, I admitted that to myself long ago. I cannot pretend this is not a disappointment, for I had hoped that she would be another Anna. She is too tall and stark, her rusty hair is coarse and untameable and stands out around her freckled face in an unbecoming manner, and when she smiles she shows her upper gums, glistening and whitely pink. With those spindly legs and big bum, that hair, the long neck especially – that is something at least she has of her mother – she always makes me think, shamefacedly, of Tenniel's drawing of Alice when she has taken a nibble from the magic mushroom. Yet she is brave and makes the best of herself and of the world. She has the rueful, grimly humorous, clomping way to her that is common to so many ungainly girls. If she were to arrive here now she would come sweeping in and plump herself down on my sofa and thrust her clasped hands so far down between her knees the knuckles would almost touch the floor, and purse her lips and inflate her cheeks and say *Poh!* and launch into a litany of the comic mishaps she has suffered since last we saw each other. Dear Claire, my sweet girl.

She accompanied me when I came down here to Ballyless for the first time, after that dream, the dream I had of walking homeward in the snow. I think she was worried I might be bent on drowning myself. She must not know what a coward I am. The journey down reminded me a little of the old days, for she and I were always fond of a jaunt. When she was a child and could not sleep at night – from the start she was an insomniac, just like her Daddy – I would bundle her in a blanket into the car and drive her along the coast road for miles beside the darkling sea, crooning whatever songs I knew any of the words of, which far from putting her to sleep made her clap her hands in not altogether derisory delight and cry for more. One time, later on, we even went on a motoring holiday together, just the two of us, but it was a mistake, she was an adolescent by then and grew rapidly bored with vineyards and chateaux and my company, and nagged at me stridently without let-up until I gave in and brought her home early. The trip down here turned out to be not much better.

It was a sumptuous, oh, truly a sumptuous autumn day, all Byzantine coppers and golds under a Tiepolo sky of enamelled blue, the countryside all fixed and glassy, seeming not so much itself as its own reflection in the still surface of a lake. It was the kind of day on which, latterly, the sun for me is the world's fat eye looking on in rich enjoyment as I writhe in my misery. Claire was wearing a big coat of dun-coloured suede which in the warmth of the car gave off a faint but unmistakable fleshy stink which distressed me, although I made no complaint. I have always suffered from what I think must be an overly acute awareness of the mingled aromas that emanate from the human concourse. Or perhaps suffer is the wrong word. I like, for instance, the brownish odour of women's hair when it is in need of washing. My daughter, a fastidious spinster – alas, I am convinced she will never marry – usually has no smell at all, that I can detect. That is another of the numerous ways in which she differs from her mother, whose feral reek, for me the stewy fragrance of life itself, and which the strongest perfume could not quite suppress, was the thing that first drew me to her, all those years ago. My hands now, eerily, have a trace of the same smell, her smell, I cannot rid them of it, wring them though I may. In her last months she smelt, at her best, of the pharmacopoeia.

When we arrived I marvelled to see how much of the village as I remembered it was still here, if only for eyes that knew where to look, mine, that is. It was like encountering an old flame behind whose features thickened by age the slender lineaments that a former self so loved can still be clearly discerned. We passed the deserted railway station and came bowling over the little bridge – still intact, still in place! – my stomach at the crest doing that remembered sudden upward float and fall, and there it all was before me, the hill road, and the beach at the bottom, and the sea. I did not stop at the house but only slowed as we went by. There are moments when the past has a force so strong it seems one might be annihilated by it.

'That was it!' I said to Claire excitedly. 'The Cedars!' On the way down I had told her all, or almost all, about the Graces. 'That was where they stayed.'

She turned back in her seat to look.

'Why did you not stop?' she said.

What was I to answer? That I was overcome by a crippling shyness suddenly, here in the midst of the lost world? I drove on, and turned on to Strand Road. The Strand Café was gone, its place taken by a large, squat and remarkably ugly house. Here were the two hotels, smaller and shabbier, of course, than in my memory of them, the Golf sporting importantly a rather grandiose flag on its roof. Even from inside the car we could hear the palms on the lawn in front dreamily clacking their dry fronds, a sound that on purple summer nights long ago had seemed to promise all of Araby. Now under the bronzen sunlight of the October afternoon – the shadows were lengthening already – everything had a quaintly faded look, as if it were all a series of pictures from old postcards. Myler's pub-post-office-grocery had swelled into a gaudy superstore with a paved parking area in front. I recalled how on a deserted, silent, sun-dazed afternoon half a century ago there had sidled up to me on the gravelled patch outside Myler's a small and harmless-seeming dog which when I put out my hand to it bared its teeth in what I mistakenly took to be an ingratiating grin and bit me on the wrist with an astonishingly swift snap of its jaws and then ran off, sniggering, or so it seemed to me; and how when I came home my mother scolded me bitterly for my foolishness in offering my hand to the brute and sent me, all on my own, to the village doctor who, elegant and urbane, stuck a perfunctory plaster over the rather pretty, purplish swelling on my wrist and then bade me take off all my clothes and sit on his knee so that, with a wonderfully pale, plump and surely manicured hand pressed warmly against my lower abdomen, he might demonstrate to me the proper way to breathe. 'Let the stomach swell instead of drawing it in, you see?'

he said softly, purringly, the warmth of his big bland face beating against my ear.

Claire gave a colourless laugh. 'Which left the more lasting mark,' she asked, 'the dog's teeth or the doctor's paw?'

I showed her my wrist where in the skin over the ulnar styloid are still to be seen the faint remaining scars from the pair of puncture marks made there by the canine's canines.

'It was not Capri,' I said, 'and Doctor ffrench was not Tiberius.'

In truth I have only fond memories of that day. I can still recall the aroma of after-lunch coffee on the doctor's breath and the fishy swivel of his house-keeper's eye as she saw me to the front door.

Claire and I arrived at the Field.

In fact it is a field no longer but a dreary holiday estate packed higgledy-piggledy with what are bound to be jerrybuilt bungalows, designed I suspect by the same cackhanded line-drawer who was responsible for the eyesores at the bottom of the garden here. However, I was pleased to note that the name given to the place, ersatz though it be, is The Lupins, and that the builder, for I presume it was the builder, even spared a tall stand of this modest wild shrub – *Lupinus*, a genus of the Papilionaceae, I have just looked it up – beside the ridiculously grand mock-gothic gateway that leads in from the road. It was under the lupin bushes that my father every other week, at darkest midnight, with spade and flashlight, muttering curses under his breath, would dig a hole in the soft sandy earth and bury the bucketful of slops from our chemical lavatory. I can never smell the weak but oddly anthropic perfume of those blossoms without seeming to catch behind it a lingering sweet whiff of nightsoil.

'Are you not going to stop at all?' Claire said. 'I'm starting to feel car-sick.'

As the years go on I have the illusion that my daughter is catching up on me in age and that by now we are almost contemporaries. It is probably the consequence of having such a clever child – had she persisted she would have made a far finer scholar than I could ever have hoped to be. Also she understands me to a degree that is disturbing and will not indulge my foibles and excesses as others do who know me less and therefore fear me more. But I am bereaved and wounded and require indulging. If there is a long version of shrift then that is what I am in need of. *Let me alone*, I cried at her in my mind, *let me creep past the traduced old Cedars, past the vanished Strand Café, past the Lupins and the Field that was, past all this past, for if I stop I shall surely dissolve in a shaming puddle of tears.* Meekly, however, I halted the car at the side of the road and she got out in a vexed silence and slammed the door behind her as if she were delivering me a box on the ear. What had I done to annoy her so? There are times when she is as wilfully moody as her mother.

And then suddenly, unlikeliest of all, behind the huddle of the Lupins' leprechaun houses, here was Duignan's lane, rutted as it always was, ambling between tangled hedges of hawthorn and dusted-over brambles. How had it survived the depredations of lorry and crane, of diggers both mechanical and human? Here as a boy I would walk down every morning, barefoot and bearing a dented billycan, on my way to buy the day's milk from Duignan the dairyman or his stoically cheerful, big-hipped wife. Even though the sun would be long up the night's moist coolness would cling on in the cobbled yard, where hens picked their way with finical steps among their own chalk-and-olive-green droppings. There was always a dog lying tethered under a leaning cart that would eye me measuringly as I went past, teetering on tiptoe so as to keep my heels out of the chicken-merd, and a grimy white cart-horse that would come and put its head over the half-door of the barn and regard me sidelong with an amused and sceptical eye from under a forelock that was exactly the same smoky shade of creamy-white as honeysuckle blossom. I did not like to knock at the farmhouse door, fearing Duignan's mother, a low-sized squarish old party who seemed fitted with a stumpy leg at each corner and who gasped when she breathed and lolled the pale wet polyp of her tongue on her lower lip, and instead I would hang back in the violet shadow of the barn to wait for Duignan or his missus to appear and save me from an encounter with the crone.

Duignan was a gangling pinhead with thin sandy hair and invisible eyelashes. He wore collarless calico shirts that were antique even then and shapeless trousers shoved into mud-caked wellingtons. In the dairy as he ladled out the milk he would talk to me about girls in a suggestively hoarse, wispy voice – he was to die presently of a diseased throat – saying he was sure I must have a little girlfriend of my own and wanting to know if she let me kiss her. As he spoke he kept his eye fixed on the long thin flute of milk he was pouring into my can, smiling to himself and rapidly batting those colourless lashes. Creepy though he was he held a certain fascination for me. He seemed always teasingly on the point of revealing, as he might show a lewd picture, some large, general and disgusting piece of knowledge to which only adults were privy. The dairy was a low square white-washed cell so white it was almost blue. The steel milk churns looked like squat sentries in flat hats, and each one had an identical white rosette burning on its shoulder where the light from the doorway was reflected. Big shallow muslin-draped pans of milk lost in their own silence were set on the floor to separate, and there was a hand-cranked wooden butter churn that I always wanted to see being operated but never did. The cool thick secret smell of milk made me think of Mrs Grace, and I would have a darkly exciting urge to give in to Duignan's wheedling and tell him about her, but held back, wisely, no doubt.

Now here I was at the farm gate again, the child of those days grown corpulent and half-grey and almost old. An ill-painted sign on the gate-post warned trespassers of prosecution. Claire behind me was saying something about farmers and shotguns but I paid no heed. I advanced across the cobbles – there were still cobbles! – seeming not to walk but bounce, rather, awkward as a half-inflated barrage balloon, buffeted by successive breath-robbing blows out of the past. Here was the barn and its half-door. A rusted harrow leaned where Duignan's cart used to lean — was the cart a misremembrance? The dairy was there too, but disused, its crazy door padlocked, against whom, it was impossible to imagine, the window panes dirtied over or broken and grass growing on the roof. An elaborate porch had been built on to the front of the farmhouse, a glass and aluminium gazebo of a thing suggestive of the rudimentary eye of a giant insect. Now inside it the door opened and an elderly young woman appeared and stopped behind the glass and considered me warily. I blundered forward, grinning and nodding, like a big bumbling missionary approaching the tiny queen of some happily as yet unconverted pygmy tribe. At first she stayed cautiously inside the porch while I addressed her through the glass, loudly enunciating my name and making excited gesticulations with my hands. Still she stood and gazed. She gave the impression of a young actress elaborately but not quite convincingly made up to look old. Her hair, dyed the colour of brown boot polish and permed into a mass of tight, shiny waves, was too voluminous for her little pinched face, surrounding it like a halo of dense thorns, and looking more like a wig than real hair. She wore a faded apron over a jumper that she could only have knitted herself, a man's corduroy trousers balding at the knees, and those zippered ankle boots of Prussian-blue mock-velvet that were all the rage among old ladies when I was young and latterly seem exclusive to beggar women and female winos. I bellowed at her through the glass how I used to stay down here as a child, in a chalet in the Field, and how I would come to the farm in the mornings for milk. She listened, nodding, a pucker appearing and disappearing at the side of her mouth as if she were suppressing a laugh. At last she opened the door of the porch and stepped out on to the cobbles. In my mood of half-demented euphoria – really, I was ridiculously excited – I had an urge to embrace her. I spoke in a rush of the Duignans, man and wife, of Duignan's mother, of the dairy, even of the baleful dog. Still she nodded, a seemingly disbelieving eye-brow arched, and looked past me to where Claire stood waiting in the gateway, arms folded, clasping herself in her big expensive fur-trimmed coat.

Avril, the young woman said her name was. Avril. She did not volunteer a surname. Dimly, like something lifting itself up that for a long time had seemed dead, there came to me the memory of a child in a dirty smock hanging back in the flagged hallway of the farmhouse, holding negligently by its chubby flexed arm a pink, bald and naked doll and watching me with a gnomic stare that nothing would deflect.

But this person before me could not have been that child, who by now would be, what, in her fifties? Perhaps the remembered child was a sister of this one, but much older, that is, born much earlier? Could that be? No, Duignan had died young, in his forties, so it was not possible, surely, that this Avril would be his daughter, since he was an adult when I was a child and . . . My mind balked in its calculations like a confused and weary old beast of burden. But Avril, now. Who in these parts would have conferred on their child a name so delicately vernal?

I asked again about the Duignans and Avril said yes, Christy Duignan had died – Christy? had I known that Duignan's name was Christy? – but Mrs D. was living still, in a nursing home somewhere along the coast. 'And Patsy has a place over near Old Bawn and Mary is in England but poor Willie died.' I nodded. I found it suddenly dispiriting to hear of them, these offshoots of the Duignan dynasty, so solid even in only their names, so mundanely real, Patsy the farmer and Mary the emigrant and little Willie who died, all crowding in on my private ceremony of remembering like uninvited poor relations at a fancy funeral. I could think of nothing to say. All the levitant euphoria of a moment past was gone now and I felt over-fleshed and incommensurate with the moment, standing there smiling and weakly nodding, the last of the air leaking out of me. Still Avril had not identified herself beyond the name, and seemed to think that I must know her, must have recognised her – but how would I, or from where, even though she was standing in what was once the Duignans' doorway? I wondered that she knew so much about the Duignans if she was not one of them, as it seemed certain she was not, or not of the immediate family, anyway, all those Willies and Marys and Patsys, none of whom could have been her parent or doubtless she would have said so by now. All at once my gloom gathered itself into a surge of sour resentment against her, as if she had for some fell reason of her own set herself up here, in this unconvincing disguise – that hennaed hair, those old lady's bootees – intentionally to usurp a corner of my mythic past. The greyish skin of her face, I noticed, was sprinkled all over with tiny freckles. They were not russet-coloured like Claire's, nor like the big splashy ones that used to swarm on Christy Duignan's strangely girlish forearms, nor, for that matter, like the worrying ones that nowadays have begun to appear on the backs of my own hands and on the chicken-pale flesh in the declivities of my shoulders on either side of the clavicle notch, but were much darker, of the same shade of dull brown as Claire's coat, hardly bigger than pinpricks and, I regret to say, suggestive of a chronic and general lack of cleanliness. They put me uneasily in mind of something, yet I could not think what it was.

'It is just, you see,' I said, 'that my wife died.'

I do not know what came over me to blurt it out like that. I hoped Claire behind me had not heard. Avril gazed into my face without expression, expecting me to say more, no doubt. But what more could I have said? On some announcements there is no elaborating. She gave a shrug denoting sympathy, lifting one shoulder and her mouth at one side.

'That's a pity,' she said in a plain, flat tone. 'I'm sorry to hear that.' She did not seem to mean it, somehow.

The autumn sun fell slantwise into the yard, making the cobbles bluely shine, and in the porch a pot of geraniums flourished aloft their last burning blossoms of the season. Honestly, this world.

In the flocculent hush of the Golf Hotel we seemed, my daughter and I, to be the only patrons. Claire wanted afternoon tea and when I had ordered it we were directed to a deserted cold conservatory at the rear that looked out on the strand and the receding tide. Here despite the glacial air a muted hint of past carousings lingered. There was a mingled smell of spilt beer and stale cigarette smoke, and on a dais in a corner an upright piano stood, incongruously bespeaking the Wild West, its lid lifted, showing the gapped grimace of its keys. After that encounter in the farmyard I felt quivery and vapourish, like a diva tottering offstage at the end of a disastrous night of broken high notes, missed prompts, collapsing scenery. Claire and I sat down side by side on a sofa and presently an awkward, ginger-haired boy tricked out in a waiter's black jacket and trousers with a stripe down the sides brought a tray and set it clattering on a low table before us and fled, stumbling in his big shoes. The tea-bag is a vile invention, suggestive to my perhaps overly squeamish eye of something a careless person might leave behind unflushed in the lavatory. I poured a cup of the turf-coloured tea and bolstered it with a nip from my hip-flask – never to be without a ready supply of anaesthetic, that is a thing I have learned in this past year. The light of afternoon was soiled and wintry now and a wall of cloud, dense, mud-blue, was building up from the horizon. The waves clawed at the suave sand along the waterline, scrabbling to hold their ground but steadily failing. There were more palm trees out there, tousled and spindly, their grey bark looking thick and tough as elephant hide. A hardy breed they must be, to survive in this cold northern clime. Do their cells remember the desert's furnace-heat? My daughter sat sunk in her coat with both hands wrapped for warmth around her tea cup. I noted with a pang her babyish fingernails, their pale-lilac tint. One's child is always one's child.

I talked about the Field, the chalet, the Duignans.

'You live in the past,' she said.

I was about to give a sharp reply, but paused. She was right, after all. Life, authentic life, is supposed to be all struggle, unflagging action and affirmation, the will butting its blunt head against the world's wall, suchlike, but when I look back I see that the greater part of my energies was always given over to the simple search for shelter, for comfort, for, yes, I admit, it, for cosiness. This is a surprising, not to say a shocking, realisation. Before, I saw myself as something of a buccaneer, facing all-comers with a cutlass in my teeth, but now I am compelled to acknowledge that this was a delusion. To be concealed, protected, guarded, that is all I have ever truly wanted, to burrow down into a place of womby warmth and cower there, hidden from the sky's indifferent gaze and the harsh air's damagings. That is why the past is just such a retreat for me, I go there eagerly, rubbing my hands and shaking off the cold present and the colder future. And yet, what existence, really, does it have, the past? After all, it is only what the present was, once, the present that is gone, no more than that. And yet.

Claire drew her head tortoise-fashion deep into the shell of her coat and kicked off her shoes and braced her feet against the edge of the little table. There is always something touching in the sight of a woman's stockinged feet, I think it must be the way the toes are bunched fatly together so that they might almost be fused. Myles Grace's toes were naturally, unnaturally, like that. When he splayed them, which he could do as easily as if they were fingers, the membranes between them would stretch into a gossamer webbing, pink and translucent and shot through leaf-like with a tracery of fine veins red like covered flame, the marks of a godling, sure as heaven.

I suddenly recalled, out of the evening's steadily densening blue, the family of teddy bears that had been Claire's companions throughout her childhood. Slightly repulsive, animate-seeming things I thought them. Leaning over her in the grainy light of the bedside lamp to bid her goodnight I would find myself regarded from above the rim of her coverlet by half a dozen pairs of tiny gleaming glass eyes, wetly brown, motionless, uncannily alert.

'Your *lares familiares*,' I said now. 'I suppose you have them still, propped on your maiden couch?'

A steep-slanted flash of sunlight fell along the beach, turning the sand above the waterline bone-white, and a white seabird, dazzling against the wall of cloud, flew up on sickle wings and turned with a soundless snap and plunged itself, a shutting chevron, into the sea's unruly back. Claire sat motionless for a moment and then began to cry. No sound, only the tears, bright beads of quicksilver in the last effulgence of marine light falling down from the high wall of glass in front of us. Crying, in that silent and almost incidental fashion, is another thing she does just like her mother did.

'You're not the only one who is suffering,' she said.

I know so little about her, really, my daughter. One day when she was young, twelve or thirteen, I suppose, and poised on the threshold of puberty, I barged in on her in the bathroom, the door of which she had neglected to lock. She was naked save for a towel wrapped tightly turban-fashion around her head. She turned to look at me over her shoulder in a fall of calm light from the frosted window, quite unflustered, gazing at me out of the fulness of herself. Her breasts were still buds but already she had that big melony behind. What did I feel, seeing her there? An inner chaos, overlaid by tenderness and a kind of fright. Ten years later she abandoned her studies in art history – Vaublin and the fête galante style; that's my girl, or was – to take up the teaching of backward children in one of the city's increasingly numerous, seething slums. What a waste of talent. I could not forgive her, cannot still. I try, but fail. It was all the doing of a young man, a bookish fellow of scant chin and extreme egalitarian views, on whom she had set her heart. The affair, if such it was – I suspect she is still a virgin – ended badly for her. Having persuaded her to throw up what should have been her life's work in favour of a futile social gesture, the black-guard absconded, leaving my misfortunate girl in the lurch. I wanted to go after him and kill him. At the least, I said, let me pay for a good barrister to prosecute him for breach of promise. Anna said to stop it, that I was only making matters worse. She was already ill. What could I do?

Outside, the dusk was thickening. The sea that before had been silent had now set up a vague tumult, perhaps the tide was on the turn. Claire's tears had stopped but stood unwiped, she seemed not to have noticed them. I shivered; these days whole church-yardsful of mourners traipse back and forth unfeel-ingly over my grave.

A large man in a morning coat came from the doorway behind us and advanced soundlessly on servant's feet and looked at us in polite enquiry and met my eye and went away again. Claire snuffled, and delving in a pocket brought out a handkerchief and stentorously blew her nose.

'It depends,' I said mildly, 'on what you mean by suffering.'

She said nothing but put the hankie away and stood up and looked about her, frowningly, as if in search of something but not knowing what. She said she would wait for me in the car, and walked away with her head bowed and her hands deep in the pockets of that coat-shaped pelt. I sighed. Against a blackening vault of sky the seabirds rose and dived like torn scraps of rag. I realised I had a headache, it had been beating away unheeded in my skull since I had first sat down in this glassed-in box of wearied air.

The boy-waiter came back, tentative as a fox cub, and made to take the tray, a carroty lock falling limply forward from his brow. With that colouring he could be yet another of the Duignan clan, cadet branch. I asked him his name. He stopped, canted forward awkwardly from the waist, and looked at me from under his pale brows in speculative alarm. His jacket had a shine, the shot cuffs of his shirt were soiled.

'Billy, sir,' he said.

I gave him a coin and he thanked me and stowed it and took up the tray and turned, then hesitated.

'Are you all right, sir?' he said.

I brought out the car keys and looked at them in perplexity. Everything seemed to be something else. I said that yes, I was all right, and he went away. The silence about me was heavy as the sea. The piano on the dais grinned its ghastly grin.

When I was leaving the lobby the man in the morning coat was there. He had a large, waxen, curiously characterless face. He bowed to me, beaming, hands clasped into fists before his chest in an excessive, operatic gesture. What is it about such people that makes me remember them? His look was unctuous yet in some way minatory. Perhaps I had been expected to tip him also. As I say: this world.

Claire was waiting by the car, shoulders hunched, using the sleeves of her coat for a muff.

'You should have asked me for the key,' I said. 'Did you think I wouldn't give it to you?'

On the way home she insisted on taking the wheel, despite my vigorous resistance. It was full night by now and in the wide-eyed glare of the headlamps successive stands of unleaving fright-trees loomed up suddenly before us and were as suddenly gone, collapsing off into the darkness on either side as if felled by the pressure of our passing. Claire was leaning so far forward her nose was almost touching the windscreen. The light rising from the dashboard like green gas gave to her face a spectral hue. I said she should let me drive. She said I was too drunk to drive. I said I was not drunk. She said I had finished the hip-flask, she had seen me empty it. I said it was no business of hers to rebuke me in this fashion. She wept again, shouting through her tears. I said that even drunk I would have been less of a danger driving than she was in this state. So it went on, hammer and tongs, tooth and nail, what you will. I gave as good, or as bad, as I got, reminding her, merely as a corrective, that for the best part, I mean the worst part – how imprecise the language is, how inadequate to its occasions – of the year that it took her mother to die, she had been conveniently abroad, pursuing her studies, while I was left to cope as best I could.

This struck home. She gave a hoarse bellow between clenched teeth and thumped the heels of her hands on the wheel. Then she started to fling all sorts of accusations at me. She said I had *driven Jerome away.* I paused. Jerome? Jerome? She meant of course the chinless do-gooder – fat lot of good he did her – and sometime object of her affections. Jerome, yes, that was the scoundrel's unlikely name. How, pray, I asked, controlling myself, how had I *driven him away?* To that she replied only with a head-tossing snort. I pondered. It was true I had considered him an unsuitable suitor, and had told him so, pointedly, on more than one occasion, but she spoke as if I had brandished a horsewhip or let fly with a shotgun. Besides, if it was my opposition that had *driven him away,* what did that say for his character or his tenacity of purpose? No no, she was better off free of the likes of him, that was certain. But for now I said nothing more, kept my counsel, and after a mile or two the fire in her went out. That is something I have always found with women, wait long enough and one will have one's way.

When we got home I went straight into the house, leaving her to park the car, and got the number of the Cedars from the telephone book and telephoned Miss Vavasour and told her that I wished to rent one of her rooms. Then I went upstairs and crawled into bed in my drawers. I was suddenly very tired. A fight with one's daughter is never less than debilitating. I had moved by then from what had been Anna's and my bedroom into the spare room over the kitchen, which used to be the nursery and where the bed was low and narrow, hardly more than a cot. I could hear Claire below in the kitchen, banging the pots and pans. I had not told her yet that I had decided to sell the house. Miss V. on the telephone had enquired how long I planned to stay. I could hear from her tone that she was puzzled, even distrustful. I maintained a deliberate vagueness. Some weeks, I said, months, perhaps. She was silent for a lengthy moment, thinking. She mentioned the Colonel, he was a permanent, she said, and set in his ways. I volunteered no comment on that. What were colonels to me? She could entertain an entire officer corps on the premises for all I cared. She said I would have to send out my laundry. I asked her if she remembered me. 'Oh, yes,' she said without inflexion, 'yes, of course, I remember you.'

I heard Claire's step on the stairs. Her anger had drained all away by now and she walked at a dragging, disconsolate plod. I do not doubt she too finds arguments tiring. The bedroom door was ajar but she did not come in, only asked listlessly through the gap if I wanted something to eat. I had not switched on the lamps in the room and the long, tapering trapezoid of light spilling across the linoleum from the landing where she stood was a pathway leading straight to childhood, hers and my own. When she was little and slept in this room, in this bed, she liked to hear the sound of my typewriter from the study downstairs. It was a comforting sound, she said, like listening to me think, although I do not know how the sound of me thinking could comfort anyone; quite the opposite, I should have said. Ah, but how far off, now, those days, those nights. All the same, she should not have shouted at me like that in the car. I do not merit being shouted at like that. 'Daddy,' she said again, with a note of testiness now, 'do you want dinner or not?' I did not answer, and she went away. Live in the past, do I.

I turned toward the wall and away from the light. Even though my knees were bent my feet still stuck out at the end of the bed. As I was heaving myself over in a tangle of sheets – I have never been able to cope with bedclothes – I caught a whiff of my own warm cheesy smell. Before Anna's illness I had held my physical self in no more than fond disgust, as most people do – hold their selves, I mean, not mine

– tolerant, necessarily, of the products of my sadly inescapable humanity, the various effluvia, the eructations fore and aft, the gleet, the scurf, the sweat and other common leakages, and even what the Bard of Hartford quaintly calls the particles of nether-do. However, when Anna's body betrayed her and she became afraid of it and its alien possibilities, I developed, by a mysterious process of transference, a crawling repugnance of my own flesh. I do not have this sense of self-disgust all the time, or at least I am not all the time aware of it, although probably it is there, waiting until I am alone, at night, or in the early morning especially, when it rises around me like a miasma of marsh gas. I have developed too a queasy fascination with the processes of my body, the gradual ones, the way for instance my hair and my fingernails insistently keep growing, no matter what state I am in, what anguish I may be undergoing. It seems so inconsiderate, so heedless of circumstance, this relentless generation of matter that is already dead, in the same way that animals will keep going about their animal business, unaware or uncaring that their master sprawled on his cold bed upstairs with mouth agape and eyes glazed over will not be coming down, ever again, to dish out the kibble or take the key to that last tin of sardines.

Speaking of typewriters – I did, I mentioned a typewriter a minute ago – last night in a dream, it has just come back to me, I was trying to write my will on a machine that was lacking the word *I*. The letter *I*, that is, small and large.

Down here, by the sea, there is a special quality to the silence at night. I do not know if this is my doing, I mean if this quality is something I bring to the silence of my room, and even of the whole house, or if it is a local effect, due to the salt in the air, perhaps, or the seaside climate in general. I do not recall noticing it when I was young and staying in the Field. It is dense and at the same time hollow. It took me a long while, nights and nights, to identify what it reminds me of. It is like the silence that I knew in the sickrooms of my childhood, when I would lie in a fever, cocooned under a hot, moist mound of blankets, with the emptiness squeezing in on my eardrums like the air in a bathysphere. Sickness in those days was a special place, a place apart, where no one else could enter, not the doctor with his shiver-inducing stethoscope or even my mother when she put her cool hand on my burning brow. It is a place like the place where I feel that I am now, miles from anywhere, and anyone. I think of the others in the house, Miss Vavasour, and the Colonel, asleep in their rooms, and then I think perhaps they are not asleep, but lying awake, like me, glooming gaunt-eyed into the lead-blue darkness. Perhaps the one is thinking of the other, for the Colonel has an idea of our chatelaine, I am convinced of it. She, however, laughs at him behind his back, not entirely without fondness, calling him Colonel Blunder, or Our Brave Soldier. Some mornings her eyes are red-rimmed as if she had been crying in the night. Does she blame herself for all that happened and grieve for it still? What a little vessel of sadness we are, sailing in this muffled silence through the autumn dark.

It was at night especially that I thought about the Graces, as I lay in my narrow metal bed in the chalet under the open window, hearing the monotonously repeated ragged collapse of waves down on the beach, the solitary cry of a sleepless seabird and, sometimes, the distant rattling of a corncrake, and the faint, jazzy moanings of the dance band in the Golf Hotel playing a last slow waltz, and my mother and father in the front room fighting, as they did when they thought I was asleep, going at each other in a grinding undertone, every night, every night, until at last one night my father left us, never to return. But that was in winter, and somewhere else, and years off still. To keep from trying to hear what they were saying I distracted myself by making up dramas in which I rescued Mrs Grace from some great and general catastrophe, a shipwreck or a devastating storm, and sequestered her for safety in a cave, conveniently dry and warm, where in moonlight – the liner had gone down by now, the storm had abated – I tenderly helped her out of her sopping swimsuit and wrapped a towel around her phosphorescent nudity, and we lay down and she leaned her head on my arm and touched my face in gratitude and sighed, and so we went to sleep together, she and I, lapped about by the vast soft summer night.

In those days I was greatly taken with the gods. I am not speaking of God, the capitalised one, but the gods in general. Or the idea of the gods, that is, the possibility of the gods. I was a keen reader and had a fair knowledge of the Greek myths, although the personages in them were hard to keep track of, so frequently did they transform themselves and so various were their adventures. Of them I had a necessarily stylised image – big, nearly naked plasticene figures all corded muscle and breasts like inverted tun-dishes – derived from the works of the great masters of the Italian Renaissance, Michelangelo especially, reproductions of whose paintings I must have seen in a book, or a magazine, I who was always on the look-out for instances of bare flesh. It was of course the erotic exploits of these celestial beings that most took my fancy. The thought of all that tensed and tensely quivering naked flesh, untrammelled save by the marmoreal folds of a robe or a wisp of gauze fortuitously placed – fortuitous, perhaps, but fully and frustratingly as protective of modesty as Rose's beach towel or, indeed, Connie Grace's swimsuit – glutted my inexperienced but already overheating imagination with reveries of love and love's transgressions, all in the unvarying form of pursuit and capture and violent overmastering. Of the details of these skirmishes in the golden dust of Greece I had scant grasp. I pictured the pump and shudder of tawny thighs from which pale loins shrink even as they surrender, and heard the moans of mingled ecstasy and sweet distress. The mechanics of the act, however, were beyond me. Once on my rambles along the thistled pathways of the Burrow, as that strip of scrubland between the seashore and the fields was called, I almost stumbled over a couple lying in a shallow sandy pit making love under a raincoat.

Their exertions had caused the coat to ride up, so that it covered their heads but not their tails – or perhaps they had arranged it that way, preferring to conceal their faces, so much more identifiable, after all, than behinds – and the sight of them there, the man's flanks rhythmically busy in the upright wishbone of the woman's lifted, wide-flung legs, made something swell and thicken in my throat, a blood-surge of alarm and thrilled revulsion. *So this*, I thought, or it was thought for me, *so this is what they do.*

Love among the big people. It was strange to picture them, to try to picture them, struggling together on their Olympian beds in the dark of night with only the stars to see them, grasping and clasping, panting endearments, crying out for pleasure as if in pain. How did they justify these dark deeds to their daytime selves? That was something that puzzled me greatly. Why were they not ashamed? On Sunday morning, say, they arrive at church still tingling from Saturday night's frolics. The priest greets them in the porch, they smile blamelessly, mumbling innocuous words. The woman dips her fingertips in the font, mingling traces of tenacious love-juice with the holy water. Under their Sunday best their thighs chafe in remembered delight. They kneel, not minding the mournfully reproachful gaze the statue of their Saviour fixes on them from the cross. After their midday Sunday dinner perhaps they will send the children out to play and retire to the sanctuary of their curtained bedroom and do it all over again, unaware of my mind's bloodshot eye fixed on them unblinkingly. Yes, I was that kind of boy. Or better say, there is part of me still that is the kind of boy that I was then. A little brute, in other words, with a filthy mind. As if there were any other sort. We never grow up. I never did, anyway.

By day I loitered about Station Road hoping for a glimpse of Mrs Grace. I would pass by the green metal gate, slowing to the pace of a somnambulist, and will her to walk out of the front door as her husband had walked out that day when I caught my first sight of him, but she kept stubbornly within. In desperation I would peer past the house to the clothesline in the garden, but all I saw was the children's laundry, their shorts and socks and one or two items of Chloe's uninterestingly skimpy under-things, and of course their father's flaccid, greyish drawers, and once, even, his sand-bucket hat, pegged at a rakish angle. The only thing of Mrs Grace's I ever saw there was her black swimsuit, hanging by its shoulder straps, limp and scandalously empty, dry now and less like a sealskin than the pelt of a panther. I looked in at the windows, too, especially the bedroom ones upstairs, and was rewarded one day – how my heart hammered! – by a glimpse behind a shadowed pane of what seemed a nude thigh that could only be hers. Then the adored flesh moved and turned into the hairy shoulder of her husband, at stool, for all I knew, and reaching for the lavatory roll.

There was a day when the door did open, but it was Rose who came out, and gave me a look that made me lower my eyes and hurry on. Yes, Rose had the measure of me from the start. Still has, no doubt.

I determined to get into the house, to walk where Mrs Grace walked, sit where she sat, touch the things that she touched. To this end I set about making the acquaintance of Chloe and her brother. It was easy, as these things were in childhood, even for a child as circumspect as I was. At that age we had no small-talk, no rituals of polite advance and encounter, but simply put ourselves into each other's vicinity and waited to see what would happen. I saw the two of them loitering on the gravel outside the Strand Café one day, spied them before they spied me, and crossed the road diagonally to where they were stand-ing, and stopped. Myles was eating an ice cream with deep concentration, licking it evenly on all sides like a cat licking a kitten, while Chloe, I suppose having finished hers, waited on him in an attitude of torpid boredom, leaning in the doorway of the café with one sandalled foot pressed on the instep of the other and her face blankly lifted to the sunlight. I did not say anything, nor did they. The three of us just stood there in the morning sunshine amid smells of seawrack and vanilla and what passed in the Strand Café for coffee, and at last Chloe deigned to lower her head and directed her gaze toward my knees and asked my name. When I told her she repeated it, as if it were a suspect coin she was testing between her teeth.

'Morden?' she said. 'What sort of a name is that?'

We walked slowly up Station Road, Chloe and I in front and Myles behind us, gambolling, I nearly said, at our heels. They were from the city, Chloe said. That would not have been hard for me to guess. She asked where I was staying. I gestured vaguely.

'Down there,' I said. 'Along past the church.'

'In a house or a hotel?'

How quick she was. I considered lying – 'The Golf Hotel, actually' – but saw where a lie could lead me.

'A chalet,' I said, mumbling.

She nodded thoughtfully.

'I've always wanted to stay in a chalet,' she said.

This was no comfort to me. On the contrary, it caused me to have a momentary but starkly clear image of the crooked little wooden outhouse standing amid the lupins across from my bedroom window, and even seemed to catch a dry, woody whiff of the torn-up squares of newsprint impaled on their rusty nail just inside the door.

We came to the Cedars, stopped at the gate. The car was parked on the gravel. It had been out recently, the cooling engine was still clicking its tongue to itself in fussy complaint. I could hear faintly from inside the house the melting-toffee tones of a palm court orchestra playing on the wireless, and I pictured Mrs Grace and her husband dancing together in there, sweeping around the furniture, she with her head thrown back and her throat bared and he mincing on his satyr's furred hind legs and grinning up eagerly into her face – he was shorter than she by an inch or two – with all his sharp little teeth on show and his ice-blue eyes alight with mirthful lust. Chloe was tracing patterns in the gravel with the toe of her sandal. There were fine white hairs on her calves but her shins were smooth and shiny as stone. Suddenly Myles gave a little jump, or skip, as if for joy but too mechanical for that, like a clockwork figure coming abruptly to life, and clipped me playfully on the back of the head with his open palm and turned and with a gagging laugh scrambled agilely over the bars of the gate and dropped down to the gravel on the other side and spun about to face us and crouched with knees and elbows flexed, like an acrobat inviting his due of applause. Chloe made a face, pulling her mouth down at one side.

'Don't mind him,' she said in a tone of bored irritation. 'He can't talk.'

They were twins. I had never encountered twins before, in the flesh, and was fascinated and at the same time slightly repelled. There seemed to me something almost indecent in such a predicament. True, they were brother and sister and so could not be identical – the very thought of identical twins sent a shiver of secret and mysterious excitement along my spine – but still there must be between them an awful depth of intimacy. How would it be? Like having one mind and two bodies? If so it was almost disgusting to think of. Imagine somehow knowing intimately, from the inside, as it were, what another's body is like, its different parts, different smells, different urges. How, how would it be? I itched to know. In the makeshift picture-house one wet

Sunday afternoon – here I leap ahead – we were watching a film in which two convicts from a chain-gang made their escape still manacled together, and beside me Chloe stirred and made a muffled sound, a sort of laughing sigh. 'Look,' she whispered, 'it's me and Myles.' I was taken aback, and felt myself blush and was glad of the dark. She might have been admitting to something intimate and shameful. Yet it was the very notion of an impropriety in such closeness that made me eager to know more, eager, and yet loath. Once – this is an even longer leap forward – when I got up the nerve to ask Chloe straight out to tell me, because I longed to know, what it felt like, this state of unavoidable intimacy with her brother – her other! – she thought for a moment and then held up her hands before her face, the palms pressed almost together but not quite touching. 'Like two magnets,' she said, 'but turned the wrong way, pulling and pushing.' After she had said it she fell darkly silent, as though this time it was she who thought she had let drop a shaming secret, and she turned away from me, and I felt for a moment something of the same panicky dizziness that I did when I held my breath for too long underwater. She was never less than alarming, was Chloe.

The link between them was palpable. I pictured

it as an invisibly fine thread of sticky shiny stuff, like spider's silk, or a glistening filament such as a snail might leave hanging as it crossed from one leaf to another, or steely and bright, it might be, and taut, like a harp-string, or a garotte. They were tied to each other, tied and bound. They felt things in common, pains, emotions, fears. They shared thoughts. They would wake in the night and lie listening to each other breathing, knowing they had been dreaming the same thing. They did not tell each other what was in the dream. There was no need. They knew.

Myles had been mute from birth. Or rather, simply, he had never spoken. The doctors could find no cause that would account for his stubborn silence, and professed themselves baffled, or sceptical, or both. At first it had been assumed he was a late starter and that in time he would begin to speak like everyone else, but the years went on and still he said not a word. Whether he had the ability to speak and chose not to, no one seemed to know. Was he mute or silent, silent or mute? Could he have a voice that he never used? Did he practise when there was no one to hear? I imagined him at night, in bed, under the covers, whispering to himself and smiling that avid, elfin smile of his. Or maybe he talked to Chloe. How they would have laughed, forehead to forehead and their arms thrown around each other's neck, sharing their secret.

'He'll talk when he has something to say,' his father would growl, with his accustomed menacing cheeriness.

It was plain that Mr Grace did not care for his son. He avoided him when he could, and was especially unwilling to be alone with him. This was no wonder, for being alone with Myles was like being in a room which someone had just violently left. His muteness was a pervasive and cloying emanation. He said nothing but was never silent. He was always fidgeting with things, snatching them up and immediately throwing them down again with a clatter. He made dry little clicking noises at the back of his throat. One heard him breathe.

His mother treated him with a sort of trailing vagueness. At moments as she weaved abstractedly through her day – although she was not a serious drinker she always looked to be mellowly a little drunk – she would stop and seem to notice him with not quite recognition, and would frown and smile at the same time, in a rueful, helpless fashion.

Neither parent could do proper sign language, and spoke to Myles by way of an improvised, brusque dumb-show that seemed less an attempt at communication than an impatient waving of him out of their sight. Yet he understood well enough what it was they were trying to say, and often before they were halfway through trying to say it, which only made them more impatient and irritated with him. Deep down they were both, I am sure, a little afraid of him. That is no wonder either. It must have been like living with an all too visible, all too tangible poltergeist.

For my part, although I am ashamed to say it, or at least I should be ashamed, what Myles put me most in mind of was a dog I once had, an irrepressibly enthusiastic terrier of which I was greatly fond but which on occasion, when there was no one about, I would cruelly beat, poor Pongo, for the hot, tumid pleasure I derived from its yelps of pain and its supplicatory squirmings. What twig-like fingers Myles had, what brittle, girlish wrists! He would goad me, plucking at my sleeve, or walking on my heels and popping his grinning head repeatedly up from under my arm, until at last I would turn on him and knock him down, which was easy to do, for I was big and strong even then, and taller than he was by a head. When he was down, however, there was the question of what to do with him, since unless prevented he would be up again at once, rolling over himself like one of those self-righting toy figures and springing effortlessly back on to his toes. When I sat on his chest I could feel the wobble of his heart against my groin, his ribcage straining and the fluttering of the taut, concave integument below his breast-bone, and he would laugh up at me, panting, and showing his moist, useless tongue. But was not I too a little afraid of him, in my heart, or wherever it is that fear resides?

In accordance with the mysterious protocols of childhood – were we children? I think there should be another word for what we were – they did not invite me into the house that first time, after I had accosted them outside the Strand Café. In fact, I do not recall under what circumstances exactly I managed eventually to get inside the Cedars. I see myself after that initial encounter turning away frustratedly from the green gate with the twins watching me go, and then I see myself another day within the very sanctum itself, as if, by a truly magical version of Myles's leap over the top bar of the gate, I had vaulted all obstacles to land up in the living room next to an angled, solid-seeming beam of brassy sunlight, with Mrs Grace in a loose-fitting, flowered dress, light-blue with a darker pattern of blue blossoms, turning from a table and smiling at me, deliberately vague,

evidently not knowing who I was but knowing nevertheless that she should, which shows that this cannot
have been the first time we had encountered each
other face to face. Where was Chloe? Where was
Myles? Why was I left alone with their mother? She
asked if I would like something, a glass of lemonade,
perhaps. 'Or,' she said in a tone of faint desperation,
'an apple . . . ?' I shook my head. Her proximity, the
mere fact of her thereness, filled me with excitement
and a mysterious sort of sorrow. Who knows the
pangs that pierce a small boy's heart? She put her
head on one side, puzzled, and amused, too, I could
see, by the tongue-tied intensity of my presence
before her. I must have seemed like a moth throbbing
before a candle-flame, or like the flame itself, shivering in its own consuming heat.

What was it she had been doing at the table?
Arranging flowers in a vase – or is that too fanciful?
There is a multi-coloured patch in my memory of
the moment, a shimmer of variegated brightness
where her hands hover. Let me linger here with her a
little while, before Rose appears, and Myles and
Chloe return from wherever they are, and her goatish
husband comes clattering on to the scene; she will be
displaced soon enough from the throbbing centre of
my attentions. How intensely that sunbeam glows.

Where is it coming from? It has an almost churchly cast, as if, impossibly, it were slanting down from a rose window high above us. Beyond the smouldering sunlight there is the placid gloom of indoors on a summer afternoon, where my memory gropes in search of details, solid objects, the components of the past. Mrs Grace, Constance, Connie, is still smiling at me in that unfocused way, which, now that I consider it, is how she looked at everything, as if she were not absolutely persuaded of the world's solidity and half expected it all at any moment to turn, in some outlandish and hilarious way, into something entirely different.

I would have said then that she was beautiful, had there been anyone to whom I would have thought of saying such a thing, but I suppose she was not, really. She was rather stocky, and her hands were fat and reddish, there was a bump at the tip of her nose, and the two lank strands of blonde hair that her fingers kept pushing back behind her ears and that kept falling forward again were darker than the rest of her hair and had the slightly greasy hue of oiled oak. She walked at a languorous slouch, the muscles in her haunches quivering under the light stuff of her summer dresses. She smelled of sweat and cold cream and, faintly, of cooking fat. Just another woman, in other words, and another mother, at that. Yet to me she was in all her ordinariness as remote and remotely desirable as any a painted pale lady with unicorn and book. But no, I should be fair to myself, child though I was, nascent romantic though I may have been. She was, even for me, not pale, she was not made of paint. She was wholly real, thick-meated, edible, almost. This was the most remarkable thing of all, that she was at once a wraith of my imagination and a woman of unavoidable flesh and blood, of fibre and musk and milk. My hitherto hardly less than seemly dreams of rescue and amorous dalliance had by now become riotous fantasies, vivid and at the same time hopelessly lacking in essential detail, of being voluptuously overborne by her, of sinking to the ground under all her warm weight, of being rolled, of being ridden, between her thighs, my arms pinned against my breast and my face on fire, at once her demon lover and her child.

At times the image of her would spring up in me unbidden, an interior succubus, and a surge of yearning would engorge the very root of my being. One greenish twilight after rain, with a wedge of wet sunlight in the window and an impossibly unseasonal thrush piping outside in the dripping lupins, I lay face down on my bed in such an intense suffusion of unassuageable desire – it hovered, this desire, like a nimbus about the image of my beloved, enfolding her everywhere and nowhere focused – that I broke into sobs, lavish, loud and thrillingly beyond all control. My mother heard me and came into the room, but said nothing, uncharacteristically – I might have expected a brusque interrogation, followed by a smack – only picked up a pillow that the thrashings of my grief had pushed off the bed and, after the briefest of hesitations, went out again, shutting the door soundlessly behind her. What did she imagine I was weeping for, I wondered, and wonder again now. Had she somehow recognised my rapturously lovesick grief for what it was? I could not believe it. How would she, who was merely my mother, know anything of this storm of passion in which I was helplessly suspended, the frail wings of my emotions burned and blasted by love's relentless flame? Oh, Ma, how little I understood you, thinking how little you understood.

So there I am, in that Edenic moment at what was suddenly the centre of the world, with that shaft of sunlight and those vestigial flowers – sweet pea? all at once I seem to see sweet pea – and blonde Mrs Grace offering me an apple that was however nowhere in evidence, and everything about to be interrupted with a grinding of cogwheels and a horrible, stomach-turning lurch. All sorts of things began to happen at once. Through an open doorway a small black woolly dog came skittering in from outside – somehow now the action has shifted from the living room to the kitchen – its nails making frantic skittling noises on the pitchpine floor. It had a tennis ball in its mouth. Immediately Myles appeared in pursuit, with Rose in turn pursuing him. He tripped or pretended to trip over a rucked rug and pitched forward only to tumble nimbly head over heel and leap to his feet again, almost knocking into his mother, who gave a cry in which were mingled startlement and weary annoyance – 'For heaven's sake, Myles!' – while the dog, its pendent ears flapping, changed tack and shot underneath the table, still grinningly gripping the ball. Rose made a feint at the animal but it dodged aside. Now through another doorway, like Old Father Time himself, came Carlo Grace, wearing shorts and sandals and with a big beach towel draped over his shoulders, his hairy paunch on show. At sight of Myles and the dog he gave a roar of sham rage and stamped his foot threateningly, and the dog let go of the ball, and dog and boy disappeared through the door as precipitately as they had entered. Rose laughed, a high whinny, and looked quickly at Mrs Grace and bit her lip. The door banged and in rapid echo another door banged upstairs, where a lavatory, flushed a moment previously, had set up its after-gulps and gurglings. The ball that the dog had dropped rolled slowly, shiny with spit, into the middle of the floor. Mr Grace, seeing me, a stranger – he must have forgotten that day of the wink – mugged a double-take, throwing back his head and screwing up his face at one side and sighting quizzically at me along the side of his nose. I heard Chloe coming downstairs, her sandals slapping on the steps. By the time she entered the room Mrs Grace had introduced me to her husband – I think it was the first time in my life I had been formally introduced to anyone, although I had to say my name since Mrs Grace had still not remembered it – and he was shaking my hand with a show of mock solemnity, addressing me as *My dear sir!* and putting on a cockney accent and declaring that any friend of his children's would always be welcome in *our 'umble 'ome*. Chloe rolled her eyes and gave a shuddering gasp of disgust. 'Shut *up*, Daddy,' she said through clenched teeth, and he, feigning terror of her, let go my hand and drew the towel shawl-like over his head and hurried at a crouch on tiptoe out of the room, making little bat-squeaks of pretend fright and dismay. Mrs Grace was lighting a cigarette. Chloe without even a glance in my direction crossed the room to the door where her father had gone out. 'I need a lift!' she shouted after him. 'I need—' The car door slammed, the engine started, the big tyres mashed the gravel. 'Damn,' Chloe said.

Mrs Grace was leaning against the table – the one with the sweet pea on it, for magically we are back in the living room again – smoking her cigarette in the way that women did in those days, one arm folded across her midriff and the elbow of the other cupped in a palm. She lifted an eyebrow at me and smiled wryly and shrugged, picking a fleck of tobacco from her lower lip. Rose stooped and wrinkling her nose picked up reluctantly the spit-smeared ball between a finger and thumb. Outside the gate the car horn tooted merrily twice and we heard the car drive away. The dog was barking wildly, wanting to be let in again to retrieve the ball.

By the way, that dog. I never saw it again. Whose can it have been?

Odd sense of lightness today, of, what shall I call it, of volatility. The wind is up again, it is fairly blowing a tempest out there, which must be the cause of this giddiness I am feeling. For I have always been strongly susceptible to the weather and its effects. As a child I loved to curl up by the wireless set of a winter eve and listen to the shipping forecast, picturing all those doughty sea-dogs in their sou'westers battling through house-high waves in Fogger and Disher and Jodrell Bank, or whatever those far-flung sea areas are called. Often as an adult, too, I would have that same feeling, there with Anna in our fine old house between the mountains and the sea, when the autumn gales groaned in the chimneys and the waves were coming over the sea wall in washes of boiling white spume. Before the pit opened under our feet that day in Mr Todd's rooms – which, come to think of it, did have about them something of the air of a sinisterly superior barber's shop – I was often surprised to ponder how many of life's good things had been granted me. If that child dreaming by the wireless had been asked what he wanted to be when he grew up, what I had become was more or less what he would have described, in however halting a fashion, I am sure of it. This is remarkable, I think, even allowing for my present sorrows. Are not the majority of men disappointed with their lot, languishing in quiet desperation in their chains?

I wonder if other people when they were children

had this kind of image, at once vague and particular, of what they would be like when they grew up. I am not speaking of hopes and aspirations, vague ambitions, that kind of thing. From the outset I was very precise and definite in my expectations. I did not want to be an engine driver or a famous explorer. When I peered wishfully through the mists from the all too real then to the blissfully imagined now, this is, as I have said, exactly how I would have foreseen my future self, a man of leisurely interests and scant ambition sitting in a room just like this one, in my sea-captain's chair, leaning at my little table, in just this season, the year declining toward its end in clement weather, the leaves scampering, the brightness imperceptibly fading from the days and the street lamps coming on only a fraction earlier each evening. Yes, this is what I thought adulthood would be, a kind of long indian summer, a state of tranquillity, of calm incuriousness, with nothing left of the barely bearable raw immediacy of childhood, all the things solved that had puzzled me when I was small, all mysteries settled, all questions answered, and the moments dripping away, unnoticed almost, drip by golden drip, toward the final, almost unnoticed, quietus.

There were things of course the boy that I was

then would not have allowed himself to foresee, in his eager anticipations, even if he had been able. Loss, grief, the sombre days and the sleepless nights, such surprises tend not to register on the prophetic imagination's photographic plate.

And then, too, when I consider the matter closely, I see that the version of the future that I pictured as a boy had an oddly antique cast to it. The world in which I live now would have been, in my imagining of it then, for all my perspicacity, different from what it is in fact, but subtly different; would have been, I see, all slouched hats and crombie overcoats and big square motor cars with winged manikins bounding from the bonnets. When had I known such things, that I could figure them so distinctly? I think it is that, being unable to conceive exactly what the future would look like but certain that I would be a person of some eminence in it, I must have furnished it with the trappings of success as I saw it among the great folk of our town, the doctors and solicitors, the provincial industrialists for whom my father humbly worked, the few remnants of Protestant gentry still clinging on in their Big Houses down the bosky side roads of the town's hinterland.

But no, that is not it either. It does not adequately account for the genteelly outmoded atmosphere that pervaded my dream of what was to come. The precise images I entertained of myself as a grown-up – seated, say, in three-piece pinstriped suit and raked fedora in the back seat of my chauffered Humber Hawk with a blanket over my knees – were imbued, I realise, with that etiolated, world-weary elegance, that infirm poise, which I associated, or which at least I associate now, with a time before the time of my childhood, that recent antiquity which was, of course, yes, the world between the wars. So what I foresaw for the future was in fact, if fact comes into it, a picture of what could only be an imagined past. I was, one might say, not so much anticipating the future as nostalgic for it, since what in my imaginings was to come was in reality already gone. And suddenly now this strikes me as in some way significant. Was it actually the future I was looking forward to, or something beyond the future?

The truth is, it has all begun to run together, past and possible future and impossible present. In the ashen weeks of daytime dread and nightly terror before Anna was forced at last to acknowledge the inevitability of Mr Todd and his prods and potions, I seemed to inhabit a twilit netherworld in which it was scarcely possible to distinguish dream from waking, since both waking and dreaming had the same penetrable, darkly velutinous texture, and in which I was wafted this way and that in a state of feverish lethargy, as if it were I and not Anna who was destined soon to be another one among the already so numerous shades. It was a gruesome version of that phantom pregnancy I experienced when Anna first knew she was expecting Claire; now it seemed I was suffering a phantom illness along with her. On all sides there were portents of mortality. I was plagued by coincidences; long-forgotten things were suddenly remembered; objects turned up that for years had been lost. My life seemed to be passing before me, not in a flash as it is said to do for those about to drown, but in a sort of leisurely convulsion, emptying itself of its secrets and its quotidian mysteries in preparation for the moment when I must step into the black boat on the shadowed river with the coin of passage cold in my already coldening hand. Strange as it was, however, this imagined place of pre-departure was not entirely unfamiliar to me. On occasion in the past, in moments of inexplicable transport, in my study, perhaps, at my desk, immersed in words, paltry as they may be, for even the second-rater is sometimes inspired, I had felt myself break through the membrane of mere consciousness into another state, one which had no name, where ordinary laws did not operate, where time moved differently if it moved at all, where I was neither alive nor the other thing and yet more vividly present than ever I could be in what we call, because we must, the real world. And even years before that again, standing for instance with Mrs Grace in that sunlit living room, or sitting with Chloe in the dark of the picture-house, I was there and not there, myself and revenant, immured in the moment and yet hovering somehow on the point of departure. Perhaps all of life is no more than a long preparation for the leaving of it.

For Anna in her illness the nights were worst. That was only to be expected. So many things were only to be expected, now that the ultimate unexpected had arrived. In the dark all the breathless incredulity of daytime – *this cannot be happening to me!* – gave way in her to a dull, unmoving amazement. As she lay sleepless beside me I could almost feel her fear, spinning steadily inside her, like a dynamo. At moments in the dark she would laugh out loud, it was a sort of laugh, in renewed sheer surprise at the fact of this plight into which she had been so piti-lessly, so ignominiously, delivered. Mostly, however, she kept herself quiet, lying on her side curled up like a lost explorer in his tent, half in a doze, half in a daze, indifferent equally, it seemed, to the prospect of survival or extinction. Up to now all her experiences had been temporary. Griefs had been assuaged, if only by time, joys had hardened into habit, her body had cured its own minor maladies. This, however, this was an absolute, a singularity, an end in itself, and yet she could not grasp it, could not absorb it. If there were pain, she said, it would at least be an authenticator, the thing to tell her that what had happened to her was realler than any reality she had known before now. But she was not in pain, not yet; there was only what she described as a general sense of agitation, a sort of interior fizzing, as if her poor, baffled body were scrabbling about inside itself, desperately throwing up defences against an invader that had already scuttled in by a secret way, its shiny black pincers snapping.

In those endless October nights, lying side by side in the darkness, toppled statues of ourselves, we sought escape from an intolerable present in the only tense possible, the past, that is, the faraway past. We went back over our earliest days together, reminding, correcting, helping each other, like two ancients tottering arm-in-arm along the ramparts of a town where they had once lived, long ago.

We recalled especially the smoky London summer

in which we met and married. I spotted Anna first at a party in someone's flat one chokingly hot afternoon, all the windows wide open and the air blue with exhaust fumes from the street outside and the honking of passing buses sounding incongruously like fog horns through the clamour and murk in the crowded rooms. It was the size of her that first caught my attention. Not that she was so very large, but she was made on a scale different from that of any woman I had known before her. Big shoulders, big arms, big feet, that great head with its sweep of thick dark hair. She was standing between me and the window, in cheesecloth and sandals, talking to another woman, in that way that she had, at once intent and remote, dreamily twisting a lock of hair around a finger, and for a moment my eye had difficulty fixing a depth of focus, since it seemed that, of the two of them, Anna, being so much the bigger, must be much nearer to me than the one to whom she was speaking.

Ah, those parties, so many of them in those days. When I think back I always see us arriving, pausing together on the threshold for a moment, my hand on the small of her back, touching through brittle silk the cool deep crevice there, her wild smell in my nostrils and the heat of her hair against my cheek.

How grand we must have looked, the two of us, making our entrance, taller than everyone else, our gaze directed over their heads as if fixed on some far fine vista that only we were privileged enough to see.

At the time she was trying to become a photographer, taking moody early-morning studies, all soot and raw silver, of some of the bleaker corners of the city. She wanted to work, to do something, to be someone. The East End called to her, Brick Lane, Spitalfields, such places. I never took any of this seriously. Perhaps I should have. She lived with her father in a rented apartment in a liver-coloured mansion on one of those gloomy backwaters off Sloane Square. It was an enormous place, with a succession of vast, high-ceilinged rooms and tall sash-windows that seemed to avert their glazed gaze from the mere human spectacle passing back and forth between them. Her Daddy, old Charlie Weiss – 'Don't worry, it's not a Jew name' – took to me at once. I was big and young and gauche, and my presence in those gilded rooms amused him. He was a merry little man with tiny delicate hands and tiny feet. His wardrobe was an amazement to me, innumerable Savile Row suits, shirts from Charvet in cream and bottle-green and aquamarine silk, dozens of pairs of handmade miniature shoes. His head, which he took to Trumper's to be shaved every other day – hair, he said, is fur, no human being should tolerate it – was a perfect polished egg, and he wore those big heavy spectacles favoured by tycoons of the time, with flanged ear-pieces and lenses the size of saucers in which his sharp little eyes darted like inquisitive, exotic fish. He could not be still, jumping up and sitting down and then jumping up again, seeming, under those lofty ceilings, a tiny burnished nut rattling around inside an outsized shell. On my first visit he showed me proudly around the flat, pointing out the pictures, old masters every one, so he imagined, the giant television set housed in a walnut cabinet, the bottle of Dom Perignon and basket of flawless inedible fruit that had been sent him that day by a business associate – Charlie did not have friends, partners, clients, but only associates. Light of summer thick as honey fell from the tall windows and glowed on the figured carpets. Anna sat on a sofa with her chin on her hand and one leg folded under her and watched dispassionately as I negotiated my way around her preposterous little father. Unlike most small people he was not at all intimidated by us big ones, and seemed indeed to find my bulk reassuring, and kept pressing close up to me, almost amorously; there were moments, while he was displaying the gleaming fruits of his success, when it seemed that he might of a sudden hop up and settle himself all comfy in the cradle of my arms. When he had mentioned his business interests for the third time I asked what business it was that he was in and he turned on me a gaze of flawless candour, those twin fish-bowls flashing.

'Heavy machinery,' he said, managing not to laugh.

Charlie regarded the spectacle of his life with delight and a certain wonder at the fact of having got away so easily with so much. He was a crook, probably dangerous, and wholly, cheerfully immoral. Anna held him in fond and rueful regard. How such a diminutive man had got so mighty a daughter was a mystery. Young as she was she seemed the tolerant mother and he the waywardly winning manchild. Her own mother had died when Anna was twelve and since then father and daughter had faced the world like a pair of nineteenth-century adventurers, a riverboat gambler, say, and his alibi girl. There were parties at the flat two or three times a week, raucous occasions through which champagne flowed like a bubbling and slightly rancid river. One night towards the end of that summer we came back from the park – I liked to walk with her at dusk through the dusty shadows under the trees that were already beginning to make that fretful, dry, papery rustle that harbinges autumn – and before we had even turned into the street we heard the sounds of tipsy revelry from the flat. Anna put a hand on my arm and we stopped. Something in the air of evening bespoke a sombre promise. She turned to me and took one of the buttons of my jacket between a finger and thumb and twisted it forward and back like the dial of a safe, and in her usual mild and mildly preoccupied fashion invited me to marry her.

Throughout that expectant, heat-hazed summer I seemed to have been breathing off the shallowest top of my lungs, like a diver poised on the highest board above that tiny square of blue so impossibly far below. Now Anna had called up to me ringingly to *jump, jump!* Today, when only the lower orders and what remains of the gentry bother to marry, and everyone else takes a partner, as if life were a dance, or a business venture, it is perhaps hard to appreciate how vertiginous a leap it was back then to plight one's troth. I had plunged into the louche world of Anna and her father as if into another medium, a fantastical one wherein the rules as I had known them up to then did not apply, where everything shimmered and nothing was real, or was real but looked fake, like that platter of perfect fruit in Charlie's flat. Now I was being invited to become a denizen of these excitingly alien deeps. What Anna proposed to me, there in the dusty summer dusk on the corner of Sloane Street, was not so much marriage as the chance to fulfil the fantasy of myself.

The wedding party was held under a striped marquee in the mansion's unexpectedly spacious back garden. It was one of the last days of that summer's heat-wave, the air, like scratched glass, crazed by glinting sunlight. Throughout the afternoon long gleaming motor cars kept pulling up outside and depositing yet more guests, heron-like ladies in big hats and girls in white lipstick and white leather knee-high boots, raffish pinstriped gents, delicate young men who pouted and smoked pot, and lesser, indeterminate types, Charlie's business associates, sleek, watchful and unsmiling, in shiny suits and shirts with different-coloured collars and sharp-toed ankle-boots with elasticated sides. Charlie bounced about amongst them all, his blued pate agleam, pride pouring off him like sweat. Late in the day a huddle of warm-eyed, slow-moving, shy plump men in headdresses and spotless white djellabas arrived in our midst like a flock of doves. Later still a dumpy dowager in a hat got stridently drunk and fell down and had to be carried away in the arms of her stone-jawed chauffeur. As the light thickened in the trees and the shadow of the next-door house began to close over the garden like a trapdoor, and the last drunken couples in their clown-bright clothes were shuffling around the makeshift wooden dance floor one last time with their heads fallen on each other's shoulders and their eyes shut and eyelids fluttering, Anna and I stood on the tattered edges of it all, and a dark burst of starlings out of nowhere flew low over the marquee, their wings making a clatter that was like a sudden round of applause, exuberant and sarcastic.

Her hair. Suddenly I am thinking of her hair, the long dark lustrous coil of it falling away from her forehead in a sideways sweep. Even in her middle age there was hardly a strand of grey in it. We were driving home from the hospital one day when she lifted a length of it from her shoulder and held it close to her eyes and examined it strand by strand, frowning.

'Is there a bird called a baldicoot?' she asked.

'There is a bandicoot,' I said cautiously, 'but I don't think it's a bird. Why?'

'Apparently I shall be as bald as a coot in a month or two.'

'Who told you that?'

'A woman in the hospital who was having treatment, the kind I am to have. She was quite bald, so I suppose she would know.' For a while she watched the houses and the shops progressing past the car window in that stealthily indifferent way that they do, and then turned to me again. 'But what is a coot?'

'That's a bird.'

'Ah.' She chuckled. 'I'll be the spitting image of Charlie when it has all fallen out.'

She was.

He died, old Charlie, of a blood clot in the brain, a few months after we were married. Anna got all his money. There was not as much of it as I would have expected, but still, there was a lot.

The odd thing, one of the odd things, about my passion for Mrs Grace is that it fizzled out almost in the same moment that it achieved what might be considered its apotheosis. It all happened on the afternoon of the picnic. By then we were going about everywhere together, Chloe and Myles and I. How proud I was to be seen with them, these divinities, for I thought of course that they were the gods, so different were they from anyone I had hitherto known. My former friends in the Field, where I no longer played, were resentful of my desertion. 'He spends all his time now with his grand new friends,' I heard my mother one day telling one of their mothers. 'The boy, you know,' she added in an undertone, 'is a dummy.' To me she wondered why I did not petition the Graces to adopt me. 'I won't mind,' she said. 'Get you out from under my feet.' And she gave me a level look, harsh and unblinking, the same look she would often turn on me after my father had gone, as if to say, *I suppose you will be the next to betray me.* As I suppose I was.

My parents had not met Mr and Mrs Grace, nor would they. People in a proper house did not mix with people from the chalets, and we would not expect to mix with them. We did not drink gin, or have people down for the weekend, or leave touring maps of France insouciantly on show in the back windows of our motor cars – few in the Field even had a motor car. The social structure of our summer world was as fixed and hard of climbing as a ziggurat. The few families who owned holiday homes were at the top, then came those who could afford to put up at hotels – the Beach was more desirable than the Golf – then there were the house renters, and then us. All-the-year-rounders did not figure in this hierarchy; villagers in general, such as Duignan the dairyman or deaf Colfer the golf-ball collector, or the two Protestant spinsters at the Ivy Lodge, or the French woman who ran the tennis courts and was said to copulate regularly with her alsatian dog, all these were a class apart, their presence no more than the blurred background to our intenser, sun-shone-upon doings. That I had managed to scramble from the base of those steep social steps all the way up to the level of the Graces seemed, like my secret passion for Connie Grace, a token of specialness, of being the one chosen among so many of the unelect. The gods had singled me out for their favour.

The picnic. We went that afternoon in Mr Grace's racy motor car far down the Burrow, all the way to where the paved road ended. A note of the voluptuous had been struck immediately by the feel of the stippled leather of the seat cover sticking to the backs of my thighs below my shorts. Mrs Grace sat beside her husband in front, half turned toward him, an elbow resting on the back of her seat so that I had a view of her armpit, excitingly stubbled, and even caught now and then, when the breeze from the open window veered my way, a whiff of her sweat-dampened flesh's civet scent. She was wearing a garment which I believe even in those demurer days was called, with graphic frankness, a halter top, no more than a strapless white woollen tube, very tight, and very revealing of the curves of her bosom's heavy undersides. She had on her film star's sunglasses with the white frames and was smoking a fat cigarette. It excited me to watch as she took a deep drag and let her mouth hang open crookedly for a moment, a rich curl of smoke suspended motionless between those waxily glistening scarlet lips. Her fingernails too were painted a bright sanguineous red. I was seated directly behind her in the back seat, with Chloe in the middle between Myles and me. Chloe's hot, bony thigh was pressed negligently against my leg. Brother and sister were engaged in one of their private wordless con- tests, tussling and squirming, plucking at each other with pincer fingers and trying to kick each other's shins in the cramped space between the seats. I never could make out the rules of these games, if rules there were, although a winner always emerged in the end, Chloe, most often. I recall, with even now a faint stirring of pity for poor Myles, the first time I witnessed them playing in this way, or fighting, more like. It was a wet afternoon and we were trapped indoors at the Cedars. What savagery a rainy day could bring out in us children! The twins were sitting on the living room floor, on their heels, facing each other, knee to knee, glaring into each other's eyes, their fingers interlocked, swaying and straining, intent as a pair of battling samurai, until at last something happened, I did not see what it was, although it was decisive, and Myles all at once was forced to surrender. Snatching his fingers from her steely claws he threw his arms around himself – he was a great clutcher of the injured or insulted self – and began to cry, in frustration and rage, emitting a high, strangled whine, his lower lip clamped over the upper and his eyes squeezed shut and spurting big, shapeless tears, the whole effect too dramatic to be entirely convincing. And what a gloatingly feline look victorious Chloe gave me over her shoulder, her face unpleasantly pinched and an eye-tooth glinting. Now, in the car, she won again, doing something to Myles's wrist that made him squeal. 'Oh, do stop, you two,' their mother said wearily, barely giving them a glance. Chloe, still grinning thinly in triumph, pressed her hip harder against my leg, while Myles grimaced, making a pursed O of his lips, this time holding back his tears, but barely, and chafing his reddened wrist.

At the end of the road Mr Grace stopped the car, and the hamper with its sandwiches and tea cups and bottles of wine was lifted from the boot and we set off to walk along a broad track of hard sand marked by an immemorial half-submerged rusted barbed-wire fence. I had never liked, even feared a little, this wild reach of marsh and mud flats where everything seemed turned away from the land, looking off desperately toward the horizon as if in mute search for a sign of rescue. The mud shone blue as a new bruise, and there were stands of bulrushes, and forgotten marker buoys tethered to slimed-over rotting wooden posts. High tide here was never more than inches deep, the water racing in over the flats swift and shiny as mercury, stopping at nothing. Mr Grace scampered ahead bandily, a folding chair clutched under each arm and that comical bucket hat tilted over his ear. We rounded the point and saw across the strait the town humped on its hill, a toy-like lavender jumble of planes and angles surmounted by a spire. Seeming to know where he was going Mr Grace struck off from the track into a meadow thronged with great tall ferns. We followed, Mrs Grace, Chloe, Myles, me. The ferns were as high as my head. Mr Grace was waiting for us on a grassy bank at the edge of the meadow, under an umbrella pine. Unnoticed, a shattered fern stalk had gouged a furrow in my bare ankle above the side of my sandal.

On a patch of grass between the low grassy bank and the wall of ferns a white cloth was spread. Mrs Grace, kneeling, a cigarette clamped in a corner of her mouth and one eye shut against the smoke, laid out the picnic things, while her husband, his hat falling further askew, struggled to draw a resistant wine cork. Myles was already off among the ferns. Chloe sat froglike on her haunches, eating an egg sandwich. Rose — where is Rose? She is there, in her scarlet shirt and dancing pumps and dancer's tight black pants with the straps that go under the soles of her feet, and her hair black as a crow's wing tied in a plume behind her fine-boned head. But how did she get here? She had not been in the car with us. A bicycle, yes, I see a bicycle asprawl in abandon among the ferns, handlebars turned side-ways and its front wheel jutting up at a somehow unseemly angle, a sly prefiguring, as it seems now, of what was to come. Mr Grace clamped the wine bottle between his knees and strained and strained, his earlobes turning red. Behind me Rose sat down at one corner of the tablecloth, leaning on a braced arm, her cheek almost resting on her shoulder, her legs folded off to the side, in a pose that should have been awkward but was not. I could hear Myles running in the ferns. Suddenly the cork came out of the wine bottle with a comical pop that startled us all.

We ate our picnic. Myles was pretending to be a wild beast and kept running in from the ferns and snatching handfuls of food and loping off again, hooting and whinnying. Mr and Mrs Grace drank their wine and presently Mr Grace was opening another bottle, this time with less difficulty. Rose said she was not hungry but Mrs Grace said that was nonsense and commanded her to eat and Mr Grace, grinning, offered her a banana. The afternoon was breezy under an as yet unclouded sky. The crooked pine soughed above us, and there was a smell of pine needles, and of grass and crushed ferns, and the salt tang of the sea. Rose sulked, I supposed because of Mrs Grace's rebuke and Mr Grace's offer of that lewd banana. Chloe was engrossed in picking at the stipples of a ruby cicatrice just below her elbow where the previous day a thorn had scratched her. I examined the fern-wound on my ankle, an angry pink groove between translucent deckle edges of whitish skin; it had not bled but in the deeps of the groove a clear ichor glinted. Mr Grace sat slumped into himself in a folding chair with one leg crossed on the other, smoking a cigarette, his hat pulled low on his forehead, shadowing his eyes.

I felt a soft small thing strike me on the cheek. Chloe had left off picking at her scabs and had thrown a breadcrumb at me. I looked at her and she looked back without expression and threw another crumb. This time she missed. I picked up the crumb from the grass and threw it back, but I missed, too. Mrs Grace was idly watching us, reclining on her side directly in front of me on the shallow incline of the verdant bank, her head supported on a hand. She had set the stem of her wine glass in the grass with the bowl wedged at an angle against a sideways lolling breast – I wondered, as so often, if they were not sore to carry, those big twin bulbs of milky flesh – and now she licked a fingertip and ran it around the rim of the glass, trying to make it sing, but no sound came. Chloe put a pellet of bread into her mouth and wetted it with spit and took it out again and kneaded it in her fingers with slow delibera-tion and took leisurely aim and threw it at me, but the wad fell short. 'Chloe!' her mother said, a wan reproach, and Chloe ignored her and smiled at me her cat's thin, gloating smile. She was a cruel-hearted girl, my Chloe. For her amusement of a day I would catch a handful of grasshoppers and tear off one of their back legs to prevent them escaping and put the twitching torsos in the lid of a polish tin and douse them in paraffin and set them alight. How intently, squatting with hands pressed on her knees, she would watch the unfortunate creatures as they seethed, boiling in their own fat.

She was making another spit-ball. 'Chloe, you are disgusting,' Mrs Grace said with a sigh, and Chloe, all at once bored, spat out the bread and brushed the crumbs from her lap and rose and walked off sulkily into the shadow of the pine tree.

Did Connie Grace catch my eye? Was that a complicit smile? With a heaving sigh she turned and lay down supine on the bank with her head leaning back on the grass and flexed one leg, so that suddenly I was allowed to see under her skirt along the inner side of her thigh all the way up to the hollow of her lap and the plump mound there sheathed in tensed white cotton. At once everything began to slow. Her emptied glass fell over in a swoon and a last drop of wine ran to the rim and hung an instant glittering and then fell. I stared and stared, my brow growing hot and my palms wet. Mr Grace under his hat seemed to be smirking at me but I did not care, he could smirk all he liked. His big wife, growing bigger by the moment, a foreshortened, headless giantess at whose huge feet I crouched in what felt almost like fear, gave a sort of wriggle and raised her knee higher still, revealing the crescent-shaped crease at the full-fleshed back of her leg where her rump began. A drumbeat in my temples was making the daylight dim. I was aware of the throbbing sting in my gouged ankle. And now from far off in the ferns there came a thin, shrill sound, an archaic pipe-note piercing through the lacquered air, and Chloe, up at the tree, scowled as if called to duty and bent and plucked a blade of grass and pressing it between her thumbs blew an answering note out of the conch-shell of her cupped hands.

After a timeless minute or two my sprawling maja drew in her leg and turned on her side again and fell asleep with shocking suddenness – her gentle snores were the sound of a small, soft engine trying and failing repeatedly to start – and I sat up, carefully, as if something delicately poised inside me might shatter at the slightest violent movement. All at once I had a sour sense of deflation. The excitement of a moment past was gone, and there was a dull restriction in my chest, and sweat on my eyelids and my upper lip, and the damp skin under the waistband of my shorts was prickly and hot. I felt puzzled, and strangely resentful, too, as if I were the one, not she, whose private self had been intruded upon and abused. It was a manifestation of the goddess I had witnessed, no doubt of that, but the instant of divinity had been disconcertingly brief. Under my greedy gaze Mrs Grace had been transformed from woman into daemon and then in a moment was mere woman again. One moment she was Connie Grace, her husband's wife, her children's mother, the next she was an object of helpless veneration, a faceless idol, ancient and elemental, conjured by the force of my desire, and then something in her had suddenly gone slack, and I had felt a qualm of revulsion and shame, not shame for myself and what I had purloined of her but, obscurely, for the woman herself, and not for anything she had done, either, but for what she was, as with a hoarse moan she turned on her side and toppled into sleep, no longer a demon temptress but herself only, a mortal woman.

Yet for all my disconcertion it is the mortal she, and not the divine, who shines for me still, with however tarnished a gleam, amidst the shadows of what is gone. She is in my memory her own avatar. Which is the more real, the woman reclining on the grassy bank of my recollections, or the strew of dust and dried marrow that is all the earth any longer retains of her? No doubt for others elsewhere she persists, a moving figure in the waxworks of memory, but their version will be different from mine, and from each other's. Thus in the minds of the many does the one ramify and disperse. It does not last, it cannot, it is not immortality. We carry the dead with us only until we die too, and then it is we who are borne along for a little while, and then our bearers in their turn drop, and so on into the unimaginable generations. I remember Anna, our daughter Claire will remember Anna and remember me, then Claire will be gone and there will be those who remember her but not us, and that will be our final dissolution. True, there will be something of us that will remain, a fading photograph, a lock of hair, a few fingerprints, a sprinkling of atoms in the air of the room where we breathed our last, yet none of this will be us, what we are and were, but only the dust of the dead.

As a boy I was quite religious. Not devout, only compulsive. The God I venerated was Yaweh, destroyer of worlds, not gentle Jesus meek and mild. The Godhead for me was menace, and I responded with fear and its inevitable concomitant, guilt. I was a very virtuoso of guilt in those younger days, and still am in these older ones, for that matter. At the time of my First Communion, or, more to the point, the First Confession that preceded it, a priest came daily to the convent school to induct our class of fledgling penitents into the intricacies of Christian

Doctrine. He was a lean, pale fanatic with flecks of white stuff permanently at the corners of his lips. I am recalling with especial clarity an enraptured disquisition he delivered to us one fine May morning on the sin of looking. Yes, looking. We had been instructed in the various categories of sin, those of commission and omission, the mortal and the venial, the seven deadly, and the terrible ones that it was said only a bishop could absolve, but here it seemed was a new category: the passive sin. Did we imagine, Fr Foamfleck scoffingly enquired, pacing impetuously from door to window, from window to door, his cassock swishing and a star of light gleaming on his narrow, balding brow like a reflection of the divine effluvium itself, did we imagine that sin must always involve the performance of an action? Looking with lust or envy or hate is lusting, envying, hating; the wish unfollowed by the deed leaves an equal stain upon the soul. Had not the Lord himself, he cried, warming to his theme, had not the Lord himself insisted that a man who looks with an adulterous heart upon a woman has as good as committed the act? By now he had quite forgotten about us, as we sat like a little band of mice gazing up at him in awed incomprehension. Although all this was as much news to me as it was to everyone else in the class – what was adultery, a sin that only adults could commit? – I understood it well enough, in my way, and welcomed it, for even at the age of seven I was an old hand, or should I say eye, at spying upon acts I was not supposed to witness, and knew well the dark pleasure of taking things by sight and the darker shame that followed. So when I had looked my fill, and look I did and filled I was, up the silvery length of Mrs Grace's thigh to the crotch of her knickers and that crease across the plump top of her leg under her bum, it was natural that I should immediately cast about for fear that all that while someone in turn might have been looking at me, the looker. Myles who had come in from the ferns was busy ogling Rose, and Chloe was still lost in vacant reverie under the pine tree, but Mr Grace, now, had he not been observing me, all along, from under the brim of that hat of his? He sat as though collapsed into himself, his chin on his chest and his furred belly bulging out of his open shirt, a bare ankle still crossed on a bare knee, so that I could see along his inner leg, too, up to the great balled lump in his khaki shorts squeezed to bursting between thick thighs. All that long afternoon, as the pine tree spread its steadily deepening purple shadow across the grass toward him, he hardly left his folding chair except to refill his wife's wine glass or fetch something to eat – I can see him, crushing half a ham sandwich between bunched fingers and thumb and stuffing the resultant mush at one go into the red hole in his beard.

To us then, at that age, all adults were unpredictable, even slightly mad, but Carlo Grace required a particularly wary monitoring. He was given to the sudden feint, the unexpected pounce. Sitting in an armchair and seemingly lost in his newspaper, he would shoot out a hand quick as a striking snake as Chloe was passing by and catch hold of her ear or a handful of her hair and twist it vigorously and painfully, with never a word or a pause in his reading, as if arm and hand had acted of their own volition. He would break off deliberately in the midst of saying something and go still as a statue, a hand suspended, gazing blank-eyed into the nothing beyond one's nervously twitching shoulder as if attending to some dread alarm or distant tumult that only he could hear, and then suddenly would make a sham grab at one's throat and laugh hissingly through his teeth. He would engage the postman, who was halfway to being a halfwit, in earnest consultation about the prospects for the weather or the likely outcome of an upcoming football match, nodding and frowning and fingering his beard, as if what he was hearing were the purest pearls of wisdom, and then when the poor deluded fellow had gone off, whistling pridefully, he would turn to us and grin, with lifted eyebrows and pursed lips, waggling his head in soundless mirth. Although all my attention seemed to have been trained upon the others, I think now that it was from Carlo Grace I first derived the notion that I was in the presence of the gods. For all his remoteness and amused indifference, he was the one who appeared to be in command over us all, a laughing deity, the Poseidon of our summer, at whose beck our little world arranged itself obediently into its acts and portions.

Still that day of licence and illicit invitation was not done. As Mrs Grace, stretched there on the grassy bank, continued softly snoring, a torpor descended on the rest of us in that little dell, the invisible net of lassitude that falls over a company when one of its number detaches and drops away into sleep. Myles was lying on his stomach on the grass beside me but facing in the opposite direction, still eyeing Rose where she was still seated behind me on a corner of the tablecloth, oblivious, as always, of his beady regard. Chloe was still standing in the shadow of the pine tree, holding something in her hand, her face lifted, looking up intently, at a bird, perhaps, or just at the latticework of branches against the sky, and those white puffs of cloud that had begun to inch their way in from the sea. How pensive she was yet how vividly defined, with that pine cone – was it? – in her hands, her rapt gaze fixed amongst the sunshot boughs. Suddenly she was the centre of the scene, the vanishing-point upon which everything converged, suddenly it was she for whom these patterns and these shades had been arranged with such meticulous artlessness: that white cloth on the polished grass, the leaning, blue-green tree, the frilled ferns, even those little clouds, trying to seem not to move, high up in the limitless, marine sky. I glanced at Mrs Grace asleep, glanced almost with contempt. All at once she was no more than a big archaic lifeless torso, the felled effigy of some goddess no longer worshipped by the tribe and thrown out on the midden, a target for the village boys with their slingshots and their bows and arrows.

Abruptly, as if roused by the cold touch of my scorn, she sat up and cast about her with a blurred look, blinking. She peered into her wine glass and seemed surprised to find it empty. The drop of wine that had fallen on her white halter had left a pink stain, she rubbed it with a fingertip, clicking her tongue. Then she looked about at us again and cleared her throat and announced that we should all play a game of chase. Everyone stared at her, even Mr Grace. '*I'm* not chasing anyone,' Chloe said from her place under the tree's shade, and laughed, a disbelieving snort, and when her mother said she must, and called her a spoilsport, she came and stood beside her father's chair and leaned an elbow on his shoulder and narrowed her eyes at her mother, and Mr Grace, old grinning goat god, put an arm around her hips and folded her in his hairy embrace. Mrs Grace turned to me. 'You'll play, won't you?' she said. 'And Rose.'

I see the game as a series of vivid tableaux, glimpsed instants of movement all rush and colour: Rose from the waist up racing through the ferns in her red shirt, her head held high and her black hair streaming behind her; Myles, with a streak of fern-juice on his forehead like warpaint, trying to wriggle out of my grasp as I dug my claw deeper into his flesh and felt the ball of his shoulder bone grind in its socket; another fleeting image of Rose running, this time on the hard sand beyond the clearing, where she was being chased by a wildly laughing Mrs Grace, two barefoot maenads framed for a moment by the bole and branches of the pine, beyond them the dull-silver glint of the bay and the sky a deep unvarying matt blue all the way down to the horizon. Here is Mrs Grace in a clearing in the ferns crouched on one knee like a sprinter waiting for the off, who, when I surprise her, instead of fleeing, as the rules of the game say that she should, beckons to me urgently and makes me crouch at her side and puts an arm around me and draws me tight against her so that I can feel the softly giving bulge of her breast and hear her heart beating and smell her milk-and-vinegar smell. 'Ssh!' she says and puts a finger to my lips – to mine, not her own. She is trembling, ripples of suppressed laughter run through her. I have not been so close to a grown-up woman since I was a child in my mother's arms, but in place of desire now I feel only a kind of surly dread. Rose discovers the two of us crouching there, and scowls. Mrs Grace, grasping the girl's hand as if to haul herself up, instead pulls her down on top of us, and there is a melee of arms and legs and Rose's flying hair and then the three of us, leaning back on our elbows and panting, are sprawled toe to toe in a star shape amid the crushed ferns. I scramble to my feet, suddenly afraid that Mrs Grace, my suddenly former beloved, will wantonly display her lap to me again, and she puts up a hand to shade her eyes and looks at me with an impenetrable, hard, unwarm smile. Rose too springs up, brushing at her shirt, and mutters something angrily that I do not catch and strides off into the ferns. Mrs Grace shrugs. 'Jealous,' she says, and then bids me fetch her cigarettes, for all of a sudden, she declares, she is dying for a fag.

When we returned to the grassy bank and the pine tree Chloe and her father were not there. The remains of the picnic, scattered on the white cloth, had a look of deliberateness to them, as if they had been arranged there, a message in code for us to decipher. 'That's nice,' Mrs Grace said sourly, 'they've left the clearing-up to us.' Myles emerged from the ferns again and knelt and picked a blade of grass and blew another reed note between his thumbs and waited, still and rapt as a plaster faun, the sunlight burnishing his straw-pale hair, and a moment later from far off came Chloe's answering call, a pure high whistle piercing like a needle through the waning summer day.

On the subject of observing and being observed, I must mention the long, grim gander I took at myself in the bathroom mirror this morning. Usually these days I do not dally before my reflection any longer than is necessary. There was a time when I quite liked what I saw in the looking-glass, but not any more. Now I am startled, and more than startled, by the visage that so abruptly appears there, never and not at all the one that I expect. I have been elbowed aside by a parody of myself, a sadly dishevelled figure in a Hallowe'en mask made of sagging, pinkish-grey rubber that bears no more than a passing resemblance to the image of what I look like that I stubbornly retain in my head. Also, there is the problem that I have with mirrors. That is, I have many problems with mirrors, but mostly they are metaphysical in nature, whereas the one I speak of is entirely practical. Because of my inordinate and absurd size, shaving mirrors and the like are always set too low for me on the wall, so that I have to lean down to be able to view the entirety of my face. Lately when I see myself peering out of the glass, stooped like that, with that expression of dim surprise and vague, slow fright which is perpetual with me now, mouth slack and eyebrows arched as if in weary astonishment, I feel I have definitely something of the look of a hanged man.

When I came here first I thought of growing a beard, out of inertia more than anything else, but after three or four days I noticed that the stubble was of a peculiar dark-rust colour – now I know how

Claire can be a redhead – nothing like the hair on my scalp, and frosted with specks of silver. This rufous stuff, coarse as sandpaper, combined with that shifty, bloodshot gaze, made me into a comic-strip convict, a real hard case, not yet hanged perhaps but definitely on Death Row. My temples where the greying hair has gone sparse are flecked with choco-latey, Avrilaceous freckles, or liver spots, I suppose they are, any one of which, I am all too well aware, might in a moment turn rampant at the whim of a rogue cell. I note too that my rosacea is coming on apace. The skin on my brow is marked all over with rubescent blotches and there is an angry rash on the wings of my nose, and even my cheeks are developing an unsightly red flush. My venerable and much thumbed copy of *Black's Medical Dictionary*, by the estimable and ever unflappable William A. R. Thomson, M.D. – Adam & Charles Black, London, thirtieth edition, with 441 black-and-white, or grey-and-greyer, illustrations and four colour plates which never fail to freeze the cockles of my heart – informs me that rosacea, a nice name for an unpleasant com-plaint, is due to *a chronic congestion of the flush areas of the face and forehead, leading to the formation of red papules*; the resultant erythema, the name we medical men give to redness of the skin, tends to wax and wane but ultimately becomes permanent, *and may*, the candid Doctor warns, *be accompanied by gross enlargement of the sebaceous glands (see SKIN), leading to the gross enlargement of the nose known as rhino-phyma (qv) or grog blossoms.* The repetition there – *gross enlargement . . . gross enlargement* – is an uncharacteristic infelicity in Dr Thomson's usually euphonious if somewhat antiquated prose style. I wonder if he does house calls. He would be bound to have a calming bedside manner and a fund of information on all sorts of topics, not all of them health-related. Medical men are more versatile than they are given credit for. Roget of *Roget's Thesaurus* was a physician, did important research on consumption and laughing gas, and no doubt cured the odd patient, into the bargain. But grog blossoms, now, that is something to look forward to.

When I consider my face in the glass like this I think, naturally, of those last studies Bonnard made of himself in the bathroom mirror at Le Bosquet towards the end of the war after his wife had died – critics call these portraits pitiless, although I do not see why pity should come into it – but in fact what my reflection most reminds me of, I have just realised it, is that Van Gogh self-portrait, not the famous one with bandage and tobacco pipe and bad hat, but that one from an earlier series, done in Paris in 1887, in which he is bare-headed in a high collar and Provence-blue necktie with all ears intact, looking as if he has just emerged from some form of punitive dousing, the forehead sloped and temples concave and cheeks sunken as from hunger; he peers out from the frame sidewise, warily, with wrathful foreboding, expecting the worst, as so he should.

This morning it was the state of my eyes that struck me most forcibly, the whites all cracaleured over with those tiny bright-red veins and the moist lower lids inflamed and hanging a little way loose of the eyeballs. I have, I note, hardly any lashes left, I who when young had a silky set a girl might have envied. At the inner extremity of the upper lids there is a little bump just before the swoop of the canthus which is almost pretty except that it is permanently yellowish at the tip, as if infected. And that bud in the canthus itself, what is that for? Nothing in the human visage bears prolonged scrutiny. The pink-tinged pallor of my cheeks, which are, I am afraid, yes, sunken, just like poor Vincent's, was made the more stark and sickly by the radiance reflected off the white walls and the enamel of the sink. This radiance was not the glow of a northern autumn but seemed more like the hard, unyielding, dry glare of the far south. It glinted on the glass before me and sank into the distemper of the walls, giving them the parched, brittle texture of cuttlefish bone. A spot of it on the curve of the hand-basin streamed outward in all directions like an immensely distant nebula. Standing there in that white box of light I was transported for a moment to some far shore, real or imagined, I do not know which, although the details had a remarkable dreamlike definition, where I sat in the sun on a hard ridge of shaly sand holding in my hands a big flat smooth blue stone. The stone was dry and warm, I seemed to press it to my lips, it seemed to taste saltily of the sea's deeps and distances, far islands, lost places under leaning fronds, the frail skeletons of fishes, wrack and rot. The little waves before me at the water's edge speak with an animate voice, whispering eagerly of some ancient catastrophe, the sack of Troy, perhaps, or the sinking of Atlantis. All brims, brackish and shining. Water-beads break and fall in a silver string from the tip of an oar. I see the black ship in the distance, looming imperceptibly nearer at every instant. I am there. I hear your siren's song. I am there, almost there.

II

WE SEEMED TO SPEND, Chloe and Myles and I, the most part of our days in the sea. We swam in sunshine and in rain; we swam in the morning, when the sea was sluggish as soup, we swam at night, the water flowing over our arms like undulations of black satin; one afternoon we stayed in the water during a thunderstorm, and a fork of lightning struck the surface of the sea so close to us we heard the crackle of it and smelt the burnt air. I was not much of a swimmer. The twins had been taking lessons since they were babies and clove the waves effortlessly, like two pairs of gleaming shears. What I lacked of skill and gracefulness I made up for in stamina. I could go long distances without stopping, and frequently did, given any kind of audience, churning along steadily in sidestroke until I had exhausted not only myself but the patience of the watchers on the strand as well.

It was at the end of one of these sad little gala displays that I had my first inkling of a change in Chloe's regard for me, or, should I say, an inkling that she had a regard for me and that a change was occurring in it. Late in the evening it was, and I had swum the distance – what, a hundred, two hundred yards? – between two of the green-slimed concrete groynes that long ago had been thrown out into the sea in a vain attempt to halt the creeping erosion of the beach. I stumbled out of the waves to find that Chloe had waited for me, on the shore, all the time that I was in the water. She stood huddled in a towel, shivering in spasms; her lips were lavender. 'There's no need to show off, you know,' she said crossly. Before I could reply – and what would I have said, anyway, since she was right, I had been showing off – Myles came leaping down from the dunes above us on wheeling legs and sprayed us both with sand and at once I had an image, perfectly clear and strangely stirring, of Chloe as I had first seen her that day when she jumped from the edge of that other dune into the midst of my life. Now she handed me my towel. We three were the only ones on the beach. The misty grey air of evening had the feel of dampened ash. I see us turn and walk away toward the gap in the dunes that led to Station Road. A corner of Chloe's towel trails in the sand. I go along with my towel draped over one shoulder and my wet hair slicked down, a Roman senator in miniature. Myles runs ahead. But who is it that lingers there on the strand in the half-light, by the darkening sea that seems to arch its back like a beast as the night fast advances from the fogged horizon? What phantom version of me is it that watches us – them – those three children – as they grow indistinct in that cinereal air and then are gone through the gap that will bring them out at the foot of Station Road?

I have not yet described Chloe. In appearance there was not much difference between us, she and I, at that age, I mean in terms of what of us might have been measured. Even her hair, almost white but darkening when it was wet to the colour of polished wheat, was hardly longer than mine. She wore it in a pageboy style, with a fringe at the front overhanging her handsome, high-domed, oddly convex forehead – like, it suddenly strikes me, remarkably like the forehead of that ghostly figure seen in profile hovering at the edge of Bonnard's *Table in Front of the Window*, the one with the fruit bowl and the book and the window that itself looks like a canvas seen from behind propped on an easel; everything for me is something else, it is a thing I notice increasingly. One of the older boys from the Field assured me one day with a snicker that a fringe like Chloe's was the certain sign of a girl who played with herself. I did not know what he meant, but I felt sure that Chloe did not play, on her own or otherwise. Not for her the games of rounders or of hunt that I had formerly enjoyed with the other youngsters in the Field. And how she sneered, flaring her nostrils, when I told her that among the families in the chalets there were girls of her age who still played with dolls. She held the majority of her coevals in high scorn. No, Chloe did not play, except with Myles, and what they did together was not really play.

The boy who had remarked on her fringe – suddenly I see him, as if he were before me here, Joe somebody, a hulking, big-boned fellow with jug ears and horrent hair – also said that Chloe had green teeth. I was outraged, but he was right; there was, I saw, the next time I had the opportunity to take a close look at them, a faint tinge to the enamel of her incisors that was green indeed, but a delicate damp grey-green, like the damp light under trees after rain, or the dull-apple shade of the undersides of leaves reflected in still water. Apples, yes, her breath too had an appley smell. Little animals we were, sniffing at each other. I liked in particular, when in time I got the chance to savour it, the cheesy tang in the crevices of her elbows and her knees. She was not, I am compelled to admit, the most hygienic of girls, and in general she gave off, more strongly as the day progressed, a flattish, fawnish odour, like that which comes out of, which used to come out of, empty biscuit tins in shops – do shops still sell loose biscuits from those big square tins? Her hands. Her eyes. Her bitten fingernails. All this I remember, intensely remember, yet it is all disparate, I cannot assemble it into a unity. Try as I may, pretend as I may, I am unable to conjure her as I can her mother, say, or Myles, or even jug-eared Joe from the Field. I cannot, in short, see her. She wavers before my memory's eye at a fixed distance, always just beyond focus, moving backward at exactly the same rate as I am moving forward. But since what I am moving forward into has begun to dwindle more and more rapidly, why can I not catch up with her? Even still I sometimes see her in the street, I mean someone who might be she, with the same domed forehead and pale hair, the same headlong and yet curiously hesitant, pigeon-toed stride, but always too young, years, years too young. This is the mystery that baffled me then, and that baffles me yet. How could she be with me one moment and the next not? How could she be elsewhere, absolutely? That was what I could not understand, could not be reconciled to, cannot still. Once out of my presence she should by right become pure figment, a memory of mine, a dream of mine, but all the evidence told me that even away from me she remained solidly, stubbornly, incomprehensibly herself. And yet people do go, do vanish. That is the greater mystery; the greatest. I too could go, oh, yes, at a moment's notice I could go and be as though I had not been, except that the long habit of living indisposeth me for dying, as Doctor Browne has it.

'*Patient*,' Anna said to me one day towards the end, 'that is an odd word. I must say, I don't feel patient at all.'

When exactly I transferred my affections – how incorrigibly fond I am of these old-fashioned formulations! – from mother to daughter I cannot recollect. There was that moment of insight and intensity at the picnic, with Chloe, under the pine tree, but that was an aesthetic rather than amorous or erotic crystallisation. No, I recall no grand moment of recognition and acknowledgment, no slipping of Chloe's hand shyly into mine, no sudden stormy embrace, no stammered profession of eternal love. That is, there must have been some or even all of these, must have been a first time we held hands, embraced, made declarations, but these first times are lost in the folds of an ever more evanescent past. Even that evening when with chattering teeth I waded out of the sea and found her waiting for me blue-lipped on the strand in the dusk I did not suffer the soundless detonation that love is supposed to set off in even a boy's supposedly unsusceptible breast. I saw how cold she was, and realised how long she had waited, registered too the brusquely tender way in which she drew the wing of the towel across my scrawny, goosefleshed ribs and draped it on my shoulder, but saw and realised and registered with little more than a mild glow of gratification, as though a warm breath had fanned across a flame burning inside me some-where in the vicinity of my heart and made it briefly flare. Yet all along a transmutation, not to say a transubstantiation, must have been taking place, in secret.

I do recall a kiss, one out of the so many that I have forgotten. Whether or not it was our first kiss I do not know. They meant so much then, kisses, they could set the whole kit and caboodle going, flares and firecrackers, fountains, gushing geysers, the lot. This one took place – no, was exchanged – no, was consummated, that is the word, in the corrugated-iron picture-house, which all along has been surreptitiously erecting itself for this very purpose out of the numerous sly references I have sprinkled through these pages. It was a barn-like structure set on a bit of scrubby waste-land between the Cliff Road and the beach. It had a steeply angled roof and no windows, only a door at the side, hung with a long curtain, of leather, I think, or somesuch stiff heavy stuff, to keep the screen from being whited-out when late-comers slipped in during matinées or at evening while the sun was shooting out its last piercing rays from behind the tennis courts. For seating there were wooden benches – we called them forms – and the screen was a large square of linen which any stray draught would set languorously asway, giving an extra undulation to some heroine's silk-clad hips or an incongruous quiver to a fearless gunslinger's gun-hand. The proprietor was a Mr Reckett, or Rickett, a small man in a Fair Isle jumper, assisted by his two big handsome teenage sons, who were a little ashamed, I always thought, of the family business, with its taint of peep-shows and the burlesque. There was only one projector, a noisy affair with a tendency to overheat – I am convinced I once saw smoke coming out of its innards – so that a full-length feature required at least two reel changes. During these intervals Mr R., who was also the projectionist, did not raise the lights, thus affording – deliberately, I am sure, for Reckett's or Rickett's Picture-House had an invitingly disreputable reputation – the numerous couples in the house, even the under-age ones, an opportunity for a minute or two of covert erotic fumbling in the pitch-dark.

On that afternoon, the rainy Saturday afternoon of this momentous kiss I am about to describe, Chloe and I were sitting in the middle of a bench near the front, so close to the screen that it seemed to tilt out over us at the top and even the most benign of the black-and-white phantoms flickering across it loomed with a manic intensity. I had been holding Chloe's hand for so long I had ceased to feel it in mine – not the primal encounter itself could have fused two fleshes so thoroughly as did those early hand-holdings – and when with a lurch and a stutter the screen went blank and her fingers twitched like fishes I twitched too. Above us the screen retained a throbbing grey penumbral glow that lasted a long moment before fading, and of which something seemed to remain even when it was gone, the ghost of a ghost. In the dark there were the usual hoots and whistles and a thunderous stamping of feet. As at a signal, under this canopy of noise, Chloe and I turned our heads simultaneously and, devout as holy drinkers, dipped our faces toward each other until our mouths met. We could see nothing, which intensified all sensations. I felt as if we were flying, without effort, dream-slowly, through the dense, powdery darkness. The clamour around us was immensely far-off now, the mere rumour of a distant uproar. Chloe's lips were cool and dry. I tasted her urgent breath. When at last with a strange little whistling sigh she drew her face away from mine a shimmer passed along my spine, as if something hot inside it had suddenly liquified and run down its hollow length. Then Mr Rickett or Reckett – perhaps it was Rockett? – brought the projector to sputtering life again and the crowd subsided into more or less quiet. The screen flared white, the film clattered through its gate, and in the second before the soundtrack started up I heard the heavy rain that had been drumming on the iron roof above us suddenly cease.

Happiness was different in childhood. It was so much then a matter simply of accumulation, of taking things – new experiences, new emotions – and applying them like so many polished tiles to what would someday be the marvellously finished pavilion of the self. And incredulity, that too was a large part of being happy, I mean that euphoric inability fully to believe one's simple luck. There I was, suddenly, with a girl in my arms, figuratively, at least, doing the things that grown-ups did, holding her hand, and kissing her in the dark, and, when the picture had ended, standing aside, clearing my throat in grave politeness, to allow her to pass ahead of me under the heavy curtain and through the doorway out into the rain-washed sunlight of the summer evening. I was myself and at the same time someone else, someone completely other, completely new. As I walked behind her amid the trudging crowd in the direction of the Strand Café I touched a fingertip to my lips, the lips that had kissed hers, half expecting to find them changed in some infinitely subtle but momentous way. I expected everything to be changed, like the day itself, that had been sombre and wet and hung with big-bellied clouds when we were going into the picture-house in what had still been afternoon and now at evening was all tawny sunlight and raked shadows, the scrub grass dripping with jewels and a red sail-boat out on the bay turning its prow and setting off toward the horizon's already dusk-blue distances.

The café. In the café. In the café we.

*

It was an evening just like that, the Sunday evening when I came here to stay, after Anna had gone at last. Although it was autumn and not summer the dark-gold sunlight and the inky shadows, long and slender in the shape of felled cypresses, were the same, and there was the same sense of everything drenched and jewelled and the same ultramarine glitter on the sea. I felt inexplicably lightened; it was as if the evening, in all the drench and drip of its fallacious pathos, had temporarily taken over from me the burden of grieving. Our house, or my house, as supposedly it was now, had still not been sold, I had not yet had the heart to put it on the market, but I could not have stayed there a moment longer. After Anna's death it went hollow, became a vast echo-chamber. There was something hostile in the air, too, the growling surliness of an old hound unable to understand where its beloved mistress has gone and resentful of the master who remains. Anna would allow no one to be told of her illness. People suspected something was up, but not, until the final stages, that what was up, for her, was the game itself. Even Claire had been left to guess that her mother was dying. And now it was over, and something else had begun, for me, which was the delicate business of being the survivor.

Miss Vavasour was shyly excited by my arrival, two small round spots like dabs of pink crêpe paper glowed high on her finely wrinkled cheeks and she kept clasping her hands before her and pursing her lips to stop herself smiling. When she opened the door Colonel Blunden was there, bobbing behind her in the hallway, now at this shoulder now at that; I could see straight away he did not like the look of me. I sympathise; after all, he was cock of the walk here before I came and knocked him off his perch. Keeping a choleric glare directed at my chin, which was on his eye-level, for he is low-sized despite the ramrod spine, he pumped my hand and cleared his throat, all bluff and manly and barking comments about the weather, rather over-playing the part of the old soldier, I thought. There is something about him that is not quite right, something too shiny, too studiedly plausible. Those glossy brogues, the Harris tweed jacket with leather patches on the elbows and the cuffs, the canary-yellow waistcoat he sports at weekends, it all seems a little too good to be true. He has the glazed flawlessness of an actor who has been playing the same part for too long. I wonder if he really is an old army man. He does a good job of hiding his Belfast accent but hints of it keep escaping, like trapped wind. And anyway, why hide it, what does he fear it might tell us? Miss Vavasour confides that she has spotted him on more than one occasion slipping into church of a Sunday for early mass. A Belfast Catholic colonel? Rum; very.

In the bay of the window in the lounge, formerly the living room, a hunting table was set for tea. The room was much as I remembered it, or looked as if it was as I remembered, for memories are always eager to match themselves seamlessly to the things and places of a revisited past. The table, was that the one where Mrs Grace had stood arranging flowers that day, the day of the dog with the ball? It was laid elaborately, big silver teapot with matching strainer, best bone china, antique creamer, tongs for the sugar cubes, doilies. Miss Vavasour was in Japanese mode, her hair done up in a bun and pierced with the two big crossed pins, making me think, incongruously, of those erotic prints of the Japanese eighteenth century in which puffy, porcelain-faced matrons suffer imperturbably the gross attentions of grimacing gentlemen with outsized members and, I am always struck to notice, remarkably pliant toes.

The conversation did not flow. Miss Vavasour was nervous still and the Colonel's stomach rumbled. Late sunlight striking through a bush outside in the blustery garden dazzled our eyes and made the things on the table seem to shake and shift. I felt over-sized, clumsy, constrained, like a big delinquent child sent by its despairing parents into the country to be watched over by a pair of elderly relatives. Was it all a hideous mistake? Should I mumble some excuse and flee to a hotel for the night, or go home, even, and put up with the emptiness and the echoes? Then I reflected that I had come here precisely so that it should be a mistake, that it should be hideous, that it should be, that I should be, in Anna's word, inappropriate. 'You're mad,' Claire had said, 'you'll die of boredom down there.' It was all right for her, I retorted, she had got herself a nice new flat – *wasting no time*, I did not add. 'Then come and live with me,' she said, 'there's room enough for two.' Live with her! Room for two! But I only thanked her and said no, that I wished to be on my own. I cannot bear the way she looks at me these days, all tenderness and daughterly concern, her head held to one side in just the way that Anna used to do, one eyebrow lifted and her forehead wrinkled solicitously. I do not want solicitude. I want anger, vituperation, violence. I am like a man with an agonising toothache who despite the pain takes a vindictive pleasure in prodding the point of his tongue again and again deep into the throbbing cavity. I imagine a fist flying out of nowhere and striking me full in the face, I almost feel the thud and hear the nose-bone breaking, even the thought of it affords me a grain of sad satisfaction. After the funeral, when people came back to the house – that was awful, almost unbearable – I gripped a wine glass so hard it shattered in my fist. Gratified, I watched my own blood drip as though it were the blood of an enemy to whom I had dealt a savage slash.

'So you're in the art business, then,' the Colonel said warily. 'A lot in that, yes?'

He meant money. Miss Vavasour, pinched-lipped, frowned at him fiercely and gave her head a reproving shake. 'He only writes about it,' she said in a whisper, gulping the words as she spoke them, as if that way I would be spared hearing them.

The Colonel looked quickly from me to her and back again and dumbly nodded. He expects to get things wrong, he is inured to it. He drinks his tea with a little finger cocked. The little finger of his other hand is hooked permanently flat against the palm, it is a syndrome, not uncommon, the name of which I have forgotten; it looks painful but he says it is not. He makes curiously elegant, sweeping gestures with that hand, a conductor calling up the woodwinds or urging a fortissimo from the chorus. He has a slight tremor, too, more than once the tea cup clacked against his front teeth, which must be dentures, so white and even are they. The skin of his weatherbeaten face and the backs of his hands is wrinkled and brown and shiny, like shiny brown paper that had been used to wrap something unwrappable.

'I see,' he said, not seeing at all.

One day in 1893 Pierre Bonnard spied a girl getting off a Paris tram and, attracted by her frailty and pale prettiness, followed her to her place of work, a *pompes funèbres*, where she spent her days sewing pearls on to funeral wreaths. Thus death at the start wove its black ribbon into their lives. He quickly made her acquaintance – I suppose these things were managed with ease and aplomb in the *Belle Époque* – and shortly afterwards she left her job, and everything else in her life, and went to live with him. She told him her name was Marthe de Méligny, and that she was sixteen. In fact, although he was not to discover it until more than thirty years later when he got round to marrying her at last, her real name was Maria Boursin, and when they had met she had been not sixteen but, like Bonnard, in her middle twenties. They were to remain together, through thick and thin, or rather say, through thin and thinner, until her death nearly fifty years later. Thadée Natanson, one of Bonnard's earliest patrons, in a memoir of the painter, recalled with swift, impressionistic strokes the elfin Marthe, writing of *her wild look of a bird, her movements on tiptoe*. She was secretive, jealous, fiercely possessive, suffered from a persecution complex, and was a great and dedicated hypochondriac. In 1927 Bonnard bought a house, Le Bosquet, in the undistinguished little town of Le Cannet on the Côte d'Azur, where he lived with Marthe, bound with her in intermittently tormented seclusion, until her death fifteen years later. At Le Bosquet she developed a habit of spending long hours in the bath, and it was in her bath that Bonnard painted her, over and over, continuing the series even after she had died. The *Baignoires* are the triumphant culmination of his life's work. In the *Nude in the bath, with dog*, begun in 1941, a year before Marthe's death and not completed until 1946, she lies there, pink and mauve and gold, a goddess of the floating world, attenuated, ageless, as much dead as alive, beside her on the tiles her little brown dog, her familiar, a dachshund, I think, curled watchful on its mat or what may be a square of flaking sunlight falling from an unseen window. The narrow room that is her refuge vibrates around her, throbbing in its colours. Her feet, the left one tensed at the end of its impossibly long leg, seem to have pushed the bath out of shape and made it bulge at the left end, and beneath the bath on that side, in the same force-field, the floor is pulled out of alignment too, and seems on the point of pouring away into the corner, not like a floor at all but a moving pool of dappled water. All moves here, moves in stillness, in aqueous silence. One hears a drip, a ripple, a fluttering sigh. A rust-red patch in the water beside the bather's right shoulder might be rust, or old blood, even. Her right hand rests on her thigh, stilled in the act of supination, and I think of Anna's hands on the table that first day when we came back from seeing Mr Todd, her helpless hands with palms upturned as if to beg something from someone opposite her who was not there.

She too, my Anna, when she fell ill, took to taking extended baths in the afternoon. They soothed her, she said. Throughout the autumn and winter of that twelvemonth of her slow dying we shut ourselves away in our house by the sea, just like Bonnard and his Marthe at Le Bosquet. The weather was mild, hardly weather at all, the seemingly unbreakable summer giving way imperceptibly to a year-end of misted-over stillness that might have been any season. Anna dreaded the coming of spring, all that unbearable bustle and clamour, she said, all that life. A deep, dreamy silence accumulated around us, soft and dense, like silt. She was so quiet, there in the bathroom on the first-floor return, that I became alarmed sometimes. I imagined her slipping down without a sound in the enormous old claw-footed bath until her face was under the surface and taking a last long watery breath. I would creep down the stairs and stand on the return, not making a sound, seeming suspended there, as if I were the one under water, listening desperately through the panels of the door for sounds of life. In some foul and treacherous chamber of my heart, of course, I wanted her to have done it, wanted it all to be over with, for me as well as for her. Then I would hear a soft heave of water as she stirred, the soft splash as she lifted a hand for the soap or a towel, and I would turn away and plod back to my room and shut the door behind me and sit down at my desk and gaze out into the luminous grey of evening, trying to think of nothing.

'Look at you, poor Max,' she said to me one day, 'having to watch your words and be nice all the time.' She was in the nursing home by then, in a room at the far end of the old wing with a corner window that looked out on a wedge of handsomely unkempt lawn and a restless and, to my eye, troubling stand of great tall blackish-green trees. The spring that she had dreaded had come and gone, and she had been too ill to mind its agitations, and now it was a damply hot, glutinous summer, the last one she would see. 'What do you mean,' I said, 'having to be nice?' She said so many strange things now-adays, as if she were already somewhere else, beyond me, where even words had a different meaning. She moved her head on the pillow and smiled at me. Her face, worn almost to the bone, had taken on a fright-ful beauty. 'You are not even allowed to hate me a little, any more,' she said, 'like you used to.' She looked out at the trees a while and then turned back to me again and smiled again and patted my hand. 'Don't look so worried,' she said. 'I hated you, too, a little. We were human beings, after all.' By then the past tense was the only one she cared to employ.

'Would you like to see your room now?' Miss Vavasour enquired. Last spikes of sunlight through the bay window before us were falling like shards of glass in a burning building. The Colonel was brush-ing crossly at the front of his yellow waistcoat where he had spilled a splash of tea. He looked put-out. Probably he had been saying something to me and I had not been listening. Miss Vavasour led the way into the hall. I was nervous of this moment, the moment when I would have to take on the house, to put it on, as it were, like something I had worn in another, prelapsarian life, a once fashionable hat, say, an outmoded pair of shoes, or a wedding suit, smelling of mothballs and no longer fitting around the waist and too tight under the arms but bulging with memories in every pocket. The hall I did not recognise at all. It is short, narrow and ill-lit, and the walls are divided horizontally by a beaded runner and papered on their lower halves with painted-over anaglypta that looks to be a hundred years old or more. I do not recall there having been a hallway here. I thought the front door opened directly into – well, I am not sure what I thought it opened into. The kitchen? As I padded behind Miss Vavasour with my bag in my hand, like the well-mannered murderer in some old black-and-white thriller, I found that the model of the house in my head, try as it would to accommodate itself to the original, kept coming up against a stubborn resistance. Everything was slightly out of scale, all angles slightly out of true. The staircase was steeper, the landing pokier, the lavatory window looked not on to the road, as I thought it should, but back across the fields. I experienced a sense almost of panic as the real, the crassly complacent real, took hold of the things I thought I remembered and shook them into its own shape. Something precious was dissolving and pouring away between my fingers. Yet how easily, in the end, I let it go. The past, I mean the real past, matters less than we pretend. When Miss Vavasour left me in what from now on was to be *my room* I threw my coat over a chair and sat down on the side of the bed and breathed deep the stale unlived-in air, and felt that I had been travelling for a long time, for years, and had at last arrived at the destination to where, all along, without knowing it, I had been bound, and where I must stay, it being, for now, the only possible place, the only possible refuge, for me.

My friendly robin appeared a moment ago in the garden and I suddenly realised what it was that Avril's freckles reminded me of, that day of our encounter in Duignan's yard. The bird as usual stops on its thirdmost perch in the holly bush and studies the lay of the land with a truculent, bead-bright eye. Robins are a famously fearless breed, and this one seems quite unconcerned when Tiddles from next door comes stalking through the long grass, and even gives what sounds like a sardonic cheep and ruffles up its feathers and expands its blood-orange breast, as if to demonstrate teasingly what a plump and toothsome morsel it would make, if cats could fly. Seeing the bird alight there I remembered at once, with a pang that was exactly the same size and as singular as the bird itself, the nest in the gorse bushes that was robbed. I was quite a bird enthusiast as a boy. Not the watching kind, I was never a watcher, I had no interest in spotting and tracking and classifying, all that would have been beyond me, and would have bored me, besides; no, I could hardly distinguish one species from another, and knew little and cared less about their history or habits. I could find their nests, though, that was my specialty. It was a matter of patience, alertness, quickness of eye, and something else, a capacity to be at one with the tiny creatures I was tracking to their lairs. A savant whose name for the moment I forget has posited as a refutation of something or other the assertion that it is impossible for a human being to imagine fully what it would be like to be a bat. I take his point in general, but I believe I could have given him a fair account of such creaturehood when I was young and still part animal myself.

I was not cruel, I would not kill a bird or steal its eggs, certainly not. What drove me was curiosity, the simple passion to know something of the secrets of other, alien lives.

A thing that always struck me was the contrast between nest and egg, I mean the contingency of the former, no matter how well or even beautifully it was fashioned, and the latter's completedness, its pristine fulness. Before it is a beginning an egg is an absolute end. It is the very definition of self-containment. I hated to see a broken egg, that tiny tragedy. In the instance I am thinking of I must inadvertently have led someone to the nest. It was in a clump of gorse on a slanted headland in the midst of open fields, I would easily have been spotted going to it, as I had been doing for weeks, so that the hen bird had grown used to me. What was it, thrush, blackbird? Some such largish species, anyway. Then one day I arrived and the eggs were gone. Two had been taken and the third was smashed on the ground under the bush. All that remained of it was a smear of mingled yolk and glair and a few fragments of shell, each with its stippling of tiny, dark-brown spots. I should not make too much of the moment, I am sure I was as sentimentally heartless as the next boy, but I can still see the gorse, I can smell the buttery perfume of its blossoms, I can recall the exact shade of those brown speckles, so like the ones on Avril's pallid cheeks and on the saddle of her nose. I have carried the memory of that moment through a whole half century, as if it were the emblem of something final, precious and irretrievable.

Anna leaning sideways from the hospital bed, vomiting on to the floor, her burning brow pressed in my palm, full and frail as an ostrich egg.

I am in the Strand Café, with Chloe, after the pictures and that memorable kiss. We sat at a plastic table drinking our favourite drink, a tall glass of fizzy orange crush with a dollop of vanilla ice cream floating in it. Remarkable the clarity with which, when I concentrate, I can see us there. Really, one might almost live one's life over, if only one could make a sufficient effort of recollection. Our table was near the open doorway from which a fat slab of sunlight lay fallen at our feet. Now and then a breeze from outside would wander in absent-mindedly, strewing a whisper of fine sand across the floor, or bringing with it an empty sweet-paper that advanced and stopped and advanced again, making a scraping sound. There was hardly anyone else in the place, some boys, or young men, rather, in a corner at the back playing cards, and behind the counter the proprietor's wife, a large, sandy-haired, not unhandsome woman, gazing off through the doorway in a blank-eyed dream. She wore a pale-blue smock or apron with a scalloped white edging. What was her name? What was it. No, it will not come – so much for Memory's prodigious memory. Mrs Strand, I shall call her Mrs Strand, if she has to be called anything. She had a particular way of standing, certainly I remember that, sturdy and four-square, one freckled arm extended and a fist pressed knuckles-down on the high back of the cash-register. The ice cream and orange mixture in our glasses had a topping of sallow froth. We drank through paper straws, avoiding each other's eye in a new access of shyness. I had a sense of a general, large, soft settling, as of a sheet unfurling and falling on a bed, or a tent collapsing into the cushion of its own air. The fact of that kiss in the dark of the picture-house – I am coming to think it must have been our first kiss, after all – sat like an amazement between us, unignorably huge. Chloe had the faintest blond shadow of a moustache, I had felt its sable touch against my lip. Now my glass was almost empty and I was afraid the last of the liquid in the straw would do its embarrassing intestinal rattle. Covertly from under lowered lids I looked at Chloe's hands, one resting on the table and the other holding her glass. The fingers were fat to the first knuckle and from there tapered to the tip:

her mother's hands, I realised. Mrs Strand's wireless set was playing some song to the swoony tune of which Chloe absently hummed along. Songs were so important then, moaning of longing and loss, the very twang of what we thought was love. In the night as I lay in my bed in the chalet the melodies would come to me, a faint, brassy blaring carried on the sea breeze from the ballrooms at the Beach Hotel or the Golf, and I would think of the couples, the permed girls in brittle blues and acid greens, the quiffed young men in chunky sportscoats and shoes with inch-thick, squashy soles, circling there in the dusty, hot half-dark. *O darling lover lonesome moonlight kisses heart and soul!* And beyond all that, outside, unseen, the beach in the darkness, the sand cool on top but keeping still the day's warmth underneath, and the long lines of white waves breaking on the bias, lit from inside themselves somehow, and over everything the night, silent, secret and intent.

'That picture was stupid,' Chloe said. She brought her face close to the rim of the glass, her fringe hanging free. Her hair was pale as the sunlight on the floor at her foot . . . But wait, this is wrong. This cannot have been the day of the kiss. When we left the picture-house it was evening, an evening after rain, and now it is the middle of an afternoon, hence that soft sunlight, that meandering breeze. And where is Myles? He was with us at the pictures, so where would he have gone, he who never left his sister's side unless driven from it? Really, Madam Memory, I take back all my praise, if it is Memory herself who is at work here and not some other, more fanciful muse. Chloe gave a snort. 'As if they wouldn't have known that highwayman was a woman.'

I looked at her hands again. The one that had been holding the glass high up had slipped down to encircle the base, in which a spiked point of pure white light steadily burned, while the other, bending the straw to her lips delicately between a thumb and forefinger, cast a pale shadow on the table in the shape of a bird's beaked and high-plumed head. Again I thought of her mother, and this time I felt briefly something sharp and burning in my breast, as if a heated needle had touched my heart. Was it a twinge of guilt? For what would Mrs Grace feel, what would she say, if she were to spy me here at this table ogling the mauve shading in the hollow of her daughter's cheek as she sucked up the last of her ice cream soda? But I did not really care, not deep down, deep past guilt and suchlike affects. Love, as we call it, has a fickle tendency to transfer itself, by a heartless, sidewise shift, from one bright object to a brighter, in the most inappropriate of circumstances. How many wedding days have ended with the tipsy and dyspeptic groom gazing miserably down on his brand-new bride bouncing under him on the king-size bed of the honeymoon suite and seeing her best friend's face, or the face of her prettier sister or even, heaven help us, of her sportive mother?

Yes, I was falling in love with Chloe – had fallen, the thing was done already. I had that sense of anxious euphoria, of happy, helpless toppling, which the one who knows he will have to do the loving always feels, at the precipitous outset. For even at such a tender age I knew that there is always a lover and a loved, and knew which one, in this case, I would be. Those weeks with Chloe were for me a series of more or less enraptured humiliations. She accepted me as a suppliant at her shrine with disconcerting complacency. In her more distracted moods she would hardly deign to notice my presence, and even when she gave me her fullest attention there was always a flaw in it, a fleck of preoccupation, of absence. This wilful vagueness tormented and infuriated me, but worse was the possibility that it might not be willed. That she might choose to disdain me I could accept, could welcome, even, in an obscurely pleasurable way, but the thought that there were intervals when I simply faded to transparency in her gaze, no, that was not to be borne. Often when I broke in on one of her vacant silences she would give a faint start and glance quickly about, at the ceiling or into a corner of the room, anywhere but at me, in search of the source of the voice that had addressed her. Was this a heartless teasing or were these moments of blankness genuine? Galled beyond bearing I would seize her by the shoulders and shake her, demanding that she see me and only me, but she would go slack in my hands and cross her eyes and let her head waggle like a rag doll's, laughing in her throat and sounding unnervingly like Myles, and when I flung her roughly from me in disgust she would fall back on sand or sofa and lie sprawled with limbs awry and pretend to be grotesquely, grinningly, dead.

Why did I put up with her caprices, her high-handedness? I was never one to suffer slights easily, and always made sure to get my own back, even on loved ones, or on loved ones especially. My forbearance in Chloe's case was due, I believe, to a strong urge of protectiveness that I had toward her. Let me explain, it is interesting, I think it is interesting. A nice, an exquisite, tactfulness was in operation here.

Since she was the one on whom I had chosen, or had been chosen, to lavish my love, she must be preserved as nearly flawless as possible, spiritually and in her actions. It was imperative that I save her from herself and her faults. The task fell to me naturally since her faults were her faults, and she could not be expected to evade their bad effects by her own volition. And not only must she be saved from these faults and their consequences for her behaviour but she must be kept from all knowledge of them, too, insofar as it was possible for me to do so. And not just her active faults. Ignorance, incapacity of insight, dull complacency, such things too must be masked, their manifestations denied. The fact for instance that she did not know that she was later in my affections than her mother, of all people, made her seem almost piteously vulnerable in my eyes. Mark, the issue was not the fact of her being a late-comer in my affections, but her ignorance of that fact. If she were somehow to find out my secret she would likely be let down in her own estimation, would think herself a fool not to have seen what I felt for her mother, and might even be tempted to feel second to her mother in having been my second choice. And that must not be.

In case I should seem to be casting myself in too benevolent a light, I hasten to say that my concern and care in the matter of Chloe and her shortcomings was not for her benefit alone. Her self-esteem was of far less importance to me than my own, although the latter was dependent on the former. If her sense of herself were tainted, by doubt or feelings of foolishness or of lack of perspicacity, my regard for her would itself be tainted. So there must be no confrontations, no brutal enlightenments, no telling of terrible truths. I might shake her by the shoulders until her bones rattled, I might throw her to the ground in disgust, but I must not tell her that I had loved her mother before I loved her, that she smelled of stale biscuits, or that Joe from the Field had remarked the green tinge of her teeth. As I walked meekly behind her swaggering figure, my fond and fondly anguished gaze fixed on the blond comma of hair at the nape of her neck or the hairline cracks in the porcelain backs of her knees, I felt as if I were carrying within me a phial of the most precious and delicately combustible material. No, no sudden movements, none at all.

There was another reason why she must be kept inviolate, unpolluted by too much self-knowledge or, indeed, too sharp a knowledge of me. This was her *difference*. In her I had my first experience of the absolute otherness of other people. It is not too much to say – well, it is, but I shall say it anyway – that in

Chloe the world was first manifest for me as an objective entity. Not my father and mother, my teachers, other children, not Connie Grace herself, no one had yet been real in the way that Chloe was. And if she was real, so, suddenly, was I. She was I believe the true origin in me of self-consciousness. Before, there had been one thing and I was part of it, now there was me and all that was not me. But here too there is a torsion, a kink of complexity. In severing me from the world and making me realise myself in being thus severed, she expelled me from that sense of the immanence of all things, the all things that had included me, in which up to then I had dwelt, in more or less blissful ignorance. Before, I had been housed, now I was in the open, in the clearing, with no shelter in sight. I did not know that I would not get inside again, through that ever straitening gate.

I never knew where I was with her, or what sort of treatment to expect at her hands, and this was, I suspect, a large part of her attraction for me, such is the quixotic nature of love. One day when we were walking along the beach at the water's edge searching after a particular kind of pink shell she needed to make a necklace she stopped suddenly and turned and, ignoring the bathers in the water and the picnickers on the sand, seized me by the shirt-front and pulled me to her and kissed me with such force that my upper lip was crushed against my front teeth and I tasted blood, and Myles, behind us, did his throaty chuckle. In a moment she had pushed me away, in high disdain, it seemed, and was walking on, frowning, her eye as before moving sharply along the waterline where the bland, packed sand greedily inhaled the outrun of each encroaching wave with a sucking sigh. I looked about anxiously. What if my mother had been there to see, or Mrs Grace, or Rose, even? But Chloe seemed not to care. I can still recall the grainy sensation as the soft pulp of our lips was ground between our teeth.

She liked to throw down dares, but was vexed when they were taken up. Early one eerily still morning, with thunder clouds on the far horizon and the sea flat and greyly lucent, I was standing before her waist-deep in the warmish wash and about to dive and swim between her legs, if she would let me, which she sometimes did. 'Go on, quick,' she said, narrowing her eyes, 'I've just done a pee.' I could not but do as she urged, aspiring little gentleman that I was. But when I surfaced again she said I was disgusting, and leaned into the water to her chin and swam slowly away.

She was prone to sudden and unnerving flashes of violence. I am thinking of one wet afternoon when we were alone together in the living room at the Cedars. The air in the room was damply chill and there was the sad, rainy-day smell of soot and cretonne curtains. Chloe had come in from the kitchen and was crossing to the window and I stood up from the sofa and went toward her, I suppose to try to get my arms around her. Immediately at my approach she stopped and brought up her hand in a quick short arc and delivered me a slap full in the face. So sudden was the blow, so complete, it seemed a definition of some small, unique and vital thing. I heard the echo of it ping back from a corner of the ceiling. We stood a moment motionless, I with my face averted, and she took a step backward, and laughed, and then pouted sulkily and went on to the window, where she picked up something from the table and looked at it with a fierce frown.

There was a day on the beach when she fixed on a townie to torment. It was a blustery grey afternoon toward the end of the holiday, the faintest of autumnal notes already in the air, and she was bored and in malevolent mood. The townie was a pale, shivering fellow in sagging black swimming trunks, with a concave chest and nipples swollen and discoloured from the cold. We cornered him, the three of us, behind a concrete groyne. He was taller than the twins, but I was taller still, and being eager to impress my girl I gave him a good hard push and knocked him back against the green-slimed wall, and Chloe planted herself in front of him and at her most imperious demanded to know his name and what he was doing here. He looked at her in slow bewilderment, unable to understand, it seemed, why he had been picked on, or what it was we wanted of him, which of course we did not know either. 'Well?' Chloe cried, hands on her hips and tapping one foot on the sand. He smiled uncertainly, more embarrassed than in fear of her. He had come down for the day, he said, mumbling, with his Mammy, on the train. 'Oh, your Mammy, is it?' Chloe said with a sneer, and as if that were a signal Myles stepped forward and smacked him hard on the side of the head with the flat of his hand, producing an impressively loud sharp *tock!* 'See?' Chloe said shrilly. 'That's what you get for being smart with us!' The townie, poor slow sheep that he was, only looked startled, and put up a hand and felt his face as if to verify the amazing fact of having been hit. There was a thrilling moment of stillness then when anything might have happened. Nothing did. The townie only gave a sort of resigned, sad shrug and shambled away, still with a hand lifted to his jaw, and Chloe turned on me defiantly but said nothing, while Myles only laughed.

What remained with me from the incident was not Chloe's glare or Myles's snigger, but the look the townie gave me at the end, before turning disconsolately away. He knew me, knew I was a townie too, like him, whatever I might try to seem. If in that look there had been an accusation of betrayal, of anger at me for siding with strangers against him, anything like that, I would not have minded, but would, in fact, have felt gratified, even if shamefacedly so. No, what unsettled me was the expression of acceptance in his glance, the ovine unsurprisedness at my perfidy. I had an urge to hurry after him and put a hand on his shoulder, not so that I might apologise or try to excuse myself for helping to humiliate him, but to make him look at me again, or, rather, to make him withdraw that other look, to negate it, to wipe the record of it from his eye. For I found intolerable the thought of being known in the way that he seemed to know me. Better than I knew myself. Worse.

I have always disliked being photographed, but I intensely disliked being photographed by Anna. It is a strange thing to say, I know, but when she was behind a camera she was like a blind person, something in her eyes went dead, an essential light was extinguished. She seemed not to be looking through the lens, at her subject, but rather to be peering inward, into herself, in search of some defining perspective, some essential point of view. She would hold the camera steady at eye-level and thrust her raptor's head out sideways and stare for a second, sightlessly, it might be, as if one's features were written in some form of braille that she was capable of reading at a distance; when she pressed the shutter it seemed the least important thing, no more than a gesture to placate the apparatus. In our early days together I was unwise enough to allow her to persuade me to pose for her on a few occasions; the results were shockingly raw, shockingly revealing. In those half dozen black-and-white head-and-shoulders shots that she took of me – and took is the word – I seemed to myself more starkly on show than I would have been in a full-length study and wearing not a stitch. I was young and smooth and not unhandsome – I am being modest – but in those photographs I appeared an overgrown homunculus. It was not that she made me look ugly or deformed. People who saw the photographs said they flattered me. I was not flattered, far from it. In them I appeared to have been grabbed and held for an instant on the point of fleeing, with cries of *Stop, thief!* ringing about me. My expression was uniformly winsome and ingratiating, the expression of a miscreant who fears he is about to be accused of a crime he knows he has committed yet cannot quite recall, but is preparing his extenuations and justifications anyway. What a desperate, beseeching smile I wore, a leer, a very leer. She trained her camera on a fresh-faced hopeful but the pictures she produced were the mug-shots of a raddled old confidence trickster. Exposed, yes, that is the word, too.

It was her special gift, the disenchanted, disenchanting, eye. I am thinking of the photographs she took in the hospital, at the end, at the beginning of the end, when she was still undergoing treatment and had strength enough to get up from her bed unaided. She had Claire search out her camera, it was years since she had used it. The prospect of this return to an old obsession gave me a strong yet unaccountable sense of foreboding. I found disturbing too, although again I could not have said exactly why, the fact that it was Claire, and not I, whom she had asked to fetch the camera, and in the tacit understanding, furthermore, that I was not to hear of it. What did it mean, all this secrecy and hugger-mugger? Claire, lately returned briefly from her studies abroad – France, the Low Countries, Vaublin, all that – was shocked to find her mother so ill, and was angry at me, of course, for not summoning her sooner. I did not tell her that Anna was the one who had not wanted her home. This too was odd, for in the past they had always been close, that pair. Was I jealous? Yes, a little, in fact more than a little, if I am to be honest. I am well aware of what I expected, what I expect, of my daughter, and of the selfishness and pathos of that expectation. Much is demanded of the dilettante's off-spring. She will do what I could not, and be a great scholar, if I have any say in the matter, and I have. Her mother left her some money, but not enough. I am the big fat goose, and costive with the golden eggs.

It was by chance that I caught Claire smuggling the camera out of the house. She tried to pass it off casually, but Claire is not good at being casual. Not that she knew, any more than I did, why it should be a secret. Anna always had an underhand way of going about the simplest things, it was the lingering influence of her father and their rackety early life together, I suppose. There was a childish side to her. I mean she was wilful, secretive, and deeply resentful of the slightest interference or objection. I can talk, I know. I think it must be that we were both only children.

That sounds odd. I mean that we were both the only children of our parents. That sounds odd too. Did I seem to disapprove of her attempts to be an artist, if taking snapshots can be considered artistry? In fact, I paid scant attention to her photographs, and she had no reason to think I would have kept the camera from her. It is all very puzzling.

Anyway, a day or two after I caught Claire with the camera I was called in by the hospital to be sternly informed that my wife had been taking photographs of the other patients and that there had been complaints. I blushed on Anna's behalf, standing in front of the Matron's desk and feeling like a schoolboy hauled up before the Head to account for someone else's misdeeds. It seemed Anna had been wandering through the wards, barefoot, in her hospital-issue bleached white smock, wheeling her drip-feed stand – she called it her dumb-waiter – in search of the more grievously marked and maimed among her fellow patients, by whose bedsides she would park the drip stand and bring out her Leica and snap away until she was spotted by one or other of the nurses and ordered back to her room.

'Did they tell you who complained?' she demanded of me sulkily. 'Not the patients, only the relatives, and what do they know?'

She had me bring the film for developing to her friend Serge. Her friend Serge, who at one time in the far past may possibly have been more than a friend, is a burly fellow with a limp and a mane of beautiful black hair which he tosses back from his forehead with a graceful sweep of both his big blunt hands. He has a studio at the top of one of those tall narrow old houses in Shade Street, by the river. He takes fashion photographs, and sleeps with his models. He claims to be a refugee from somewhere or other, and speaks with a lisping accent which the girls are said to find irresistible. He does not use a surname, and even Serge, for all I know, may be a *nom-d'appareil*. He is the kind of person we used to know, Anna and I, in the old days, which were still new then. I cannot think now how I tolerated him; nothing like disaster for showing up the cheapness and fraudulence of one's world, one's former world.

There seems to be something about me that Serge finds irresistibly funny. He keeps up a stream of unamusing little jokes, which I am convinced are a pretext for him to laugh without seeming to be laughing at me. When I came to collect the developed prints he set off on a search for them amidst the picturesque disorder of the studio – it would not surprise me if he arranges the disorder, like a window display – picking his way about nimbly on his disproportionately dainty feet despite a violent list to the left at every other step. He slurped coffee from a seemingly bottomless mug and talked to me over his shoulder. The coffee is another of his trademarks, along with the hair and the limp and the Tolstoyan baggy white shirts that he favours. 'How is the beautiful Annie?' he asked. He glanced at me sidelong and laughed. He always called her Annie, which no one else did; I suppress the thought that it might have been his old love name for her. I had not told him of her illness – why should I? He was scrabbling about in the chaos on the big table he uses as a work desk. The vinegary stink of developing fluid from the darkroom was stinging my nostrils and my eyes. '*Any news of Annie*,' he warbled to himself, making a jingle of it, and gave another snuffly laugh down his nostrils. I saw myself run forward with a cry and hustle him to the window and heave him headlong down into the cobbled street. He gave a grunt of triumph and came up with a thick manila envelope, but when I reached out to take it he held back, considering me with a merrily speculative eye, his head cocked to the side. 'These things she is taking, they are some pictures,' he said, hefting the envelope in one hand and flapping the other limply up and down in his studied Mitteleuropan way. Through a skylight above us the sun of summer shone full on the work table, making the strewn sheets of photographic paper burn with a hot white glare. Serge shook his head and whistled soundlessly through pursed lips. 'Some pictures!'

From her hospital bed Anna reached up eagerly with fingers childishly splayed and snatched the envelope from my hands without a word. It was over-warm and humid in the room and there was a glistening grey film of sweat on her forehead and her upper lip. Her hair had begun to grow again, in a half-hearted fashion, as if it knew it would not be needed for long; it came out in patches, lank and black and greasy-seeming, like a cat's licked fur. I sat on the side of the bed and watched her tear impatiently with her fingernails at the flap of the envelope. What is it about hospital rooms that makes them so seductive, despite all that goes on in them? They are not like hotel rooms. Hotel rooms, even the grandest of them, are anonymous; there is nothing in them that cares for a guest, not the bed, not the refrigerated drinks cabinet, not even the trouser-press, standing so deferentially at attention with its back to the wall. Despite all efforts of architects, designers, managements, hotel rooms are always impatient for us to be gone; hospital rooms, on the contrary, and without anybody's effort, are there to make us stay, to want to stay, and be content. They have a soothing suggestion of the nursery, all that thick cream paint on the walls, the rubberised floors, the miniature hand-basin in the corner with its demure little towel on a rail underneath, and the bed, of course, with its wheels and levers, that looks like a kiddie's complicated cot, where one might sleep and dream, and be watched over, and cared for, and never, not ever, die. I wonder if I could rent one, a hospital room, that is, and work there, live there, even. The amenities would be wonderful. There would be the cheery wake-up call in the mornings, meals served with iron regularity, one's bed made up neat and tight as a long white envelope, and a whole medical team standing by to cope with any emergency. Yes, I could be content there, in one of those white cells, my barred window, no, not barred, I am getting carried away, my window looking down on the city, the smokestacks, the busy roads, the hunched houses, and all the little figures, hurrying endlessly, to and fro.

Anna spread the photographs around her on the bed and pored over them avidly, her eyes alight, those eyes that by then had come to seem enormous, starting from the armature of the skull. The first surprise was that she had used colour film, for she had always favoured black-and-white. Then there were the photographs themselves. They might have been taken in a field hospital in wartime, or in a casualty ward in a defeated and devastated city. There was an old man with one leg gone below the knee, a thick line of sutures like the prototype of a zip fastener traversing the shiny stump. An obese, middle-aged woman was missing a breast, the flesh where it had been recently removed all puckered and swollen like a giant, empty eye-socket. A big-bosomed, smiling mother in a lacy nightdress dis-played a hydrocephalic baby with a bewildered look in its otter's bulging eye. The arthritic fingers of an old woman taken in close-up were knotted and knobbed like clusters of root ginger. A boy with a canker embossed on his cheek, intricate as a mandala, grinned into the camera, his two fists lifted and giving a double thumbs-up sign, a fat tongue cheekily stuck out. There was a shot angled down into a metal bin with gobs and strings of unidentifiable dark wet meat thrown into it – was that refuse from the kitchen, or the operating theatre?

What was most striking to me about the people pictured was the calmly smiling way in which they dis-played their wounds, their stitches, their suppurations.

I recall in particular a large and at first sight formal study, in hard-edged shades of plastic pinks and puces and glossy greys, taken from low down at the foot of her bed, of a fat old wild-haired woman with her slack, blue-veined legs lifted and knees splayed, showing off what I presumed was a prolapsed womb. The arrangement was as striking and as carefully composed as a frontispiece from one of Blake's prophetic books. The central space, an inverted triangle bounded on two sides by the woman's cocked legs and along the top by the hem of her white gown stretched tight across from knee to knee, might have been a blank patch of parchment in wait of a fiery inscription, heralding perhaps the mock-birth of the pink and darkly purple thing already protruding from her lap. Above this triangle the woman's Medusa-head seemed by a subtle trick of perspective to have been severed and lifted forward and set down squarely in the same plane as her knees, the clean-cut stump of the neck appearing to be balanced on the straight line of the gown's hem that formed the upturned base of the triangle. Despite the position in which it found itself the face was perfectly at ease, and might even have been smiling, in a humorously deprecating fashion, with a certain satisfaction and, yes, a certain definite pride. I recalled walking in the street with

Anna one day after all her hair had fallen out and she spotted passing by on the opposite pavement a woman who was also bald. I do not know if Anna caught me catching the look they exchanged, the two of them, blank-eyed and at the same time sharp, sly, complicit. In all that endless twelvemonth of her illness I do not think I ever felt more distant from her than I did at that moment, elbowed aside by the sorority of the afflicted.

'Well?' she said now, keeping her eyes on the pictures and not bothering to look at me. 'What do you think?'

She did not care what I thought. By now she had gone beyond me and my opinions.

'Have you shown them to Claire?' I asked. Why was that the first thing that came into my head?

She pretended not to have heard, or perhaps had not been listening. A bell was buzzing somewhere in the building, like a small insistent pain made audible.

'They are my dossier,' she said. 'My indictment.'

'Your indictment?' I said helplessly, feeling an obscure panic. 'Of what?'

She shrugged.

'Oh, everything,' she said, mildly. 'Everything.'

*

Chloe, her cruelty. The beach. The midnight swim. Her lost sandal, that night in the doorway of the dancehall, Cinderella's shoe. All gone. All lost. It is no matter. Tired, tired and drunk. No matter.

We have had a storm. It went on all night long and into the middle of the morning, an extraordinary affair, I have never known the like, in these temperate zones, for violence or duration. I enjoyed it outrageously, sitting up in my ornate bed as on a catafalque, if that is the word I want, the room aflicker around me and the sky stamping up and down in a fury, breaking its bones. At last, I thought, at last the elements have achieved a pitch of magnificence to match my inner turmoil! I felt transfigured, I felt like one of Wagner's demi-gods, aloft on a thunder-cloud and directing the great booming chords, the clashes of celestial cymbals. In this mood of histrionic euphoria, fizzing with brandy-fumes and static, I considered my position in a new and crepitant light. I mean my general position. I have ever had the conviction, resistant to all rational considerations, that at some unspecified future moment the continuous rehearsal which is my life, with its so many misreadings, its slips and fluffs, will be done with and that the real drama for which I have ever and with such earnestness been preparing will at last begin. It is a common delusion, I know, everyone entertains it. Yet last night, in the midst of that spectacular display of Valhallan petulance, I wondered if the moment of my entrance might be imminent, the moment of my *going on*, so to say. I do not know how it would be, this dramatic leap into the thick of the action, or what exactly might be expected to take place, onstage. Yet I anticipate an apotheosis of some kind, some grand climacteric. I am not speaking here of a posthumous transfiguration. I do not entertain the possibility of an afterlife, or any deity capable of offering it. Given the world that he created, it would be an impiety against God to believe in him. No, what I am looking forward to is a moment of earthly expression. That is it, that is it exactly: I shall be expressed, totally. I shall be delivered, like a noble closing speech. I shall be, in a word, *said*. Has this not always been my aim, is this not, indeed, the secret aim of all of us, to be no longer flesh but transformed utterly into the gossamer of unsuffering spirit? Bang, crash, shudder, the very walls shaking.

By the way: the bed, my bed. Miss Vavasour insists it has always been here. The Graces, mother and father, was it theirs, is this where they slept, in this very bed? What a thought, I do not know what to do with it. Stop thinking it, that would be best; least unsettling, that is.

Another week done with. How quickly the time goes as the season advances, the earth hurtling along its groove into the year's sharply descending final arc. Despite the continuing clemency of the weather the Colonel feels the winter coming on. He has been unwell of late, has caught what he says is a cold on the kidneys. I tell him that was one of my mother's complaints – *one of her favourites, in fact,* I do not add – but he gives me a queer look, thinking I am mocking him, perhaps, as perhaps I am. What is a cold on the kidneys, anyway? Ma was no more specific than the Colonel on the subject, and even *Black's Medical* can offer no enlightenment. Maybe he wants me to think this is the reason for his frequent shufflings to the lavatory by day and night and not the something more serious that I suspect. 'I'm not the best,' he says, 'and that's a fact.' He has taken to wearing a muffler at mealtimes. He turns over his food listlessly and greets the mildest attempt at levity with a soulful, suffering glance that drops wearily away to the accompaniment of a faint sigh that is almost a moan. Have I described his fascinatingly chromatic nose? It changes hue with the time of day and the slightest variation of the weather, from pale lavender through burgundy to the deepest imperial purple. Is this rhinophyma, I suddenly wonder, are these Dr Thomson's famous grog blossoms? Miss Vavasour is sceptical of his complaints, and makes a wry face at me when he is not looking. I think he is losing heart in his attempts to woo her. In that bright-yellow waistcoat, the bottom button always punctiliously undone and the pointed flaps open over his neat little paunch, he is as intent and circumspect as one of those outlandishly plumed male birds, peacock or cock pheasant, who gorgeously stalk up and down at a distance, desperate of eye but pretending indifference, while the drab hen unconcernedly pecks in the gravel for grubs. Miss V. bats aside his ponderously coy attentions with a mixture of vexation and flustered embarrassment. I surmise, from the injured looks he throws at her, that previously she gave him some grounds for hope which were immediately whipped from under him when I came along to be a witness to her folly, and that now she is cross at herself and eager I should be convinced that what he may have taken for encouragement was really no more than a display of a landlady's professional politesse.

Often at a loss myself to know what to do with my time, I have been compiling a schedule of the Colonel's typical day. He rises early, for he is a poor sleeper, suggesting to us by expressive silences and tight-lipped shrugs a fund of battleground nightmares that would keep a narcolept from sleep, although I have an idea the bad memories that beset him were gathered not in the far-flung colonies but somewhere nearer home, for example on the boreens and cratered side roads of South Armagh. Breakfast he takes alone, at a small table in the ingle-nook in the kitchen – no, I did not recall an ingle, not to speak of a nook – solitude being the preferred mode in which to partake of what he frequently and portentously pronounces *the most important meal of the day*. Miss Vavasour is content not to disturb him, and serves him his rashers and eggs and black pudding in a sardonic silence. He keeps his own supply of condiments, unlabelled bottles of brown and red and dark-green sluggish stuffs, which he doles on to his food with an alchemist's niceness of measurement. There is a spread too that he prepares himself, he calls it slap, a khaki-coloured goo involving anchovies, curry powder, a great deal of pepper, and other, unnamed things; it smells, curiously, of dog. 'A great scourer for the bag,' he says. It took me a while to realise that this bag of which he often speaks, though never in Miss V.'s presence, is the stomach and environs. He is ever alive to the state of the bag.

After breakfast comes the morning constitutional, taken in all weathers down Station Road and along the Cliff Walk past the Pier Head Bar and back again the long way round by the lighthouse cottages and the Gem, where he stops to buy the morning paper and a roll of the extra-strong peppermints which he sucks on all day, and the faint sickly smell of which pervades the house. He goes along at a brisk clip with what I am sure he intends to be a military bearing, although the first morning I saw him setting off I noted with a jolt how at every step he swings out his left foot in a tight sideways curve, exactly as my long-lost father used to do. For the first week or two of my stay here he would still bring back from these route marches a token for Miss Vavasour, nothing fancy, nothing cissyish, a spray of russet leaves or a sprig of greenery, nothing that could not be presented as merely an item of horticultural interest, which he would place without remark on the hall table beside her gardening gloves and her big bunch of house keys. Now he returns empty-handed, save for his paper and his peppermints. That is my doing; my arrival put paid to the ceremony of the nosegays.

The newspaper consumes what is left of his morning, he reads it from first page to last, gathering intelligence, missing nothing. He sits by the fireplace in the lounge, where the clock on the mantelpiece has a hesitant, geriatric tick and pauses at the half hour and the two quarter hours to deliver itself of a single, infirm, jangling chime but on the hour itself maintains what seems a vindictive silence. He has his armchair, his glass ashtray for his pipe, his box of Swan Vestas, his footstool, his paper rack. Does he notice those brassy beams of sunlight falling through the leaded panes of the bay window, the desiccated bunch of sea-blue and tenderly blood-brown hydrangea occupying the grate where even yet the first fire of the season has not needed to be lit? Does he notice that the world he reads about in the paper is no longer the world he knew? Perhaps these days all his energies, like mine, go into the effort of not noticing. I have caught him furtively crossing himself when the tolling of the angelus bell comes up to us from the stone church down on Strand Road.

At lunchtime the Colonel and I must shift for ourselves, for Miss Vavasour retires to her room every day between noon and three, to sleep, or read, or work on her memoirs, nothing would surprise me. The Colonel is a ruminant. He sits at the kitchen table in shirt-sleeves and an antique sleeveless pullover munching away at an ill-made sandwich – hacked lump of cheese or chunk of cold meat between two door-stoppers smeared with his slap, or a daub of Colman's fieriest, or sometimes both if he feels in need of a jolt – and tries out feints of conversation on me, like a canny field commander searching for a bulge in the enemy's defences. He sticks to neutral topics, the weather, sporting fixtures, horse racing although he assures me he is not a betting man. Despite the diffidence his need is patent: he dreads the afternoons, those empty hours, as I dread the sleepless nights. He cannot make me out, would like to know what really I am doing here, who might be anywhere, if I chose, so he believes. Who that could afford the warm south – 'The sun's the only man for the pains and aches,' the Colonel opines – would come to do his grieving at the Cedars? I have not told him about the old days here, the Graces, all that. Not that all that is an explanation. I get up to leave – 'Work,' I say solemnly – and he gives me a desperate look. Even my unforthcoming company is preferable to his room and the radio.

A chance mention of my daughter provoked an excited response. He has a daughter too, married, with a pair of little ones, as he says. They are going to come for a visit any day now, the daughter, her husband the engineer, and the girls, who are seven and three. I have a premonition of photographs and sure enough the wallet comes out of a back pocket and the snaps are shown, a leathery young woman with a dissatisfied mien who looks not at all like the Colonel, and a little girl in a party frock who misfortunately does. The son-in-law, grinning on a beach with babe in arms, is unexpectedly good-looking, a big-shouldered southern type with an oiled quiff and bruised eyes – how did mousey Miss Blunden get herself such a he-man? Other lives, other lives. Suddenly somehow they are too much for me, the Colonel's daughter, her man, their girls, and I return the pictures hastily, shaking my head. 'Oh, sorry, sorry,' the Colonel says, harrumphing embarrassedly. He thinks that talk of family stirs painful associations for me, but it is not that, or not only that. These days I must take the world in small and carefully measured doses, it is a sort of homeopathic cure I am undergoing, though I am not certain what this cure is meant to mend. Perhaps I am learning to live amongst the living again. Practising, I mean. But no, that is not it. Being here is just a way of not being anywhere.

Miss Vavasour, so assiduous in other areas of her

care of us, is capricious, not to say cavalier, in the matter not only of luncheon but of meals in general, and dinner especially at the Cedars can be an unpredictable refection. Anything might appear on the table, and does. Tonight for instance she served us breakfast kippers with poached eggs and boiled cabbage. The Colonel, sniffing, ostentatiously wielded his condiment bottles turn and turn about like a spot-the-pea artist. To these wordless protests of his Miss Vavasour's response is invariably one of aristocratic absent-mindedness verging on disdain. After the kippers there were tinned pears lodged in a gritty grey lukewarm substance which if childhood memory serves I think was semolina. Semolina, my goodness. As we made our way through this stodge, with nothing but the clicking of cutlery to disturb the silence, I had a sudden image of myself as a sort of large dark simian something slumped there at the table, or not a something but a nothing, rather, a hole in the room, a palpable absence, a darkness visible. It was very strange. I saw the scene as if from outside myself, the dining room half lit by two standard lamps, the ugly table with the whorled legs, Miss Vavasour absently at gaze and the Colonel stooped over his plate and baring one side of his upper dentures as he chewed, and I this big dark indistinct shape, like the shape that no one at the séance sees until the daguerreotype is developed. I think I am becoming my own ghost.

After dinner Miss Vavasour clears the table in a few broad fanciful passes – she is altogether too good for this kind of menial chore – while the Colonel and I sit in vague distress listening to our systems doing their best to deal with the insults with which they have just been served. Then Miss V. in stately fashion leads the way to the television room. This is a cheerless, ill-lit chamber which has a somehow subterranean atmosphere, and is always dank and cold. The furnishings too have an underground look to them, like things that subsided here over the years from some brighter place above. A chintz-covered sofa sprawls as if aghast, its two arms flung wide and cushions sagging. There is an armchair upholstered in plaid, and a small, three-legged table with a dusty potted plant which I believe is a genuine aspidistra, the like of which I have not seen since I do not know when, if ever. Miss Vavasour's upright piano, its lid shut, stands against the back wall as if in tight-lipped resentment of its gaudy rival opposite, a mighty, gunmetal-grey Pixilate Panoramic which its owner regards with a mixture of pride and slightly shamed misgiving. On this set we watch the comedy shows, favouring the gentler ones repeated from twenty or thirty years ago. We sit in silence, the canned audiences doing our laughing for us. The jittering coloured light from the screen plays over our faces. We are rapt, as mindless as children. Tonight there was a programme on a place in Africa, the Serengeti Plain, I think it was, and its great elephant herds. What amazing beasts they are, a direct link surely to a time long before our time, when behemoths even bigger than they roared and rampaged through forest and swamp. In manner they are melancholy and yet seem covertly amused, at us, apparently. They lumber along placidly in single file, the trunk-tip of one daintily furled around the laughable piggy tail of its cousin in front. The young, hairier than their elders, trot contentedly between their mothers' legs. If one set out to seek among our fellow-creatures, the land-bound ones, at least, for our very opposite, one would surely need look no further than the elephants. How is it we have allowed them to survive so long? Those sad little knowing eyes seem to invite one to pick up a blunderbuss. Yes, put a big bullet through there, or into one of those huge absurd flappy ears. Yes, yes, exterminate all the brutes, lop away at the tree of life until only the stump is left standing, then lovingly take the cleaver to that, too. Finish it all off.

You cunt, you fucking cunt, how could you go and leave me like this, floundering in my own foulness, with no one to save me from myself. *How could you.*

Speaking of the television room, I realise suddenly, I cannot think why it did not strike me before now, so obvious is it, that what it reminds me of, what the whole house reminds me of, for that matter, and this must be the real reason I came here to hide in the first place, is the rented rooms my mother and I inhabited, were forced to inhabit, throughout my teenage years. After my father left she was compelled to find work to support us and pay for my education, such as it was. We moved to the city, she and I, where she thought there would surely be more opportunities for her. She had no skills, had left school early and worked briefly as a shop-girl before she met my father and married him to get away from her family, nevertheless she was convinced that somewhere there awaited her the ideal position, the job of jobs, the one that she and only she was meant to fill but maddeningly could never find. So we shifted from place to place, from lodging house to lodging house, arriving at a new one always it seemed on a drizzly Sunday evening in winter. They were all alike, those rooms, or are so at least in my memory of them. There was the armchair with the broken arm, the pock-marked lino on the floor, the squat black gas stove sullen in its corner and smelling of the previous lodger's fried dinners. The lavatory was down the hall, with a chipped wooden seat and a long brown rust-stain on the back of the bowl and the ring-pull missing from the chain. The smell in the hall was like the smell of my breath when I breathed and rebreathed it into my cupped hands to know what it would be like to be suffocated. The surface of the table we ate at had a tacky feel under the fingers no matter how hard she scrubbed at it. After our tea she would clear away the tea things and spread out the *Evening Mail* on the table under the wan glow of a sixty-watt bulb and run a hairpin down the columns of job ads, ticking off each ad and muttering angrily under her breath. '*Previous experience essential . . . references required . . . must be university graduate . . .* Huh!' Then the greasy pack of cards, the matches divided into two equal piles, the tin ashtray overflowing with her cigarette butts, the cocoa for me and the glass of cooking sherry for her. We played Old Maid, Gin Rummy, Hearts. After that there was the sofa bed to be unfolded and the sour under-sheet pulled tight, and the blanket to be pinned up somehow from the ceiling to hang along the side of her bed for privacy. I lay and listened in helpless anger to her sighs, her snores, the squeaks of broken wind that she let off. Every other night, it seemed, I would wake to hear her as she wept, a knuckle pressed against her mouth and her face buried in the pillow. My father was rarely mentioned between us, unless he was late with the monthly postal order. She could not bring herself to speak his name; he was Gentleman Jim, or His Lordship, or, when she was in one of her rages or had taken too much sherry, Phil the Flute-player, or even Fart-arse the Fiddler. Her conceit was that he was enjoying a lavish success, *over there*, a success he cruelly refused to share with us as he should and as we deserved. The envelopes bringing the money orders – never a letter, only a card at Christmas or on my birthday, inscribed in the laboured copperplate of which he had always been so proud – bore the postmarks of places which even yet, when I am *over there* and see them signposted on the motorways his labour helped to build, provoke in me a confusion of feelings that includes a sticky sort of sadness, anger or its after-shock, and a curious yearning that is like nostalgia, a nostalgia for somewhere I have never been to. Watford. Coventry. Stoke. He too would have known the dingy rooms, the lino on the floor, the gas stove, the smells in the hall. Then the last letter came, from a strange woman – Maureen Strange, her name! – announcing *the very sad news I have to tell you*. My mother's bitter tears were as much of anger as of grief. 'Who's this,' she cried, 'this *Maureen?*' The single sheet of blue-lined notepaper shook in her hand. 'Blast him,' she said through gritted teeth, 'blast him anyway, the bastard!' In my mind I saw him for an instant, in the chalet, as it happens, at night, turning back from the open door in the thick yellow glow of the paraffin lamp and giving me an oddly quizzical glance, almost smiling, a spot of light from the lamp shining on his forehead and beyond him through the doorway the velvety depthless dark of the summer night.

Last thing, when the television stations are about to plunge into their unacceptably lurid late-night schedules, the set is firmly switched off and the Colonel has a cup of herbal tea prepared for him by Miss Vavasour. He tells me he hates the stuff – 'Not a word, mind!' – but dares not refuse. Miss Vavasour stands over him as he drinks. She insists it will help him sleep; he is gloomily convinced the opposite is the case, yet makes no protest, and drains the cup with a doomed expression. One night I persuaded him to accompany me to the Pier Head Bar for a nightcap, but it was a mistake. He grew anxious in my company – I did not blame him, I grow anxious in it myself – and fidgeted with his tobacco pipe and his glass of stout and kept easing back his cuff surreptitiously to check the time by his watch. The few locals who were there glowered at us, and we soon left, and walked back to the Cedars in silence under a tremendous October sky of stars and flying moon and tattered clouds. Most nights I drink myself to sleep, or attempt to, with half a dozen bumpers of brandy from the jeroboam of best Napoleon I keep in my room. I suppose I could offer him a drop of that, but I think not. The idea of late-night chats with the Colonel about life and related matters does not appeal. The night is long, my temper short.

Have I spoken already of my drinking? I drink like a fish. No, not like a fish, fishes do not drink, it is only breathing, their kind of breathing. I drink like one recently widowed – widowered? – a person of scant talent and scanter ambition, greyed o'er by the years, uncertain and astray and in need of consolation and the brief respite of drink-induced oblivion. I would take drugs if I had them, but I have not, and do not know how I might go about getting some. I doubt that Ballyless boasts a dope dealer. Perhaps the Pecker Devereux could help me. The Pecker is a fearsome fellow all shoulders and barrel chest with a big coarse weathered face and a gorilla's bandy arms. His huge face is pitted all over from some ancient acne or pox, each cavity ingrained with its speck of shiny black dirt. He used to be a deep-sea sailor, and is said to have killed a man. He has an orchard, where he lives in a wheelless caravan under the trees with his scrawny whippet of a wife. He sells apples and, clandestinely, a cloudy, sulphurous moonshine made from windfalls that sends the young men of the village crazy on Saturday nights. Why am I speaking of him like this? What is the Pecker Devereux to me? In these parts the x is pronounced, *Devrecks*, they say, I cannot stop. How wild the unguarded fancy runs.

Our day today was lightened, if that is the way to put it, by a visit from Miss Vavasour's friend Bun, who joined us for Sunday lunch. I came upon her at noon in the lounge, overflowing a wicker armchair in the bay window, lolling as if helpless there and faintly panting. The space where she sat was thronged with smoky sunlight and at first I could hardly make her out, although in truth she is as unmissable as the late Queen of Tonga. She is an enormous person, of indeterminate age. She wore a sack-coloured tweed dress tightly belted in the middle, which made her look as if she had been pumped up to bursting at bosom and hips, and her short stout cork-coloured legs were stuck out in front of her like two gigantic bungs protruding from her nether regions. A tiny sweet face, delicate of feature and pinkly aglow, is set in the big pale pudding of her head, the fossil remains, marvellously preserved, of the girl that she once was, long ago. Her ash-and-silver hair was done in an old-fashioned style, parted down the centre and pulled back into an eponymous bun. She smiled at me and nodded a greeting, her powdered wattles joggling. I did not know who she was, and thought she must be a guest newly arrived – Miss Vavasour has half a dozen vacant rooms for rent at this off-peak season. When she tottered to her feet the wicker chair cried out in excruciated relief. She really is of a prodigious bulk. I thought that if her belt buckle were to fail and the belt snap her trunk would flop into a perfectly spherical shape with her head on top like a large cherry on a, well, on a bun. It was apparent from the look she gave me, of mingled sympathy and eager interest, that she was aware of who I was and had been apprised of my stricken state. She told me her name, grand-sounding, with a hyphen, but I immediately forgot it. Her hand was small and soft and moistly warm, a baby's hand. Colonel Blunden came into the room then, with the

Sunday papers under his arm, and looked at her and frowned. When he frowns like that the yellowish whites of his eyes seem to darken and his mouth takes on the out-thrust blunt squareness of a muzzle.

Among the more or less harrowing consequences of bereavement is the sheepish sense I have of being an impostor. After Anna died I was everywhere attended upon, deferred to, made an object of special consideration. A hush surrounded me among people who had heard of my loss, so that I had no choice but to observe in return a solemn and pensive silence of my own, that very quickly set me twitching. It started, this singling-out, at the cemetery, if not before. With what tenderness they gazed at me across the grave-mouth, and how gently yet firmly they took my arm when the ceremony was done, as if I might be in danger of falling in a faint and pitching headlong into the hole myself. I even thought I detected a speculative something in the warmth with which certain of the women embraced me, in the lingering way they held on to my hand, gazing into my eyes and shaking their heads in wordless commiseration, with that melting stoniness of expression that old-style tragic actresses would put on in the closing scene when the harrowed hero staggered on stage with the heroine's corpse in his arms. I felt

I should stop and hold up a hand and tell these people that really, I did not deserve their reverence, for reverence is what it felt like, that I had been merely a bystander, a bit-player, while Anna did the dying. Throughout lunch Bun insisted on addressing me in tones of warm concern, muted awe, and try as I might I could modulate no tone in response that did not sound brave and bashful. Miss Vavasour, I could see, was finding all this gush increasingly annoying, and made repeated attempts to foster a less soulful, brisker atmosphere at the table, without success. The Colonel was no help, although he did try, breaking in on Bun's relentless flow of solicitude with weather forecasts and topics from the day's papers, but every time was rebuffed. He was simply no match for Bun. Showing his tarnished dentures in a ghastly display of grins and grimaces, he had the look of a hyena bobbing and squirming before the heedless advance of a hippo.

Bun lives in the city, in a flat over a shop, in circumstances which, she would firmly have me know, are far beneath her, daughter of the hyphen-ated gentry that she is. She reminds me of one of those hearty virgins of a bygone age, the housekeep-ing sister, say, of a bachelor clergyman or widowed squire. As she twittered on I pictured her in bombazine, whatever that is, and button-boots, seated in state on granite steps before a vast front door in the midst of a tiered array of squint-eyed domestics; I saw her, the fox's nemesis, in hunting pink and bowler hat with a veil, astride the sagging back of a big black galloping horse; or there she was in an enormous kitchen with range and scrubbed deal table and hanging hams, instructing loyal old Mrs Grub on which cuts of beef to serve for the Master's annual dinner to mark the Glorious Twelfth. Diverting myself in this harmless fashion I did not notice the fight developing between her and Miss Vavasour until it was well under way, and I had no idea how it might have started or what it was about. The two normally muted spots of colour on Miss Vavasour's cheekbones were burning fiercely, while Bun, who seemed to be swelling to even larger proportions under the pneumatic effects of a growing indignation, sat regarding her friend across the table with a fixed, froggy smile, her breath coming in fast little plosive gasps. They spoke with vengeful politeness, barging at each other like an unfairly matched pair of hobbyhorses. *Really, I fail to see how you can say . . . Am I to understand that you . . .? The point is not that I . . . The point is that you did . . . Well, that is just . . . It most certainly is not . . . Excuse me, it most certainly is!*

The Colonel, increasingly alarmed, looked wildly from one of them to the other and back again, his eyes clicking in their sockets, as if he were watching a tennis match that had started in friendly enough fashion but had suddenly turned murderous.

I would have thought Miss Vavasour would emerge the easy victor from this contest, but she did not. She was not fighting with the full force of the weaponry I am sure she has at her command. Something, I could see, was holding her back, something of which Bun was well aware and which she leaned upon with all her considerable weight and to her strong advantage. Although they seemed in the heat of the argument to have forgotten about the Colonel and me, the realisation slowly dawned that they were conducting this struggle at least partly for my benefit, to impress me, and to try to win me over, to one side or the other. I could tell this from the manner in which Bun's little eager black eyes kept flickering coyly in my direction, while Miss Vavasour refused to glance my way even once. Bun, I began to see, was far more sly and astute than I would at first have given her credit for. One is inclined to imagine that people who are fat must also be stupid. This fat person, however, had taken the measure of me, and, I was convinced, saw me clearly for what I was, in all my essentials. And what was it that she saw? In my life it never troubled me to be kept by a rich, or richish, wife. I was born to be a dilettante, all that was lacking was the means, until I met Anna. Nor am I concerned particularly about the provenance of Anna's money, which was first Charlie Weiss's and is now mine, or how much or what kind of heavy machinery Charlie had to buy and sell in the making of it. What is money, after all? Almost nothing, when one has a sufficiency of it. So why was I squirming like this under Bun's veiled but knowing, irresistible scrutiny?

But come now, Max, come now. I will not deny it, I was always ashamed of my origins, and even still it requires only an arch glance or a condescending word from the likes of Bun to set me quivering inwardly in indignation and hot resentment. From the start I was bent on bettering myself. What was it that I wanted from Chloe Grace but to be on the level of her family's superior social position, however briefly, at whatever remove? It was hard going, scaling those Olympian heights. Sitting there with Bun I recalled with an irresistible faint shudder another Sunday lunch at the Cedars, half a century before. Who had invited me? Not Chloe, surely. Perhaps her mother did, when I was still her admirer and it amused her to have me sitting tongue-tied at her table. How nervous I was, really terrified. There were things on the table such as I had never seen before, odd-shaped cruets, china sauce-boats, a silver stand for the carving knife, a carving fork with a bone handle and a safety lever that could be pulled out at the back. As each course arrived I waited to see which pieces of cutlery the others would pick up before I would risk picking up my own. Someone passed me a bowl of mint sauce and I did not know what to do with it – mint sauce! Now and then from the other end of the table Carlo Grace, chewing vigorously, would bend a lively gaze on me. What was life like at the chalet, he wanted to know. What did we cook on? A Primus stove, I told him. 'Ha!' he cried. 'Primus *inter pares*!' And how he laughed, and Myles laughed too, and even Rose's lips twitched, though no one save he, I am sure, understood the sally, and Chloe scowled, not at their mockery but at my haplessness.

Anna could not sympathise with my sensitivities in these matters, she being the product of a classless class. She thought my mother a delight – fearsome, that is, unrelenting, and unforgiving, but for all that delightful, in her way. My mother, I need hardly say, did not reciprocate this warm regard. They met no more than two or three times, disastrously, I thought. Ma did not come to the wedding – let me admit it, I did not invite her – and died not long afterwards, at about the same time as Charlie Weiss. 'As if they were releasing us, the two of them,' Anna said. I did not share this benign interpretation, but made no comment. That was a day in the nursing home, she suddenly began to speak about my mother, with nothing to prompt her that I had noticed; the figures of the far past come back at the end, wanting their due. It was a morning after storm, and all outside the window of the corner room looked tousled and groggy, the dishevelled lawn littered with a caducous fall of leaves and the trees swaying still, like hungover drunks. On one wrist Anna wore a plastic tag and on the other a gadget like a wristwatch with a button that when pressed would release a fixed dose of morphine into her already polluted bloodstream. The first time we came home for a visit – home: the word gives me a shove, and I stumble – my mother hardly spoke a word to her. Ma was living in a flat by the canal, a dim low place that smelled of her landlady's cats. We had brought her gifts of duty-free cigarettes and a bottle of sherry, she accepted them with a sniff. She said she hoped we were not expecting her to put us up. We stayed in a cheap hotel nearby where the bath water was brown and Anna's handbag was stolen. We took Ma to the Zoo. She laughed at the baboons, nastily, letting us know they reminded her of someone, me, of course. One of them was masturbating, with a curiously lackadaisical air, looking off over its shoulder. 'Dirty thing,' Ma said dismissively and turned away.

We had tea in the café in the grounds, where the blaring of elephants mingled with the clamour of the bank holiday crowd. Ma smoked the duty-free cigarettes, ostentatiously stubbing each one out after three or four puffs, showing me what she thought of my peace offerings.

'Why does she keep calling you Max?' she hissed at me when Anna had gone to the counter to fetch a scone for her. 'Your name is not Max.'

'It is now,' I said. 'Did you not read the things I sent you, the things that I wrote, with my name printed on them?'

She gave one of her mountainous shrugs.

'I thought they were by somebody else.'

She could show her anger just by her way of sitting, skewed sideways on the chair, stiff-backed, her hands clamped on the handbag in her lap, her hat, shaped like a brioche and with a bit of black netting around the crown, askew on her unkempt grey curls. There was a little grey fuzz on her chin, too. She glanced contemptuously about her. 'Huh,' she said, 'this place. I suppose you'd like to leave me here, put me in with the monkeys and let them feed me bananas.'

Anna came back with the scone. Ma looked at it scornfully.

'I don't want that,' she said. 'I didn't ask for that.'

'Ma,' I said.

'Don't *Ma* me.'

But when we were leaving she wept, backing for cover behind the open door of the flat, lifting a forearm to hide her eyes, like a child, furious at herself. She died that winter, sitting on a bench by the canal one unseasonably mild mid-week afternoon. Angina pectoris, no one had known. The pigeons were still worrying at the crusts she had strewn for them on the path when a tramp sat down beside her and offered her a swig from his bottle in its brown-paper bag, not noticing she was dead.

'Strange,' Anna said. 'To be here, like that, and then not.'

She sighed, and looked out at the trees. They fascinated her, those trees, she wanted to go out and stand amongst them, to hear the wind blowing in the boughs. But there would be no going out, for her, any more. 'To have been here,' she said.

Someone was addressing me. It was Bun. How long had I been away, wandering through the chamber of horrors in my head? Lunch was done and Bun was saying goodbye. When she smiles her little face becomes smaller still, crinkling and contracting around the minute button of her nose. Through the window I could see clouds massing although a wettish sun low in the west still glared out of a pale sliver of leek-green sky. For a second I had that image of myself again, hunched hugely on my chair, pink lower lip adroop and enormous hands lying helplessly before me on the table, a great ape, captive, tranquillised and bleary. There are times, they occur with increasing frequency nowadays, when I seem to know nothing, when everything I did know seems to have fallen out of my mind like a shower of rain, and I am gripped for a moment in paralysed dismay, waiting for it all to come back but with no certainty that it will. Bun was gathering her things preparatory to the considerable effort of unbunging those mighty legs of hers from under the table and getting herself to her feet. Miss Vavasour had already risen and was hovering by her friend's shoulder – it was as big and round as a bowling-ball – impatient for her to be gone and trying not to show it. The Colonel was at Bun's other side, leaning forward at an awkward angle and making vague feints in the air with his hands, like a removals man squaring up to a weighty and particularly awkward item of furniture.

'Well!' Bun said, giving the table a tap with her knuckles, and looked up brightly first at Miss Vavasour, then at the Colonel, and both pressed a step more closely in, as if they might indeed be about to put a hand each under her elbows and heave her to her feet.

We went outside into the copper-coloured light of the late-autumn evening. Strong gusts of wind were sweeping up Station Road, making the tops of the trees thrash and flinging dead leaves about the sky. Rooks cawed rawly. The year is almost done. Why do I think something new will come to replace it, other than a number on a calendar? Bun's car, a nippy little red model, bright as a ladybird, was parked on the gravel inside the gate. It gasped on its springs as Bun inserted herself rearways into the driving seat, first pushing in her enormous behind then heaving up her legs and falling back heavily with a grunt against the fake tiger-skin upholstery. The Colonel drew open the gate for her and stood in the middle of the road and directed her out with broad dramatic sweeps of his arms. Smells of exhaust smoke, the sea, the garden's autumn rot. Brief desolation. I know nothing, nothing, old ape that I am. Bun sounded the car horn gaily and waved, her pinched face grinning through the glass at us, and Miss Vavasour waved back, not gaily, and the car buzzed away lopsidedly up the road and over the railway bridge and was gone.

'That's a perisher,' the Colonel said, rubbing his hands and heading indoors.

Miss Vavasour sighed.

We would have no dinner, lunch having lasted so long and having been so fraught. Miss V. was still agitated, I could see, from that bandying of words with her friend. When the Colonel followed her into the kitchen, angling for afternoon tea, at least, she was quite sharp with him, and he scuttled off to his room and the commentary to a football match on the wireless. I too retreated, to the lounge, with my book – Bell on Bonnard, dull as ditch-water – but I could not read, and put the book aside. Bun's visit had upset the delicate equilibrium of the household, there was a sort of noiseless trilling in the atmosphere, as if a fine, taut alarm wire had been tripped and was vibrating still. I sat in the bay of the window and watched the day darken. Bare trees across the road were black against the last flares of the setting sun, and the rooks in a raucous flock were wheeling and dropping, settling disputatiously for the night. I was thinking of Anna. I make myself think of her, I do it as an exercise. She is lodged in me like a knife and yet I am beginning to forget her. Already the image of her that I hold in my head is fraying, bits of pigments, flakes of gold leaf, are chipping off. Will the entire canvas be empty one day? I have come to realise how little I knew her, I mean how shallowly I knew her, how ineptly. I do not blame myself for this. Perhaps I should. Was I too lazy, too inattentive, too self-absorbed? Yes, all of those things, and yet I cannot think it is a matter of blame, this forgetting, this not-having-known. I fancy, rather, that I expected too much, in the way of knowing. I know so little of myself, how should I think to know another?

But wait, no, that is not it. I am being disingenuous – for a change, says you, yes yes. The truth is, we did not wish to know each other. More, what we wished was exactly that, not to know each other. I said somewhere already – no time to go back and look for it now, caught up all at once as I am in the toils of this thought – that what I found in Anna from the first was a way of fulfilling the fantasy of myself. I did not know quite what I meant when I said it, but thinking now on it a little I suddenly see. Or do I. Let me try to tease it out, I have plenty of time, these Sunday evenings are endless.

From earliest days I wanted to be someone else. The injunction *nosce te ipsum* had an ashen taste on my tongue from the first time a teacher enjoined me to repeat it after him. I knew myself, all too well, and did not like what I knew. Again, I must qualify. It was not what I was that I disliked, I mean the singular, essential me – although I grant that even the notion of an essential, singular self is problematic – but the congeries of affects, inclinations, received ideas, class tics, that my birth and upbringing had bestowed on me in place of a personality. In place of, yes. I never had a personality, not in the way that others have, or think they have. I was always a distinct no-one, whose fiercest wish was to be an indistinct someone. I know what I mean. Anna, I saw at once, would be the medium of my transmutation. She was the fairground mirror in which all my distortions would be made straight. 'Why not be yourself?' she would say to me in our early days together – *be*, mark you, not *know* – pitying my fumbling attempts to grasp the great world. *Be yourself!* Meaning, of course, *Be anyone you like*. That was the pact we made, that we would relieve each other of the burden of being the people whom everyone else told us we were. Or at least she relieved me of that burden, but what did I do for her? Perhaps I should not include her in this drive toward unknowing, perhaps it was only I who desired ignorance.

The question I am left with now, anyway, is precisely the question of knowing. Who, if not ourselves, were we? All right, leave Anna out of it. Who, if not myself, was I? The philosophers tell us that we are defined and have our being through others. Is a rose red in the dark? In a forest on a far planet where there are no ears to hear does a falling tree make a crash? I ask: who was to know me, if not Anna? Who was to know Anna, if not I? Absurd questions. We were happy together, or not unhappy, which is more than most people manage; is that not enough? There were strains, there were stresses, as how would there not be in any union such as ours, if any such there are. The shouts, the screams, the flung plates, the odd slap, the odder punch, we had all that. Then there was Serge and his ilk, not to mention my Sergesses, no, not to mention. But even in our most savage fights we were only violently at play, like Chloe and Myles in their wrestling matches.

Our quarrels we ended in laughter, bitter laughter, but laughter all the same, abashed and even a little ashamed, ashamed that is not of our ferocity, but our lack of it. We fought in order to feel, and to feel real, being the self-made creatures that we were. That I was.

Could we, could I, have done otherwise? Could I have lived differently? Fruitless interrogation. Of course I could, but I did not, and therein lies the absurdity of even asking. Anyway, where are the paragons of authenticity against whom my concocted self might be measured? In those final bathroom paintings that Bonnard did of the septuagenarian Marthe he was still depicting her as the teenager he had thought she was when he first met her. Why should I demand more veracity of vision of myself than of a great and tragic artist? We did our best, Anna and I. We forgave each other for all that we were not. What more could be expected, in this vale of torments and tears? *Do not look so worried*, Anna said, *I hated you, too, a little, we were human beings, after all.* Yet for all that, I cannot rid myself of the conviction that we missed something, that I missed something, only I do not know what it might have been.

Lost track. Everything is mixed up. Why do I

torment myself with these insoluble equivocations, have I not had enough of casuistry? Leave yourself alone, Max, leave yourself alone.

Miss Vavasour came in, a moving wraith in the shadows of the twilit room. She enquired if I was warm enough, if she should light a fire. I asked her about Bun, who was she, how had they met, just for the sake of asking something. It was a while before she gave an answer, and when she did it was to a question I had not asked.

'Well, you see,' she said, 'Vivienne's people own this house.'

'Vivienne?'

'Bun.'

'Ah.'

She bent to the fireplace and lifted the bunch of dried hydrangea, crackling, from the grate.

'Or perhaps it is she who owns it now,' she said, 'since most of her people have passed on.' I said I was surprised, I had thought the house was hers. 'No,' she said, frowning at the brittle flowers in her hands, then looked up, almost impish, showing the tiniest tip of a tongue. 'But I come with it, so to speak.'

Faintly from the Colonel's room we heard the crowd cheering and the commentator's excited squawks; someone had scored a goal. They must be playing in the almost dark by now. Injury time.

'And you never married?' I said.

She smiled a frugal smile at that, casting down her eyes again.

'Oh, no,' she said. 'I never married.' She glanced at me quickly and away. The two spots of colour on her cheekbones glowed. 'Vivienne,' she said, 'was my friend. Bun, that is.'

'Ah,' I said again. What else could I say?

She is playing the piano now. Schumann, *Kinderszenen*. As if to prompt me.

Strange, is it not, the way they lodge in the mind, the seemingly inconsidered things? Behind the Cedars, where a corner of the house met the tussocked lawn, under a crooked black drainpipe, there stood a water butt, long gone by now, of course. It was a wooden barrel, a real one, full-size, the staves blackened with age and the iron hoops eaten to frills by rust. The rim was nicely bevelled, and so smooth that one could hardly feel the joins between the staves; smoothly sawn, that is, and planed, but in texture the sodden grain-end of the wood there was slightly furry, or napped, rather, like the pod of a bulrush, only tougher to the touch, and chillier, and more moist. Although it must have held I do not know how many scores of gallons it was always full almost to the brim, thanks to the frequency of rain in these parts, even, or especially, in summer. When I looked down into it the water seemed black and thick as oil. Because the barrel listed a little the surface of the water formed a fat ellipse, that trembled at the slightest breath and broke into terror-stricken ripples when a train went past. That ill-tended corner of the garden had a soft damp climate all of its own, due to the presence of the water barrel. Weeds in profusion flourished there, nettles, dock leaves, convolvulus, other things I do not know the name of, and the daylight had a greenish cast to it, particularly so in the morningtime. The water in the barrel, being rain water, was soft, or hard, one or the other, and therefore was considered good for the hair, or the scalp, or something, I do not know. And it was there one glittering sunny morning that I came upon Mrs Grace helping Rose to wash her hair.

Memory dislikes motion, preferring to hold things still, and as with so many of these remembered scenes I see this one as a tableau. Rose stands bent forward from the waist with her hands on her knees, her hair hanging down from her face in a long black shining wedge dripping with soap suds. She is bare-foot, I see her toes in the long grass, and is wearing one of those vaguely Tyrolean short-sleeved white linen blouses that were so popular at the time, full at the waist and tight at the shoulders and embroidered across the bust in an abstract pattern of red and prussian-blue stitching. The neckline is deeply scallo-ped and inside it I have a clear glimpse of her pendent breasts, small and spiked, like the business ends of two spinning-tops. Mrs Grace wears a blue satin dressing gown and delicate blue slippers, bringing an incongruous breath of the boudoir into the out-of-doors. Her hair is pinned back at the ears with two tortoise-shell clasps, or slides, I think they were called. It is apparent she is not long out of bed, and in the morning light her face has a raw, roughly sculpted look. She stands in the very pose of Vermeer's maid with the milk jug, her head and her left shoulder inclined, one hand cupped under the heavy fall of Rose's hair and the other pouring a dense silvery sluice of water from a chipped enamel jug. The water where it falls on the crown of Rose's head makes a bare patch that shakes and slithers, like the spot of moonlight on Pierrot's sleeve. Rose gives little hooting cries of protest – '*Oo! Oo! Oo!*' – at the cold shock of the water on her scalp.

Poor Rosie. I can never think of her name without that epithet attached. She was, what, nineteen, twenty at the most. Tallish, remarkably slender, narrow at waist and long of hip, she was possessed of a silky, sulky gracefulness from the height of her pale flat brow to her neat and shapely and slightly splay-toed feet. I suppose someone wishing to be unkind – Chloe, for instance – might have described her features as sharp. Her nose, with its tear-shaped, pharaonic nostrils, was prominent at the bridge, the skin stretched tight and translucent over the bone. It is deflected, this nose, a fraction to the left, so that when one looks at her straight-on there is the illusion of seeing her at once full-face and in profile, as in one of those fiddly Picasso portraits. This defect, far from making her seem misproportioned, only added to the soulful expressiveness of her face. In repose, when she was unaware of being spied on – and what a little spy I was! – she would hold her head at an acute downward tilt, her eyes hooded and her shallowly cleft chin tucked into her shoulder. Then she would seem a Duccio madonna, melancholy, remote, self-forgetting, lost in the sombre dream of all that was to come, of all that, for her, was not to come.

Of the three central figures in that summer's salt-bleached triptych it is she, oddly, who is most sharply delineated on the wall of my memory. I think the reason for this is that the first two figures in the scene, I mean Chloe and her mother, are all my own work while Rose is by another, unknown, hand. I keep going up close to them, the two Graces, now mother, now daughter, applying a dab of colour here, scumbling a detail there, and the result of all this close work is that my focus on them is blurred rather than sharpened, even when I stand back to survey my handiwork. But Rose, Rose is a completed portrait, Rose is done. This does not mean she was more real or of more significance to me than Chloe or her mother, certainly not, only that I can picture her with the most immediacy. It cannot be because she is still here, for the version of her which is here is so changed as to be hardly recognisable. I see her in her pumps and sheer black pants and shirt of a crimson shade – although she must have had other outfits, this is the one she wears in almost every one of my recollections of her – posed among inconsequentials, the arbitrary props of the studio, a dull drape, a dusty straw hat with a blossom in the band, a bit of mossed-over wall that is probably made of cardboard, and, high up in one corner, an umber doorway where, mysteriously, deep shadows give on to a white-gold blaze of empty light. Her presence was not as vivid for me as that of Chloe or Mrs Grace, how could it be, yet there was something that set her apart, with that midnight-black hair of hers and that white skin the powdery bloom of which the strongest sunlight or harshest sea breeze seemed incapable of smudging.

She was I suppose what in the old days, I mean days even older than those of which I speak, would have been called a governess. A governess, however, would have had her modest spheres of power, but poor Rosie was helpless before the twins and their unheeding parents. For Chloe and Myles she was the obvious enemy, the butt of their cruellest jokes, an object of resentment and endless ridicule. They had two modes by which they treated her. They were either indifferent, to the point that she might have been invisible to them, or else they subjected everything she did or said, however trivial, to a relentless scrutiny and interrogation. As she moved about the house they would follow after her, crowding on her heels, watching closely her every action – putting down a plate, picking up a book, trying not to look at herself in a mirror – as if what she was doing were the most outlandish and inexplicable behaviour they had ever witnessed. She would ignore them for as long as she could bear but in the end would turn on them, flushed and trembling, and implore them please, please, to leave her alone, keeping her voice to an anguished whisper for fear the elder Graces should hear her losing control. This was just the response the twins had wanted, of course, and they would press up to her more closely still and peer eagerly into her face, feigning wonderment, and Chloe would bombard her with questions – what had been on the plate? was that a good book? why did she not want to see herself in the glass? – until tears welled up in her eyes and her mouth sagged askew in sorrow and impotent rage, and then the two of them would run off in delight, laughing like demons.

I discovered Rose's secret one Saturday afternoon when I came to the Cedars to call for Chloe. As I arrived she was getting into the car with her father and about to leave for a trip to town. I stopped at the gate. We had made an arrangement to go and play tennis – could she have forgotten? Of course she could. I was dismayed; to be abandoned like this on an empty Saturday afternoon was not a thing lightly to be borne. Myles, who was opening the gate for his father to drive through, saw my dismay and grinned, like the malignant sprite that he was. Mr Grace peered out at me from behind the windscreen and inclined his head toward Chloe and said something, and he also was grinning. By now the day itself, breezy and bright, seemed to exude derision and a generalised merriment. Mr Grace trod hard on the accelerator and the car with a loud report from its hindquarters bounded forward on the gravel so that I had to step smartly out of the way – although they shared nothing else, my father and Carlo Grace had the same truculently playful sense of fun – and Chloe through the side window, her face blurred behind the glass, looked out at me with an expression of frowning surprise, as if she had just that moment noticed me standing there, which for all I knew she had. I waved a hand, with as much carelessness as I could feign, and she smiled with down-turned mouth in a fakely rueful way and gave an exaggerated shrug of apology, lifting her shoulders level with her ears. The car had slowed for Myles to get in and she put her face close to the window and mouthed something, and raised her left hand in an oddly formal gesture, it might have been a sort of blessing, and what could I do but smile and shrug too, and wave again, as she was borne away in a swirl of exhaust smoke, with Myles's severed-seeming head in the rear window, grinning back at me gloatingly.

The house had a deserted aspect. I walked past the front door and down to where the diagonal row of trees marked the end of the garden. Beyond was the railway line paved with jagged loose blue shale and giving off its mephitic whiff of ash and gas. The trees, planted too close together, were spindly and misshapen, their highest branches confusedly waving like so many arms upflung in wild disorder. What were they? Not oaks – sycamores, perhaps. Before I knew what I was doing I was clambering up the middlemost one. This was not like me, I was not daring or adventurous, and had, and have, no head for heights. Up I went, however, up and up, hand and instep, instep and hand, from bough to bough. The climb was exhilaratingly easy, despite the foliage hissing in scandalised protest around me and twigs slapping at my face, and soon I was as near the top as it was possible to go. There I clung, fearless as any jack tar astride the rigging, the earth's deck gently rolling far below me, while, above, a low sky of dull pearl seemed close enough to touch. At this height the breeze was a steady flow of solid air, smelling of inland things, earth, and smoke, and animals. I could see the roofs of the town on the horizon, and farther off and higher up, like a mirage, a tiny silver ship propped motionless on a smear of pale sea. A bird landed on a twig and looked at me in surprise and then flew away again quickly with an offended chirp.

I had by now forgotten Chloe's forgetfulness, so exultant was I and brimful of manic glee at being so high and so far from everything, and I did not notice Rose below me until I heard her sobbing.

She was standing underneath the tree next to the one in which I was perched, her shoulders hunched and her elbows pressed into her sides as if to keep herself upright. Her agitated fingers clutched a wadded handkerchief, but so novelettishly was she posed, weeping there amidst the soughing airs of afternoon, that I thought at first it must be a crumpled love letter and not a hankie she was holding. How odd she looked, foreshortened to an irregular disc of shoulders and head – the parting in her hair was the same shade of off-white as the sodden handkerchief she was holding – and when she turned hastily at the sound of a step behind her she wobbled briefly like a ninepin that the bowl has succeeded only in striking a glancing blow. Mrs Grace was approaching along the pathway worn in the grass under the clothesline, her head bowed and her arms folded cruciform over flattened breasts and a hand clasped crosswise on each shoulder. She was barefoot, and wore shorts, and one of her husband's white shirts that was flatteringly far too big for her. She stopped a little way off from Rose and stood a moment silent, turning from side to side in quarter turns on the pivot of herself, still with her hands on her shoulders, as if she too like Rose were holding herself up, herself a child that she was rocking in her arms.

'Rose,' she said in a playfully coaxing tone, 'oh, Rose, what is it?'

Rose, who had resolutely turned her face to the far fields again, gave a liquid snort of not-laughter.

'What is it?' she cried, her voice flying up on the final word and spilling over on itself. 'What is it?'

She blew her nose indignantly on the rim of the balled-up hankie and finished with a hair-tossing snuffle. Even from this angle I could see that Mrs Grace was smiling, and biting her lip. Behind me from afar came a hooting whistle. The afternoon train from town, matt-black engine and half a dozen green wooden carriages, was blundering toward us through the fields like a big mad toy, huffing bulbous links of thick white smoke. Mrs Grace moved forward soundlessly and touched a fingertip to Rose's elbow but Rose snatched her arm away as if the touch were burning hot. A flurry of wind flattened the shirt against Mrs Grace's body and showed distinctly the fat outlines of her breasts. 'Oh, come on now, Rosie,' she coaxed again, and this time managed to insinuate a hand into the crook of the girl's arm and with a series of soft tugs made her turn, stiff and unwilling though she was, and together they set off pacing under the trees. Rose went stumblingly, talking and talking, while Mrs Grace kept her head down as before and seemed hardly to speak at all; from the set of her shoulders and a stooping drag to her gait I suspected she was suppressing an urge to laugh. Of Rose's tremulous hiccupy words the ones I caught were *love* and *foolish* and *Mr Grace*, and of Mrs Grace's responses only a shouted *Carlo?* followed by an incredulous whoop. Suddenly the train was there, making the trunk of the tree vibrate between my knees; as the engine passed I looked into the cabin and saw distinctly the white of an eye flash up at me from under a gleaming, smoke-blackened brow. When I turned back to them the two had stopped pacing and stood face to face in the long grass, Mrs Grace smiling with a hand lifted to Rose's shoulder and Rose, her nostrils edged with pink, gouging into her teary eyes with the knuckles of both hands, and then a blinding plume of the train's smoke blew violently into my face and by the time it cleared they had turned and were walking back up the path together to the house.

So there it was. Rose was lost in love for the father of the children in her charge. It was the old story, although I do not know how it was old for me, who was so young. What did I think, what feel? I recall most clearly the wadded handkerchief in Rose's hands and the blue filigree of incipient varicose veins on the backs of Mrs Grace's strong bare calves. And the steam engine, of course, that had come to a clanking stop over in the station, and stood now seething and gasping and squirting jets of scalding water from its fascinatingly intricate underparts as it waited impatiently to be off again. What are living beings, compared to the enduring intensity of mere things?

When Rose and Mrs Grace were gone I climbed down from the tree, a harder thing to do than climbing up had been, and went softly past the silent and unseeing house and walked down Station Road in the polished pewter light of the emptied afternoon. That train had pulled out of the station and by now was already somewhere else, somewhere else entirely.

Naturally I lost no time in telling Chloe of my discovery. Her response was not at all what I had expected it would be. True, she seemed shocked at first, but quickly assumed a sceptical air, and even appeared to be annoyed, I mean annoyed at me, for having told her. This was disconcerting. I had depended on her greeting my account of the scene under the trees with a delighted cackle, which in turn would have allowed me the assurance to treat the matter as a joke, instead of which I was forced to reflect on it in a more serious and sombre light. A sombre light, imagine that. But why a joke? Because laughter, for the young, is a neutralising force, and tames terrors? Rose, although nearly twice as old as we were, was still on this side of the gulf that separated us from the world of the adults. It was bad enough to have to entertain the thought of them, the real grown-ups, at their furtive frolics, but the possibility of Rose cavorting with a man of Carlo Grace's years – that paunch, that bulging crotch, that chest-fur with its glints of grey – was hardly to be entertained by a sensibility as delicate, as callow, as mine still was. Had she declared her love to Mr Grace? Had he reciprocated? The pictures that flashed before me of pale Rose reclining in her satyr's rough embrace excited and alarmed me in equal measure. And what of Mrs Grace? How calmly she had received Rose's blurted confession, with what lightness, what amusement, even. Why had she not scratched out the girl's eyes with her glistening, vermilion claws?

Then there were the lovers themselves. How I marvelled at the ease, the smooth effrontery, with which they masked all that was going on between them. Carlo Grace's very insouciance seemed now a mark of criminal intent. Who but a heartless seducer would laugh like that, and tease, and thrust out his chin and scratch rapidly in the grizzled beard underneath it, his fingernails making a rasping sound? The fact that in public he paid no more attention to Rose than he did to anyone else who happened to cross his path was only a further sign of his cunning and his skilful dissimulation. Rose had only to hand him his newspaper, and he had only to accept it from her, for it to seem to my hotly vigilant eye that a clandestine, indecent exchange had taken place. Her mild and diffident demeanour in his presence was to me that of a debauched nun, now that I knew of her secret shame, and images moved in the deeper reaches of my imagination of her glimmering pale form joined with him in dim coarse couplings, and I heard his muffled bellows and her muted moans of dark delight.

What had driven her to confess, and to her beloved's spouse, at that? And what did she think, poor Rosie, the first time her eye fell on the slogan that Myles scrawled in chalk on the gate posts and on the footpath outside the gate – *RV loves CG* – and the accompanying rudimentary sketch of a female torso, two circles with dots in the centre, two curves for the flanks, and, below, a pair of brackets enclosing a curt, vertical gash? She must have blushed, oh, she must have burned. She thought it was Chloe, not I, who had somehow found her out. Strangely, though, it was not Chloe whose power was thus increased over Rose, but the contrary, or so it seemed. The governess's eye had a new and steelier light when it fell on the girl now, and the girl, to my surprise and puzzlement, appeared cowed under that look as she had never been before. When I think of them like that, the one glinting, the other shying, I cannot but speculate that what happened on the day of the strange tide was in some way a consequence of the uncovering of Rose's secret passion. After all, why should I be less susceptible than the next melodramatist to the tale's demand for a neat closing twist?

The tide came up the beach all the way to the foot of the dunes, as though the sea were brimming over its bounds. In silence we watched the water's steady advance, sitting in a row, the three of us, Chloe and Myles and me, with our backs against the peeling grey boards of the disused groundsman's hut beside the first tee of the golf course. We had been swimming but we had given up, made uneasy by this waveless, unstoppable tide, the sinister, calm way it kept coming on. The sky was misted white all over with a flat, pale-gold disc of sun stuck motionless in the middle of it. Gulls swooped, shrieking. The air was still. Yet I distinctly recall how the single blades of marram grass growing up through the sand round-about had each inscribed a neat half circle in front of itself, which suggests a wind was blowing, or at least a breeze. Perhaps that was another day, the day I noticed the grass marking the sand like that. Chloe was in her swimsuit, with a white cardigan draped over her shoulders. Her hair was darkly wet and plastered to her skull. In that unshadowed milky light her face seemed almost featureless, and she and Myles beside her were as alike as the profiles on a pair of coins. Below us in a hollow in the dunes Rose lay on her back on a beach towel with her hands behind her head and seemed to be asleep. The sea's scummed edge was within a yard of her heels. Chloe considered her, smiling to herself. 'Maybe she'll be washed away,' she said.

It was Myles who got the door of the hut open, twisting the padlock until the bolt broke from its screws and came away in his hand. Inside, there was a single tiny room, empty, and smelling of old urine.

A wooden bench seat was set along one wall, and above it there was a small window, the frame intact but the glass long gone. Chloe knelt on the bench with her face in the window and her elbows on the sill. I sat on one side of her, Myles on the other. Why do I think there was something Egyptian about the way that we were posed there, Chloe kneeling and looking out and Myles and I on the bench and facing into the little room? Is it because I am compiling a Book of the Dead? She was the Sphinx and we her seated priests. There was silence, save for the crying of the gulls.

'I hope she gets drowned,' Chloe said, speaking through the window, and gave one of her sharp little nicking laughs. 'I hope she does' – *nick nick* – 'I hate her.'

Last words. It was early morning, just before dawn, when Anna came to consciousness. I could not rightly tell if I had been awake or just dreaming that I was. Those nights that I spent sprawled in the armchair beside her bed were rife with curiously mundane hallucinations, half dreams of preparing meals for her, or talking about her to people I had never seen before, or just walking along with her, through dim, nondescript streets, I walking, that is, and she lying comatose beside me and yet managing to move, and keep pace with me, somehow, sliding along on solid air, on her journey toward the Field of Reeds. Waking now, she turned her head on the damp pillow and looked at me wide-eyed in the underwater glimmer of the nightlight with an expression of large and wary startlement. I think she did not know me. I had that paralysing sensation, part awe and part alarm, that comes over one in a sudden and unexpected solitary encounter with a creature of the wild. I could feel my heart beating in slow, liquid thumps, as if it were flopping over an endless series of identical obstacles. Anna coughed, making a sound like the clatter of bones. I knew this was the end. I felt inadequate to the moment, and wanted to cry out for help. Nurse, nurse, come quick, my wife is leaving me! I could not think, my mind seemed filled with toppling masonry. Still Anna stared at me, still surprised, still suspicious. Away down the corridor someone unseen dropped something that clattered, she heard the noise and seemed reassured. Perhaps she thought it was something I had said, and thought she understood it, for she nodded, but impatiently, as if to say *No, you're wrong, that is not it at all!* She reached out a hand and fixed it claw-like on my wrist. That monkeyish grasp, it holds me yet. I blundered forward from the chair in a sort of panic and scrambled to my knees beside the bed, like one of the dumbstruck faithful falling in adoration before an apparition. Anna was still clutching my wrist. I put my other hand on her brow, and it seemed to me I could feel her mind behind it feverishly at work, making the last tremendous effort of thinking its final thought. Had I ever looked at her in life, with such urgent attention, as I looked at her now? As if looking alone would hold her here, as if she could not go so long as my eye did not flinch. She was panting, softly and slowly, like a runner pausing who still has miles to run. Her breath gave off a mild, dry stink, as of withered flowers. I spoke her name but she only closed her eyes briefly, dismissively, as if I should know that she was no longer Anna, that she was no longer anyone, and then opened them and stared at me again, harder than ever, not in surprise now but with a commanding sternness, willing that I should hear, hear and understand, what it was she had to say. She let go of my wrist and her fingers scrabbled briefly on the bed, searching for something. I took her hand. I could feel the flutter of a pulse at the base of her thumb. I said something, some fatuous thing such as *Don't go*, or *Stay with me*, but again she gave that impatient shake of the head, and tugged my hand to draw me closer. 'They are stopping the clocks,' she said, the merest thread of a whisper, conspiratorial. 'I have stopped time.' And she nodded, a solemn, knowing nod, and smiled, too, I would swear it was a smile.

It was the deft, brusque way that Chloe shrugged off her cardigan that prompted me, that permitted me, to put my hand against the back of her thigh where she knelt beside me. Her skin was chill and stippled with gooseflesh but I could feel the busy blood swarming just below the surface. She did not respond to my touch but went on looking out at whatever it was she was looking at – all that water, perhaps, that inexorable slow flood – and cautiously I slid my hand upward until my fingers touched the taut hem of her bathing suit. Her cardigan, that had settled on my lap, now slithered off and tumbled to the floor, making me think of something, a spray of flowers let fall, perhaps, or a falling bird. It would have been enough for me just to go on sitting there with my hand under her bottom, my heart beating out a syncopated measure and my eyes fixed on a knot-hole in the wooden wall opposite, had she not in a tiny, convulsive movement shifted her knee a fraction sideways along the bench and opened her lap to my astonished fingertips. The wadded crotch of her swimsuit was sopping with sea water that felt scalding to my touch. No sooner had my fingers found her there than she clenched her thighs shut again, trapping my hand. Shivers like tiny electric currents ran from all over her into her lap, and with a wriggle she pulled herself free of me, and I thought it was all over, but I was wrong. Quickly she turned about and climbed down from the bench all knees and elbows and sat beside me squirmingly and turned up her face and offered me her cold lips and hot mouth to kiss. The straps of her swimsuit were tied in a bow at the back of her neck, and now without moving her mouth from mine she put up a hand behind her and undid the knot and tugged the wet cloth down to her waist. Still kissing her, I inclined my head to the side and looked with the eye that could see past her ear down along the ridges of her spine to the beginnings of her narrow rump and the cleft there the colour of a clean steel knife. With an impatient gesture she took my hand and pressed it to the barely perceptible mound of one of her breasts the tip of which was cold and hard. On her other side Myles sat with his legs loosely splayed before him, leaning his head back against the wall with his eyes closed. Blindly Chloe reached out sideways and found his hand lying palm-upwards on the bench and clasped it, and as she did so her mouth tightened against mine and I felt rather than heard the faint mewling moan that rose in her throat.

I did not hear the door opening, only registered the light altering in the little room. Chloe stiffened against me and turned her head quickly and said something, a word I did not catch. Rose was standing in the doorway. She was in her bathing suit but was wearing her black pumps, which made her long pale skinny legs seem even longer and paler and skinnier. She reminded me of something, I could not think what, one hand on the door and the other on the door-jamb, seeming to be held suspended there between two strong gusts, one from inside the hut driving against her and another from outside pressing at her back. Chloe hastily pulled up the flap of her swimsuit and retied the straps behind her neck, speaking that word again harshly under her breath, the word I could not catch – Rose's name, was it, or just some imprecation? – and made a low dive from the bench, fast as a fox, and ducked under Rose's arm and was gone through the door and away. 'You come back here, Miss!' Rose cried in a voice that cracked. 'Just you come back here this instant!' She gave me a look then, a more-in-sorrow-than-in-anger look, and shook her head, and turned and stalked off stork-like on those stilted white legs. Myles, still sprawled on the bench beside me, gave a low laugh. I stared at him. It seemed to me that he had spoken.

All that followed I see in miniature, in a sort of cameo, or one of those rounded views, looked on from above, at the off-centre of which the old painters would depict the moment of a drama in such tiny detail as hardly to be noticed amidst the blue and gold expanses of sea and sky. I lingered a moment on the bench, breathing. Myles watched me, waiting to see what I would do. When I came out of the hut Chloe and Rose were down on the little semi-circle of sand between the dunes and the water's edge, squared up to each other and shrieking in each other's face. I could not hear what they were saying. Now Chloe broke away and stamped in a furious, tight ring around herself, churning the sand. She kicked Rose's towel. It is only my fancy, I know, but I see the little waves lapping hungrily at her heels. At last, with one last cry and a curious, chopping gesture of a hand and forearm, she turned and walked to the edge of the waves and, scissoring her legs, plumped down on the sand and sat with her knees pressed against her breast and her arms wrapped about her knees, her face lifted toward the horizon. Rose with hands on hips stood glaring at her back, but seeing she would get no response turned away and began angrily to gather up her things, pitching towel, book, bathing cap into the crook of her arm like a fishwife throwing fish into a creel. I heard Myles behind me, and a second later he passed me by at a headlong sprint, seeming to cartwheel rather than run. When he got to where Chloe was sitting he sat down beside her and put an arm across her shoulders and laid his head against hers. Rose paused and cast an uncertain glance at them, wrapped there together, their backs turned to the world. Then calmly they stood up and waded into the sea, the water smooth as oil hardly breaking around them, and leaned forward in unison and swam out slowly, their two heads bobbing on the whitish swell, out, and out.

We watched them, Rose and I, she clutching her gathered-up things against her, and I just standing. I do not know what I was thinking, I do not remember thinking anything. There are times like that, not frequent enough, when the mind just empties. They were far out now, the two of them, so far as to be pale dots between pale sky and paler sea, and then one of the dots disappeared. After that it was all over very quickly, I mean what we could see of it. A splash, a little white water, whiter than that all around, then nothing, the indifferent world closing.

There was a shout, and Rose and I turned to see

a large red-faced man with close-clipped grey hair coming down the dunes toward us, high-stepping flurriedly through the sliding sands with comical haste. He wore a yellow shirt and khaki trousers and two-tone shoes and was brandishing a golf club. The shoes I may have invented. I am sure however of the glove that he wore on his right hand, the hand that held the golf stick; it was light brown, fingerless, and the back of it was punched with holes, I do not know why it caught my attention particularly. He kept shouting that someone should go for the Guards. He seemed extremely angry, gesturing in the air with the club like a Zulu warrior shaking his knobkerrie. Zulus, knobkerries? Perhaps I mean assegais. His caddy, meanwhile, up on the bank, an ageless emaciated runt in a buttoned-up tweed jacket and a tweed cap, stood contemplating the scene below him with a sardonic expression, leaning casually on the golf bag with his ankles crossed. Next, a muscle-bound young man in tight blue swimming trunks appeared, I do not know from where, he seemed to materialise out of the very air, and without preliminary plunged into the sea and swam out swiftly with expert, stiff strokes. By now Rose was pacing back and forth at the water's edge, three paces this way, stop, wheel, three paces that way, stop, wheel, like poor demented Ariadne on the Naxos shore, still clutching to her breast the towel, book and bathing cap. After a time the would-be life-saver came back, and strode toward us out of the waveless water with that swimmer's hindered swagger, shaking his head and snorting. It was no go, he said, no go. Rose cried out, a sort of sob, and shook her head rapidly from side to side, and the golfer glared at her. Then they were all dwindling behind me, for I was running, trying to run, along the beach, in the direction of Station Road and the Cedars. Why did I not cut away, through the grounds of the Golf Hotel, on to the road, where the going would have been so much easier? But I did not want the going to be easier. I did not want to get where I was going. Often in my dreams I am back there again, wading through that sand that grows ever more resistant, so that it seems that my feet themselves are made of some massy, crumbling stuff. What did I feel? Most strongly, I think, a sense of awe, awe of myself, that is, who had known two living creatures that now were suddenly, astoundingly, dead. But did I believe they were dead? In my mind they were held suspended in a vast bright space, upright, their arms linked and their eyes wide open, gazing gravely before them into illimitable depths of light.

Here at last was the green iron gate, the car

standing on the gravel, and the front door, wide open as so often. In the house all was tranquil and still. I moved among the rooms as if I were myself a thing of air, a drifting spirit, Ariel set free and at a loss. I found Mrs Grace in the living room. She turned to me, putting a hand to her mouth, the milky light of afternoon at her back. This all is silence, save for the drowsy hum of summer from without. Then Carlo Grace came in, saying, 'Damned thing, it seems to be . . .' and he stopped too, and so we stood in stillness, we three, at the end.

Was't well done?

Night, and everything so quiet, as if there were no one, not even myself. I cannot hear the sea, which on other nights rumbles and growls, now near and grating, now afar and faint. I do not want to be alone like this. Why have you not come back to haunt me? It is the least I would have expected of you. Why this silence day after day, night after interminable night? It is like a fog, this silence of yours. First it was a blur on the horizon, the next minute we were in the midst of it, purblind and stumbling, clinging to each other. It started that day after the visit to Mr Todd when we walked out of the clinic into the deserted car park, all those machines ranked neatly there, sleek as porpoises and making not a sound, and no sign even of the young woman and her clicking high heels. Then our house shocked into its own kind of silence, and soon thereafter the silent corridors of hospitals, the hushed wards, the waiting rooms, and then the last room of all. Send back your ghost. Torment me, if you like. Rattle your chains, drag your cerements across the floor, keen like a banshee, anything. I would have a ghost.

Where is my bottle. I need my big baby's bottle. My soother.

Miss Vavasour gives me a pitying look. I blench under her glance. She knows the questions I want to ask, the questions I have been burning to put to her since I first came here but never had the nerve. This morning when she saw me silently formulating them yet again she shook her head, not unkindly. 'I can't help you,' she said, smiling. 'You must know that.' What does she mean by must? I know so little of anything. We are in the lounge, sitting in the bay of the bow window, as so often. The day outside is bright and cold, the first real day of winter we have had. All this in the historic present. Miss Vavasour is mending what looks suspiciously like one of the Colonel's socks. She has a wooden gadget, shaped like a large mushroom, on which she stretches the heel to darn the hole in it. I find it restful to watch her at this timeless task. I am in need of rest. My head might be packed with wet cotton wool and there is an acid taste of vomit in my mouth which all Miss Vavasour's plyings of milky tea and soldiers of thin-sliced toast cannot rid me of. Also there is a bruise on my temple that throbs. I sit before Miss V. sheepish and contrite. I feel more than ever the delinquent boy.

But what a day it was yesterday, what a night, and, heavens! what a morning-after. It all began with fair enough promise. Ironically, as it would turn out, it was the Colonel's daughter who was supposed to come down, along with Hubby and the children. The Colonel tried to be nonchalant, putting on his gruffest manner – 'We'll be rightly invaded!' – but over breakfast his hands shook so with excitement that he set the table to trembling and the tea cups rattling in their saucers. Miss Vavasour insisted that his daughter and her family should all stay for lunch, that she would cook a chicken, and asked what kind of ice cream the children would like. 'Oh, now,' the Colonel blustered, 'really, there's no need!' It was plain to see he was deeply affected, however, and was damp-eyed for a moment. I looked forward myself with some anticipation to getting a look at last at this daughter and her he-man husband. The prospect of the children was somewhat daunting, though; kiddies in general, I am afraid, bring out the not so latent Gilles de Rais in me.

The visit was due for midday, but the noontide bell tolled, and the lunch hour came and went, and no car had pulled up at the gate and no joyous shouts of the Little Ones had been heard. The Colonel paced, wrist clasped in a hand behind him, or stationed himself before the window, muzzle thrust forward, and shot a cuff and lifted his arm to eye level and glared reproachfully at his watch. Miss Vavasour and I went about on tenterhooks, not daring to speak. The aroma of roasting chicken in the house seemed a heartless gibe. It was late in the afternoon when the telephone in the hall rang, making us all start. The Colonel leaned his ear to the receiver like a despairing priest in the confessional. The exchange was brief. We tried not to hear what he was saying. He came into the kitchen clearing his throat. 'Car,' he said, looking at no one. 'Broke down.' Clearly he had been lied to, or was lying now to us. He turned to Miss Vavasour with a desolate smile. 'Sorry about the chicken,' he said.

I encouraged him to come out for a drink with me but he declined. He was feeling a bit tired, he said, had a bit of a headache all of a sudden. He went off to his room. How heavy his tread was on the stair, how softly he closed the bedroom door. 'Oh, dear,' Miss Vavasour said.

I went to the Pier Head Bar by myself and got sozzled. I did not mean to but I did. It was one of those plangent autumn evenings streaked with late sunlight that seemed itself a memory of what some-time in the far past had been the blaze of noon. Rain earlier had left puddles on the road that were paler than the sky, as if the last of day were dying in them. It was windy and the skirts of my overcoat flapped about my legs like Little Ones of my own, begging their Da not to go to the pub. But go I did. The Pier Head is a cheerless establishment presided over by a huge television set, fully the match of Miss V.'s Panoramic, permanently switched on but with the sound turned down. The publican is a fat soft slow man of few words. He has a peculiar name, I cannot remember it for the moment. I drank double bran-dies. Odd moments of the evening stand out in my memory, fuzzily bright, like lamp standards in a fog. I remember provoking or being provoked into an argument with an old fellow at the bar, and being remonstrated with by a much younger one, his son, perhaps, or grandson, whom I pushed and who threatened to summon the police. When the publican intervened – Barragry, that is his name – I tried to push him, too, lunging at him across the counter with a hoarse shout. Really, this is not like me at all, I do not know what was the matter, I mean other than what is usually the matter. At last they calmed me down and I retreated grumpily to a table in the corner, under the speechless television set, where I sat mumbling to myself and sighing. Those drunken sighs, bubbly and tremulous, how like sobs they can sound. The last light of evening, what I could see of it through the unpainted top quarter of the pub window, was of that angry, purplish-brown cast that I find both affecting and troubling, it is the very colour of winter. Not that I have anything against winter, indeed, it is my favourite season, next to autumn, but this year that November glow seemed a presagement of something more than winter, and I fell into a mood of bitter melancholy. Seeking to assuage my heaviness of heart I called for more brandy but Barragry refused it, advisedly, as I now acknowledge, and I stormed out in rageful indig-nation, or tried to storm but staggered really, and came back to the Cedars and my own bottle, which I have fondly dubbed the Little Corporal. On the stairs I met Colonel Blunden and had some converse with him, I do not know what about, exactly.

It was night by now, but instead of staying in my room and going to bed I put the bottle under my coat and went out again. Of what happened after that I have only jagged and ill-lit flickers of recollection. I remember standing in the wind under the shaking radiance of a street light awaiting some grand and general revelation and then losing interest in it before it could arrive. Then I was on the beach in the dark, sitting in the sand with my legs stuck out before me and the brandy bottle, empty now or nearly, cradled in my lap. There seemed to be lights out at sea, a long way from shore, bobbing and swaying, like the lights of a fishing fleet, but I must have imagined them, there are no fishing boats in these waters. I was cold despite my coat, the thickness of which was not enough to protect my hindparts from the chill dampness of the sand in which I was sitting. It was not the damp and the chill, however, that made me struggle to my feet at last, but a determination to get closer to those lights and investigate them; I may even have had some idea of wading into the sea and swimming out to meet them. It was at the water's edge, anyway, that I lost my footing and fell down and struck my temple on a stone. I lay there for I do not know how long, fluttering in and out of consciousness, unable or unwilling to move. It is a good thing the tide was on the ebb. I was not in pain, not even very much upset. In fact, it seemed quite natural to be sprawled there, in the dark, under a tumultuous sky, watching the faint phosphorescence of the waves as they pattered forward eagerly only to retreat again, like a flock of inquisitive but timorous mice, and the Little Corporal, as drunk it seemed as myself, rolling back and forth on the shingle with a grating sound, and hearing the wind above me blowing through the great invisible hollows and funnels of the air.

I must have fallen asleep then, or passed out even, for I do not remember the Colonel finding me, although he insists I spoke to him quite sensibly, and allowed him to help me up and walk me back to the Cedars. This must have been the case, I mean I must have been in some way conscious, for he would not have had the strength, surely, to get me to my feet unassisted, much less to haul me from the beach to my bedroom door, slung across his back, perhaps, or dragging me by the heels behind him. But how had he known where to find me? It seems that in our colloquy on the stairs, although colloquy is not the word, since according to him I did the most part of the talking, I had dwelt at length on the well-known fact, well-known and a fact according to me, that drowning is the gentlest death, and when by a late hour he had not heard me returning, and fearing that I might indeed in my inebriated state try to make away with myself, he had decided he must go and look for me. He had to scout the beach for a long time, and had been about to give up the search, when some gleam from moon or brightest star fell upon my form, supine there on that stony littoral. When, after much meandering and many pauses for expatiation by me on numerous topics, we arrived at the Cedars at last, he had helped me up the stairs and seen me into my room. All this reported, for of that faltering anabasis I recall, as I have said, nothing. Later he had heard me, still in my room, being uproariously sick – not on the carpet but out of the window into the back yard, I am relieved to say – and then seeming to fall down heavily, and had taken it upon himself to come into my room, and there had discovered me, for the second time that night, in a heap, as they say, at the foot of the bed, lost to consciousness and, so he judged, urgently in need of medical attention.

I woke at some early hour of the still-dark

morning to a strange and unnerving scene which I at first took to be an hallucination. The Colonel was there, spick as usual in tweed and cavalry twill – he had not been to bed at all – pacing the floor with a frown, and so, far more implausibly, was Miss Vavasour, who, it would turn out, also had heard, or felt, more likely, in the very bones of the old house, the crash I made as I collapsed after that bout of vomiting at the window. She was wearing her Japanese dressing-gown, and her hair was gathered under a hair-net the like of which I had not seen since I was a child. She sat on a chair a little way off from me, against the wall, sideways on, in the very pose of Whistler's mother, her hands folded on her lap and her face bowed, so that her eye sockets seemed two pits of empty blackness. A lamp, which I thought was a candle, was burning on a table before her, shedding a dim globe of light upon the scene, which overall – a dimly radiant round with seated woman and pacing man – might have been a nocturnal study by Gericault, or de la Tour. Baffled, and abandoning all effort to understand what was going on or how the two of them came to be there, I fell asleep again, or passed out again.

When I next awakened the curtains were open and it was day. The room had a chastened and somewhat abashed aspect, I thought, and everything looked pale and featureless, like a woman's unmade-up morning face. Outside, a uniformly white sky sat sulkily immobile, seeming no more than a yard or two higher than the roof of the house. Vaguely the events of the night came shuffling back shamefaced to my addled consciousness. Around me the bed-clothes were tossed and twisted as after a debauch, and there was a strong smell of sick. I put up a hand and a shot of pain went through my head when my fingers found the pulpy swelling on my temple where it had struck upon the stone. It was only then, with a start that made the bed creak, that I noticed the young man seated on my chair, leaning forward with his arms folded on my desk, reading a book lying open before him on my leather writing pad. He wore steel-framed spectacles and had a high, balding brow and sparse hair of no particular colour. His clothes were characterless too, although I had a general impression of jaded corduroys. Hearing me stir he lifted his eyes unhurriedly from the page and turned his head and looked at me, quite composed, and even smiled, though cheerlessly, and enquired as to how I was feeling. Nonplussed – that is the word, surely – I struggled up in the bed, which seemed to wobble under me as if the mattress were filled with some thick and viscous liquid, and gave him what was intended to be an imperiously interrogative stare. However, he continued calmly regarding me, quite unruffled. The Doctor, he said, making it sound as though there were only one in the world, had been to see me earlier, while I was out – *out*, that was how he put it, and I wondered wildly for a moment if I had been down to the beach again, without knowing it – and had said I seemed to be suffering from a concussion compounded by severe but temporary alcohol poisoning. Seemed? Seemed?

'Claire drove us down,' he said. 'She's sleeping now.'

Jerome! The chinless inamorato! Now I knew him. How had he wormed his way back into my daughter's favour? Had he been the only one she could think of to turn to, in the middle of the night, when the Colonel or Miss Vavasour, whichever of them it was, had called to tell her of the latest scrape her father had got himself into? If so, I thought, I shall be to blame, although I could not see exactly why. How I cursed myself, sprawled there on that Doge's daybed, crapulent and woozy and altogether lacking the strength to leap up and seize the presumptuous fellow by the scruff and throw him out a second time. But there was worse to come. When he went out to find if Claire had wakened yet, and she came back with him, drawn and red-rimmed and wearing a raincoat over her slip, she informed me straight away, with the air of one hastily drawing fire so as to be able all the better to deflect it, that they were engaged. For a moment, befuddled as I was, I did not know what she meant – engaged by whom, and as what? – a moment which, as it proved, was sufficient for my vanquishment. I have not managed to bring up the subject again, and every further moment that passes further consolidates her victory over me. This is how, in a twinkling, these things are won and lost. Read Maistre on warfare.

Nor did she stop there, but, flushed with that initial triumph, and seizing the advantage offered by my temporary infirmity, went on to direct, a figurative hand cocked on her hip, that I must pack up and leave the Cedars forthwith and let her take me home – home, she says! – where she will care for me, which care will include, I am given to understand, the withholding of all alcoholic stimulants, or soporifics, until such time as the Doctor, him again, declares me fit for something or other, life, I suppose. What am I to do? How am I to resist? She says it is time I got down seriously to work. 'He is finishing,' she informed her betrothed, not without a gloss of filial pride, 'a big book on Bonnard.' I had not the heart to tell her that my Big Book on Bonnard – it sounds like something one might shy coconuts at – has got no farther than half of a putative first chapter and a notebook filled with derivative and half-baked would-be aperçus. Well, it is no matter. There are other things I can do. I can go to Paris and paint. Or I might retire into a monastery, pass my days in quiet contemplation of the infinite, or write a great treatise there, a vulgate of the dead, I can see myself in my cell, long-bearded, with quill-pen and hat and docile lion, through a window beside me minuscule peasants in the distance making hay, and hovering above my brow the dove refulgent. Oh, yes, life is pregnant with possibilities.

I suppose I shall not be allowed to sell the house, either.

Miss Vavasour says she will miss me, but thinks I am doing *the right thing*. Leaving the Cedars is hardly of my doing, I tell her, I am being forced to it. She smiles at that. 'Oh, Max,' she says, 'I do not think you are a man to be forced into anything.' That gives me pause, not because of the tribute to my strength of will, but the fact, which I register with a faint shock, that this is the first time she has addressed me by my name. Still, I do not think it means that I can call her Rose. A certain formal distance is necessary for the good maintenance of the dainty relation we have forged, re-forged, between us over these past weeks. At this hint of intimacy, however, the old, unasked questions come swarming forward again. I would like to ask her if she blames herself for Chloe's death – I believe, I should say, on no evidence, that it was Chloe who went down first, with Myles following after, to try to save her – and if she is convinced their drowning together like that was entirely an accident, or something else. She would probably tell me, if I did ask. She is not reticent. She fairly prattled on about the Graces, Carlo and Connie – 'Their lives were destroyed, of course' – and how they, too, died, not long after losing the twins. Carlo went first, of an aneurysm, then Connie, in a car crash. I ask what kind of crash, and she gives me a look. 'Connie was not the kind to kill herself,' she says, with a faint twist of the lips.

They were good to her, afterwards, she says, never a reproach or the hint of an accusation of duty betrayed. They set her up at the Cedars, they knew Bun's people, persuaded them to take her on to look after the house. 'And here I am still,' she says, with a grim small smile, 'all these long years later.'

The Colonel is moving about upstairs, making

discreet but definite noises; he is glad I am going, I know it. I thanked him for his help last night. 'You probably saved my life,' I said, thinking suddenly it was probably true. Much huffing and clearing of the throat – *Faugh, sir, only doin' me demned duty!* – and a hand giving my upper arm a quick squeeze. He even produced a going-away present, a fountain pen, a Swan, it is as old as he is, I should think, still in its box, in a bed of yellowed tissue paper. I am graving these words with it, it has a graceful action, smooth and swift with only the occasional blot. Where did he come by it, I wonder? I did not know what to say. 'Nothing required,' he said. 'Never had a use for it myself, you should have it, for your writing, and so on.' Then he bustled off, rubbing his white old dry hands together. I note that although it is not the weekend he is wearing his yellow waistcoat. I shall never know, now, if he really is an old army man, or an impostor. It is another of those questions I cannot bring myself to put to Miss Vavasour.

'It's her I miss,' she says, 'Connie – Mrs Grace – that is.' I suppose I stare, and she gives me another of those pitying glances. 'It was never him, with me,' she says. 'You didn't think that, did you?' I thought of her standing below me that day under the trees, sobbing, her head sitting on the platter of her foreshortened shoulders, the wadded hankie in her hand. 'Oh, no,' she said, 'never him.' And I thought, too, of the day of the picnic and of her sitting behind me on the grass and looking where I was avidly looking and seeing what was not meant for me at all.

Anna died before dawn. To tell the truth, I was not there when it happened. I had walked out on to the steps of the nursing home to breathe deep the black and lustrous air of morning. And in that moment, so calm and drear, I recalled another moment, long ago, in the sea that summer at Ballyless. I had gone swimming alone, I do not know why, or where Chloe and Myles might have been; perhaps they had gone with their parents somewhere, it would have been one of the last trips they made together, perhaps the very last. The sky was hazed over and not a breeze stirred the surface of the sea, at the margin of which the small waves were breaking in a listless line, over and over, like a hem being turned endlessly by a sleepy seamstress. There were few people on the beach, and those few were at a distance from me, and something in the dense, unmoving air made the sound of their voices seem to come from a greater distance still. I was standing up to my waist in water that was perfectly transparent, so that I could plainly see below me the ribbed sand of the seabed, and tiny shells and bits of a crab's broken claw, and my own feet, pallid and alien, like specimens displayed under glass. As I stood there, suddenly, no, not suddenly, but in a sort of driving heave, the whole sea surged, it was not a wave, but a smooth rolling swell that seemed to come up from the deeps, as if something vast down there had stirred itself, and I was lifted briefly and carried a little way toward the shore and then was set down on my feet as before, as if nothing had happened. And indeed nothing had happened, a momentous nothing, just another of the great world's shrugs of indifference.

A nurse came out then to fetch me, and I turned and followed her inside, and it was as if I were walking into the sea.

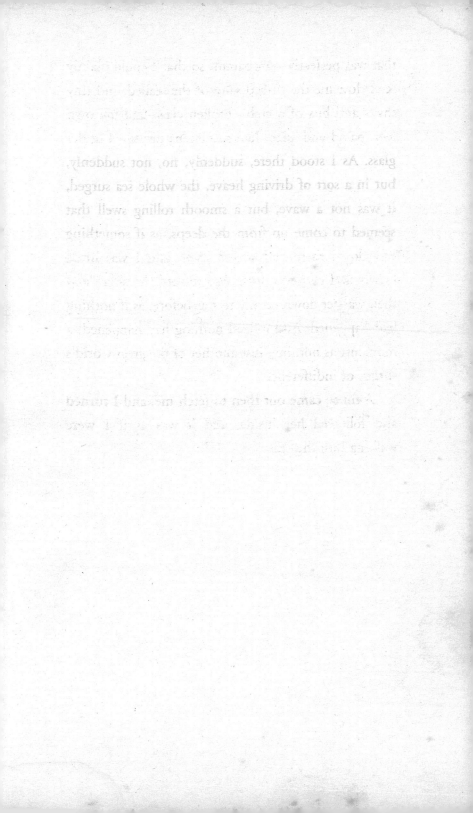

Praise for *The S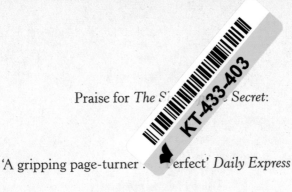e Secret*:

'A gripping page-turner . . . erfect' *Daily Express*

'I really enjoyed this novel . . . Utterly ingenious' *Observer*

'Glorious fun' *Independent on Sunday*

'Insider knowledge lends atmosphere to this hugely enjoyable thriller' *Mail on Sunday*

'A seductively mystifying tale of a highly intelligent serial killer who is fashioning his murders after Shakespeare's plays' *Good Book Guide*

'A hide-and-seek chase of murder and mayhem' *The Times*

Also by J.L. Carrell

The Shakespeare Secret

THE SHAKESPEARE CURSE

J. L. CARRELL

sphere

SPHERE

First published in Great Britain in 2010 by Sphere

A CIP catalogue record for this book
is available from the British Library.

ISBN 978-0-7515-4222-6

Typeset in Horley by M Rules
Printed and bound in Great Britain by
Clays Ltd, St Ives plc

Papers used by Sphere are natural, renewable and
recyclable products sourced from well-managed forests and certified
in accordance with the rules of the Forest Stewardship Council.

Mixed Sources
Product group from well-managed
forests and other controlled sources
www.fsc.org   Cert no. SGS-COC-004081
© 1996 Forest Stewardship Council

Sphere
An imprint of
Little, Brown Book Group
100 Victoria Embankment
London EC4Y 0DY

An Hachette UK Company
www.hachette.co.uk

www.littlebrown.co.uk

For Johnny

'I can call spirits from the vasty deep.

Why, so can I, or so can any man;
But will they come when you do call for them?'

—William Shakespeare

An it harm none, do what ye will.

—The Wiccan Rede (or Witches' Counsel)

PROLOGUE

November, 1606
Hampton Court Palace

Wrapped in a gown of blue-green velvet trimmed with gold, a queen's crown on his head, the boy sat drowsing in the throne near the centre of the Great Hall, just at the edge of the light. Tomorrow, it would be the king who sat there. Not a player king, but the real one, His Majesty King James I of England and VI of Scotland. Tonight, however, someone among the players had been needed to sit there and see just what the king on his throne would see as Mr Shakespeare's new Scottish play, blood-spattered and witch-haunted, conjured up a rite of nameless evil.

The boy, who was not in this scene, had volunteered. But the rehearsal had been unaccountably delayed, stretching deep into the frigid November night, until it was almost as cold inside the unheated hall as it was in the frost-rimed courtyards below. The heavy gown, though, was warm, and as the hours crawled on, the boy found it hard to keep his eyes open.

Well out of the torchlight illuminating the playing area, a grizzled man-at-arms in a worn leather jerkin, gaunt as a figure of famine, leaned against the wall at the edge of a tapestry, seeming to drowse as well.

At last, movement stirred in the haze of light. Three figures, cloaked head to toe in black, skimmed in a circle about the cauldron set in the centre of the hall, their voices melding into a single chant somewhere between a moan and a hiss.

'*What is it you do?*' rasped the player king as he entered, eyes wide with horror.

The answer whined through the echoing hall like the nearly human sound of the wind, or maybe the restless dead, seeking entry at the eaves: *A deed without a name.*

Not long afterwards, a phalanx of children, eerily beautiful, had drifted into the light, gliding one by one past the throne. In the rear, the smallest held up a mirror.

On the throne, the boy-queen sat bolt upright.

Against the wall, barely visible in the outer darkness, the old soldier's eyes flickered open.

A few moments later, the boy slid from the throne and melted into the darkness at the back of the hall. Behind him, the man followed like an ill-fitting shadow.

Robert Cecil, Earl of Salisbury, was wakened by his manservant in the small hours of the morning. Behind him in the darkness, two more faces floated in a double halo of candlelight. One slipping from black hair toward grey age, and the other just rising into the fullness of his prime, but both Howards, and both smug. The Earl of Northampton and his nephew the Earl of Suffolk.

Salisbury was instantly awake. He did not know what the Howards had to look smug about at such an hour of the morning, but anything that happened in the palace without his knowledge disturbed him. When it involved the Howards, it invariably meant danger.

'It's the boy, my lord,' said his manservant, coughing discreetly.

'The players' boy,' Suffolk specified.

'He is missing,' purred Northampton. 'Along with the mirror.'

Wherever that boy is, Salisbury thought with an inward sigh, *the Howards know about it.* Aloud, he said, 'Rouse Dr Dee,' and painfully sat up, aware of Northampton's stare aimed at the hump on his back. 'And send for the captain on duty.'

To the captain, he simply said, 'Find him.'

Half an hour later, Salisbury led the way, splay-footed and limping, towards the waiting chamber off the Great Hall, aware at every step of the proud, straight stalking of the tall Howard earls flanking him. He did not like working with either of them, especially Northampton. Generally speaking, Salisbury was fastidious about his person and his apparel, small and misshapen though he was, but not about people, whose talents he assessed with a cold, accurate eye and then used as necessary. But the Howards curdled something within his soul, making him long to step out into the

3

nearest rose garden, whatever the weather, to rid himself of some not-quite-detectable stench. The king, however, had fallen under Northampton's spell, and had made the occasional partnership unavoidable. Witness this unsavoury business of the boy. When it came to the kingdom's safety, Salisbury was not above using anybody, but he did not enjoy baiting traps with children.

Dr Dee was waiting for them, his dark robe and long white beard fairly shaking with indignation. 'You told me you were keeping them here for their safety,' he charged. 'The boy and the mirror both.'

Salisbury sighed. Not for *their* safety. For the king's. For the kingdom's. Why couldn't men as undoubtedly brilliant as Dr Dee make that distinction?

The earl did not give much credence to such things as magic mirrors and conjuring spirits. But just in case, he kept his finger on the pulse of what was happening among the kingdom's conjurors, John Dee foremost among them. His brilliance as a mathematician and navigator was, after all, unmatched, and he had done Salisbury's father and the old queen good service in the field of cryptology. If even a fraction of Dee's claims about conjuring angels or transmuting base metal into gold turned out to be true, Salisbury wanted a handle on the old man.

So when Dee had come running, spouting a wild tale of blood and fire seen in one of his show-stones, Salisbury had listened with a seriousness that had shaken Dr Dee even as it gratified him, and then he had interviewed the boy who claimed to have done the actual seeing. For, as Salisbury already knew, but Dr Dee did not, there were indeed plans afoot among some renegade Catholics to blow up Parliament and with it, the king.

To Dr Dee's chagrin, however, Salisbury had kept the boy who seemed to have foreseen not only the Gunpowder Plot, but also a mysterious woman holding a knife. And he had kept, too, the mirror the boy claimed to have seen it in.

That had been a year ago. The Powder Plot had not come off, as Salisbury had all along known it would not. The plotters had been caught and either killed in the capture or executed with the full ferocity of the law. Only one figure was still at large: the kingmaker that Salisbury was certain had been behind the plot from the beginning, but had never been able to identify. Someone among the great of the kingdom who had meant to take the reins of rule amid the chaos. Someone who was most certainly among those who fawned daily on the king he had plotted to kill.

Salisbury had naturally assumed that this person was a man, but the boy's vision of a woman with red hair and dark eyes, holding a knife engraved with letters the boy could not read, had brought him up short. If the earl had believed in ghosts, he might almost have said that the boy had seen old Queen Elizabeth. But the enemy he sought was surely still among the living. The old queen's blood ran in other veins, though – thinly, to be sure, but there. Women with Tudor and Plantagenet ancestry, and the telltale red-gold colouring to prove it, were not hard to come by at court. The king's widely scattered family of Stewarts among them.

When it came to these royal families, that touch of flame in the hair often came with a Machiavellian ruthlessness that made the Howards, dangerous as they were, seem as innocent as kittens. It was one reason the Plantagenets, Tudors and Stewarts had occupied thrones for centuries, Salisbury reflected sourly, while the Howards had lost the lone dukedom that had been their pinnacle of achievement – unless you counted the two queens whose crowns Henry VIII had cut off, along with their heads. Tudors and Stewarts, though, had produced women of more formidable mettle: Queen Elizabeth and her cousin, the present king's mother, Mary, Queen of Scots, prime among them. So why not a woman?

Or a woman in concert with a still unknown man.

So Salisbury had set out to discover the identity of the face in the mirror. He'd tried the boy in various positions at court – but there were limited opportunities for a young boy to observe great ladies unnoticed, and the child had never encountered her. In the end, it had been another of Mr Shakespeare's plays that gave the earl the idea of installing the boy among the King's Men, giving him both a perfect excuse and a prime vantage point from which to observe the courtiers drawn around the king. He'd had to use Suffolk, the Lord Chamberlain, whose job it was to organise the king's palace and all the entertainments within it, for that. But he'd bypassed the Howards when commissioning a play to touch on plots against a king's life; that he had done himself. It wouldn't be only the boy, of course, scanning the crowds for reactions. But only the boy could identify the particular face of his dreams.

Except that now, on the eve of the performance, the young idiot had gone missing. If it hadn't been for the Howards, he'd have concluded that the young rascal was in the kitchen pinching puddings, and gone right back to sleep. As it was, he listened wearily to the tramping feet of soldiers fanning through the palace.

An hour later, the captain skidded back into his presence. 'We've found something, your lordship,' he panted. But when demanded what, he just shook his head. 'I think, sir, you had better come and see for yourself.'

And so they had marched through long winding ways back into the oldest part of the palace. The chamber where they stopped was marked as unassigned on the Lord Chamberlain's list, but the door was locked from the inside. Stranger still, several of the captain's men swore up and down to have heard an ungodly cry from somewhere in this corridor – though all the other rooms were open and empty. Grown men, all of them, but Salisbury could sense the ooze of fear on their breath.

'Break it open,' he said shortly, aware of the Howards clenching in anticipation beside him.

It took axe-work: Hampton Court had been made to last. With a wrenching groan, the door at last split down the centre and the soldiers stood aside, allowing the earls to pass.

Even from the threshold, it could be seen that the room was empty. There were no rushes on the floor, no hangings on the walls, and no furniture cluttering the space. A fire, however, had recently warmed the grate, though it had been allowed to die out. The air still bore faint traces of some stew or broth that had seethed here. In the midst of this emptiness, the only object to stop the eye was a body lying stretched out on the flagged floor in front of the hearth. Draped over it was a heavy gown of peacock blue.

Dr Dee darted forward, plucking a small slice of darkness from a fold in the velvet. With precise fingers, he held up a dark disc of polished stone: his missing mirror. The old conjuror rubbed it with his sleeve, peering into its depths as Suffolk leaned forward with unseemly eagerness. 'What do you see?'

Dr Dee looked up, the skin below his watery eyes sagging, and shook his head. 'There is a dark veil drawn across it.' A shudder passed through his entire body. 'Whatever this mirror has seen, it is evil.'

A boy is dead, thought Salisbury. *We need no magic to tell us that*. In a flicker of irritation, he twitched the gown aside.

Beside him, Suffolk and Northampton went preternaturally still. Their surprise was momentary, so quickly

8

smoothed over that they would have fooled almost any other man, but Salisbury could often tell what a man was thinking before he was aware of the drifts of his own thoughts – to the point that some men muttered that it was he, not Dr Dee, who bent strange spirits to his will. Now, beneath his rigid mask of revulsion, he felt a sly curiosity waken and stretch through every vein and sinew. Whatever the Howards had been expecting, this was not it.

The body at their feet was naked, and strangely bound. But it was not the boy.

BLADE

Is this a dagger which I see before me,
The handle toward my hand?

1

October, 2009
Scotland

It's the oldest temptation. Not gold or the power it can buy, not love, not even the deep, drumming fires of lust: what we coveted first was knowledge. Not just any knowledge, either, but forbidden, more-than-mortal knowledge, as seductive and treacherous as a will-o'-the-wisp glimmering like unearthly fruit amid dark branches.

At least, that's the tale that Genesis suggests. Not that I believe everything the Bible says. But it's a good story, and I love stories. Besides, whether or not knowledge is the oldest temptation, it's beyond doubt one of the most dangerous. Spellbinding in the full, old sense of the word. That much I can swear to. I've felt the pull of it myself, and come closer than I like to admit to being lured into the abyss.

For me, it was a voice, low and musical, that first enthralled me; at least, that's how I remember it. I can see her still, crossing to a tall window, throwing back curtains of pale blue silk embroidered with Chinese dragons, opening the casement to the chill Scottish night. The sharp scent of pines swept through the room, stirring the silk, so that the dragons seemed to writhe and coil around her.

Nearing seventy, Lady Nairn's face was lined with the fine-china crackling of very fair skin in old age. Awash in moonlight, with her hands thrust deep into the pockets of her jacket, a gauzy scarf at her neck, and hair of the palest gold swept up in a graceful French twist, she seemed to be shining with a light of her own.

'It's one of the Sidlaws,' she mused, staring out the window at the hill that dominated the landscape. A strangely shaped hill sitting apart from its fellows, capped with a turret-like top. '*Law*, from Old English *hlaew*, meaning hill, mountain, or mound, and also the hollow places inside them, like caves or barrows. And *sid*, from the Gaelic *sidhe*' – which she pronounced like 'she'. 'The Good Folk,' she said without turning. 'The Fairies . . . It's a fairy hill.'

She was tall, taller than me, and still imposing – not someone you expected to hear musing about fairies.

She shrugged slightly, as if brushing off my thoughts. 'People have disappeared from it, from time to time. Caught up by the Good Folk riding out on one of their hunts, and swept off to feast in enchanted halls where time passes differently, and the golden air is laced with laughter and song. Most never return. Those who do come back touched. Fairy-stricken, as it's said around here. That's what the old legends say, at any rate.'

14

She glanced around. 'Not the gossamer-winged flower-mites the Victorians liked to draw, mind you. The Scottish fairies, I'm talking about. Sometimes confused with the weird sisters or with witches – but not hags, as Shakespeare makes them. In Scotland, the fairies are bright and beautiful and fey. Dangerous.'

It struck me suddenly that standing there silvered with moonlight, she looked like one of them herself.

'We have one rule in this house. *Don't go up the hill alone.*'

I'd met her for the first time earlier that evening. It was Athenaide who engineered it, of course: who else?

Athenaide Dever Preston was a small, white-haired woman with an outsized personality more in keeping with the expanse of her ranch than with the diminutive scale of her person. The ranch encompassed a wide swathe of south-western New Mexico; she lived there in an improbable palace modelled on Hamlet's Elsinore, concealed within a ghost-town by the name of Shakespeare. Since the death of her cousin Rosalind Howard, once my mentor at Harvard, Athenaide had decided that I needed a family, and that she was the best candidate for the job.

That morning, the phone had pulled me from a deep blanket of sleep in my flat in London.

'I have a friend who wants to meet you,' she said.

'Athenaide?' I'd croaked, sitting up. I peered at the clock. 'It's five a.m.'

'I don't mean at this instant, *mija*. Tonight. Dinner. Are you busy?'

All week, I'd been looking forward to a rendezvous with Chopin at my piano, a velvety glass of cabernet, and maybe later some mindless TV. But I owed Athenaide more than I could ever count. 'No,' I said reluctantly.

'Not even with the redoubtable Mr Benjamin Pearl?'

I swallowed hard against a pang of irritation. Ben Pearl and I had met two years before, trying to outrun a killer while tracking down one of Shakespeare's lost plays – an experience that might as well have been a lightning bolt fusing us together. At first, we'd met whenever we could, with a fizz and sparkle that felt like champagne and fireworks. For a week or ten days, we'd be as inseparable as we were insatiable. But then one career or the other would come calling, pulling us down separate paths. In the end, the strain was too great. Six months earlier, we'd parted ways for good, but Athenaide stubbornly refused to absorb that fact.

'Ah well,' she clucked. 'As some bright young thing once said, the course of true love never did run smooth. Now write this down: Boswell's Court, off Castle Hill.'

I was halfway through scribbling out the address when I stopped. London had no Castle Hill that I knew of. 'You mean Parliament Hill? Tower Hill?'

'No, I mean Castle Hill, *mija*. Edinburgh.'

'*Edinburgh?*' My uncaffeinated voice cracked.

16

'How far is that from London – three hundred miles?' She sniffed. 'Wouldn't get you from the ranch up to Santa Fe. A jaunt, not a journey.'

'But—'

'Boswell's Court at eight-thirty,' she said firmly. 'There's a train from King's Cross at three-thirty. A ticket will be waiting for you. Gets in at quarter past eight, I'm told. Just enough time to get up the hill.'

'Athenaid.'

'*Bon appétit*, Katharine. Lady Nairn is quite possibly the most glamorous person I know. You'll have fun.' Laughter burbling through the phone, she hung up.

I stared at the phone in mute disbelief as its blue glow faded to darkness. So much for Chopin and *Project Runway*. I collapsed back in the bed with a groan that sputtered into laughter. Athenaide, whose parents had been costume designers for the likes of Bette Davis and Grace Kelly, and who had since made herself a billionaire, had spent her life running in glamorous circles. If this woman was at the pinnacle of Athenaide's league, she was way out of mine.

After a few minutes, I threw back the covers and padded towards the kitchen and coffee. I'd signed up for Athenaide's ride – or at least failed to throw myself off. I might as well enjoy it. Even without the redoubtable Mr Benjamin Pearl.

*

By the time the train pulled into Edinburgh, darkness had long since fallen. Across the wide boulevard of Princes Street, the New Town paraded away in neat, if rainswept, Georgian elegance. On the other side of the station, the medieval town jostled stubbornly up a steep hill, crowding towards the castle perched atop its summit in brooding golden defiance against the night.

Minutes later, I was in the back of a taxi winding up the hill, the street a dark chasm between tall houses of grey stone slick with damp. Just before the buildings fell away into the open space in front of the castle, the taxi drew to a stop. 'Boswell's Court,' the driver said, pointing to an open doorway.

Overhead, a placard like an old-fashioned inn sign glistened in the rain, sporting two rampant goats and a leering devil's head above gilded letters that spelled out *The Witchery*.

Beneath this, a low stone archway led through to a little courtyard. At the far end sat a small wooden house dominated by a great black door; just inside, a wide stair led down into an opulent fantasia on a Jacobean palace. Mute courtiers hunted stags across tapestries, heavy furniture swelled with dark carving, and, everywhere, candles flickered in iron stands that looked to have been rifled from either cathedrals or dungeons.

Making my way through the restaurant in the wake of the hostess, I wound towards a back corner. *One of the most glamorous women I know,* Athenaide had said, but through some trick of the shadows and flickering light, I did not see her until I was very close. And then I found myself face to face with a legend.

'L-Lady Nairn?' I'd stammered in confusion.

'You must be Kate Stanley,' she'd said, rising. 'Yes, I'm Lady Nairn,' she added, extending her hand. 'Better known as Janet Douglas,' she added with a disarming smile. 'Once upon a very long time ago.'

Janet Douglas had once had beauty to make Helen of Troy burn with envy. In the 1950s, she'd had a meteoric acting career, coming to the world's attention as Viola, the silver-tongued heroine of *Twelfth Night*. After that, she'd made five or six films in quick succession, all of them classics. But it was her live performance of Lady Macbeth, Shakespeare's fiend-like queen, in London's West End, that had seared her face into the consciousness of a generation. If Lady Macbeth had been her greatest role, it was also her last. In the audience at the premiere, a Scottish lordling had fallen in love with her – nothing unusual in itself. What set his passion apart was that she returned it. A month later, she'd abruptly left stage and screen to marry him. From that day forward, her disappearance from the world's stage had been more mysterious and complete than any other since Greta Garbo's.

Yet here she was, shaking my hand with an amused look on her face. 'I've been looking forward to this moment for a long time,' she said, her voice just as I remembered it from films and interviews, husky for a woman, with a honeyed golden timbre. 'I saw your *Cardenio*. And your *Hamlet*.'

The plays I'd directed at London's Globe Theatre.

Disbelief jangled through my bones. *Janet Douglas had been in the audience at the Globe, and nobody noticed?* In London, tabloid capital of the universe?

But then, nobody seemed to be noticing her here, either. I glanced around. Not a single diner or waiter appeared to have registered her presence, needling our table with side-long glances and surreptitious whispers.

And then I saw that I was wrong. From a booth across the room where he sat alone, one man gazed steadily in our direction. I'd noticed him as I walked in; an impression of height and dark hair had made me think, for a fleeting instant, that he was Ben. I'd stopped and glanced back: but his face was thin, with a long, patrician nose and eyes so pale they might have been silver; he was nobody I knew. Now he sat staring in our direction, a half-smile playing on his mouth, but there was no amusement in his eyes – only something feral and hungry that had nothing to do with food.

If Lady Nairn noticed, she gave no inkling of it. 'Thank you for coming such a long way, on an old woman's whim.'

I smiled, thinking of Athenaide's acid tongue: *A jaunt, not a journey.*

'I'd like you to meet my granddaughter. Lily MacPhee.

Though perhaps I should say I want her to meet you.' She spread her hands in mock dismay. 'Fifteen going on twenty-five. She's at rehearsal at the moment, but I'm to walk up and collect her after dinner . . . She's had a hard year of it, as I have. Her mother – my daughter Elizabeth – and father were killed in a car crash six months ago.'

A jagged sorrow ripped through the universe.

I laid my spoon down; it was shaking. 'I lost my parents at about her age,' I said carefully. *What was wrong with me? That grief was fifteen years old, yet it had washed over me with the raw intensity of newness.*

Lady Nairn nodded. 'Athenaide told me. It's one reason I pushed for this meeting.'

'And the other?'

She sighed. 'It's been a gloomy year in the Nairn household. Our own *annus horribilis*, I suppose. I also lost my husband recently.'

It dawned on me that she was wearing her black silk dress as if it were armour. 'I'm sorry,' I said.

Those famous turquoise eyes grew bright, but she did not look away. 'It's not well known, but Angus – my husband – spent his life collecting all kinds of flotsam and jetsam to do with – well, with the Scottish Play.'

Macbeth, she meant. In the theatrical world, there was a strong taboo against naming it. The Scottish Play, the Plaid Play, even MacDaddy, and MacBeast, it was called – but somehow it surprised me that forty years after she'd walked away from the theatre, the worldly woman sitting across from me would indulge in the old superstition.

'He was fascinated by both the historical king and Shakespeare's play,' she went on. 'Anything to do with the story. Including, I'm afraid, me.' She glanced down with a self-deprecatory smile. When she raised her eyes again, though, they were dark with worry. 'I sometimes wonder whether the curse is clinging to me.'

I frowned. In the theatre, the spiralling evil of Shakespeare's witch-haunted tragedy is held to be so strong that it cannot be contained by the frail walls of the stage, but spills over into reality. By long tradition, it may not be quoted within a theatre beyond what is necessary for rehearsal and performance. Even the play's title and its lead characters' names are forbidden. Lady M, she is, while her husband is the Scottish King. Or just the King and the Queen, as if no other royalty, imagined or real, matter. There are elaborate rites to exorcise the ill luck of violating that taboo.

Anthropologically, I found it intriguing. Practically, I found it absurd and even irritating. 'I'm sorry. I can't believe that.'

'No.' She sighed. 'Nor do I, most of the time.' She took a sip of wine. 'We'd been planning to put his collection on exhibit. I'd like to go ahead with it, as a memorial of sorts. And I'd like your help.'

I shifted uncomfortably. 'Sounds like you'd be better off

with a historian. Or a curator. Someone from the British Museum, maybe.'

She shook her head. 'Not that kind of exhibit.' Her voice slid into the cadence of poetry. '*How dull it is to pause, to make an end, to rust unburnished, not to shine in use . . .* I want Angus's collection burnished, you might say, in performance. In a production of *Macbeth.* And I want you to direct.'

In the midst of a sip of wine, I spluttered and set down the glass.

'I haven't yet set a date,' she was saying. 'But it's to be a one-off, by invitation only, at Hampton Court. Sybilla Fraser has signed on as Lady M. And Jason Pierce has agreed to play the King.'

I knew Sybilla by sight; everybody did. She was the UK's latest 'it' girl, a rising star – or diva-in-training, said some – with deep golden skin and dark golden hair that cascaded around her in luxurious ringlets. Even her eyes were amber, as aloof and inscrutable as a lioness's. Jason, though, I knew personally. He cultivated the aura of an Australian bad boy film star, but he was a more serious actor than he liked to admit, with a hankering for proving his dramatic chops on stage, through Shakespeare. I'd directed him as both Hamlet and Cardenio, and both times, he'd often seemed more like my nemesis than my colleague.

I raised an eyebrow, and Lady Nairn sighed. 'He's the inveterate philanderer, you know—'

'Epic,' I interjected.

'But as I understand it, she's the one who's already got someone new on the line. With luck, they'll channel their tension into the fire and ice between Macbeth and his Lady.'

'And without luck?'

'Free fireworks, I suppose.'

'So, Jason and Sybilla—'

'And myself,' said Lady Nairn. I did a double take. 'One last time,' she went on, 'I mean to take the stage. Not as the Queen, obviously. At least, not the Scottish Queen. Bit past the expiry date for that.' She set her wine glass down with a small click. 'I mean to play Hecate, Queen of Witches.'

So withered, and so wild in their attire, Shakespeare had written of his hags, *that look not like the inhabitants of the earth, and yet are on it.*

'Hecate doesn't suit you,' I said suddenly.

'A backhanded compliment if ever there was one,' said Lady Nairn with a smile.

'Athenaide told me that you're the most glamorous person she knows.'

'Did she now?' She raised one brow. '"Glamour" is an old Scots word for magic. In particular, the power to weave webs of illusion. *All was delusion, nought was truth,* as Sir Walter Scott put it.'

This entire evening was beginning to feel like a delusion. Janet Douglas was returning to the stage in *Macbeth*? And she wanted *me* to direct?

'Why me?' I blurted out. 'You could have anyone you ask.'

'I'm asking you. Or do you know another director with expertise in occult Shakespeare?'

Hell and damnation, I thought. *So that's it.* What now seemed like a lifetime ago, I had written a dissertation on that subject, by which I meant the codes and clues that various people believed were hidden in the Bard's works. The twisting meanings of that small word, *occult*, it seemed, would haunt me as long as I lived.

'Lady Nairn, don't get me wrong, I don't mean to disappoint, but by "occult" I mean—'

She waved me off. 'You mean the old sense of the word: hidden, obscured, secret. *Not* magical. Yes, I know. I've listened to your interviews. But it's not magic I want you for.' She leaned forward. 'I told you that my husband collected anything and everything to do with *Macbeth*. Well, a week or ten days before we lost him, he grew tense and excited in a way that meant one thing. He was closing in on a find.'

Somewhere within, a small seed of misgiving sprouted warily into life. 'What kind of find?'

She sat back, eyeing me in silence. Then she rose from her chair with an elusive smile. For a moment, her hand rested lightly on my shoulder. 'Come to Dunsinnan.'

I didn't recognise the word.

'Better known as Dunsinane. Macbeth's castle of evil.

25

Surely you remember that,' she said with a smile. 'I live there.' Turning abruptly, she headed for the stairs.

Knowledge, the oldest temptation. Caught in the tug of curiosity, I rose and followed her out.

2

Outside, the rain had stopped, but the air was still damp, thick with the sharp bracken scent of autumn, even up here in the high stone heart of the old city. We turned left, up the hill towards the castle.

Lady Nairn had invited the entire prospective cast up to her house for a weekend of 'atmospheric research', as she put it, with the intention of carting them back down here, two nights hence, for the Fire Festival of Samhuinn, the old Celtic holy night that Christianity had co-opted and turned into Halloween. Pronounced 'Sow-en', more or less, by English speakers, *Samhuinn* means 'summer's end' in Scottish Gaelic, she explained. It was the turning of the year, when the door between the living and the dead was said to thin to a transparent veil. The Edinburgh festival was a winter carnival, a street pageant in which masked players mimed a modern version of the ancient pagan myth of the Summer King meeting the Winter King in battle.

Her granddaughter Lily had a part in it. 'As a torchbearer,' she said. 'More or less the Shakespearean equivalent of a spear-carrier. Necessary, but nearly invisible. Someday, though, I expect she'd like to be the kayak.'

That's what I thought I heard, at any rate.

Lady Nairn laughed at my confusion. '*Cailleach*,' she explained. 'Not kayak. Another Gaelic word. Sounds to English ears like an Eskimo canoe, but it means "old woman". The old woman of winter, who comes into her power as summer wanes and dies.' She wrapped her coat closer around herself. 'The Queen of Darkness and Death,' she went on quietly, 'but also of renewal. Most people forget about that part. But there is no life without death, and no spring without the great die-off of winter . . .'

For a moment we walked in silence, our footsteps ringing against the pavement. 'The old myths personify that conundrum,' she said. 'And the festival dramatises the myths. The Cailleach chooses the Winter King as her champion and eggs him on into battle against the old King of Summer. All in mime. So archetypal, really, that words are superfluous.'

The image of a terrible queen urging a warrior in his prime to kill an old king and take his place skimmed through my head. 'But that's the story of *Macbeth*,' I said slowly.

'It's the myth behind it,' she specified.

'But *Macbeth* is based on history,' I protested. 'Scottish history.'

She sniffed. 'History rearranged – cut and pasted – to fit myth. Scholars have forgotten that part, if they ever knew it.

But myth is not so easily cornered and tamed into neat academic fact.'

In all the years I'd spent in the ivory tower, working towards being a professor of Shakespeare before falling in love with the Bard on stage and running off to the theatre, I'd never heard any version of Lady Nairn's theory. But it fitted. It fitted with the simplicity of truth. 'You think Shakespeare knew?' I asked quietly.

She looked straight ahead, a mischievous smile upending the corners of her mouth. 'I think he knew a great deal more than we credit him with.'

The buildings fell away as we came to the dark emptiness of the Esplanade. At the far end, the castle reared into the night. In the centre of the parade ground, a crowd roiled and milled. Under a loose netting of laughter, torches flickered here and there, and somewhere in the middle, someone in a stag's mask was tossing their head so that antlers reared into the night. Now and again, unearthly howls rose in waves of loneliness towards the moon.

The crowd shifted and for an instant I saw the dark-haired man from the restaurant. His eyes met mine, and then the crowd shifted again, and he disappeared. A girl detached herself from the outer fringes, loping over to us with adolescent gangliness.

Lily MacPhee had her grandmother's wide-set eyes and high cheekbones, though her colouring was entirely different.

Flame-red hair spilled in waves past her shoulders. Her milk-white skin was scattered with freckles like stars, and her eyes were a pale sea-green. A small jewel winked in her nose. The Pre-Raphaelites, I thought, would have fought bitter duels among themselves for the right to paint her as Guinevere or the Lady of the Lake.

'You said yes!' she said with girlish pleasure.

'She said maybe,' said her grandmother. 'More or less.'

Dunsinnan Hill, Lady Nairn told me as we drove, lay fifty miles ahead, just north of the Tay. It had been fortified since the Iron Age, but a thousand years ago, the old histories said, the historical King Macbeth had rebuilt it.

For a generation, he'd ruled Scotland from its heights, until his young cousin Malcolm had come north in the year 1054, at the head of an army of the hated Sassenach – Anglo-Saxons from northern England, along with a fair few Vikings. Charging up the hill, Malcolm's Saxons had clashed with Macbeth's Scots in a pitched battle that raged from sunrise to sunset, leaving the slopes scattered with crow's bait. It was not the end – though Macbeth lost both the battle and the hill, he lived to lead his battered men in retreat – but it was the beginning of the end. Two years later, Malcolm finally caught up with him, and this time the knife went home. Malcolm had mounted Macbeth's head on a pole and claimed the kingship of Scotland for himself.

Macbeth had been a good king, famed for both generosity

and bravery – by some reckonings, the last truly Celtic king of Scotland, ruling in the old ways. But among the most lasting spoils of victory is the right to write history, and Macbeth's legacy had quickly darkened. It was Shakespeare, though, who'd made him a byword for evil.

It was a tragic arc, I thought as Lady Nairn's voice faded away: to fall, after death, from hero-king to reviled tyrant. At least Shakespeare's fictionalised Macbeth made the plunge during his life, of his own accord.

'There,' said Lady Nairn presently. She pointed to a rounded hilltop with a small turreted summit, set a little apart from the others. We'd left the main roads and were hurtling south on a narrow lane across fields and through hedgerows. The road led straight for the hill, veering at the last minute around the western slope, plunging into a pine wood and past a quarry, and then left along the south side of the hill. Soon after that, we turned off the lane, away from the hill, and into a gravel drive.

Dunsinnan House stood in a high saddle, looking north across the road to the hill for which it was named and south to the glimmering waters of the Firth of Tay. At its heart, the tall rectangle of an old Scottish castle could still be seen, though in ensuing centuries it had sprouted several new wings, not to mention towers and cupolas, balconies and bay windows seemingly at random, giving it the air of an aged grande dame proudly squeezed into a gown from her youth, now haphazardly adorned with gewgaws and baubles collected from every period of her life.

Lady Nairn led me swiftly up four flights of stairs to a bedroom in a high corner. Its walls were covered in watered blue silk; along the northern wall marched three tall windows curtained in more blue silk embroidered with Chinese dragons. 'I thought you might like a view,' she'd said, crossing the room to throw open the middle window, so that both the sound and the scent of pines blew through the room. Beyond, the hill was visible mostly as an absence of stars.

Don't go up the hill alone. The sentence hung on the air between us.

'I told you I lost my husband,' she said. 'I meant it more literally than you perhaps realised.' She looked back towards the hill. 'He disappeared up there one night three months ago. We went to the police, of course. They poked around a bit, but didn't find anything. Suggested, in a roundabout way, that maybe he'd gone off for a bit of something on the side. He was not that sort of man.

'Auld Callie – a woman from the village, someone he'd known from childhood – found him the following week, sitting on the hilltop, dangling his legs like a child's over the ramparts. He was rocking back and forth, muttering one phrase over and over: *Dunsinnan must go to Birnam Wood.*'

'Macbeth's riddle,' I said quietly.

32

'No,' she said with a slight shake of the head. 'The witches' riddle.' She launched into the Shakespeare:

Macbeth shall never vanquished be, until
Great Birnam Wood to high Dunsinnan Hill
Shall come against him.

In the play, King Macbeth assumes the riddle is a metaphor for 'never', only to learn, when confronted by a forest on the move, that the witches meant it literally. '*The equivocation of the fiend that lies like truth,*' I murmured.

She gave me a sad smile. 'I'm not sure it counts as equivocation if there's no clear answer at all, rather than too many. And in any case, Angus reversed it . . . *Dunsinnan must go to Birnam Wood.* His title, you know, was Nairn of Dunsinnan, so I thought he was referring to himself. And you can see the Wood, or what's left of it, from the hilltop, so it seemed to me that he was saying that *he* must go to Birnam. I took him there . . . he'd known the place since childhood, but he didn't recognise it. Stood there turning round and round beneath the great oak, looking bewildered.'

Her voice dipped into bitterness. 'He died a fortnight after that. A month ago, that was. Blessing, really. His mind was gone, or mostly so. Just enough left to understand that he wasn't right. Made him desperate, near the end.'

Her voice had begun to waver, and she paused to steady it, turning to the window and brushing damp cheeks with the back of one hand. 'I'm sorry,' she said, giving herself a little shake and going on. 'The doctors said he had a stroke. No doubt they're right. But that it isn't the whole story. When we found him, he'd been missing for a week, but he was clean-shaven, and his clothes were immaculate.' Her chin went up. *'As if he'd just left.'*

She pinned me with her gaze. 'Do you know Aleister Crowley's definition of magic? It's "the science and art of causing change to occur in conformity with will".'

I frowned. It was a famous – and famously baggy – definition. By its lights, just about everything was magic. Crowley himself had included potato-growing and banking in the list, along with ritual magic and spells. Where was this going?

She leaned forward. 'There were those who wished Angus ill,' she said with quiet intensity. 'Mostly, I'm afraid, for my sake.'

'Wishing doesn't make it so.'

'Perhaps not.'

Beyond her, through the window, I saw something – a weasel or a stoat, maybe – undulating across the corner of the lawn, a furtive shadow in darkness. Almost in rhythm with it, a prickle of foreboding crept across my skin. *What was she suggesting? That someone had murdered Sir Angus by magic?*

'Lady Nairn, if you suspect foul play in Sir Angus's death, you should go to the police.'

'I think it must be dealt with by other means.' She cocked her head. 'How much do you know about the writing of *Macbeth*? Not the story. The writing of it.'

I frowned. 'There's not much to know. It's Shakespeare's shortest tragedy. Published posthumously, in the First Folio.'

'The first collected edition of his works,' she said, nodding. 'Dated 1623, seven years after Shakespeare's death. But that's about its printing. Not its writing.'

'We don't know anything about the writing of any of his plays.'

'There was an earlier version.' She said it defiantly, a gauntlet thrown down.

'Many scholars think so,' I said carefully. That much was true, mostly because of the witches. Eerie and terrifying at one moment, they are, and broad comedy at the next – not to mention Hecate, Queen of Witches, who seems to have been pulled wholesale from another, later play by Thomas Middleton, and slapped down haphazardly into Shakespeare's play, for all that her brand of gleefully cackling evil would be more at home in a Disney film. 'But there's no real evidence one way or an—'

She cut me off. 'As a child, my husband's grandfather met an old woman on the hill. She told him that long ago, Shakespeare had come here with a company of English players, and met a dark fairy – a witch – who lived in a boiling lake. She taught him all her dark arts; in return, he stole her soul and fled.

'She searched high and low, but he had hidden it well. It was not in a stone or an egg, a ring or a crown: not in any of the places one normally hides such a thing. She found it at last, though, written into a play, mixed into the very ink scrawled across the pages of a book. Snatching up the book, she cursed his words to scatter misery rather than joy, and then she vanished back to her lake.

'Some time earlier, the boy's grandfather had vanished on the hill, so when the old woman told him her tale and made him repeat it back to her, he decided she was the dark fairy of her own story, and the book, if he could find it, was her payment for his grandfather . . . in later years, he – Angus's grandfather – came to believe she had been talking about *Macbeth*.'

I gazed at her in silence. How could I put what I had to say tactfully? 'Lady Nairn – with all due respect to your husband's grandfather: as wonderful as his story is, it's a child's half-remembered tale, a hundred years old. It hardly counts as evidence for an earlier version of the play.'

'Not by itself. But it fits with this.' She went to the desk and opened an archival folder, handing me a photocopied page. 'From the old Dunsinnan House account book,' she said. 'Half ledger, half diary.'

Under an entry dated 1 November, 1589, someone had written *The English players departit hence*. But it mentioned no names.

'Read the next sentence,' said Lady Nairn.

The same day, the Lady Arran reportit a mirror and a book
stolen, and charged that the players had taken them. But
they could not be found.

I looked up quickly. I knew of Lady Arran. Elizabeth
Stewart, Lady Arran, her contemporaries had sneered, was
a greedy, avaricious, and ambitious woman. A Lady Jezebel
who consorted with witches. For a time, young King James
had been besotted with her and her husband both; there
had been whispers in some corners that she was the reason
the king would not take a wife. Other whispers charged that
she'd kill him if she could: that she desired, above all else, to
be queen. She was, said some, the historical figure standing
in the shadows behind the character of Lady Macbeth.

Lady Nairn smiled. 'I thought you might recognise that
name. So you see, we do have evidence.'

'Of what?' It was all I could do to stay calm. 'That Lady
Arran was here, yes. That Shakespeare was, no. He knew *of*
her, almost surely – almost twenty years later. But we don't
know that he ever knew her in person. We don't know anything at all about him in 1589, actually, beyond the fact that
he was alive. That's right in the middle of what's called his
lost years. No record of his whereabouts whatsoever.'

'Unless he was here. You might at least be gracious
enough to admit it's suggestive,' she said reproachfully.
'As it happens, it also dovetails with my family legends.'
She looked out at the night. 'I am descended, in a direct

mother-to-daughter line, from Elizabeth Stewart. From Lady Macbeth.'

I must have been gaping in disbelief, because she shot me a wry smile. 'My husband found my heritage quite alluring. Lily, on the other hand, doesn't know, and I'd like to keep it that way. It's not information that's necessarily . . . useful . . . to a fifteen-year-old.'

'You have family legends about her?' I asked, feeling a little faint.

'Elizabeth Stewart didn't consort with witches. She *was* one. Not a cackling devil-worshipping crone, but a serious student of magic. As my mother and grandmother would have it, the Bard once saw her at work and later put his rec-ollections – quite accurately – in a play. It was not easy to dissuade him from performing it, but it was done. And the manuscript made to disappear.'

My mind was reeling.

'You can make of the witchcraft whatever you like, Kate. It's not the magic I'm trying to interest you in,' she said patiently. 'It's the manuscript.' She drew the archival folder off the desk, holding it out to me. 'Three days ago, shuffled among Angus's papers, I found this.'

I opened the folder. Inside was a postcard, and a single sheet of heavy ivory notepaper. The postcard was a copy of one of my favourite paintings in Britain, John Singer Sargent's portrait of Ellen Terry as Lady Macbeth. Terry had been one of the three or four all-time great Lady

Macbeths. The last, before Janet Douglas. Sargent had somehow made her gown shimmer between blue and green. With her long red braids, a gleam of gold low on her waist, and the blue-green gown accentuating the curve of her hips and then narrowing as it cascaded towards the floor, I'd always thought she looked more like a mermaid than a queen.

Behind the card, the notepaper was covered with writing in a large looping hand of confidence and passion, and something stubbornly childlike, too. I glanced at the signature. *Nell*, it read, with a long tail like a comet.

The pet name used among family and friends by Ellen Terry. I glanced up.

'As much as can be discerned from a fax, both signature and letter are genuine,' said Lady Nairn. She turned to look out the window. 'Read it. Take your time.'

It was dated 1911. 'My dear Monsieur Superbe Homme,' it began. *My dear Superb Man. My dear Superman.*

My dear Monsieur Superbe Homme,

I am forwarding to you a curious letter I have recently received from a fellow denizen of the drama whose personal tale is as tragic as any role she might encharacter on the stage. Indeed, I am not at all certain that her long woes have not in the end loosened her hold upon sanity. As you will see, she believes, poor soul, not only that Mr Shakespeare first circulated a version of Macbeth

*substantially different from the one that has come down to
us, but that this earlier version has survived (!) – and that
she is the guardian of its whereabouts.*

'Surely you don't bel—'

'I think my husband believed that his grandfather's mysterious old lady and Ellen's "poor soul" were one and the same.'

Our eyes locked in silence. 'Go on,' she said presently. I
looked back down.

*I would conclude out of hand that she is lunatic, were it
not for the enclosure which she gave to me along with her
tale, and which I now send on to you. I think the book
queer enough, but it is the letter inside that you will find
most curious. Unfortunately, all it conveys about the nature
of this supposed earlier version is that its differences lie
chiefly with the witches, especially Hecate, who is said to
be 'both there and not there'.*

I glanced up. 'Thus Hecate?'

'I'm an actress,' she said with a small shrug. 'I learn characters by playing them. Finish it.'

There wasn't much more:

*A riddling sentiment of an appropriately
Shakespearean fashion, I suppose, but exasperating all the
same. I cannot make head or tail of it.*

*As it is, I am hoping that you can glimpse the Forest
through the Trees.*

Nell

I lifted the letter, but there was nothing else in the folder.
'The enclosure?'

'Missing.' She sighed. 'And no indication where, when, or
how he acquired the letter, either. So you see, I don't know
what Angus found.' She cocked her head. 'But I know what
he was looking for.'

For a moment, I sat in stunned silence. Someone – a real
woman, not a witch or a fairy – had believed not only that an
earlier version of *Macbeth* had existed, but that it had survived to the dawn of the twentieth century. And while Ellen
Terry had been sceptical, she had not been able to dismiss
the woman's tale out of hand, either. On top of that, it was
the witches – the magic – that was said to be different: the
very aspect of the surviving play that bothered scholars
most.

A tremor of excitement, or maybe it was dread, went
through me. What if it were true? The *Cardenio* manuscript
I'd helped to find had had caché as a lost play . . . but
this . . . we were talking about one of the great plays. One of
the most profound explorations of evil in all human history.
A play most people could quote, even people who'd never
seen it – or any Shakespeare at all, for that matter. *Double,
double toil and trouble, fire burn and cauldron bubble . . .*

41

Lady Nairn cut into my reverie. 'What do you suppose it would be worth?' she asked.

Cardenio had gone at auction for many millions; a lost version of *Macbeth* would very possibly fetch more. A *Macbeth* that linked Shakespeare to magic actually practised, not just cackled on a stage . . . I shook my head, running my tongue around dry lips. 'I have no idea.'

'Surely it would reach to a sum worth frightening an old man to death, at least in some quarters.'

I looked up sharply. 'You think . . .?'

'I don't know what to think. But I would like to know what happened to my husband. And if he did find what Ellen Terry was talking about – *I want it.*' She drew about herself all the hauteur of a queen. 'I want you to find it. And then I want you to stage it.'

She straightened, erect as a queen heading for execution. 'I loved Angus, Kate. I left the stage for him. The adulation of the world . . . And he was enough. He was worth it. You, of all people, might understand the measure of that. I am not asking you to find his killer. I am asking you to find the manuscript. Will you help me?'

Something about her strange mix of pride and fragility tugged at the heart. And however disturbing her charge of murder might be, the manuscript had just enough plausibility to pluck at my curiosity.

'*Dunsinnan must go to Birnam Wood,*' I said quietly. 'You took him there?'

She nodded.

'I had no idea it was a real place – at least, not one that still existed . . . I suppose we should start there.'

She let out a long, slow breath, bowing her head with relief. 'Thank you.' Straightening, she rose to leave. 'I'll take you there first thing in the morning.' At the door, she turned back, her eyes gleaming, though whether with tears or with triumph it was hard to say. 'Meanwhile, don't go up the hill alone.'

My head still spinning, I changed into a pair of striped silk pyjamas laid out for me, and climbed into bed. On the bedside table was a copy of *Macbeth*.

I sat for a moment with my arms wrapped around my knees. My agreement to help Lady Nairn was already beginning to look like folly. Her charge of murder, for one, was a dark return to superstition, the sort of stuff that had spawned witch hunts. Even the more rational parts of her story were dubious. For all I knew, Terry's letter was a forgery. Nobody could authenticate something like that by looking at a fax; I doubted that reputable experts would even consent to try.

How had the grandfather's story gone? That a dark fairy had told him that Shakespeare had learned magic here, from a witch who lived in a boiling lake?

I want you to find it. And then I want you to stage it. Out of her presence, Lady Nairn's demand seemed little less lunatic

43

than the old fairy's geography. A task, set by an angry and sorrowing goddess: find what her husband had found. Or hadn't. More likely, she'd set me to catch a dead man's dream.

And she wasn't a goddess. She was Lady Macbeth, in a deeper way than anyone imagined. What would it be like, to have that past running through your veins?

I sighed and opened the play. It took a scene or two for the rush of adrenalin to clear from my head. A scene or two after that, I was nodding. Before I reached the end of the first act, I was asleep.

Aware that I was walking through a dream, I picked my way up a steep hill that levelled off into a wide field. In the distance rose a castle. High on its battlements, a woman with red hair stood staring into the night, ignoring a jeering crowd below, her gown whipping about in the wind as if she were riding out a storm on the prow of some immense ship. Around her, I sensed malice closing in so thickly that it became hard to breathe.

I woke in darkness, gasping for air, and for a moment I had no idea where I was. Then I remembered Lady Nairn's voice: '*Dunsinnan. Dunsinane. Macbeth's castle of evil.*'

I rose and filled a glass of water from the bathroom tap. On the way back to bed, I passed the dressing table, its mirror reflecting the three tall windows, the middle curtain still drawn open to the sky. I stood there a moment, watching the reflection of the night. I could still see a faint glow from the moon in the west, though the moon itself had set. As I watched, though, a yellow star winked into being. I whirled to the window. *Not a star.* Across the road, high up, flames kindled and caught, blossoming into what must have been a great bonfire atop the hill.

I stood there rapt, staring at it for I don't know how long. All around that point of light, the night was dark and still. Then I glimpsed movement closer in. Peering down, I saw a shadow striding across the grass. A woman in a short coat and trousers, a pale scarf fluttering at her neck. Twisted into a neat knot, her hair was paler still.

Lady Nairn crossed the lawn and disappeared into the shadows of the drive. Going where at this time of night – alone?

Maybe half an hour later, I saw movement again, but this time it was high and farther away. Perhaps it was the wind and some odd trick of the damp Scottish air. Perhaps I was dreaming. But I could have sworn that silhouetted against the fire I saw the shadowy form of someone dancing with arms outstretched to the moonless night.

3

I watched as long as I could, but sleep eventually dragged at me and I stumbled back to bed. I curled up facing the window, propping myself up with pillows, watching the hill until I could stay awake no longer.

When I woke again, much later, the fire on the hill had gone out. Suddenly, both mirror and window seemed ominous staring eyes. Rising, I drew the curtains and cast my robe over the mirror. Then I lay back down and slept till morning.

I woke late but did not feel rested. It had been a fitful sleep at best. I dressed in a hurry, eager to be off to Birnam Wood. Downstairs, I had the dining room all to myself. Breakfast – though by rights it was closer to lunch – was served by the cook. I poked at oatmeal and an egg, and tried to finish reading the play, but both my mind and my stomach were jumping around like excited rabbits. On the subject of the whereabouts of either the lady of the house or her granddaughter, however, the cook was polite but noncommittal, and I saw no one else about.

I had no choice but to wait; I might as well make use of

the time. Leaving my breakfast half-eaten, I took an apple and let myself out into the garden. The morning was unseasonably warm; surely there would be a bench somewhere where I could tackle *Macbeth*, which I hadn't read all the way through in a long time.

On either side of the drive that swooped up from the road to the house lay thick lawns bordered by tall conifer woods. On the left a Renaissance knot garden had been laid out, its gravel paths and low hedges marking out beds shaped as lozenges and triangles and filled with lavender, rosemary, thyme, and many more herbs I couldn't name. I wandered for a while, not seeing a soul, and eventually I found a bench at the bottom of the slope. Once again, I sat down to read the play from the beginning.

When shall we three meet again,
In thunder, lightning, or in rain?

On the other side of the road, Dunsinnan Hill loomed over the words. It was thrilling to read the play in its shadow, but surely it would be even more stirring to read it at the summit where Macbeth had battled all those years ago.

Suddenly, I remembered Lady Nairn saying *You can see Birnam Wood, or what's left of it, from the top.* As if the hill itself had pulled me up, I rose and took two steps toward it, and then stopped. *Don't go up the hill alone,* she'd also said. *People disappear from it, from time to time.* Her husband,

47

among them. I shuddered, thinking of the fire I'd seen in the night. But that had been well past midnight, I told myself firmly. Probably a dream from beginning to end, for that matter. Surely on a bright warm day, more like late August than late October, there couldn't be any harm in a short hike – if one could even call it a hike. More like a walk. I rose and made my way down to the bottom of the garden.

Across the road, the slopes were sheer exposed rock. There was no climbing the hill from this direction. But as we'd driven in, I'd seen a stile over the fence, and a path winding up its northern slope. It had been a short drive from there to the house. It wouldn't be a bad walk.

I hesitated, glancing back. The windows of the house stared back blindly.

I want your help, Lady Nairn had said. Well, she would have it. Shoving the play in my coat pocket, I stepped purposefully from the drive and out into the lane.

It took twenty minutes to reach the stile. Beyond it, the path led up along the edge of a steep grassy field and past a thick plantation of pine. The grass gave way to heather clumped with gorse, and then even the gorse disappeared, leaving russet brown waves of heather unbroken by anything but wind. Topping a rise, I heard the grind and clatter of the quarry splattering through the morning. At my feet, the heather ended abruptly at the edge of a large meadow. To the west, it was edged with a fence labelled DANGER; all that was visible through the fence was sky. To the south, though, the meadow lapped against the sheer grassy slopes of the hill's strange cylindrical summit, rising into the sky like an emerald ziggurat. All that was left of the ancient fortress at its top were the worn tracks of its earthen ramparts, visible in outline as terraces circling the hilltop like a road spiralling into the heavens.

I caught my breath. Macbeth, the real Macbeth, had stood atop that summit.

Ten minutes later, I scrambled over a slight lip and found myself at the edge of a shallow grassy bowl on top of the world. A sweet wind swept endlessly up over the edge, and for a moment I stood looking about me, breathing it in.

I stepped down into the bowl. It was instantly quieter and warmer, almost as if I'd stepped into a different place and time. I walked towards the cairn, meaning to use it as a backrest, but a few steps on, I stopped. Just beyond, hidden from first sight by a small hummock, was a ring of fire-blackened stones. As if pulled against my will, I drew near it and bent down. The ash in the middle was still warm.

I jumped back, my heart thudding in my chest. So there *had* been a fire up here last night. And from the grass beaten down in a circle just outside the fire ring, a dancer, too. For a moment, I stood poised to run.

But the day was bright and beautiful, and I was clearly alone. Besides, I told myself, there's nothing inherently ominous about a bonfire atop a hill on a clear autumn night. No need to bolt like an addled antelope, at any rate. I'd come this far – I might as well look at what I'd come to see.

I turned and looked northward. Far across the valley, the Highlands rose in waves of deepening purple. Somewhere out there, fringing the feet of the mountains, lay Birnam Wood. *Dunsinnan must go to Birnam Wood*, Sir Angus had said. What the hell was that supposed to mean?

The reverse had not been good news for King Macbeth, at least in Shakespeare's telling.

For a while I stood roiling with frustration, staring across the valley. At last, though, I made myself sit down in the grass with my back to the cairn and pull out both my apple and the book. If Sir Angus's words were any indication, the play itself worked in some manner as a clue. I couldn't reach Birnam Wood without wings, but there was no better place to read the *Macbeth* than here.

When shall we three meet again,
In thunder, lightning, or in rain?
When the hurly-burly's done,
When the battle's lost and won.
That will be ere the set of sun.
Where's the place?
                  Upon the heath.
There to meet with Macbeth . . .
Fair is foul and foul is fair,
Hover through the fog and filthy air.

50

Even read silently, the words had the eerie rhythmic quality of a spell. In the distance, I could still hear snatches of the tractor's droning, its sound winding around the clank of the quarry closer to hand and the trill of birds swooping overhead. Somehow they all seemed to twine together in a rhythmic accompaniment to the Shakespeare.

The bird calls grew harsh and more insistent. Lower down the hill, I heard the whinny of a horse, and then a sound I knew only from the stage: the clash of swords.

I woke with a start. How long I'd dozed before tipping over into dreams, I had no idea, but it must have been some time, because the warm afternoon had dissolved, leaving behind a world swathed in a cold grey blanket of mist. Low in the south-west, the sun had become a silk-wrapped pearl. By its position, the time looked to be late afternoon. If that was right, I'd slept a long time. I was gathering up my book and my half-eaten apple when I heard the whisper drifting on the wind, so that I couldn't even tell from which direction it came: *Thou shalt be queen hereafter.*

I froze. But all I heard was the wordless sweep of the wind up over the summit. *I still have one foot in my dreams,* I thought. Gingerly, I stepped toward the path leading down through the old ramparts of the fortress. And stopped. At my feet was a gleam of metal.

I bent down for a closer look. A long single-edged blade of blue-grey steel lay half hidden in the grass. The hilt,

51

lying towards me, was black with glints of silver. I was reaching out to grasp it when I saw the foot.

At the edge of one of the old trenches, someone lay stretched out in the grass, covered by a heavy blue-green gown shimmering like peacock feathers, except that it wasn't feathered. It was scaled. I stepped closer. It looked like Ellen Terry's gown, the one she'd been painted in as Lady Macbeth. It seemed to ripple in the grass like a long serpent, draped lengthwise, as it was, over – over whoever it was. By the narrow delicacy of the foot, a woman, and young.

Instinctively, my fingers wrapped around the hilt. Sliding the knife from the grass, I stepped closer. She didn't move.

I lifted a corner of the gown and saw a fall of flame-red hair. Aware of a dull thudding that must be my heart, I lifted the gown farther. What lay beneath I glimpsed only for an instant, but it is branded in my memory: her hands bound behind her back, a length of cloth passed lengthwise around her torso, passing through her groin and knotted around her neck, smeared thickly with blood.

It was Lily, and she was dead.

Floating on the wind, came another whisper. *She must die.* And then, drifting closer, a third: *Nothing is but what is not.* Whoever they were, they were closing in.

The blue gown slipped from my grasp. Tightening my grip on the knife, I backed away slowly for a few paces, and then I turned and ran.

4

Still gripping the knife, I stumbled through the mist, slipping and sliding down the ramparts and on down through the heather. A gorse bush loomed out of the swirling greyness. As I swerved to avoid it, someone grabbed me from behind. I swung around with the knife, but it was knocked from my grasp, thudding off into the heather. A broad hand clapped over my mouth, and I was forced to the ground and dragged from the path.

'You've kent what you shouldna,' whispered a voice in my ear. Broad Scots for *You have known what you should not*. Twisting around to look at my captor, I saw a wild-eyed, grey-haired woman, broadly built, at least twenty years my senior.

I lunged away, but she jerked my arms back so expertly that the pain nearly knocked the wind from me.

'Lie still,' she said, 'if you don't want to get the both of us killed.'

A few seconds later, I heard what she must have sensed earlier: hoofbeats coming fast down the hill. I twisted around to face the path, just in time to see a white horse emerge from the mist not five feet away. Spooked by the gorse, the animal whinnied and reared. The rider threw his weight forward, fighting for control, his focus so intent on the horse that I don't think he ever saw us. But the horse did.

Its hooves crashed down no more than a foot from my head. Backing a few paces, it bolted. But not before I'd seen the rider's face. He was the dark-haired man.

For what seemed like aeons, my captor and I lay in silence beneath the bush. At last, she raised her head. I sat up, but she shook her head. 'Hush,' she said, her head cocked, listening.

Footsteps were coming back this way, up the hill. Footsteps, not hoofbeats. This time, she did not have to pull me down; I crouched next to her, as small as I could make myself.

Bent low to the ground, the man ran right past us. Then he stopped and looked back, reaching down to pick something up.

My book. Hot panic flooded through me.

Stealthily, he crept towards us and then stopped. *Go,* I prayed with every sinew of my body. *Go, and don't look back.*

He turned and took one step away, and then another, and then without warning his hand darted out, grabbing me by one wrist.

Behind me, the grey-haired Fury cried out. Shoving me forward so that I stumbled right into his arms, she darted across the heather, flapping like a broken-winged bird as she disappeared into the mist.

I jerked away from the hands grasping me, but he held tight. 'Hello, Professor,' said a voice I knew, and I realised that his hair, though dark, was curly, and his eyes were green. It was Ben, and he was laughing.

'*You!*' was all I could manage to croak.

Something in my voice cut through his hilarity. 'Are you all right?'

My breath came out in a sob. 'Lily,' I gasped, pulling free at last.

'Your friend?' He nodded in the direction the old woman had run.

'*No.* Lady Nairn's fifteen-year-old granddaughter. On the hilltop,' I said. 'Dead.' I bent down, scrabbling through the heather for the knife.

'Whoa,' said Ben, crouching down with me. 'Slow down.'

I sat back on my heels, brushing away a hot squeeze of tears. 'Up on top of the hill. I found a knife. And then Lily, lying there dead, with her throat cut. And a voice, or maybe two voices. Whispers. I don't know. So I ran. The woman you saw, the grey-haired woman – I don't know who she is – knocked the knife away and dragged me off the path, and then the dark-haired man nearly rode me down on a spooked horse . . .' I waved wildly in the direction of the hilltop. 'And now I can't find the knife.' The last sentence was nearly a wail.

Dropping to his hands and knees, Ben began combing the heather for it.

'Did you hear me? She's fifteen. She's *dead*.'

'I heard you.' Two minutes later he plucked the knife from a clump of heather. It gleamed darkly, a pattern of whorls in the steel catching the strange grey light, so that the blade seemed to ripple and undulate almost as if it were alive. 'Jesus, Kate,' he said, staring down at it with a low whistle. 'Where did you say you found the girl?'

'On the hilltop.'

He was suddenly terse. 'Show me.'

'We need to call the police.'

He was gazing upwards through the mist. Slowly, he shook his head. 'Are you sure she's dead?'

'*I saw her.*'

'Did you check her pulse?'

'She's dead.'

'You said her throat was cut. But there's no blood on this knife.'

'So maybe the killer used another . . .' My voice trailed off. There hadn't been enough blood around the body, either.

I began running back up the hill. Ben followed.

It didn't take long to reach the summit. For a moment we crouched just below the rim, listening, but all we heard was wind in the grass. Silently, Ben eased out the sharp-edged black pistol I had never seen him without and cautiously peered up over the edge. After a moment, he jumped up and strode over. I followed.

The cairn was there, and beside it the fire ring. But where the body had lain, nothing was visible but grass.

Other than Ben and me, there was no one, living or dead, atop the hill.

5

'But she was here,' I said. 'I found her. Over there. By one of the pits. It was only a few minutes ago.' I pointed towards where I had seen her.

His gun drawn and ready, we slowly circled the hill just below the rim, Ben bending to look at the grass as we went. When we'd come full circle, he peered over the edge once again. 'Stay here.'

Bent low to the ground, he slid silently across the grass, glancing into each of the pits in turn. At the last one, he straightened, motioning me over. They, too, were empty of everything but grass and wind.

'*She was here*,' I insisted.

Ben crouched down to the ground, scanning the grass with a tracker's fine eye. 'I see no sign of it,' he said after a while, sitting back on his heels. 'A few footsteps – but nothing like the weight of a body.'

'She was here,' I said again. 'It was Lily. She was dead.' I glared at him for a moment in silence, and then, feeling the hot swell of tears, I turned on my heel, speeding back down the hill.

'Where are you going?' he asked as he caught up with me.

'Back to the house,' I said shortly. Lily would be there, or she would not. 'And you?'

'I was looking for you. Now that I've found you, I don't exactly know.'

I stopped. 'You knew I was up here?'

'Lady Nairn told me that she'd told you not to come up the hill. So it was the first place I looked.'

'Not funny.'

'But accurate.'

Trained in some branch of the British special forces that he'd never identified to me in all our time together, he'd left it to found a high-tech security company. 'As in guns,' he'd told me when we first met. 'Not stocks and bonds.' That Lady Nairn would need someone like Ben made sense. The moment the merest hint of her show got out, she'd be hounded by paparazzi. No doubt she'd worried about Sir Angus's collection as well, at least the part that she meant to move down to Hampton Court and back.

But it was Lily who had needed protection, I thought. And had not had it. Ben hadn't even known who she was.

By the time we got down to the lay-by, dusk was quickly fading to dark. Ben drove me back to the house in silence.

I leapt out of the car as soon as it came to a stop and raced inside, taking the stairs two at a time, up one flight and then down a wide passageway towards the sound of the party. *I'd completely forgotten about Lady Nairn's dinner.*

The company had already gathered in the old great hall, now laid out as a comfortable drawing room, filled with sofas and chairs, a fire of some sweet-smelling wood crackling in the immense fireplace. I scanned the room for Lady Nairn; she was holding court among three men in front of a long bank of windows.

'Where's Lily?' My voice felt ragged in my throat.

Around the room, conversation faltered and the clink of glassware and ice stilled as everyone turned to stare.

Lady Nairn's eyes flickered across the room in the direction of a grand piano in a far corner. A man bent over it, laughing. Jason Pierce. Registering the silence, he straightened and turned, revealing Lily in green velvet at the keyboard, flushed with delight. 'Oh,' she said. 'It's you.'

I felt a wash of loose-limbed relief, followed by a flush of confusion. The dead girl wasn't Lily . . . but in that case, who was she?

At the piano, Lily launched into the dark, downward sweep of Bach's Toccata and Fugue in D minor. '*By the pricking of my thumbs,*' she chanted, '*something wicked this way comes.*'

Flat-footed and heavy, silence smothered the room . 'The play,' gasped a small white-haired woman, clutching at a silver cross on a chain around her neck. 'You've quoted the play.'

'Worse than that,' said Sybilla Fraser, her fingers

wrapped gracefully around a champagne flute. 'She's quoted the witches.' Sybilla was draped in fiery silk that set off her golden hair and skin; her eyes were smouldering. She was, if anything, more beautiful in person than on screen.

But I could not get the girl on the hill out of my head. Neither Ben nor I had found any trace of her. Maybe she'd been a dream. Or maybe I'd left someone up there, dead or dying, alone on the hill as darkness fell.

I turned to leave, only to find that someone had stepped into the doorway behind me, blocking my way. The grey-haired Fury from the hill. In dark accusation, she raised her arm to point at Lily. At least, most people in the room seemed to think that she was pointing at Lily. But from my vantage, she was pointing straight at me. 'You've brought evil into this house,' she cried.

For a moment, no one moved.

'The curse only works in a theatre,' said Lily, rising. When no one answered, her bravura faltered. 'Doesn't it?'

'As of today,' said Sybilla, 'this house *is* a theatre.' She pointed at the door. '*Out.*'

'Christ, Syb,' protested Jason. 'She's just a kid. And it's not like we've started rehearsals. You don't have to do the bloody fiend-like queen thing yet.'

Sybilla's eyes flashed. 'You, too! Out.'

'*Fiend-like queen?*' he scoffed. 'You think that counts?'

Behind Sybilla, a large man with a paunch and grizzled ginger hair balded into a tonsure rose to his feet. 'A quote's a quote, laddie. And as the lady says, I gather we're to rehearse in this room. Informal-like, but, still, rehearsal's rehearsal. So out with the both of you.'

'Hell,' said Jason. Brushing by me and then past the grey-haired woman, he flung himself out the door. Eyes spitting fire, Lily followed.

The grey-haired Fury never moved. With Lily gone, she was now clearly pointing at me.

'Does either of them ken the ritual to counter the curse?' asked the ginger-haired man, of no one in particular.

It seemed an easy way out of the room. 'I'll show them,' I said. As I came to the old woman, she leaned in close. 'Put it back,' she said in my ear.

Put it back? Did she know about the knife? And if she knew about the knife, did she know about the body? 'Did you see anyone on the hill this afternoon? A body?' I asked, low enough that no one else could hear.

She shook her head. 'It's the blade you should be worried about,' she said, and then she scooted me through the door in Lily's wake. Behind me, it closed with a resounding thud.

'You *believe* all that voodoo twaddle?' growled Jason out in the passageway.

'It's about respect, not belief,' I said shortly.

'Tell that to Medusa in grey,' Jason retorted.

'Auld Callie,' said Lily. Standing there in a green dress with faux-medieval trumpet sleeves, her flame-red hair floating about her face, she was near tears of fury. 'She's playing one of the witches. The kids in the village think she *is* one.'

Auld Callie, I thought suddenly. *That was the name of the woman who'd found Sir Angus.*

'I thought I saw you this afternoon,' I said to Lily. 'On the hill.'

'Well, you didn't. You just saw Sybilla make a fool of me. And my grandmother *let* her.'

Had I been dreaming? Or was there someone else out there? The only way to find out was to go back. I started down the passage.

'Oh no,' said Jason, grabbing my arm. 'You're not going anywhere till you get us out of this.'

His grip tightened. It was going to be faster to give in than argue. There were rules that existed in the theatre that one must follow to avoid the curse. Silly as it may have seemed, when actors were faced with the curse they often decided it was just better to follow orders. Under my terse direction, Jason turned three times clockwise and then pounded on the door to the hall, asking to be let back in. Sybilla opened the door. *'Fair thoughts and happy hours attend on you,'* he said as he stepped back through it. Sybilla gave him a smile of incandescent triumph, and then, without acknowledging Lily at all, she shut the door behind him.

'Cow,' shot Lily. She spun around three times and crossed to the door, her knuckles paused a few inches out. 'What should I say?'

I glanced anxiously down the corridor. 'You have to quote from one of the lucky plays. Jason went with *Merchant of Venice*. Why don't you do *Midsummer*?'

She shrugged. 'Sure.'

'An old standby is *Hand in hand with fairy grace, will we sing and bless this place.*'

She looked back, her sea-green eyes alight with mischief. 'You should have said that up on the hill. It's a fairy hill, you know.' Before I could respond, she rapped sharply on the door, which opened to reveal Lady Nairn.

'Enter Lilidh Gruoch MacPhee,' said Lily's grandmother, and Lily stepped through the door, pulling me with her. Around the room, the gathered company strained forward to hear.

Exhaling sharply, Lily blew a strand of red from her face and fixed Sybilla with her gaze.

What you see when you awake,
Do it for your true love take;
Love and languish for his sake.
Be it lynx, or cat, or bear,
Leopard or boar with bristled hair:
In your eye, whate'er appears
When you wake, it is your dear:
Wake when some vile thing is near.

Whirling on her heel, Lily strode from the room, slamming the door so hard that the antlers rattled on the walls.

The company stood stunned. She'd known, of course, what to do, I realised. One would, growing up in this house. Her question to me had been no more than a tease; she'd known exactly what she meant to say. She'd altered a few bits here and there, remembering sense rather than exact phrasing, but the words were recognisably Oberon's – the King of Fairies to his sleeping wife Titania, the Fairy Queen. A love-trick, you could say, if you were in a charitable mood. A magical practical joke with razored humiliation at its core, though, would be more accurate.

'But that's not a blessing,' quavered the woman with the silver cross. 'That's another curse.'

Sybilla rose, coolly surveying the company, her eyes coming to rest at last on Jason. 'And how does the curse end? Oh that's right: *Titania waked, and straightway loved an ass.*' Sweeping across the room, she disappeared through a narrow door onto a balcony.

With a groan, Jason strode after her.

'Gallus lass,' said a deep Scottish voice. The ginger-haired man.

'Sybilla or Lily?' snapped Lady Nairn. She wore her hair swept back again today, and she was again in black, this time in a pantsuit.

'Take your pick,' the man said with a grin. '*Gallus*, from gallows,' he said in my direction. 'A compliment, in Scots. Cheeky, mischievous, daring.'

'As in "worthy of hanging", if you want to be literal

65

about it,' said Lady Nairn darkly. 'I will be raising gallows myself if we begin shedding actors before we ever get to rehearsals . . . Kate, meet the gallus Eircheard.' His name sounded like Air Cart, though with the breathy back-of-the-throat 'c' at the end of *loch* and *Bach*. 'The king's loyal servant Seyton in our production. And also the doomed King of Summer in the Samhuinn festival. Emphasis on "doomed".'

He winked at me. 'Marching merrily – if a wee bit hirplty-pirplty – to the sacrifice.' He took a few steps towards me, extending his hand, and I saw that he had the rolling gait of someone with a lifelong limp. One foot was encased in a strangely shaped and heavily built-up shoe.

'Eircheard,' Lady Nairn went on, 'meet Kate Stanley. Whom you may *not* monopolise until you have given her the chance to escape upstairs and freshen up.' To me, she added, 'I laid something out on your bed. I hope it fits.'

He raised his drink in my direction. '*Slàinte mhath*,' he said. 'When you're suitably tarted up to be given a drink, you can toast me back. I'll teach ye how.' His eyes bright with laughter, he turned away.

Before anyone else could stop me, I slipped out, running downstairs and out into the night.

6

I'd just reached the lane when a car turned into it up ahead and drew alongside me. It was Ben.

'She's not there, Kate.'

I started walking again, and he jumped out of the car and caught me by both shoulders, spinning me around to face him.

'I *saw* her,' I said stubbornly. 'Not Lily, obviously – but that doesn't mean she wasn't somebody else.'

'That's why I went back.'

I blinked. 'You . . .?'

'Went back,' he said. 'Checked every inch of the hilltop and as much as I could of the surrounding slope, just to be sure. She's not there . . . She was a nightmare, Kate.'

'She was real. And the gown that was draped over her was real, too. I touched it . . . It was blue. It had weight. It had *sound*, for Christ's sake.' It had cascaded back over her with the dry, rattling sound of rain in the desert.

'They do, sometimes.'

I let him drive me back up to the house, watching him as he drove. He'd battled demons of his own, once, in the aftermath of some operation turned bloody fiasco in Africa. I'd never learned the full details, only bits and pieces as his worry about me had come out and after I'd seen a few gruesome sights myself in the wake of searching for a killer two years before. I caught my breath. Was that what he was worried about? That this was some kind of delayed reaction to that experience?

'It wasn't a hallucination,' I said defensively as we walked across the terrace. At a bench near the door, I stopped and sat down, blinking back tears. 'I mean, the knife is real.'

'Another reason I went back.' He pulled the blade from his knapsack and lay it on the bench. Its pattern of coils and scrolls gleamed in the moonlight. 'You have no business going up there alone, Kate. No jacket. No torch. And no weapon. For Christ's sake, if she *is* real, there was – and maybe is – a killer up there. If you want to go back, at least ask me to go with you.'

'Where I need to go, actually, is Birnam Wood.'

He sat down on the bench, the knife between us. 'Kate – we need to talk.'

I stiffened. 'Not now.' I'd been afraid this was coming.

'I—'

'*Not now.*' I wanted to think about the knife. About the girl on the hill, dreamed or real. About the manuscript and Sir Angus's mysterious death. About anything but our parting. 'What are you doing here, anyway?'

'Consulting.'

I was used to the half-truths and tangents that were all he could or would tell me about the black hole of his career. The secrecy at the centre of his life was the only thing I'd hated about him, even though I understood it. 'For Lady Nairn,' I said, working it out for myself. 'Did Athenaide put you up to this?'

He smiled noncommittally.

Just then a slim figure walked around the corner of the terrace. Lily, still mad at the world, by the look on her face. 'Hullo,' she said sourly. 'Didn't expect to find you two out here.'

'We were just going in to dinner,' I said.

'Then I hope you're quick change artists. Gran's a stickler for dress in the evening. Show up in jeans, and she'll turn you away hungry at the dining room door.' Catching sight of the knife glinting on the bench between us, she sucked in a quick breath. 'Bit Tristan and Isolde, don't you think?'

Ben sighed and rose. 'Would you like me to keep it under my wing?' he asked me with a nod at the knife. 'Or do you mean to wear it into dinner? Presupposing that there's not a weapons check, along with a dress check, at the door.'

'This is Gran's house,' said Lily. 'Jeans, no. Daggers, yes. Though that's usually with kilts.'

'I think the company's jittery enough,' I said, handing the knife back to Ben, 'without giving them reason to wonder whether they've got a mad slasher in their midst.'

He dropped it back in his knapsack. 'See you inside,' he said, striding up the stairs and into the house.

Lily plopped down beside me. 'So tell me . . . why do you even *like* this stupid play? I mean, all Shakespeare does is rip off the old myths, stain a good king's reputation, and shove a really interesting woman out of the way.' She kicked at the stone pavement. 'Who in their right mind would just let a creature like Lady Macbeth fade out, off stage? I get my grandparents' obsession, living where they do, and with Gran's past on the stage, and all. But why you?'

I took a deep breath and forced my thoughts in her direction. 'I've loved Shakespeare since childhood, I suppose. Loved the stories. And it was mostly encouraged by my family. But *Macbeth* – that was different. That was rebellion. My mother hated it. Wouldn't allow a copy of it in the house. So I went looking for it. Naturally.'

Lily threw her head back and laughed. '*That's* the way to get kids to read Shakespeare. Tell them they can't.' She rose, dusting off her hands. 'Are you coming in?'

'In a few minutes.'

With a shrug, she flitted up the stairs in Ben's wake.

I leaned back against the wall, watching the moonlight play in the trees. *Tristan and Isolde*, she'd said, likening us to guilty lovers eager to proclaim their innocence with a symbol no one could mistake, laying a sword between them on the bed just before spies burst into their love nest. The reference attested to some fine schooling, probably private and outrageously pricey, but as for Ben and me, the kid was so far off base it was laughable. Epic lovers didn't let oceans or deadly feuds, or even death come between them. Ben and I had let the small twists and tugs of two careers pull us apart.

An American freelance theatre director with a specialty in Shakespeare and a home-base in London, I went wherever the jobs were – and in the wake of finding *Cardenio*, they were scattered all over the globe. As for Ben, it wasn't easy to explain what he did, especially since the word 'mercenary' made him snort in derision. Before we'd met, he'd left whatever special ops part of the British military or secret service had trained him, and formed a private security company whose bread and butter was protection of the sort he was probably discussing with Lady Nairn. But he also had a quiet side-specialty in missions too delicate or dicey for politicians to stomach. Missions that, being his own commander-in-chief, he could accept or decline at will. I thought of him as a modern-day Drake or Raleigh. 'You think I'm a pirate?' he'd asked, his voice cracking in amusement, when I'd told him that once, as we lay in bed one rainy afternoon.

'Not a pirate. A privateer.'

He'd shrugged off the distinction. 'What's a swash? Perhaps I should know, in case I ever need to buckle one.'

'I like you unbuckled, thank you very much,' I'd said. He'd risen over me, naked and beautiful, and I'd sunk back into the sheets, laughing. A week later, he had disappeared, and I had not known where he was – or whether he was still alive, for that matter – for two months.

In atonement, he'd arranged a week in a cottage in Ireland, overlooking the sea: just the two of us, he promised, some friendly horses, and a long unspoiled stretch of beach. And then I'd had a call from my agent.

'*Coriolanus?*' Ben had said in disbelief when I phoned to cancel the trip. 'In St Petersburg? Nobody even likes *Coriolanus.*'

And so it went, growing increasingly hard to make time for each other, and increasingly easy to chafe at the other's absence. In the calendar year-and-a-half that we'd been together, I figured that we'd actually been in each other's company for two months. Three, tops.

Then, on a bright morning in June, I'd walked to Ben's flat through showers of birdsong to find him staring absently out the big front window overlooking the Thames. He was wearing jeans and a green T-shirt that made his eyes look like a malachite sea.

'Do you want this?' At first I'd thought he was talking about breakfast. 'Us,' he'd specified in a voice that cancelled my hunger.

'Of course,' I'd said, swallowing hard. 'Look, about last night, I'm sorry. But I'm not the only one to—'

'God knows I'm no model of steady presence. But I miss one date for every three times you stand me up.' It wasn't an accusation, just a fact stated with a flat calm that I found far more frightening than recrimination or clever retort.

'At least you know where I am.' I'd tried for insouciance, but it came out with a peevishness that made me wince.

'Not here.' He'd given me a wry smile.

'But I'm starting to get really interesting work,' I protested. 'Chances that won't come around twice. In a few years, I might be more established. Able to line more things up in advance.' *Able to say no to the stray, wind-borne chance.* I'd left that last thought unsaid.

He'd watched the sunlight rippling like scales of gold on the river. 'What you and I have, Kate, it's . . . unusual. I'll wait, at least for a while, if you can tell me that you'll be there at the end of this tunnel – if you can tell me that there'll *be* an end.'

But I could not give him a date, and I would not make up the false spectre of one. In truth, I wasn't even sure I wanted one to exist. In perverse stubbornness, I stood mute, and in the silence, something snapped, sending a million invisible cracks spidering across the sky.

It was an amicable, if bittersweet parting. Very adult. I walked home in a small grey shroud.

'How long is "a while"?' Athenaide had asked. When I reported the rift I didn't know. I'd thrown myself into my work, which was thankfully plentiful all through the summer. I'd had no more than a few days of downtime when I'd had to fend off the foreboding that I'd made a terrible mistake.

Until now.

I rose and went upstairs to dress.

Laid out on my bed was a deeply V'd halter dress in silk of peacock blue. I very nearly turned around and went down to dinner in my grass-stained khakis. Only the notion of trying to explain why I'd done so made me shed them and slip the dress over my head. Pulling on the black heels I'd worn the night before, I smoothed down my hair and glanced in the mirror.

I was no majestic beauty like Ellen Terry, but given the afternoon I'd had, I was fairly presentable. In my mind's eye, though, the image that floated up to cloud the mirror wasn't the mermaid painting of a ferocious queen, but a girl with flame-red hair and a red slash across her throat, naked and bound beneath a fall of blue silk.

Tossing a bathrobe over the mirror, I went downstairs to dinner.

The crowd had filtered into the dining room, but people were still milling about, finding their places. At the door, Lady Nairn introduced me to Effie Summers, the white-haired lady who'd protested when Lily quoted the play. Effie's eyes widened. She looked from side to side as if my presence might make someone else burst into dangerous quotation, and scuttled away.

The table, set for well over twenty, was a Victorian

fantasy of china and crystal, with a pyramid of sugared fruit as a centrepiece. Before each plate a small enamelled bird held a card in its beak with the name. I found mine in the beak of a swan near the centre of the table; Jason was to my right. Eircheard was down at the end of the table, near a mutely sullen Lily. So much for learning to toast in Gaelic from Eircheard; I'd be toasting in Australian instead.

'Where am I to sit?' Sybilla asked with a pout.

Lady Nairn motioned to a still vacant place across from me. Frowning, Sybilla picked up the bird – a raven – with the card in its beak, turning it around so the whole table could read the neat black lettering:

HAL BERRIDGE.

'Who's Hal Berridge?' asked Jason.

Down near the end of the table, Effie Summers rose. 'The boy,' she gasped, clutching at her throat, finding the cross that hung on her necklace. *'The boy who died.'*

7

A cry of surprise rose and then died over the table.

'The first Lady M,' said Effie, her voice edging near hysteria.

Lady Nairn had been staring at Sybilla's card in consternation, but eyeing Effie's panic, she cut in briskly. 'He was a boy actor with Shakespeare's company, when women were banned from the stage and boys played all the female roles. The night before the premiere in front of the king at Hampton Court, he took ill and died.'

Effie leaned across the table towards Sybilla, her eyes wide and dark. 'Mere hours before the show was to start, this was. Only one other actor knew the role well enough to step into it: Shakespeare.' Her hands scrabbled like claws across the table. 'Don't you see? The death of Hal Berridge is what started the curse. *It's a warning.*'

Still holding the raven with the offending place-card in its beak, Sybilla was within a breath of tossing it into the fire and making a grand, irrecoverable exit.

'Who put it there?' asked a slightly amused Jason Pierce. No one answered.

With a sigh, I put down my napkin and rose. 'I'm sorry to have to disagree with Ms Summers, but that tale is – and was – no more than a hoax.'

All eyes swivelled to me. Even Lady Nairn looked confused.

'I have no idea who's to blame for its appearance tonight,' I went on, 'but the name Hal Berridge was first dreamed up at the end of the nineteenth century, by a theatre critic named Max Beerbohm.'

'The cartoonist?' asked Lady Nairn, her face pinched with concentration.

I nodded. 'Caricaturist, critic, novelist, man-about-town. A satirist at heart, and a brilliant wit. More in demand to liven up London dinner parties than Oscar Wilde. Shakespeare bored him. One night, he baulked at picking apart a production he disliked, and devoted most of his review to anecdotes about Shakespeare. Including Hal Berridge. Larded the whole thing with quotations from obscure historical sources, which made it convincing. So convincing, that his stories were swallowed whole by generations of actors, unchallenged by scholars. Problem was, he made them all up.'

'Do you mean to say that the curse – the whole history of it – is based on a lie?' asked Sybilla.

'A jest.' I smiled. 'I don't discount that some productions have been dogged by terrible luck. My personal favourite involves Charlton Heston's tights. But the bad luck did not have its origins in the demise of Hal Berridge.'

It was a strange prank, I thought. Not in good taste, for starters – mean-spirited, really. But obscure, as well. So obscure that it failed the first test of a good joke: that its audience should get it without reference to footnotes. The jester had surely been counting on someone to explain the joke: but in which direction? Effie's superstition or my scepticism?

The small enamelled bird trembled in Sybilla's hand. She was not yet ready to give up her grand scene.

Ben walked over and plucked the card from the raven's beak. Pulling a pen from his pocket, he turned it over, scrawled *HM the Scottish Queen* across the back, and tucked it back into the bird's mouth. 'Your Majesty,' he said to Sybilla with a little bow, holding out his arm.

Thank you, I mouthed.

She gave him a smile of such radiance that I winced. And then she reached up and ran a hand down the side of his face. 'Thank you, darling,' she said in a voice purring with satisfaction and promise.

Darling?

Small details of the past few days floated loose from their moorings and fell back down to earth in a new arrangement. I heard Lady Nairn's voice, as if in an echo chamber: *she's the one who's already got someone new on the line*. And Ben – he'd tried to talk to me, but I'd refused to listen, and then ducked behind Lily.

Bit Tristan and Isolde, she'd said, peering at the tableau of the two of us separated by the knife. Had she known? Had everyone known but me?

I felt myself flush and looked down. If I could have, I would have fled to upper Siberia, to cool off in the permafrost. But I was hemmed in by the ritual of a formal dinner. If I left now, I'd only make the scene worse, and my part in it more pathetic.

'So what happened to Charlton Heston's tights?' asked Lily from the far end of the table.

'Somebody doused them with kerosene,' I heard myself say, as if from far away. 'He was in an outdoor production that involved riding a horse. It can't have been very far, but the combination of friction and horse sweat heated up the tights to the point that Heston had to dash off stage crying *Get them off me, get them off* . . . Not very nice, for Heston, I suppose, but it makes for a mental picture that sticks.'

There was some laughter, and blessedly the focus drifted elsewhere. Normally, the nervous chatter about strange happenings during *Macbeth* productions would have fascinated me, but tonight the various Macbeths who'd accidentally stabbed Macduffs, and vice versa, the Lady Macbeths who'd taken tumbles during the sleepwalking scene – even the patron who'd committed suicide by diving headfirst from the balcony of the Met during a performance of Verdi's Scottish Opera – it all sounded dull as dust. At one point, Jason – not the world's most sensitive man – leaned over and asked whether I felt all right.

I could not look at Ben, but I couldn't keep myself from stealing the occasional glance at Sybilla. She had eyes only for Ben, whom she proceeded to monopolise all the way through dinner, without once acknowledging Jason's existence.

Or mine, for that matter.

I excused myself at the first possible moment, stumbling blindly down the corridor, finding myself in the deserted drawing room. I stood there for I don't know how long, numb and hollow, the very air scraping my skin raw. After a while, I heard voices approaching. Footsteps and laughter. The company coming back in for after-dinner coffee, no doubt.

I wanted neither coffee nor company. A small door near the front of the room led to a steep spiral staircase. I took it. It wound up and up through what I supposed must be one of the corner towers to a cramped landing and from there into a circular room. I stopped just inside. The whole room seemed to be singing. Directly across, a large window perfectly framed the hill. To the right, another window was open to the night, hung with wind chimes that gave the room its voice, from a high silvery ring to a rich dark bass. A wall fountain added the quiet laughter of water. Before a small fireplace stood two comfortable armchairs and a small table, and an antique carved chest sat beneath the hill-filled window. Other than that, the room was empty of furniture.

It was the chest that riveted my attention. In the middle

sat an immense silver bowl, flanked on one side by a rectangular mirror in an ornate carved frame, the glass spotted and dim with age; on the other side was a knife with a black hilt and strange undulating whorls running through the steel of the blade.

From even a short distance, it looked exactly like the knife I'd found on the hill. Had Ben given it to Lady Nairn?

I stepped through the room and bent close. Only then could I see that this knife had no runes running down the blade, and its edge was rounded and smooth. Oddly thick, too. It had never been honed.

'You've found my inner sanctum,' said Lady Nairn over my shoulder, and I jumped. 'The pieces at the heart of our collection. Cauldron, Mirror, and Blade. The inspiration for the production, too. The cauldron is Iron-Age Celtic. At least, the original is – dug up out of a bog in the Highlands in the eighteenth century. Too fragile for use, though, so what you see is a reproduction. The mirror is Elizabethan. Said to have belonged to the King's Men.'

'And the knife?' I asked, my breath tight in my throat.

'A modern copy.'

'Of what?'

'Of one found on the hill.'

'Tell me about it,' I said.

She was watching me as if she could see through me to the past and maybe also the future. 'I had it made for the stage—'

'The original.'

Crossing to the chest, she set it in my hand and motioned me to one of the armchairs by the little fireplace. Turning to sit, I saw on a hook by the door a shimmering length of blue silk, scaled like a dragon. Knife in hand, I stared at it as if at a ghost.

'Ellen Terry's Lady M costume,' said Lady Nairn with some amusement. 'Or an approximation thereof. Made of silk embroidered with beetle wings. How perfect is that, for a queen who was a witch in all but name? Though perhaps the beetles would disagree.'

I was still staring at it, open-mouthed, remembering the peculiar dry pattering sound of the gown over the body on the hill, when she started her tale. The knife had been found at the end of the eighteenth century, she said, during the first archaeological dig on the hill. It had not turned up in a spadeful of earth, though. Instead, it had been plucked, early one morning, from the grass where it lay gleaming in the weak sun. How it got there was never discovered. Even to amateur eyes, though, it was clearly ancient, fitted with a black hilt and etched with letters no one could read.

'What happened to it?' I asked, my mouth dry.

'Evil rumours gathered around it – mostly whispers that it was the blade that had killed Macbeth. The real one.

'Grim,' she went on, 'but it made it valuable. For nearly fifty years, it passed from father to son, as one of the great treasures of the house. Then it was sold to pay a gambling debt. Soon after that, the family very nearly lost the entire estate.'

She cleared her throat. 'Coincidence, no doubt, though not everyone thought so. By the time a son of the house tried to trace the knife, however, it had passed beyond reach. Then, in 1857, William Nairn, my husband's great-great-grandfather and the paterfamilias at the time, claimed to have found it, once again, just lying in the grass on the hill-top. This raised some eyebrows – not least his wife's – even at the time, but he never wavered in his story.

'However he came by the knife, thereafter he would not let it out of his sight. By the following summer, when his son – my husband's great-grandfather – was born, the knife seemed to have taken an uncanny hold over him that not even a new child could shake. He spent his days watching the play of light across the blade. At night, he grew restless, walking the battlements at all hours, knife in hand, looking towards the hill. His wife began to wonder whether the thing had bewitched him.

'On the eve of Samhuinn in 1859, he disappeared in a gale. A young servant girl later claimed she had seen him struggling up the hill, though how she could have seen through the lashing rain that night put her story in some doubt. In any case, neither William Nairn nor his knife were ever seen again.

'To the end of her days, his wife believed that he had been taken by the Good Folk, who had reclaimed the knife as theirs, and had taken him along in the bargain.'

The tale faded slowly, lingering long after her voice had stilled. 'It was William's grandson who met the dark fairy on the hill,' she said presently.

The old woman that Sir Angus believed had sent something along to Ellen Terry. The phrases I'd heard whispered on the wind swirled around in my head. *You shall be queen here-after . . . Nothing is but what is not . . . She must die.* Chased by a few clearer phrases: *Evil rumours gathered around it . . .* Most strident of all: *You have brought evil into this house.*

I shifted uncomfortably. 'Lady Nairn . . . do you think the knife could have anything to do with whatever Sir Angus found?'

'I shouldn't think so. Why?'

I looked up from the knife in my hand. 'I found a knife very like this today.'

Her eyes narrowed. 'Where?' Before I could reply, she answered her own question. 'You went up the hill.'

'I'm sorry.' I swallowed. 'It – the knife wasn't all I found. I also found a body, or at least I thought I did. I thought – at first – it was Lily.'

'My God, Lily?'

'Obviously, it wasn't,' I quickly explained. 'It must have been a dream or a nightmare.'

She drew in a sharp breath. 'That explains some of your rushing about, I suppose.'

'There was no body.' I got up and went to the window. 'Ben went back, to make sure.'

'And the knife?'

'He has it.'

'Is that where you met Auld Callie?'

I nodded. 'Lily says the kids in the village think she's a witch.'

'As the saying goes, *you say witch, I say wise* . . . If she's a witch, she's a white one. Caledonia Gorrie is worth heeding.'

'Where did you get this?'

She put out her hand for knife, and I gave it back. 'My husband had it made for me. It's a copy of the original.'

I frowned. 'But if the knife was lost in 1859,' I said slowly, 'how could he have a copy of it made?'

'We still have the dig notes from 1799. There's a full-scale drawing.'

My heart turned over. 'May I see it?'

'Come,' she said, heading swiftly out of the room.

8

As we neared the foot of the stairs, we heard a strange, almost inhuman keening, and every hair on my body rose. Ducking back into the hall, we found that most of the company had drifted off to their rooms and the lights had been dimmed. Those who remained had gathered at the French doors, thrown wide open to the night. The sound was drifting in from outside.

Among them was the white-haired woman who'd been so nervous about the curse, Effie Summers . . . another of the witches. Looking back at us now, her mouth shaped into a long narrow O of fear and a low, whining sob laid a line of guttural bass under the strange song filling the air.

'Effie,' said Lady Nairn, 'what's happened?' Gripping my wrist, she drew me through the room.

Shaking her head, Effie pointed at the doors.

I eased forward to look outside. The moon had set, leaving the night sky awash in stars. The pines ringing the house seemed to scour the horizon as they swayed in the wind. On the lawn below, candles marched in a flickering circle, and in its midst stood a woman.

No – a girl. Lily, her dress rippling in the wind. Slowly, she began to raise her arms skyward, and I realised that the keening was swelling from her throat. At her feet lay what looked like a small gleaming fountain. I stepped onto the balcony, squinting through the darkness. It was a mirror, laid on the grass.

Behind me, a voice cracked into prayer. '*Our Father, who art in heaven, hallowed be thy Name . . .*' Gripping her cross before her, Effie sank to her knees. Beside her, Lady Nairn raised one hand to her mouth and went still.

On the lawn below, Lily swayed a little. Her arms, still rising, had reached shoulder height, the long sleeves streaming behind her. Still singing her wordless song, she began to spin.

'*Thy kingdom come, thy will be done, on earth as it is in heaven . . .*' Effie growled.

Lily's spinning quickened, her feet stamping the ground.

All along the front of the house, other windows were thrown open, filled with dark figures staring into the night. Still others, I realised, were gathering in the hall behind us.

'. . . *Deliver us from evil,*' whispered Effie. '*For thine is the kingdom, the power, and the glory, for ever and ever. Amen.*'

Down on the lawn, Lily noticed neither Effie nor the gathering crowd. Her voice had lost all contact with individual sounds, stretching into an inhuman whine, a moaning of wind or of ghosts. Arms stretched high over her head, she was spinning so quickly that she'd become a blur.

Holding the cross out before her, Effie suddenly rose and strode to the balustrade, lifting her voice with all the wrath of a prophet. '*Thou shalt not suffer a witch to live!*'

A gust circled the lawn, rattling the windows, and most of the candles went out. With a great cry, Lily flung down her arms and fell to the ground.

For a moment, there was no sound but the wind roaring in the trees. Her face taut, small flecks of foam caught at the corners of her mouth, Effie turned to Lady Nairn. 'Thou shalt not suffer—'

Lady Nairn rounded on her, cutting her off. '*Effie!*'

She blinked. Her voice had dissolved to a dry whisper. 'This is what comes of allowing satanic rituals under your roof.'

'Wiccan, not satanic,' said Lady Nairn shortly. 'There's a difference. As for "allowing", I wasn't consulted, and, technically speaking, she's not under my roof.'

Still clutching the crucifix, Effie was panting a little. 'Pray for her,' she said quietly. Turning around, she glimpsed the gathered crowd, scanning it from one end to the other. 'Pray for her,' she said again. 'Pray for us all.' With one last glance of reproach at Lady Nairn, Effie stumbled back through the room, the crowd parting to let her through in silence.

'Puts the "effing" in "complete effing lunatic",' said Jason as she disappeared through the door. Around him, the silence splintered into nervous laughter.

Down on the lawn, Lily stirred. Lady Nairn had seen it,

too. 'Exhibitionist little fool,' she said under her breath. 'If I ever get my hands on Corra Ravensbrook, I'll bloody well throttle her.' She glanced at me. 'Meanwhile, if you see Ben, tell him I want to see him. And that blasted knife.' With that, she hurried out.

So much for seeing the drawing of the original knife, I thought with irritation. And who the hell was Corra Ravensbrook? Not knowing what else to do with myself, I wandered back up towards my room.

'Kate,' said Ben as I reached the top, and I stopped as if I'd run into glass. He was perched on a sofa in a small sitting room just off the landing. He'd changed back into jeans and a sweater. Resting his chin on both fists, he was staring at a low table before him.

I went to the doorway and stopped again. Sybilla was nowhere to be seen. He rose. 'I'm sorry.'

'You're a colossal bastard, you know that? You should have told me.'

'I tried.'

'You should have made sure.'

'Fair enough.' He eyed me in silence for a moment. 'Look, I didn't know you would be here, or I wouldn't have come. I won't stay.'

'Surely we can both act like professionals for the length of one weekend,' I said stiffly.

'In that case, you want to take a look at this?' He

motioned towards the table in front of him. On it lay my knife, his BlackBerry, and a pad of paper crossed with a line of bold lettering. He'd transcribed the runes from the knife onto the paper.

I crossed the room and looked down at the pad:

ᚱᛁᚠᛞᛏᚨᚱ

'You read runes, Professor?' His old nickname for me, from my roots in academia, though I'd left the ivory tower for the theatre long before I'd achieved that exalted status.

'Two R's, a couple of slanted F's, and some butterflies,' I said shortly. 'In other words, no.'

'Thank God for Google,' he said, handing me the BlackBerry. On the web, he'd pulled up a table of runes and their modern equivalents. In spite of myself, I was interested. Staring at the small screen, I lowered myself onto the arm of the sofa. 'The F's turn out to be A's,' he said, 'and the butterflies are D's.'

Letter by letter, I translated the word into the modern Roman alphabet, and he wrote them in large block letters beneath the runes:

RIADNADR

'Make any sense to you?'

I shook my head. 'Couldn't even tell you the language.'

'Bloody useless. Don't you at least know a bona fide professor of runes we can call?'

'Past midnight?'

'How about Eircheard?' asked Lady Nairn.

I jumped. She was standing right over us. Next to her stood Sybilla, in jeans and a jacket, her hair floating about her face in wild ringlets. She was impossibly, preposterously beautiful. I could have throttled her.

'Is that it?' Lady Nairn asked, with a glance at the knife.

I nodded and Ben held it out to her, but she just stared, as if it might bite. It was Sybilla who reached for it in the end, her fingers drifting across Ben's.

'Eircheard is a professor?' I asked.

'He'd find that amusing,' said Lady Nairn. 'No. He's a swordsmith. Which means he actually *uses* runes, in addition to studying them.'

'What does it say?' asked Sybilla, looking wide-eyed at Ben.

'That, *bella donna*, is what we're trying to figure out.'

Bella donna? I got saddled with 'professor' and she got 'bella donna'? Okay, so it meant 'beautiful lady' in Italian. Like it or not, that was accurate. But I had a sudden savage jolt of pleasure that belladonna was also the name of an ancient and potent poison.

Lady Nairn touched my arm. 'It was Eircheard who made the stage knife. The one you saw downstairs. My husband let him refit an old byre down the road into a smithy, and took the knife in payment. Eircheard researched it for months, poring over every bit of knowledge he could glean about the knife William Nairn found on the hill. He must know as much about it as anyone.'

'Do you think he made this one?' asked Ben.

Lady Nairn tapped her chin with one finger, thinking. 'Do you know, I believe a late-night visit to the gallus Eircheard is in order.'

'I'll come too,' announced Sybilla.

The house was quiet and dark. On the lawn, the candles still stood in Lily's circle, though their flames had long since blown out. Leaning at crazy angles, some of them had spilled wax onto the grass.

It was one of those startlingly clear nights of late autumn, hushed as if waiting. A faint scent of wood smoke, thin as a dim memory, haunted air otherwise clean and crisp. Something about the star-scattered depth of the blackness overhead squelched small talk. I tried not to notice Sybilla holding Ben's hand.

We stepped quietly down the drive, footsteps crunching on the gravel, and into the road. With the hill looming over us, we turned left, skirting its steep slopes. Five minutes later, we came to the road that we'd driven in on the night before, leading off around the hill to the right. Crossing it, we stayed on the lane which plunged straight ahead into thick woods on either side.

We heard the smithy before we saw it, the rhythmic clank of steel hammering steel gradually separating itself from the measureless moan of the trees. *Clang, clang, clang. Pause.* And then again.

I glimpsed lights through the branches, and then the trees fell away. In the midst of a wide field sat a low stone building with only three sides; the fourth was open, like a doll's house, to the Scottish elements. Inside, the forge glowed white, yellow, and orange in the night. Eircheard, in a leather apron, gloves, and goggles, was hammering a long rod of white-hot steel against an anvil.

We strode up to the edge of the smithy. Though the night was crisp and the building was entirely open at one end, the heat coming off the forge made the whole place uncomfortably warm. 'Eircheard,' called Lady Nairn, but got no answer through the hammering. With every stroke, bright burning flakes of scale scattered around the anvil like falling stars, as if we'd walked unawares into the midst of some creation myth, watching a squat god forge new constellations for the deeps of space. 'Eircheard,' Lady Nairn called again. Still no answer.

Taking the knapsack from Ben, I drew out the knife, brushed past Lady Nairn, and slid it onto the anvil alongside the long piece of steel he was shaping into a sword. The whorls and curls in the finished blade undulated like a living thing in the firelight.

For a split second, the hammer stilled midair before

clattering to the ground. Pulling me close, Eircheard wrapped an arm around my neck. Something flashed in his other hand, and I felt the prick of cold steel against my throat.

'Where'd you come by that blade?' he demanded.

9

Against my back, I could feel Eircheard's chest heaving for breath, the dry skitter of his heart. He gave me a quick shake. '*Where?*' he growled.

Before I could answer, Lady Nairn stepped into the light. 'Not from me,' she said.

'Fegs,' said Eircheard, dropping me so quickly it almost felt like a shove. 'It's yourself. Why didn't you say so?' Tossing his knife on a large round table, he stared at it, panting. Then he turned to me. 'Saw the knife, lassie, not yourself. Thought you'd taken what wasn't yours to take. No harm done, though, eh?' He extended a meaty hand, now empty.

Still dazed, I shook it.

Ben had seized the rune-engraved knife from the anvil the moment Eircheard grabbed me. With a nod at him, Eircheard pulled out a handkerchief and wiped his brow, beaded with sweat. 'I'd still like to hear where ye came by that blade, though.'

'On the hill,' said Lady Nairn. Behind her, Sybilla was pale.

The handkerchief stilled in the middle of Eircheard's face. He peeped out from under it. 'Dunsinnan Hill?' When Lady Nairn said nothing, his glance slid to me.

'I fell asleep. It was there when I woke.'

'You ken it's a fairy hill?'

I nodded.

'Then you're either gallus, lass, or goamless. Foolhardy, or just plain foolish.' He shook his head, thrusting the handkerchief back into his pocket.

His eyes flashing, he thrust out his other hand. 'Let's have a wee look at it, then.'

Ben glanced at Lady Nairn, who nodded. Reluctantly, he set the knife in Eircheard's hand.

Eircheard moved so that the blade caught the firelight better. Pulling off his goggles, he drew a pair of wire-rimmed glasses from another pocket and shoved them on his nose, which he put right down near the blade. He looked, I couldn't help thinking, like some young, ginger-bearded Santa Claus.

He looked up, his eyes locking on Lady Nairn, his breath exhaling in a long, whistling sigh. 'I'd like to say I made it, but no. I've made another very like it, but mine has no runes. Nor an edge, neither.'

'Edges can be honed,' said Lady Nairn softly, 'and runes can be added.'

'So they can,' he replied, 'but the pattern in the blade is forged into the steel in its making, and cannot be changed.

And that pattern's not mine. You ken your own, see, like you ken your own bairns.'

'Can you read the runes?' asked Sybilla.

He ran a stubby finger down the centre of the blade. Almost a caress.

'We tried,' I said, 'but all we came up with was RIAD-NADR. Which I can't make head or tail of.'

Eircheard cocked his head, his eyes suddenly twinkling, the way they had when he'd teased me before dinner. 'So that's what the delegation's about it, is it?' His gaze rested on me. 'Don't sell yourself short. You've used Norse instead of Anglo-Saxon runes, but other than that, you've got the tail – the last half of the word – right. It's the head, I expect, where you went wrong. The first three letters are worn, see, and you missed some strokes.' Handing me the knife, he went to a workbench and rustled about, returning with a rag and a can of some kind of grease. As the four of us leaned in around him, he dipped the rag into the grease and passed it over the bright surface of the blade. As if he'd revealed invisible ink, other lines appeared, faint but there, so that:

ᚱᛁᚠ

became

ᛒᛚᚠ

97

In other words, he explained, RIA became BLO, so that the inscription read not RIADNADR but BLODNÆDR. 'Runic shorthand,' he said, rubbing his chin thoughtfully, 'for *Blod Nædder*. Blood Adder.'

'Blackadder's vampire brother,' quipped Ben.

Eircheard looked up in reproach. 'Ye can say *Blood Serpent*, if it'll keep you from laughing like a daftie at what's not funny. Likely it's the knife's name. A common kenning – poetic metaphor, that is – for *sword*.' He ran a finger along the back of the knife. 'Makes sense. It's a classic Sassenach shape, this. Called a *seax*. A single-edged short sword or long knife, often with this angle along the back. Terrible fierce cutters, these are.' He glanced up at Ben. 'Nothing funny about the damage they can do.'

'Whoever made this knife,' I said slowly, 'must have seen Lady Nairn's.'

'Or the dig notebook,' said Lady Nairn.

With a grunt, Eircheard limped into the shadows at the far end of the building and rummaged about, returning presently with a roll of photocopies in oversized paper. Dropping it on the table, he thumbed through the pages and drew one out, unrolling it and weighting its corners with an old coffee mug, a small hammer, and two twisted bits of steel. It was flecked with burn marks and ringed with coffee-cup stains. 'Working copy,' he said sheepishly, smoothing a hand over the stains, as if he might wipe them away. 'Never left this building.'

98

The drawing was life-sized, delicate lines done in pen and ink, and though the ink had faded a bit, it was a near photographic copy of the knife in my hand. The runes were smudged, as if someone had rubbed them out. But the pattern in the blade was remarkably exact.

'But that's a drawing of this knife,' I said slowly, 'not the other way round.'

Eircheard sat down suddenly, running a hand over his bald head. 'So it is, lassie, so it is.'

Lady Nairn frowned. 'That drawing was made in 1799. Are you suggesting that this is an eighteenth-century knife?'

A grumble of dissent rose from deep in Eircheard's throat. 'Cannot be,' he said, shaking his head. 'It's pattern-welded, like I said. A process that was lost for centuries before archaeologists and smiths put their heads together in the twentieth century and worked it out again.' He touched the knife with one finger, as if might disappear. 'So you see, it's either under a hundred years old, probably well under – or nigh on a thousand.'

The fire had cooled from white and lemony yellow to richer oranges. In the silence, the whole room seemed to flicker. The knife, too, seemed to be flickering.

'So if it's the original of these drawings—' I swallowed hard.

'Then nigh on a thousand would be right.'

I stared at the blade, its strange markings exactly mirrored in the drawing. 'That's impossible,' I said slowly. 'Isn't it?'

For a moment, all of us stood in a circle staring down at the knife.

'Could a blade survive that long in this condition?' asked Ben. 'Still bright, still holding an edge?'

'I don't ken of any,' said Eircheard. 'But I don't ken any reason why one couldn't, were it taken care of properly. Not on a Scottish hill, mind. Or *in* one, at any rate. Our hills are a wee bit damp, if you haven't noticed, and damp's no friend to a bonnie bright blade such as this. But taken care of – well, steel's wonderful strong stuff.'

The heat of the forge was suddenly making me dizzy. The battle in 1054 had pitted Macbeth's Scots against Malcolm's invading army of Sassenach Northumbrians – a combination of northern Anglo-Saxons and Viking mercenaries. Had one of them carried this knife?

Nigh on a thousand years old. I found myself staring at a corner of the drawing. In a fine copperplate hand, someone had written a few lines of description. I read them aloud: *Black hilt of fine-grained wood. A polished steel guard. Barbarian inscription down the centre of the blade, and another around the hilt.*

I looked up. 'Another inscription?'

'Well now,' Eircheard said, stroking his beard. 'I'd forgotten about that.'

I picked up the rag and dipped it in the oil, brushing it around the metal ring at the base of the hilt, where it joined the blade. Very faintly, runes appeared, running around the perimeter in an unbroken ring. No beginning, no end – not even any divisions between words. 'It's a round,' said Eircheard softly. 'A phrase that begins and ends with the same word or syllable. But on the blade, see, that word'll only be engraved once. So that the phrase runs round and round in a never-ending circle. Strong magic, that was thought to be.'

Pulling a pad of paper towards him, Eircheard turned the knife slowly until he found a word he recognised, and began transcribing, first dividing the runes into words, and then putting them into the modern alphabet:

ᛒᚢᛏᚠ ᚦᛏᛗ ᚾᚠ ᛏᛗ ᛒᛁᚦ ᚾᚠᛈᛁᚾᛏ ᚠ

BUTO THTE NA NE BITH NAWIHT A

He bit his lip, concentrating. '*Buto* plus an abbreviation for *Thætte*, "Except that",' he murmured. 'Northumbrian dialect. Then you skip to *Bith*, or "is", negated by *na ne*, or "not". Then *nawiht*, "nothing" and *a*, or "always".' He scribbled out the whole sentence in block letters:

EXCEPT THAT WHICH IS NOT NOTHING ALWAYS

'Sounds more Eeyore than Warrior,' said Ben.
Eircheard ignored him. 'Like I said, it'll make a phrase

101

that begins and ends with the same word. Let me think . . .'
He sat staring at the blade, his fingers rubbing his temples.

'Jesus, Mary, and Joseph,' he said after a few minutes, his breath coming out in a long whistle. 'It's *Bith*.' Hunching over the pad, he wrote out another line, rearranging the words:

BITH NAWIHT A BUTO THÆTTE NA NE BITH

'What's it mean?'

It was Sybilla who'd asked the question, but it was me he looked at as he answered it. 'Nothing ever is but that which is not,' he translated.

'Begins and ends with "not",' said Ben. 'I like it. It's even a round in modern English.'

The whole smithy seemed to be rising, spinning around me.

'You know it in its shorter form, lass, no?' Eircheard asked softly.

I nodded, and my throat moved, but no words came out. It was Lady Nairn who spoke, her voice no more than a dry whisper. '*Nothing is but what is not.*'

Ben frowned. 'Sounds familiar.'

'It's Shakespeare,' said Lady Nairn.

'It's *Macbeth*,' I said, the words seeming heavy, slow, impossible as they floated away from me.

Sybilla glanced at all of us in turn, frowning. 'But I

thought you said the knife was a thousand years old. How can it quote *Macbeth* if it's a thousand years old?'

'It can't,' I said. 'It would have to be the other way around.'

'Runes can be added,' Lady Nairn said again, her voice harsh as a crow's.

'In Old English verse?' shot Eircheard. 'Complete with alliteration, correct stress, and decent meter? Possible, not likely.'

I ran a hand through my hair. 'But that means swallowing the notion that Shakespeare not only marched up to Scotland and saw this knife, but that he could read Anglo-Saxon – in runes, no less. It's absurd.'

The blade winked mockingly in the light. *Nothing is but what is not.*

Eircheard went to a cupboard where he drew down five mismatched tumblers and a squat, wide-shouldered bottle of single-malt Scotch. 'A blade called Blood Serpent, ringed with an unbroken verse about the intertwined web of being and not being – that's a blade that has killed plenty,' he said as he splashed a finger of amber whisky into each glass and shoved them around the table. 'But Ben's right. The inscription doesn't read like a warrior's thought.' His eyes met Lady Nairn's.

'It reads like magic,' she said.

He nodded. 'I think you've found a ritual blade. Never seen one, mind you, but there are whispers of them in the old stories. If that's the case, maybe it wasn't this blade that Shakespeare somehow knew. Maybe it was the ritual it was used for.

'Religious rites have longer lives and a wider reach than any single object used within them. If you found a thousand-year-old chalice engraved with a line from the Latin Mass, should you infer that someone who'd quoted the Mass in English yesterday, or four hundred years ago, for that matter, had seen that particular cup? Or only that they both knew some form of the same rite?'

The fire in the forge had cooled even further, to a simmering red that brought the pattern of the blade to life. It seemed to writhe and undulate, coiling and uncoiling like the creature it was named for.

'What ritual could the blade be used for?' Sybilla's eyes glittered.

He shrugged. 'Hard to say.' He poured out another splash of whisky and wiped his forehead with his arm. 'Neither the Anglo-Saxons nor the Celts were shy about sacrifice, though. There's a Roman account of Celtic priestesses dressed all in white, moving through sacred groves dispatching victims with sacred blades, cutting their throats and letting the blood run into a cauldron.' He drained his glass, sucking the last drop of whisky through his teeth. 'Like I said, I haven't seen a ritual blade. But I've handled a fair few that've seen hard use in battle. Something strange happens to blades that have drunk a fair lot of blood. They wake. Not quite alive, but, still – sentient, somehow. And some of them grow to want more. Blood, I mean.'

For a moment, there was no sound between us save the guttering of the fire. Then, from the back of the smithy, came a shrill cry. We turned to hear a grating sound floating in through a narrow window high up in the wall. The noise grew into a rumbling, rattling slide like a sudden fall of rock, and then faded to silence.

For an instant, no one moved. Then Eircheard and Ben sprinted out of the open front and around the corner towards the rear of the building. Snatching up the knife from the table, I followed close behind. A stack of crates and pallets under the window had collapsed in a heap that was still groaning and settling. Just beyond, what looked like a small shed clung to the back wall. *He lives in a lean-to backing up to the smithy*, Lady Nairn had said. It looked like a closet barely big enough for Eircheard to lie down in. The door was ajar.

'Come out, you wee rotten scunner,' growled Eircheard.

Inside, nothing moved.

He yanked the door open wide, shining a flashlight inside. The bedroom, neat as a monk's cell and as small, was empty.

'Can't've gone far,' said Eircheard.

Ben turned and shone the flashlight about the area around the back of the smithy. Patiently, he and Eircheard began scanning the ground for clues.

They'd just disappeared around the far corner, heading into the field beyond, when something caught my eye off to the right. Someone moving stealthily back into the woods that divided the smithy from the hill, and from Dunsinnan House.

If I yelled, the intruder would take off. If I waited for Ben and Eircheard, or went to fetch them, the intruder would be long gone.

My grip on the knife tightening, I slipped into the woods in the wake of the shadow.

The woods turned out to be a stand no more than ten feet thick, after which they opened up again. At the edge of this clearing, I paused. It was not a work of nature. It was a carefully shaped circle, lined on the inside with a ring of immense old beech trees, the last of their leaves rustling like dry paper. Inside the trees hunched a circle of standing stones. Not as tall or as massive as Stonehenge. Lumpier, somehow. Older and less refined. And in the darkness, far more powerful. A brooding, ancient power.

Wind swept through the treetops. I glanced up, watching them bend and lash against the star-scattered circle of night overhead, their moaning rising from a low murmur to the howl of an oceanic gale. Leaves floated downwards in large, eddying flakes, as if the sky were snowing darkness. I shivered, and drew my jacket closer around me.

When I looked back down, a figure stood in the centre of

the stones. The silhouette, black on black, of a woman from an earlier century, her long hair and gown stirring in the wind. A dry hiss left her lips, and she began to glide towards me.

10

The blade in my hand burned with a cold fire; it seemed to buzz at a pitch so low that I felt rather than heard it, as if it were resonating with some strong source of energy. Backing a few paces I turned to run, but her hand whipped out and gripped my wrist. I yelped, but only a squeak came out.

'It's me, Kate,' she whispered. '*Lily*.'

Lily alive, or Lily dreamed and dead? My heart thudding hard in my chest, I slowly turned around.

Her face was pale in the faint light, her wide-set eyes large and dark. What had looked like the gown of a Renaissance lady resolved into a coat with a tight bodice and long flaring skirts. Above the coat, her throat was a pale column, unmarked.

'Do you think it's true?' she asked in a low voice. 'Do you think that's a ritual knife?'

I glanced down at the dagger and then back up. 'How much did you overhear?'

'All of it.' She grinned sheepishly.

From over at the smithy came a shout. '*Kate!*' It was Lady Nairn.

'Damn,' said Lily. Her grip on my arm tightened. 'Please don't tell her I was here. I'm already entry A-1 on her shit list.'

I was staring at her wrist, gripping my arm. On it was a small tattoo I hadn't noticed before. A delicate five-pointed star. A pentacle, the symbol of witches – of Wicca, the neo-pagan religion of witchcraft.

Lady Nairn called again. 'Please,' whispered Lily, her eyes pleading. 'I won't tell a soul.'

Fifteen going on twenty-five, Lady Nairn had said of her. In the days following my parents' death, I'd been very like her. Unpredictable, and a little wild. But she was, at heart, a good kid. 'Go on, then,' I said with a wave of the hand.

She flashed a wide smile. 'Thanks. You're awesome.' She dashed across the circle, in the direction of Dunsinnan House.

In a bright, evil flare the image of her body, bound and naked on the hilltop, flashed across my mind. 'Lily,' I said, stepping after her. At the far edge of the clearing, she looked back. 'You'll be all right?' I asked, feeling suddenly both frightened and foolish.

'No worries. We're practically in the back garden. Besides, we're too bloody far out in the sticks for a bogey-man to bother in the first place.' And then she was gone, her passing barely stirring up a rustle amid the deep bracken.

I was turning to head back to the forge when a voice whispered out from the woods at my back. *Why did you bring the dagger from that place?*

I whirled. 'Who's there?'

Another voice snaked from the right. *It must lie there . . .*

And a third voice came from the left. *Dunsinnan must go to Birnam Wood.*

The wind tossed in the trees, and I thought I saw shadows glide in towards the stones as all three voices spoke at once: *She must die . . .*

Gripping the knife close, I turned slowly about.

'*Kate!*' This time, it was Ben's voice. Flashlight beams criss-crossed the night, and footsteps pounded across the field towards the woods.

Thirty seconds later, a flashlight beam strafed through the clearing. Eircheard and Ben crashed through the trees in its wake.

Ben took one glance at the knife and looked up at my face. 'Are you all right?'

'Someone was here.' I swallowed hard.

'What happened?' asked Eircheard.

I shook my head. 'Nothing. Voices. I saw nothing but shadows.'

Ben was scanning the ground around the stones.

'Kids,' said Eircheard with contempt. 'At a certain age, the village kids love to scare themselves silly telling ghost stories in the circle. Make a night of it, they do, by heading over to snoop about the forge. A few of them, you can see their eyes all starry with dreams of lame smiths forging magic rings and dragon chains. Most of them, though, are just idling, hoping to see me burn the place down, maybe the woods with it. Sodding little pyros.'

'Not kids,' I said. *Lily had been here, only moments before. Was I sure of that?*

I looked at Ben. 'They were the same voices I heard on the hill this morning.' That time, there had also been a body.

I told them what I'd heard, thinking through the words as I did. *Why did you bring the dagger from that place? It must lie there . . .* Lady Macbeth's cry to her husband after he's killed the king, with the dagger made singular. 'Put it back,' was the gist of it.

Auld Callie's words, exactly.

But the voices had stolen Sir Angus's words, too. *Dunsinnan must go to Birnam Wood.*

All in all, a fairly clear message: drop the dagger, go after the manuscript – or whatever it was that Sir Angus had been after.

Who would need to tell me that in the guise of ghosts in a stone circle? And tack on a death threat, besides.

She must die.

Who must die?

'Jesus,' said Eircheard. 'No, not kids.'

Lady Nairn and Sybilla walked into the clearing. 'A stone circle,' cried Sybilla, clasping her hands in delight. 'I knew it. I *knew* there was a place of power hereabouts.'

'Everything all right?' asked Lady Nairn.

'I'd like to go to Birnam Wood,' I said.

She looked from me to Ben and Eircheard and nodded. 'I've organised a reading of the play on the hill at sunrise,' she said. 'To begin the celebration of Samhuinn. We'll head to Birnam directly after that.'

It would do. It would have to.

Sybilla was standing in the middle of the circle, swaying a little. 'The knife belongs here,' she said. 'I can *feel* it.'

Irritation suddenly overwhelmed me. 'The stone circles of Britain – and I am assuming this is one of them – are Neolithic,' I said crossly. 'Stone Age. The druids were Iron Age Celts. And if Eircheard is right about the knife, it's late Anglo-Saxon, which makes it medieval, at least five hundred years after the fall of Rome. So where that knife belongs is anybody's guess, but it isn't here.'

Sybilla wasn't fazed. 'It's a sacred knife, and this is a sacred place. *It belongs.*'

I gave up. 'I'm heading back to bed.'

'High time we all followed suit,' said Lady Nairn.

At the smithy, Eircheard gave me a leather scabbard for the knife, and then we made our way back to the house in silence. Orion the hunter, his star-studded knife at his belt, was just rising into the south-eastern sky. To our left, the hill seemed to lean down over us, heavy with menace. Or maybe it was just mockery.

We said goodnight to each other at the upstairs landing. Sybilla's hand lingered on Ben's arm in unspoken invitation, but he discreetly disengaged himself and walked me down the hall. Just outside my door, he stopped.

His clean, slightly spicy scent sped through me until my whole body ached for him.

Nothing is but what is not.

'Hide it,' he said, with a glance at the scabbard in my hand. 'Are you okay with that? Or would you like some help?'

'I can take it from here, thanks.' *Bastard.*

He opened his mouth to say something, but thought better of it. 'Goodnight, Kate.' Turning the corner, he walked ten feet down the corridor. Lady Nairn had given him the room right next to mine.

In that, I thought I saw the long hand of Athenaide.

Just inside my room, I leaned back against the door, wondering whether I was about to cry or scream. In the end I did neither, splashing water on my face at the sink instead.

A small fire was burning cheerily in the fireplace; the luxuries of life with staff, I thought. Towelling off, I sank into one of the armchairs before the fire and drew the knife out of the sheath, watching it ripple in the light. My outburst in the circle had left me shaken. Not just because it had been childish, but because for all that my facts were right, it was Sybilla who had hit, however messily, upon some truth. Not about the knife, but about the place. There *was* something strange about that circle in its clearing in the woods. A place of power, she'd said. And she was right. I'd felt it too. But I wasn't as sure as she was that the power there was entirely benign.

'She must die,' the voices had chanted. *Who must die?*

The phrase was Shakespeare's, I was certain of that. But not from *Macbeth*. On my phone, I pulled up the web and entered it into a Shakespearean search engine. *Othello*, *Caesar*, and *Henry VIII*, came the answer. Spoken about Desdemona, Portia, and Queen Elizabeth.

I frowned. It had been an old jest between my mentor Roz Howard and myself that my auburn hair and dark eyes, the tiniest hint of a hook in my nose made me look like Shakespeare's queen, in her days as a princess. It was a jest that Ben had kept alive. But the voices couldn't have known that. Could they?

I clicked on *Henry VIII*, pulling up the phrase in its context.

She must die
She must, the saints must have her; yet a virgin,
A most unspotted lily shall she pass
To the ground, and all the world shall mourn her.

Lily, I thought raggedly. They hadn't threatened me: *they'd threatened Lily*. And I'd let her walk out of that circle alone.

I stood up, filled with sudden dread. I had no idea where

114

her bedroom was. On this floor, I thought. I had to find it –
and her – if it meant knocking on every door in the goddamned house. I was already striding for the door when I
heard a quiet tap from the other side and flung it open.

11

Lily stood in the hall in loose flannel trousers and an old black Belle and Sebastian sweatshirt, a book and a small wooden box under her arm, her face bright with excitement. 'I couldn't sleep. I've had an idea, and, well, I saw your light on, so I thought I might as well run it by you.' She bounded into the room. 'You aren't angry with me, are you?'

In my confusion, I felt as if I'd been bounced by Tigger. 'For listening? I would've done the same thing at your age. Maybe at my age.'

'I'm not normally so nosy. Only, I saw the knife out on the terrace before dinner, and afterwards I heard you talking about it in the little sitting room, and I was so curious . . . is that it?'

It lay where I'd left it on the table, shining in the firelight. 'Yes.' Setting the book and the box on the table, she caught it up, hefting it in her hand.

I glanced at the book. The cover showed a tall stone standing alone in a green field under lowering clouds, a single bright ray of sun illuminating the scene. It was titled *Ancient Pictland*, by Corra Ravensbrook.

Using both hands, Lily began waving the knife in slow motion, almost like Tai Chi. 'Do you think it's really a thousand years old?'

'I don't know.' How could it be? How could it *not* be?

'It'd be really cool to use this in the Festival, don't you think? For the fight between the kings.'

'For a stage fight?'

She smiled. 'You heard Eircheard. It's a ritual knife. And it's an old ritual we're staging.'

'Lily – it's a *real* knife. An edged weapon.'

'I know. But it's a king-sacrifice we're staging, just like the one that killed Macbeth.'

'Staging being the operative word.'

'It would be *authentic*.'

'It would be insanely reckless,' I said incredulously. She was from a theatrical family, for heaven's sake.

'You know Eircheard and Jason are taking those roles? If anyone could handle a real knife, it'd be those two.' She gave me a wicked smile. 'And there'd be those who'd be happy enough if Jason came out a little the worse for wear, I can tell you that. It's one thing for Sybilla to have been asked to be the Cailleach; she's been a member of the Beltane Fire Society – the festival organisers – since long before she hit the big time. It was idiotic, though, when Jason was cast as the Winter King. That role has always been cast from members of the Fire Society. Like Eircheard as the Summer King. Amateurs who really care about the show and the myths behind it. But Sybilla wrote a big cheque, and *voilà*, we're saddled with Jason. Bit uncomfortable, now that they're not speaking. On the other hand, there's no speaking in the show, either, so maybe their feuding won't matter a toss.'

She blew a strand of coppery hair from her face. 'But I'm in no position to complain, or even say *I told you so*, because I'm an exception to the rule myself. Too young, you know. Gran pulled some strings for me.'

Holding the knife tightly, she raised both hands towards the ceiling, as she had out on the lawn. 'I'd like to be the Cailleach one day. Ever so much more than Lady Macbeth. I mean, the Cailleach's, like, the real thing, isn't she? It's her show. She chooses the champions who will be kings, and she sets them against each other. They're fighting for the right to marry her, at least in her young person of the Bride, as much as anything else.'

She brought her hands down to her hips. 'Do you know what the name Dunsinnan means?'

'No.'

She marched over to the windows. I'd drawn the curtains wide, letting the windows frame the hill. 'Fort of the Nipple,' she said with a flourish. '*Dun* means fort in Gaelic, and *sine* means nipple. You can't really tell from this side, but next time you drive in from the main road, have a look. The whole hill looks like a woman's breast.' She threw open the middle window and leaned out into the night. 'Weird name, for a military hill.'

I had my doubts, having met a few of Ben's friends. Some of them were capable of seeing breasts and penises in the void of outer space. But I held my tongue.

'The archaeologists all say that the ramparts on the hilltop are the remains of an Iron Age hill fort . . . but there's no evidence of that. I mean, buildings, yes. But not of a fort or castle specifically. And it doesn't seem, militarily speaking, the best place around. I mean, the hill just to the east, the King's Seat, is higher. So if the point is really male and military, like all the histories say, don't you think you'd build your fort next door?'

Privately, I doubted her expertise in judging suitable spots for fortification from an Iron Age point of view, but it didn't seem the right time to remark on it.

'But they didn't.' Pulling back inside, she turned and hopped up to sit on the sill. 'For over a thousand years, the stronghold was on Dunsinnan. Which would make all the sense in the world if it were less a fort and more, say, a *spiritual* stronghold. Especially given its shape and the stone circle at its base.' She crossed her arms in triumph. 'I think it was a temple complex.'

She was looking at me as if daring me to disagree. As I made no move to shout her down, she went on. 'There are records, you know, of Macbeth coming here to consult with witches. But, like, change that title to priestesses, and you've got a Stronghold of the Lady. The great Goddess worshipped in this land for millennia before the coming of

Christianity . . . I'm not talking about *Scot*land, mind you.'
Her nose wrinkled in contempt. 'The Scots are newcomers,
invaders from Ireland.' She threw her arms wide. 'This – the
whole of central Scotland – was Pictland, the kingdom of
the Picts. That's what the Romans called them. The Priteni,
they called themselves – or something like it. Their actual
language is lost. Celtic, but closer to Welsh than Gaelic,
apparently. In any case, it's where we get the word
"Britain",' she said proudly. 'Dunsinnan – or the stretch of
country from Dunsinnan to Scone – was once the spiritual
centre of Pictland, the land of the Priteni. The spiritual
centre of *Britain*. Ground zero for Goddess worship, right
here. How cool is that?'

How much of this was being regurgitated from Corra
Ravensbrook, whoever she was? No matter – Lily was
clearly very taken with her version of history. If I wanted
her to consider another viewpoint – a sane one, say – I'd
have to proceed with caution. 'But isn't Dunsinnan where
the battle was?' I asked aloud. 'The great battle between
Malcolm and Macbeth in 1054? Sounds military to me.'

She shrugged. 'Wouldn't be the first battle fought at a
temple. Think about it: Malcolm's army came down from
Birnam, just this side of the river from Dunkeld, where his
grandfather had been the lay abbot. Even then, way back in
the eleventh century, Dunkeld, see, was a bastion of
Christianity.' She jumped down from the sill and began to
pace before it. 'Don't you see? They weren't just fighting for

the throne, Malcolm and Macbeth. It was a holy war. A Christian crusade against the old faith. Against the Goddess. A war to enforce Christianity and disinherit women. To banish the old Pictish ways that properly belong to this place.'

She pointed at the book with the knife. 'That's where Ravensbrook's so interesting. The usual Wiccan stuff – well, it tends to be airy-fairy. All about how gentle and good Wicca is, in tune with the earth, and the natural rhythms of life, you know? Which is fine – more than fine. But the old Goddess religion, it could be *fierce*. It didn't just pay lip service to the notion that death is a part of life. It embraced that fact fully. If you know what I mean.'

I frowned. 'You mean sacrifice?'

'*Blood* sacrifice,' she said with teenage relish. 'Sacrifice of the king. There are a lot of stories about king sacrifice, you know,' she babbled on. 'The Samhuinn Fire Festival among them, but they weren't always just stories. Corra says the myths are memories of old rites.'

She held up the knife. 'According to Eircheard, this is a ritual knife. And it's also the knife that killed Macbeth. *King* Macbeth.' For a moment, we both stared at the firelight and moonlight playing on its surface. 'Ergo, the knife killed Macbeth in a ritual killing. *Macbeth was killed as part of a ritual sacrifice of the king.*' She let one finger stray across the runes on the blade. 'I mean, what is a ritual knife *for*, but ritual?'

Who was this Corra Ravensbrook, I wondered again. The ideas of king-sacrifice she seemed to have planted in Lily had been discredited among academics long ago. A growing number of neo-pagans, especially the more intellectual sort, dismissed much of it as wishful thinking. But Lily, I realised, was in no mood to hear the voice of reason.

'Seems like rotten timing,' I said mildly, 'to slice up your leader and feed his lifeblood to the gods, just when you're on the run, looking for a place to make a last desperate stand.'

'King sacrifice would never have been common. Performed only in times of great need, to settle some extraordinary debt with the gods. And what greater need than the destruction of your whole civilisation?' She grinned. 'Hey, apocalypse threatens, you'll do anything. Reason goes right out the window.'

It was the most sensible thing she'd said in some time. I sighed. 'All the old histories say that it was Macduff, fighting for Malcolm, who killed Macbeth and set his head on a pole. Not priestesses. Even Shakespeare used that part of the story.' It was one of his most blunt stage directions: *Enter Macduff with Macbeth's head.* So preposterous that it was a dicey moment, on stage: audiences had been known to laugh.

Lily waved off the authorities. 'And who wrote those histories? Monks! Christians. Busily writing the goddess and her priestesses out of existence. I imagine Macduff found the pole, all right, and took it up as a trophy, waving it

122

about. But it was the Celts, not the Christians, who worshipped heads. Decorated their sacred spaces with them. Submerged them in wells, boiled them in cauldrons, believed they could speak. It would have been Macbeth's own people who wanted his head as a talisman. By taking it, I reckon Macduff ripped the heart out of whatever will to fight they had left. A sort of grim Capture the Flag, if you like.'

'If you're right, it didn't work out any better for them than for him, did it?'

'No,' she said sadly, 'not much.' She crossed the room and set the knife back down on the table and stood with her hands on her hips, staring into the fire. 'He was the last Celtic king. The last king of the Priteni. But because of him, not everything was lost.'

She was starting to make Macbeth out to be a Scottish King Arthur.

'The old religion survived, you know. It just went underground. Really deep. Especially in places like this. Out in the sticks now – think what it would have been like in the eleventh century.' She turned to me, her eyes gleaming with excitement. 'So . . . imagine Shakespeare coming through with a troupe of travelling players. Imagine him glimpsing, somehow, a rite preserved from the old days by women descended from the priestesses of the ancient Pictish goddess. What would he do with it, do you think?'

Presupposing all her ridiculousness were true, I knew

exactly what Shakespeare would have done with it. He was a magpie, a pack rat, when it came to plot, borrowing and stealing from everywhere. And magic made good theatre. Spectacular.

'He would have written it into a script,' I said quietly.

'Now *that* would make your bloody play interesting,' said Lily.

No, I thought, that would make it explosive. It was titillating enough to suggest that he'd put in a real spell or some rite of casting a circle – at least one that people once thought was real. But those could be found on the pages of grimoires and witch-hunting manuals. They weren't entirely lost. Putting in a rite of sacrifice preserved from an otherwise lost pagan religion – hell, if we were talking about the Picts, it was pretty much a lost civilisation – that was something else entirely. Never mind the obvious fascination for Shakespeareans. Every neo-pagan, every Christian, every scholar of Britain's history, every journalist who wanted to sell papers or air-time would be salivating over it.

I cleared my throat and said aloud what a responsible adult ought to say. 'That's a lot of ifs.'

'And one cold, hard, thousand-year-old piece of evidence,' she said with shining eyes.

Nothing is but what is not.

'I'll tell you one thing,' she said, 'even if he got it wrong – painting something as evil that wasn't, really, I'd still want to read it. I'd even forgive the irritating old git for tormenting every schoolkid in modern Britain, just for preserving it at all.' She turned to me. 'So, what do you think?'

'That I need to think.' I felt as if she'd just gone after me with a baseball bat.

Picking up the wooden box she'd brought along, she opened it. Inside was something covered in black silk. 'I brought my tarot cards,' she said. 'Want a reading, while you think?'

I glanced over at the clock. I'd have to be up in three hours. 'Could I take a rain check on that?'

She jumped up. 'Oh lord. So sorry. You've got to get up for Gran's early morning hike up the hill, haven't you?'

'You're not coming?'

She snorted. 'Let's see. *Macbeth* and a cold walk up the hill, or my warm bed and a nice morning's lie-in. No bloody contest. But I don't think you have a choice. So of course we can do it later . . . just as long as you let me corner you at some point. I bet your cards will be really interesting. Besides, you'll like my deck. It's a *Macbeth* deck.'

She started for the door. 'Lily – what were you doing out on the lawn tonight?'

Halfway across the room, she stopped. 'Charging the mirror.'

The mirror that had been in the middle of her dance. 'What does that mean?'

She sighed. 'I'm trying to learn to scry. To see things in a mirror. But you have to learn how to empty your mind, first. And also charge your mirror. Fill it with energy. Kind

125

of like you'd charge a mobile phone, but the energy's different. Natural. Mostly, you charge them with moonlight.'

She turned back with a mischievous smile. 'Like I said, goddess-worship had to go underground. But it never entirely died out. Not through all the battles, not through all the burning years. And now, it's coming back. People are returning to the old ways.'

'Including you?'

'Among others.'

'What do you want to see?'

She shrugged. 'Same as everyone else. My first love. My future.' Her eyes met mine. 'My parents.'

I took a deep breath, but said nothing. There was nothing useful I could say.

'I heard you lost yours,' she said in a small voice. 'What happened to them?'

I sighed. 'They were diplomats. A small plane and bad weather in the foothills of the Himalayas. A lethal combination. I was fifteen.'

Her eyes were growing glassy. 'Better than the motorway outside Preston.'

In the fireplace, a log disintegrated in a shower of sparks. 'There's no good place for it.'

Her voice shrank. 'They were driving home from visiting me down at school.'

I locked my eyes on hers and held them. 'It wasn't your fault, Lily.'

After a moment she shrugged. 'I *know* that. Lots of expensive therapy.' She gave me a watery smile and looked away. 'But sometimes it's hard to feel it. When did you stop missing them?'

Was this it? Was this why she had sought my company? A toxic combination of guilt and longing. Poor kid. No wonder she was acting out. 'Never.'

She looked back sharply.

'Only the hurt loses its sharpness, gradually,' I said more gently. 'And other things grow up and change the balance of things. It doesn't go away. But it does become bearable. Does that make sense?'

'Thank you for not saying it will all be fine.'

'You're welcome.'

'Did I tell you that you look nice in that dress?'

I'd followed her to the door. Having entirely forgotten what I was wearing, I looked down and saw Lady Nairn's peacock-blue silk. 'Thanks. Your grandmother lent it to me.'

'It was my mother's.'

I looked up aghast. *What the hell had Lady Nairn been thinking?* 'I'm so sorry. I had no idea.'

She smiled. 'It's okay. You look a little like her. Besides, she'd have liked you. I like you too.' Squeezing me in an impulsive hug, she opened the door and pattered off down the hall.

And I like you, I thought, staring after her.

*

I was turning back into the room when I heard another door open and glanced back. Sybilla emerged from Ben's room in a flame-coloured kimono. Seeing me, she nodded, her eyes sly with triumph as she swayed silently down the hall. As if the flames from her kimono had brushed me with kerosene, I felt waves of heat sweeping around me, the blue silk disappearing in a whoosh of yellow and red, my skin liquefying, melting into puddles at my feet.

I looked up to see Ben standing in the doorway, watching me, his face a blank.

12

I closed the door and shut my eyes, squeezing Ben from my thoughts.

Imagine Shakespeare coming through with a troupe of travelling players, Lily had said. *Imagine him glimpsing, somehow, a rite preserved from the old days by women descended from the priestesses of the ancient Pictish goddess. What would he do with it, do you think?*

Now that would make your bloody play interesting.

That was the understatement of the season.

Her notion echoed the Nairn legends, but one-upped them.

It was plausible, or at least possible, that Shakespeare had at some point come north. It was plausible that had he ever glimpsed a real magical rite, some hocus-pocus current during his lifetime, he would have slipped it into a play. But a survival of some pagan sacrificial rite, kept alive by a secret line of priestesses?

That was entirely fucking preposterous.

Except for the knife gleaming on my table.

A knife that was, according to Eircheard, a thousand years old.

Nothing is but what is not.

It would make sense of the manuscript's disappearance, I thought. Had anyone recognised it for what it was, it would have been deemed demon-worship, in those days.

Which made putting such a thing in the script in the first place entirely inexplicable, even if he had it at his fingertips. Why court such disaster, with a king who fancied himself both a target and a skilled hunter of witches?

And in any case, he wouldn't have had such a thing at his fingertips, because it didn't exist. It couldn't.

And besides, a cook wanting paper to line a pastry tin or start the day's fire made equal sense of the disappearance . . . except that in 1911 Ellen Terry had passed on evidence that the manuscript still existed.

Dunsinnan must go to Birnam Wood.

I looked out the window, willing day to come. But the moon just hung there in the west, a wide teasing smile in the night.

Suddenly exhausted, I slipped the knife in its scabbard under my pillow, and fell instantly to sleep.

I woke with a shriek to find myself on my knees in front of the mirror, the drawn blade in my hand. I dropped it, and it fell to the deep carpeted floor with a soft thud.

I scooted back, staring at it as I might stare at a snake.

It must have been five minutes before I could move.

What was it Eircheard said about blades that had killed? *Some of them grow to want more. Blood, I mean.*

When I finally dressed, I walked in a wide circle around it.

Only at the last minute could I bring myself to touch it. I couldn't just leave it there, after all, lying in the middle of the carpet.

I threw a towel over it, scooped it up, deposited it in the bottom drawer of the dresser, and shoved a small pillow on top of it. And then I fairly ran down the stairs.

We'd been told to gather in the hall at six-thirty sharp, ready for a brisk walk. Auld Callie, who lived in the village on the other side of the hill, was meeting us at the top. Everyone else had wandered in by 6:35 – except Effie Summers. A check of her room revealed a bed that hadn't been slept in. 'I thought I calmed her down enough to at least stay the night,' said Lady Nairn in irritation.

'Gone off to pray for all our sins,' said Jason.

'God knows you could use it,' snapped Sybilla.

Ten minutes later, we left without Effie.

In the grey light of dawn, the hill was quiet. In wellies and an old green Barbour jacket, Lady Nairn led the way. The rest of us straggled behind her in a long line. Laughter rippled up the hillside. It was hard to reconcile this slope, quietly drowsing, with the menacing creature that had loomed over us in the night, much less the mist-shrouded nightmare I'd traversed yesterday afternoon.

The Fort of the Nipple. The Stronghold of the Goddess.

The only goddess around this morning was Sybilla, who looked as if she'd just walked off a Ralph Lauren shoot, with high caramel-coloured boots, khaki trousers, and a short tweed jacket that fitted so well it appeared to have grown on her. She'd pulled her thick curls back into a pony-tail.

Why couldn't it have been her, I thought savagely, *whom I saw dead on the hill, instead of Lily?*

I strode forward to catch up with Lady Nairn. 'I had a talk with Lily last night,' I said, panting a little. She'd meant it when she'd said the walk would be brisk. 'After everyone went to bed.'

'Oh?'

'I hadn't realised she was Wiccan.'

'Wiccan, my foot,' said Lady Nairn, stabbing the hill with an ivory-handled walking stick. 'She's read a few books. Lit some candles. Had that ridiculous tattoo incised into her wrist.' She looked sideways at me. 'If she'd done that on my watch, it would've cost her a month of Sundays in pun-ishment, but that was when her parents were still alive. Did she show you the book?'

'If you mean *Ancient Pictland*, yes.'

She snorted. 'Wretched woman. Here Lily is, having barely outgrown Harry Potter, reaching for something else in the weeks after her mum and dad died. Lights upon Corra Ravensbrook.' She said the name as if it were poison in her mouth. 'Next thing I know it's Corra this and Corra

132

that. Equally fictional as Potter, you know, but a lot less amusing. And pretending to be *history*.'

We'd reached the base of the final summit, and she stopped to rest for a bit, letting the remainder of the company catch up. 'She has glamour, though. I'll give her that. In her prose, at any rate. No idea what she looks like.'

She gave me another sideways glance. '*All is delusion, nought is truth.* One might be able to forgive it as a dram of piss-poor scholarship and a whole damned cask of wishful thinking, except that it's not – *she's* not delusional. It's deliberate. She's making money, hand over fist as I understand it, off people who are . . . are reaching out for something. And more than the money, I suspect, she's feeding on their admiration. Which makes her, in some ways, frankly vampiric. I'm not coming from the same place as Effie, you understand. I'm not equating what Ravensbrook does – or Wicca proper, for that matter – with demonic evil. I'm speaking about misleading vulnerable people, many of them still half children. A much more mundane, infuriating, and hard-to-pinpoint evil. You can't exorcise it. You can't prosecute it. You can just hope the child comes to her senses.'

We crested the summit and stood watching the straggling line of people below. Beyond, the sun slowly crept across the valley. 'It's not that people shouldn't yearn for something more. Especially young people who are hurting, like Lily. It's that Ms Ravensbrook offers easy, pat answers. Recipes, really.' She turned and wiggled her fingers, her voice taking on the witchy tones of a Disney fortuneteller. 'Take a pinch of dragon's blood, add a little nakedness under the full moon or the dark of the moon, and throw in nine knots in a red thread, and *poof*, you will tap your true power. And find wealth and happiness, too.' She sniffed. 'It doesn't work like that. No religion works like that.' She stopped again, hands on her hips, the walking stick jutting out at an awkward angle. 'If you want the truth, I suspect Ms Ravensbrook isn't much of a Wiccan herself. Probably a bored housewife.'

She took a deep breath and forced a smile on her face. 'Apologies for the rant. You hit a sore spot, as you might have guessed by now.' The others were catching up, filing into the bowl of the summit in ones and twos.

'You said she feeds on her readers' admiration,' I said. 'How?'

Lady Nairn groaned. 'She has a website, with an email address. You can write to her. So Lily did. Or does, I should probably say.'

'They have a regular correspondence?'

'God no. Or I *would* be ballistic. But I know Lily's written to her more than once. And that she's responded. Wouldn't surprise me, you know, if Lily's antics on the lawn last night were Corra-directed.'

'Why?'

She looked out over the valley below. 'I've read a little about Wicca myself. And what Lily was doing: it was

134

sloppy. Maybe that's just a teenager, improvising. On the other hand, Lily also improvises her clothing. That should give you a good indication of her style in general.'

Sloppy was not a word that went with her fashion statement. Romantic, one might say. But not sloppy.

Lady Nairn pointed north-west across the valley. 'Birnam Wood. Right about there.'

What had drawn Sir Angus there?

Behind me, I heard shouts of laughter. Ben and Sybilla were playing some private game of tag. Bright-eyed and golden, Sybilla was running, I realised with sudden misgiving, straight towards the pit where yesterday I'd seen Lily lying dead. Or thought I had.

Glancing back like some eager Daphne luring on her Apollo, she did not see the hole opening just in front of her. Ben shouted, and she caught herself right at the edge. She looked down, and her mouth opened wide in surprise, and then horror; a cry caught in her throat. A swarm of flies rose around her like dark thoughts, and Sybilla took one step back and simply wilted.

Ben, already running, reached her first, catching her mid-faint. '*Jesus God*,' said Eircheard. Behind him, a scream rose in waves of panic.

I knew before I got there what they were seeing. A naked young woman, strangely bound, with her throat cut. Surely the body by now beginning to decay. Steeling myself, I walked forward and looked down into the trench.

But there was no body, naked or clothed. There was only blood, curdling from red to brown, filling the trench like a shallow bath. Next to me, Lady Nairn's face was taut with revulsion. '*Blood will have blood,*' she murmured.

Interlude

30 April, 1585
Dirleton Castle, Scotland

The countess had the English lord shown up to her in her private aerie in the old lord's hall, a circular room beneath a vaulted dome high in one of the oldest towers of the castle. The servants were terrified of the place, thinking it haunted, and she'd made no effort to combat that fear, finding it useful. She was content, up here, to be served by her old nurse and one faithful manservant, both of whom would die for her.

Lord Henry Howard was dark of complexion and stealthy in demeanour, a battle between disdain and hope permanently etched in his face. On one finger he flaunted a signet she recognised: a phoenix. The emblem of Mary of Guise, the mother of Mary, Queen of Scots.

It was both unmistakable and deniable, and she admired its combination of cleverness and discretion.

For it was unsafe, most decidedly unsafe, to carry a token pointing to Queen Mary, the king's mother, who'd been forced to abdicate the throne of Scotland in his favour when he was thirteen months old. Eighteen years ago, that had been, or nearly so. Long imprisoned in England and persona non grata in Scotland, the queen remained a focus of rebellion in both kingdoms at once.

'A true king of Scotland would not baulk at delivering real support to the rightful queen of England,' said Lord Henry. Setting down his wine, he rose to go. 'The throne, of course, must belong only to Stewarts, and of royal blood.' He cleared his throat. 'Such a king, the queen would back.' He looked at the countess with mocking eyes, but hers could be as cold as his were.

He had left soon after, and she'd watched him go with a coolness that belied the froth boiling in her blood. *Stewarts of royal blood*: it described both herself and her husband, another Jamie Stewart, older and braver than the pigeon-hearted boy who occupied the throne. And yet a man whom she had, more or less, under her thumb.

The message, of course, had been from Queen Mary. *Support me, and I will support you.* Or at least, *I will not contest you, if you can win and hold the crown.* The countess had little sympathy for the queen languishing in comfortable imprisonment in a remote English castle. The woman had just signed her son's death warrant, so badly did she want a crown: and not the Scottish one, which she had always thought beneath her.

It was less the queen's ruthlessness than her incompetence, however, that irritated the countess. For it was the countess's misfortune to be born with the capacity to rule that Mary lacked, but a lineage that gave her no real road to power: her Stewart blood, though royal, was bastard, and through the female line. Even so, in her youth in her father's Highland strongholds, she had listened more than once as old powers of darkness decreed that one day she would be a queen. She had exulted at the thought, even at the age of ten or twelve, and she had been doing her best to help fate along ever since.

Now she went to a chest and pulled from its velvet wrapping a dark mirror. This she fixed to the end of a long leather strap hanging down from the apex of the dome, allowing it to twirl a little, this way and that, over the centre of her work table.

She had taken the mirror, long ago, in payment from the English wizard, Dr Dee. Unknown to her parents, who thought she was frequenting the warehouses full of the world's silks and jewels, feathers and spices, she'd spent that cold February in Antwerp working her fingers to the bone, helping Dr Dee copy a rare manuscript of angelic magic. But when she had finished, he'd refused to pay the price they'd agreed upon: knowledge. She'd wanted teaching: to learn the Great Art. What he offered, in the end, was a purse of silver. As if she were a whore. She, an earl's daughter.

She'd burned the pages she'd copied one by one till he was on his knees and weeping. And then she'd tossed the rest into the air above the hearth. As he hurried to pick them up, she'd taken the mirror and left.

She did not know what it was made of, or who had made it. It seemed a work of magic in itself. But she'd taught herself to scry in it. Quite a feat, as Dr Dee had told her it was known to show fire and blood to those who could not wrest it to their will.

At a nod, the old nurse banked down the fire, moved one chair near to the table, and left. Palms down on the table, the countess sat still before the dangling mirror, gazing obliquely at its surface, barely brushed by firelight and moonlight, letting her mind touch upon Lord Henry and then drift. Letting the question form and shift like clouds: *Is he the one? Is he the man who will make me, at long last, a queen?*

Clouds misted the surface of the mirror though she knew there were none, or few, in the sky. And then they dissolved and she saw, quite clearly, a face with dark half-moon brows and a high forehead. A pointed chin. Delicate features and pale skin. What made this face arresting was a luminous, yet precise, quality of eye.

A young man, barely more than a boy. The king's age, or thereabouts. Perhaps a year or two older. He was not a face in her mind, she realised suddenly. He was a reflection of flesh and blood, caught in the mirror.

She turned, and he froze, caught stepping from the space between tapestry and wall. He'd thought her sleeping, perhaps, or entranced. *How long had he been there? How much had he heard and seen?* The consequences of treason, which the conversation with Lord Henry most certainly was, were unspeakable. The consequences of witchcraft, which is what the mirror-gazing would be counted, were worse.

If he'd run, she'd have called the guard and had him killed before he could say a word. But he stepped out and bowed with a brash flourish and a flush in his cheeks that was oddly beautiful. One of the English players, she saw.

Young, expendable, and eminently unbelievable in his word against the countess, a favourite of the king.

She summoned him forward with a crook of one finger, and obediently, he came. Diane de Poitiers had been only a year or two younger than she when she'd first seduced her king, twenty years younger than herself. This boy, common though he might be, looked to be the same age, or thereabouts, as James. Hitching the king to her skirts as her lover was not, at present, the likeliest road to consolidating her power: but the countess believed in keeping all roads open. A little practice with a boy would do no harm, and it might cool the sudden burning in her blood.

She ran a finger down his cheek. He trembled under her touch, and not from fear. She untied one lace of his plain doublet, and then another. Saw a sardonic brow half lift. He would neither fight nor flee, then. But would he rise?

She was down to his fourth lace before his hand closed around her wrist, and he drove her back against the wall, the tapestries billowing out from the force of it as young, strong hands slid up around her.

He pulled her back to the table, clearing it with one arm,

lowering her on her back before him. Even now, in the twilight of her beauty, she knew she was resplendent, showed to best advantage in low firelight and candle flame. She let him watch, savouring for a moment the appreciation in his eyes, and then, beneath the dark mirror now swaying above them like a pendulum, she pulled him into her.

She saw, once, much later, their reflection in the mirror. A beast with two backs. She said as much, under her breath, and he looked up and laughed. And then they rolled to the floor.

She lost count, after a time, of the rising carillons of pleasure that beat through her blood at the insistence of fingers and lips, eyelashes and tongue. He was a master of tension and release. He was not, as she'd thought, inexperienced at love.

As the first traces of dawn lightened the horizon, even he lay sated and spent. Standing at the window, she could see the Beltane fires kindling in the distance on the low rises that passed for hills in this flat land bordering the sea. The preachers could thunder all they liked, but even when the farmers listened to them quaking in fear, when it came to the fertility and well-being of their land, their crops, and their herds, they feared to break with tradition more. No matter how pious they might be at other times, on two nights of the year, Samhuinn and Beltane, they kept stubbornly to the old ways. Older, in fact, than all but a very few could possibly imagine.

There was a knock at the door. She nudged the boy with her foot, and he grunted and pulled himself behind a tapestry. A messenger stood just outside, the sheen of sweat from a hard ride still glistening on his face. 'My lady,' he said with a quick bow. 'The king comes here tonight.'

She caught the tip of her tongue between her teeth in her excitement. 'Madness,' she said under her breath. 'You're mad to say it.'

'The plague has broken out in Edinburgh; His Majesty rides hence with his lordship, your husband.'

As she dismissed the man, a wild surge of elation coursed through her. By nightfall, the king would ride under her battlements, but if she had her way, he would not ride out again. At least, not this king.

The king is dead, long live the king.

She hardly noticed as the player picked up his doublet, and with a sly smile, bowed and left.

WOOD

Who can impress the forest, bid the tree
Unfix his earth-bound root?

13

Yesterday there hadn't been enough blood; today its thick, metallic scent was suffocating. No one could survive the loss of that much of it. Whoever she'd been that I'd seen the evening before, she was dead now. *But where was she? And who?*

Whoever she was, I'd left her alone, dead or dying on the hill as dusk fell. And now she was gone.

I glanced from the blood-spattered trench back to Sybilla lying on the bank. On the grass, for a moment, she lay like the body I'd seen the day before. But she was dressed, her arms and legs unbound, her neck intact, and her chest rising and falling. She was coming to, Ben right beside her. I felt a twinge of regret. *Why couldn't it have been Sybilla?* I'd thought, as we started up the hill: something one shouldn't wish on anyone, even in passing, even in a private moment of jealousy.

'We need to find Effie,' Ben said quietly.

I did a double take. I'd been thinking of the unknown woman seen at the edge of a dream, but Effie was also missing.

Her voice shrilled through my memory: *Thou shalt not suffer a witch to live*. I'd assumed – I think we all assumed – that her words were aimed at Lily. Maybe so. But suddenly they seemed a double-edged sword. Effie, after all, had been set to *play* a witch.

Next to me, Lady Nairn said, 'Oh dear God.' She tried Effie's cell phone, but it went straight to voicemail. Her next call was to the police.

My eye drifted back down the trench. On the far side, a bit of paper fluttered in the grass. Stepping around, I bent down to look at it.

It was a playing card. No – too long and thin. A tarot card. One of the major arcana, or face cards, showing a young man in jaunty yellow and red trousers, hanging upside down by one foot from a tree, his free leg crooked at the knee, foot tucked up against the opposite leg, so that his body made the shape of an upside down four. The Hanged Man.

'Symbol of sacrifice and prophetic wisdom,' said Eircheard over my shoulder.

The figure on the card looked more like a boy than a man – a jester even, with particoloured trousers of red and yellow, his face oddly serene. In his hand he held a knife with an angled back and runes on the blade.

'Look at the knife,' I said.

'Aye,' said Eircheard, gently taking the card from me. 'But it's not just the blade that's over-familiar. It's the tree as

148

well.' It was an ancient spreading oak, its scalloped leaves minutely detailed. Crutches held up its massive lower limbs, giving it a distinctive silhouette. 'It's the Birnam oak,' he said.

Dunsinnan must go to Birnam Wood.

I looked up sharply. 'Is that part of Birnam Wood?'

'Part?' scoffed Eircheard. 'It's all that's left. That, and two sycamores. But they're bairns – children – by comparison. The oak, now, he was already mature in Shakespeare's day. There's an outside chance he was a sapling when Malcolm's men were stripping branches for their march on Macbeth.'

Lady Nairn had finished her phone call and was stepping around towards us, a look of annoyance on her face. 'We're not to touch—' She stopped in her tracks, her face going white.

'The card,' she said, her voice rasping. 'It's Lily's.'

You'll like my deck, she'd said to me. *It's a Macbeth deck.*

'There's writing on the back,' said Ben, from the other side of the trench. I turned it over. The design on the back was a tangle of Celtic knots. Across it, someone had scrawled a phrase in red ink: *Blood will have Blood.*

Lady Nairn's words, as we'd first seen the blood.

Macbeth's words.

The image of Lily naked and bound beneath the blue gown flashed across my mind. And voices in the darkness: *She must die.* 'Where is she?' I asked.

'Still in bed,' said Lady Nairn, already calling Lily's cell. *'Did you see her?'*

'I—' This call went to voicemail too. Lady Nairn's eyes grew wide. 'No.'

I began to walk down the hill. And then I started to run.

14

Lady Nairn had started out with me, but I was younger and faster. At the base of the summit, she tossed me the keys to her car and said '*Go.*'

Back at the house near the top of the stairs, I startled a maid who pointed out Lily's room. The bed was unmade, the duvet half hanging to the floor. But Lily was not there. For a moment I stood panting on the threshold, and then I turned on my heel and went down the hall to my own room.

Someone had tossed it. The mattress had been pulled off the bed, the bedding left in forlorn heaps on the floor. Pillows had been slit and every drawer pulled out and turned over.

The drawer where I'd hidden the knife was at the top of the heap. The pillow I'd put over it was still there, and the towel in which I'd wrapped it, but the knife was gone.

Had there been enough time, after I'd left for breakfast, for someone to take it and get up the hill before us? And use it?

Just barely.

Whether or not it had been mine, some knife had certainly been used up there. *She must die, she must . . . A most unspotted lily shall she pass to the ground, and the all the world shall mourn her.*

Where the hell was Lily?

The Hanged Man of her tarot deck had pictured not only the knife, but the oak that was, according to Eircheard, all that was left of Birnam Wood. *Dunsinnan must go to Birnam Wood,* Sir Angus had said.

I turned on my heel and went back downstairs. Just as I was climbing back into Lady Nairn's Range Rover, she and Ben pulled up in his car. 'I can't find Lily, and the knife's gone,' I said, as the passenger window zipped down. In the car, her eyes met Ben's.

'Have you searched the whole house?' she asked.

'No. But I'm going to that goddamned wood.'

'I'm staying here,' she said. 'You two go.'

'Do you know the way?' Ben asked.

I shook my head no.

'Then let me drive,' he said. 'It'll be faster.'

I got back out of Lady Nairn's car and slipped into Ben's. 'Why aren't you with Sybilla?'

'She had a shock and she fainted,' he said shortly. 'But she's safe.'

'Which is more than can be said for Lily,' I said, buckling up.

'Or you, Kate.'

152

I glanced over at him, but he was watching the road, his expression inscrutable as we pulled out of the drive and headed down the lane.

Last night, he'd stopped me from going back up the hill, more or less pointing out that I'd been a fool. 'That card was Lily's,' I said a little defensively. 'And it points straight at Birnam Wood. I mean to follow the trail.'

'Yes. But not alone. Is it a trail only, Kate, or also an invitation? Especially since you've already heard what might amount to a death threat, twice.'

'If you mean *She must die*, that's aimed at Lily.'

'Maybe,' he said with a shrug as I explained the context. 'But it was you they spoke to.'

I looked out the window, my heart thudding as we sped along in silence between hedgerows lining close-shorn golden fields.

'About the knife,' he said after a while. 'It's gone from your room, but not exactly gone.'

I turned sharply. 'That was you? *You* took it?'

'Lady Nairn has it.'

'*You tossed my room?*'

'I didn't exactly toss it, Kate. Didn't have to. It was the first place I looked.' His faintly amused calm was infuriating.

'You complete fucking bastard,' I burst out.

He looked across at me, startled. '*Has* someone tossed it?'

153

'Of course somebody's tossed it. Bedding in tatters, every drawer emptied.'

'Good thing I got there first, then. Though I am sorry about the room.'

That he was right did nothing to lessen my fury. Nor did the fact that he was having a hard time keeping a smile off his face.

'Come on, Kate. It's fair enough to be angry. But not so much with me . . . tell me about the tarot card. What do you know about the Hanged Man?'

For Lily's sake, I had to set aside my anger. 'Not much,' I said tightly. 'She had the deck last night, though. Offered to read my cards.'

He raised one eyebrow. 'How much of a twist have your occult studies taken?'

'I put her off.'

'So you don't actually know if that card was still in the deck.'

'No.' Tarot wasn't something I knew very much about. I phoned Lady Nairn and put her on speaker.

'Lily's not here,' she said, her voice tense with worry.

'We'll find her,' said Ben.

'The tarot card is hers,' she said. 'The deck's spread out on her bed, and the Hanged Man is missing.' She'd found nothing else missing, and no further clue to where Lily had gone, but she could tell us a fair amount about the card's meaning.

'The Hanged Man,' she explained, 'symbolises sacrifice and prophecy – not death, as novices often assume. He's a reference to Odin, chief of the Norse gods. A divinity of war and wisdom who wrested secret, possibly forbidden knowledge from the underworld.'

'How?' asked Ben.

'By sacrificing himself to himself, hanging nine nights on a tree, pierced with a spear, until he'd sunk deep enough into the realm of death to seize runes and, screaming, pull them up into the world of light.'

'Got to love the Norse,' said Ben, shaking his head.

The Hanged Man, Lady Nairn went on, always had a serene face. He symbolised the surrender and acceptance that led to clarity of vision, and to wisdom. Unless he was reversed, and then he symbolised passivity, or the tendency to get lost in a labyrinth of idle dreams.

'Where'd Lily get that deck?' I asked.

'From Corra bloody Ravensbrook,' she snapped. 'Who else? Ordered it off her website.'

'How did the card come to have the Birnam oak on it? And the Nairn knife?'

'No idea. All I care about is finding Lily.' Her voice cracked as she hung up.

We drove a while in silence. On either side of us, fields stretched into the distance, stacked with cylindrical bales of hay. Now and then the road shot through thinning arch-ways of russet and yellow trees. Halfway across the plain of

Strathmore, we headed west and wound into the foothills of the Highlands.

'Who would do this?' I asked suddenly.

'Do *what*? Do we actually know what's been done?'

I took a deep breath. 'Lily's missing, for one. And yesterday, I saw a body I thought was hers.'

'Yes. But it wasn't her. And whoever she was, she wasn't there when we went back, and she isn't there this morning. We don't even know that the blood is human, Kate.'

'There's the knife.'

'Which was clean yesterday, and has been in either your possession or mine or Lady Nairn's ever since.'

'And there were the voices, both on the hill, and in the stone circle. Which told me, more or less, in the circle, to put the damned thing back, or else.' *Or else she must die.*

'Auld Callie told you that straight out, didn't she?'

We looked at each other. She was supposed to have met us up on the hill that morning.

'Did you see her?' asked Ben.

'No.'

That made three missing people. What was going on?

'There's also Sybilla's card,' said Ben.

The Hal Berridge card. I sighed. 'At the very least, someone's doing a damned fine job of trying to sabotage Lady Nairn's production. Is that why you're here?'

'She's spoken to me. She has some legitimate concerns.'

'Do they have names?'

'A Reverend Calvin Gosson. On the far, fire and brimstone fringe of the Kirk. The Church of Scotland. Currently filling in as minister at the Cathedral of Dunkeld, while the regular man recovers from heart surgery. I'm told that he believes we're all engaged in a great battle between good and evil, only most people can't or won't see the battlefield any longer. Which, in his view, means the odds have tipped in favour of the forces of darkness.'

'Would he have any connection to Effie Summers?'

'Yes. He's said to favour the quotation *Thou shalt not suffer a witch to live* in his sermons, for one.'

'Charming. Is there a "two"?'

Ben looked sideways at me. 'Gosson found his calling late, it seems. He used to be an actor. He was in Lady Nairn's famous *Macbeth*. Played Fleance.'

'The boy who got away.' Banquo's son, the young boy who escapes Macbeth's murderers – played in many productions by the witches, or at least by the same actors who play the witches.

'The boy who lived,' said Ben with a wry smile. 'Like Harry Potter, he's dedicated his life to the war against evil. Unlike Harry, he counts witches among his enemies.'

'Even the stage variety?'

'He warned Lady Nairn off the play. Told her it gathered dark powers strongly around itself, especially in the hands of gifted performers.'

'A compliment in reverse, I suppose . . . If Effie's under

his spell – so to speak – why would she take the role of a witch?'

'Dunno. Maybe she's only recently been swayed by him. Maybe she's a mole.'

'A spy? Are you serious?'

He smiled. 'Admittedly not a very good one.'

'Did Lady Nairn mention anyone else?' I asked.

'One other. Lucas Porter.'

'The film director?'

He nodded.

Lucas Porter was a Hollywood legend – all the more mythic for his reclusiveness. He'd been a great film director, *auteur* of a dozen or so classic films from the fifties and sixties. Cult films, most of them. Four or five of them, including two starring Janet Douglas, perennially showed up fairly high in lists of the greatest films of all time.

Janet Douglas – Lady Nairn – had left the stage for Sir Angus. She'd also left Lucas Porter.

'Her next project,' said Ben, 'would have been a film version of *Macbeth*, directed by Porter. He was furious, apparently. Told her she'd ruined the picture he'd meant to make his magnum opus, the crowning achievement of his career.'

'Jesus. There must have been any number of actresses who would've killed for that part,' I said.

'That's what she told him, but he wouldn't make the picture with anyone else. He told her that he'd ruin

– personally – any production of *Macbeth* that she got anywhere near.'

'But that was over forty years ago.'

'That's what I said. She said, "You don't know Lucas." She and Sir Angus apparently kept watch on him from a distance.'

'He scared her that much?'

'Mmm. Two years ago, she says, he faded from view. Not that he was ever flash. More like a recluse. But he just quietly disappeared. They waited for a year and a half—'

'And then they figured it was safe to mount their show?'

He nodded. 'And then Sir Angus died. And you know the rest.'

Coming through some trees, we turned down through the tiny, ancient town of Dunkeld, which clung to the River Tay as it tumbled out of the hills. Far away, at the bottom of the steep main street, I glimpsed a graceful bridge of stone arches curving over the river, deep blue and swift, rushing its way towards the sea. On the far side lay the village of Birnam and the wood from which it took its name. From Eircheard's description, I'd thought there were only the oak and two sycamores left. But the riverbank was thick with trees, their canopy orange and red, yellow and russet, all the colours of fire.

At the bottom of the road, just before the bridge, the light turned yellow. Walking towards it, two people broke into a run, crossing just as the light turned red. One was a tall man with black hair; he was pulling along with him a girl with long flame-red hair that seemed to float about her of its own accord.

I leaned forward, pointing. 'That looks like Lily.'

We drew to a stop several cars back from the light, which seemed interminable. As long as Lily and her companion were on the bridge, we could at least keep tabs on them from a distance. Once they reached the other side, they could scatter in any direction. They neared the other side, and the light still showed no signs of changing. Ben jerked the car out of the line. One wheel up on the sidewalk, we careened around the cars in front, shooting through the morning traffic on the cross street and onto the bridge. At the far end, the man pulled Lily into a run, disappearing into the woods on the left.

We skidded to a stop just past the foot of the bridge and leapt out of the car, following in their wake. The bank here was still far below; steep steps led downwards from the road into dimness. 'Lily!' I called, but got no answer. With a glance at Ben, I chased after her.

The chill of dawn still lingered beneath the eaves of the wood, though the sun was well up in the world beyond. Deeply carpeted in coppery leaves and roofed by the arching trees, the path was a long tunnel lit by a scattershot sun. No one was on it. 'Lily!' I called again as I ran, glimpsing flashes of the river through laced branches. Save for our footfalls and breathing, and the rush of the water, however, the wood was silent and seemingly empty.

Stirred by our passing, leaves swirled up in eddies that looked, from the corner of the eye, like small animals herding us onward. Rounding a bend, we came to an enormous tree, green with moss, its trunk gnarled into the silhouette of a giant's bulbous face staring sadly at the ground. 'The sycamores,' said Ben as we passed another, equally immense.

Beyond that, I looked up to see the ancient oak, unmistakable in its majesty. There was no sign of Lily, or of anyone else. I bent down panting, hands on my knees, gazing at the tree, an aged emperor asleep in the watery morning sun, crutches propping up low branches thicker than most of the other trees in the wood. 'It' was not a pronoun that came to mind. *He* was recognisably the same tree as the one pictured in Lily's tarot card. Around him, the air was golden and heavy and silent, thick not only with a strange heavy sleepiness, but with something old and anguished, even angry, despite the sweet haze of autumn.

Three trees left, from the primordial forest that had once covered much of central Scotland. Three trees, set apart from their fellows by something more than sheer size. *Like creatures from an elder world*, I thought, and caught my breath as I recognised the phrase. It came from Holinshed, Shakespeare's source for *Macbeth*, talking about the weird sisters.

There had been three of them, too.

'You really think it was her?' asked Ben.

I nodded.

'Who was the bloke?'

'Don't know.'

Where could they have gone?

As Ben scanned the ground for tracks, I gazed at the tree. What about this tree – or this place – had drawn Sir Angus?

Wind stirred its branches, which creaked and groaned. I slid down the bank and put a hand on the tree, trailing around it; its trunk must have been at least ten feet in diameter. A hollow gaped in the far side, opening into a room I could stand up in. It smelled of damp and decay.

As I ducked out, I felt a drop on my hand and looked down. It wasn't rain; it was red. A splatter of blood.

Backing away from the tree, I looked up and my voice caught in my throat. Glancing over, Ben slid quickly down towards me. All I could do was point. Twenty feet overhead, just where the trunk began to branch and entirely invisible from the path, a body was hanging, swaying a little in the wind, which made the branch creak.

It was an old woman with wild grey hair. Auld Callie.

Someone had clearly looked at a tarot deck before arranging her. Auld Callie's hands were tied behind her back, and her left foot had been tied up behind her right knee, making the shape of a 4. But she was not the Hanged Man, upside down, with mask of serenity on her face. She hung by her neck. Her abdomen had been slashed through her dress, dripping blood in slow, heavy drops, and her face looked as if she had died cursing all the demons of hell. She was Odin, pierced with a sword and screaming.

'Call the police,' said Ben, brushing past me and hoisting himself into the tree. He'd reached her in what seemed like no more than three moves. Holding himself to the tree with one arm, he felt for a pulse. But from the crook of her neck, it was pointless. She was dead.

15

I called the police and told them about Auld Callie and her link to the mess on Dunsinnan Hill, as well. We were told in no uncertain terms to stay right where we were.

And not to cut the body down.

Which was just as well, as we had no knife that would cut that rope.

The knife from the hill would do it, I thought suddenly. But it was in Lady Nairn's safekeeping.

The day before, Auld Callie had pulled me from the hill as I'd run down the path with the knife in my hands, and seconds later the dark-haired man had cantered by. She'd quite possibly saved my life. And now she was dead.

No one, surely, would kill Auld Callie just to torment Lady Nairn. That seemed to rule Lucas Porter out, at any rate. What about the Reverend Mr Gosson?

Thou shalt not suffer a witch to live.

'There's a paper here,' said Ben quietly. 'Clipped to her dress.' He pulled it loose. It was a single sheet, folded loosely in quarters. He let it go, and it floated slowly downwards, eddying and bouncing a little in the air like an oversized butterfly, landing gently in the dying bracken at my feet.

I stared at it warily. There was a smear of blood across it, already dried to brown. Beneath that, someone had written my name. *Kate Stanley*.

I bent and picked it up, my fingers shaking a little. It was a single sheet of thick buff-coloured paper. My name was written on the otherwise blank reverse. Inside the folds, the front was thick with ink. The top third was covered with tiny writing in old ink faded to brown. The bottom was blank – or had been, until someone had filled it with a drawing in pen, deep black ink and wash: a fierce-looking Shakespeare in doublet and hose reached in a fencing lunge toward a kilted Scottish King. Both figures wielded leafy branches instead of swords.

Beneath the picture, in the same ink as the drawing, someone had scrawled a line from *Macbeth*:

Who can impress the Forrest, bid the Tree unfix his earth-bound root?

The impish curves of the drawing and the proud folly of the expressions were one of a kind. I was staring at a Max Beerbohm caricature, an original by the looks of it, probably penned sometime during the nineteenth century's fitfully wanton *fin de siècle*. For all that, it was the cramped writing above the caricature that riveted me.

'What is it?' Ben asked quietly.

'A page from a diary, I think.'

'Can you read it?' asked Ben.

'Not easily.' The hand was seventeenth-century, at a guess, and the messy scrawl of a voluminous writer, on top of that: someone who wrote too much and too fast to bother with neatness. A magpie who recorded everything as he heard it, without any attempt at organisation or culling.

At the top of the page a single legible line stood out:

I once heard Sir William Davenant say that the Youth who was to have first taken the parte of Lady Macbeth fell sudden sicke of a Pleurisie and died, wherefor Master Shakspeare himself did enacte in his steade.

I was staring at a page from the notes of the prattling seventeenth-century antiquarian John Aubrey. A page that scholars had never found, but Max Beerbohm had. A page that said the origin of the play's curse was not a hoax, after all.

A page on which someone had written my name. Who? And why?

I glanced up at Auld Callie, thinking of Odin hanging for nine nights from his tree. Not for love or release from death, like Christ, though he was sometimes compared to Christ. For knowledge. All for the sake of knowledge, in the shape of runes. I looked back down at the page trembling in my hands. What had Auld Callie been so brutally made to toss back, screaming, from the underworld?

Ben dropped beside me, and I became aware of a whirl of sirens in the distance and booted feet pounding down the path.

What are you trying to tell me? I asked Auld Callie silently. And then I folded the page and shoved it into the pocket of my jacket. Auld Callie – or someone – meant for me to see this; I had no intention of handing it over to the police till I'd had a chance to do so.

Ben raised one eyebrow. 'I take it we are not mentioning the knife, either.'

We, I thought. Was this what it took to bind Ben and me together into the first person plural? Murder?

Aloud, all I said was, 'Not yet.'

'And Lily?'

'Leave her out of it.'

'Do we know she was in it?'

He wasn't really looking for an answer, and I didn't give him one.

16

The wood was quickly teeming with police. Forensic officers in white suits and blue gloves tented off the tree as best they could, while uniformed officers cordoned off the path for a long way in both directions. Plainclothes detectives from CID weren't far behind. A sergeant took down our names and information.

Detective Inspector Sheena McGregor arrived from Dunsinnan House, marching straight for us with a face of cold contempt. In her late thirties or early forties, she had short brown hair, a wiry build, and brittle eyes; she smelled of cigarettes and coffee. She already knew who we were, and her questions were blistering. Why hadn't we waited, as asked, atop Dunsinnan Hill, and what in God's name did we think we'd been doing tramping into a crime scene at the Birnam Tree?

'We didn't know it *was* a crime scene, Detective Inspector,' said Ben, all solemn contrition.

'What sort of fool do you take me for, Mr Pearl?' she said coldly. 'You took one look at the slaughterhouse arrangement on top of that hill and drove straight here. Why?' She looked from him to me.

She must have seen the tarot card. She couldn't be asking 'Why Birnam Wood?' She was asking 'Why you? Why come?' I felt my chin going up. 'We thought we were looking at an ugly prank. We didn't expect to find murder.'

'A prank,' she said, her face tightening in displeasure. 'That's a lot of blood for a prank, Ms Stanley.'

'We were up there to read *Macbeth*.'

Her eyes narrowed. 'A bloody prank for a bloody play, eh?'

'It's said to be cursed. I don't expect you to believe that, but a lot of actors do. Someone had already tweaked the cast's jitters on that subject. I thought this was another . . . tease.'

Her foot tapped impatiently on the ground. 'Come with me,' she said suddenly, striding down the bank.

A forensics squad had shielded much of the tree from the path, but the way the body was placed, there was no way to tent it entirely from view. From the riverbank, Auld Callie was still plainly visible, dangling from a high branch, her crooked knee bumping against the trunk, her grizzled hair lifting, now and again, in the wind. A wide streak of reddish-brown blood spilled down her dress, falling in a long vertical stroke down the trunk of the tree. With flashbulbs going off, and white-suited crime-scene officers swarming up and down ladders, the scene looked like a surreal film shoot.

'That doesn't look like a prank to me,' said DI McGregor. 'That looks like ritual murder.'

169

What's a ritual knife for, but ritual? Lily had asked, the night before. Only the ritual knife had not been anywhere near Callie: it had been under my pillow, or safe in Ben's and then Lady Nairn's possession.

Lily, on the other hand, was another story. Was it her I'd seen scurrying into this wood? What was she doing here, and where had she gone?

McGregor was looking at me with a strange mix of distaste and grim triumph. Ritual murder was probably what she lived for. Solve this case quickly, and she'd move up from Detective Inspector to Detective Chief Inspector, in a blink.

One of the white-suited forensics officers approached, pulling McGregor aside for a moment. They were ready to remove the body. Turning back to us, she motioned over one of her underlings. 'I'll have more questions for you presently, but in the meantime you will wait, please, with my sergeant. But I should like to have one thing straight, first. I've heard a bit about you. Both of you.' She took a step towards me. 'If you know anything – anything at all – about what happened up on that hill or in this wood and are withholding it, you will do time for it. I will see to it per-sonally. Is that clear, Ms Stanley?'

The page from Aubrey's diary seemed to tingle and flare in my pocket, the letters of my name scrawling across the page in lines of fire.

'Yes, ma'am,' I said.

*

170

There wasn't much we could tell them about Auld Callie's death beyond the time when we'd found her, and the eerie emptiness of the wood when we had. Other witnesses told of a man and a woman ducking into the trees before us; there was no point in denying that. The police didn't find any more trace of them than we had, however. About Lily, both Ben and I remained mute. If McGregor and company wanted to draw the same inference that I had based on reports of a red-headed woman, there was nothing I could do about it. Meanwhile I saw no need to point them in her direction. Not yet.

She was fifteen years old. Whatever she was up to, it couldn't be murder, I told myself. It was one thing to relish the beauty and power of ancient pagan ritual. It was quite another to participate in a ritualised kill.

Was it a sacrifice? Who had clipped the page from Aubrey's diary to her dress, and marked it 'Kate Stanley'? The urge to look at it was so strong that at times I had to find something else to do with my hands, to keep them from drawing it out of my pocket of their own accord.

DI McGregor had no intention of letting us go easily or soon, however. The sun rose in the sky and curved towards the west again before she would release us. Only the obvious fact that Auld Callie had been dead a few hours before we arrived stalled her from arresting us both for the murder, I thought glumly. Even then, we were sent home like naughty schoolchildren. She'd declared the entire verge at the end of the bridge, including Ben's car, part of the crime scene. It was a stretch, but not one Ben was willing to contest. 'Let her look,' he said quietly to me. 'There's nothing for her to find, and it won't do us any harm to cooperate.' We were driven back to Dunsinnan House in the back of a police car.

It was a quiet ride.

17

Late slanted light had fired the battlements of Dunsinnan House to gold by the time we arrived. We were ushered into the hall, where the police, under the orders of DI McGregor, were still working their way through what seemed like interminably thorough statements from everyone in the company. Apparently, the statements Ben and I had given at Birnam Wood were not going to excuse us being last in line at Dunsinnan. Two crime scenes, McGregor said briskly. Two statements. We were asked, politely but firmly, to remain in the hall until we'd been seen to.

Lady Nairn had fresh tea brought in, serving it herself from a pot of Georgian silver. 'I thought I saw Lily earlier,' I said quietly. 'Going into the wood. I don't know what she's up to, but she's not safe.'

For an instant, her hand stilled. Then she nodded. 'Point taken,' she said, leaving me with a rich, steaming cup of tea.

She'd cancelled the trip into Edinburgh to see the Samhuinn Fire Festival. Sybilla, Jason, and Eircheard, as the three leads, were still going, as were one or two others. Most everyone else had given their statement and quietly

173

departed for home; raucous celebration did not have quite the right ring to it in the face of murder.

Jason had driven off before we returned. Sybilla, however, was waiting for Ben. As dusk draped blue shadows across the lawn, she began to get restive. Scudding across the room, she came to a stop before the table where McGregor sat. 'I have a *performance*,' she announced.

'And I have a murder,' said DI McGregor, glancing up from a clipboard. 'In any case, no one is stopping you.'

'You are stopping Ben. And he is driving me.'

'Find someone else.'

'He's my bodyguard,' said Sybilla.

I almost choked. *Who did she think she was, Whitney Houston?* I glanced over at Ben. A lot of men would have been mortified; he clearly thought the whole scene was funny.

Sybilla never wavered. 'There are ten thousand people massing along the Royal Mile in Edinburgh,' she said, her voice low and silky, 'waiting to see the Samhuinn Fire Festival. Stopping it in its tracks, I assure you, will guarantee you publicity you do not want.'

McGregor was irritating and driven, but she wasn't a fool. Sybilla was playing diva to the hilt, but she was right. Setting her jaw, McGregor sent Ben on his way.

Watching from the doorway, Eircheard hobbled over to me, shaking his head. 'Born diva, that one. Would you like me to try something similar for you?'

174

'Are you in need of a bodyguard?' I asked acidly.

'Ah well, I seem to have mislaid my vulnerable side. But I'm sure I could find it, would it come in handy.'

'Thanks,' I said with a smile. 'But I'm running on about three hours sleep as it is. I think I'll stay here and collapse.' *Kate Stanley*, whispered the paper in my pocket. All I wanted was to be alone so I could figure out what this page meant. It would never happen in a crowd of ten thousand.

Eircheard laughed. 'Sweet dreams, lass.'

McGregor motioned me over, and we went over a set of questions remarkably similar to those I'd already answered. Finally, I was free.

I fairly ran up the stairs towards my room. Would anyone have put it back together again? So long as there was a single working lamp, I didn't much care.

As I came up to the top landing, I heard a wail through the corridor and stopped. 'Bollocks!' burst out Lily. 'Jason, Sybilla, and Eircheard are going. Why can't I?'

I heard Lady Nairn's voice reply. 'For starters, Jason, Sybilla, and Eircheard have the lead roles. The festival won't go on without them. Like it or not, the same can't be said for a torchbearer. Furthermore, none of them grew up with Auld Callie in and out of their homes since before they were born. She was murdered this morning, Lily. You will pay your respects.'

'Eircheard knew her. Better than me.'

'Eircheard is not my granddaughter.'

175

'Auld Callie, of anyone, would *want* me to go.'

'I'm sorry, Lily,' Lady Nairn said firmly.

'No, you're not. You're a . . . you're a . . .'

'*Secret, black, and midnight hag?*' prompted Lady Nairn with a sigh.

I heard a quick intake of breath. 'That's a quote.'

'The taboo is in effect for the hall, darling. Extending it to the entire house does seem a bit excessive.'

I stifled a chuckle, but Lily clearly didn't see the humour in the situation.

'You are trying to live up to your part in that bloody play, aren't you?' she cried. Footsteps ran down the hall, and a door slammed.

Lady Nairn appeared around the corner.

'Is it safe?' I asked.

'So long as you avoid the dragon's lair,' she said with a rueful smile. 'Third door on the left, that would be.' For the first time since I'd met her, she looked her age.

I hesitated. On the one hand, I really just wanted to read the page in my pocket. On the other, I needed to know who had directed it to me, and for that, I needed Lady Nairn's help. She was gliding past me, heading down the stairs when I heard myself call her back.

'Today on the hill, you said *blood will have blood*.'

Two steps below me, she turned.

'You asked me to help you. But I can't unless you tell me what's going on.'

176

'You think I know?'

'You know more than you're telling. Lady Nairn, Lily's been threatened three times in two days.'

'*Three* times? You've heard another?'

'Effie.'

'*Thou shalt not suffer a witch*?' She shook her head. 'Effie's harmless. She's got nothing to do with this.'

'Lady Nairn, there is a long, bloody history of Christians killing witches.'

'You think I don't know that?'

'Like it or not, Effie has fallen in with a radically conservative arm of the church.'

She looked down. With a deep breath she looked back up. 'What I am going to tell you is private. Not for other ears. Not even Lily's. *Especially* not Lily's.'

I nodded. Coming back up the stairs, she led me to the little sitting room off the landing. It was empty; even so, she beckoned me to some chairs in a far corner, settling into one of them with a sigh.

'Forty-odd years ago now, when I left theatre and film to marry Angus . . . it wasn't just my career I left behind. I also left a man.'

'Lucas Porter.'

She raised an eyebrow.

'Ben told me a little,' I said.

She clasped her hands together in her lap. 'I felt I had to tell him about my decision in person. We'd been lovers for three years; I would not send him a Dear John letter, or the Hollywood form of it, a call from my agent. So I flew to New York and told him myself. Lucas was furious. I've never seen anyone that angry before or since. As I left, he made – well, he called it a promise, but it was a threat. Any production of *Macbeth* that I got anywhere near, he said, he would ruin.

'For many years, I didn't mind. I was in love, I was raising a child, and building myself another life in which playing a blood-soaked queen did not figure into my priorities. But in the last few . . . well, Angus and I had collected some remarkable pieces, and one night we had the notion that it would be interesting to see them in use, you know. Not just displayed like so many butterflies on a placard.

'But the spectre of Lucas was worrisome. Through the years, you know, there'd been times when Angus was very near purchasing something for the collection, either at auction or through a private deal, and suddenly, the object would be bought out from under us at an outrageous price. We never knew who it was . . . or even that it was one person – these things happen, at times, in the life of a collector. But we both found it odd, and we both suspected Lucas.'

She cocked her head. 'I like to think that neither one of us is – was – particularly cowardly, but we shelved the idea because of him. And then, two years ago, I read a small article in the paper. Lucas Porter had disappeared. He'd gone sailing one day in waters north of Boston, and never came back. I'm sorry to say it, but I read that article with hope. We waited a year, Angus and I, to see whether he'd reappear. Walk into some police office and tell a strange story of dodging taxes or fighting sharks, or something. But a year went by, and he was still missing.

'Neither of us was getting any younger. So we decided to put together the show. But then Angus died, the Hal Berridge card showed up, and the blood on the hill . . . and now Auld Callie. My God, Kate, I've known Auld Callie since I married Angus. How could anyone do that to her?'

The fire crackled, and I watched her face slowly line with tears.

'*Blood will have blood*,' she said, brushing the damp from her face. 'It was a phrase Lucas used that day in New York. He referred to what I was doing to his picture as an abortion, in rather graphic terms. As a stillbirth. Murder. I'd killed his picture and his career.'

'You really believe he's capable of this? The card, the blood, Auld Callie?'

She rose and crossed to the fireplace, staring into the glowing embers. 'Just before I left him to start rehearsals for *Macbeth* in London, we'd been talking about children. He wanted them right away; I wasn't ready. One day I was looking through some things at his studio, and I found a picture

I hadn't seen. One of those Victorian photos of dead children dressed in their Christening robes, laid out in their cribs, just before burial. At least, that's what I thought it was at first. But then I realised it wasn't Victorian, it was one of his own staged photographs. He used to like to do that, you know. Mimic photographs or paintings from other periods. He might have had a stellar career as a forger, except that he always marked his work. He'd put in some little detail, buried in the background, that pinpointed the year he'd made it. In this case, it was a bolo tie slung over a mirror in the background. The clasp of the tie was a political badge that read *Let's back Jack*. With a stylised line-portrait, almost a cartoon, of JFK's face.'

'So when you found it, the photograph was recent?' I asked.

'The badge was from the 1960 Presidential election. This would have been 1964. The thing was, he'd also made a film. It documented the child's death from what looked like fever. It showed the mother rocking him, holding him through chills and then a seizure, and then stillness.'

'So he staged a child's death?'

She sniffed. 'There was a copy of a death certificate pasted to the back of the photo.'

I stared at her for a moment. 'You mean the child actually died?'

Her voice was almost a monotone. 'I mean, Kate, it was a snuff film.' Her eyes met mine. 'I have no proof, of course.

But I knew it then, and I know it now. He arranged that child's death as a work of art, and he filmed it happening.'

I could hear the blood pulsing in my neck.

'So you see, after he threatened me, I avoided *Macbeth* for forty years,' she said. 'He's capable of anything.'

18

'Have you told this story to the police?'

'Yes. They did not seem overly impressed with the notion of forty-year-old vengeance on the part of a missing and possibly dead ex-lover. Even so, you should leave Lucas to the police, Kate. Just find the manuscript. Because if it is him, he'll be after it, too.'

I nearly showed her the Aubrey; perhaps I should have. But it had my name on it, not hers, and I wanted to think about it in private first, uncluttered by other reactions. So I let her go back down the stairs without saying anything.

As I turned into the corridor leading to my room, I saw Ben and Sybilla coming out of his room and froze. I thought they'd left ages ago. Glancing down at me, she leaned in and drew him into a deep kiss, her whole body rippling with the force of it.

Desire and jealousy and anger – at her, at him, and maybe most of all at myself – shot through me in a blinding flush of red and I stumbled backwards. There was a door next to me. Groping for the handle, I ducked inside.

A narrow stairwell led upwards. Wanting to be anywhere

but where I was, I took it, following it up two storeys, where it opened onto the roof.

Night had fallen while I spoke to Lady Nairn. I stood in the darkness, feeling as if I'd left my skin behind. Up ahead, the battlements carved up the starlit sky. Atop them hunched a gargoyle whose head slowly twisted to face me.

'Oh,' said Lily dourly. 'It's you.'

'Come down from there.'

'Bothered by heights?'

'By the possibility of you going splat, yes.'

She shrugged. 'I like it up here.' She pulled her knees in even closer to her chest. 'I don't suppose you have the knife, do you?' Her voice was taut with wistful eagerness.

'On me?'

She sighed. 'I suppose not. But I'd like to see it again. I'd come down for that.'

'Your grandmother has it.'

She made a sour face. 'That's that, then. I won't see it till I'm eighteen. She'd keep me a child till I'm eighty, if she could. Hey . . . *you* could head down the Fire Festival if you liked. I bet she'd even lend you a car. And I could stow away—'

'I'm heading to bed, Lily.' The adrenaline flush I'd felt downstairs was draining away, leaving me hollow with exhaustion.

'How boring. Or is it that you're taking her side?'

'I'm staying out of it.'

She sighed, laying a cheek on one knee. 'I thought you were *way* cooler than that.'

'Sorry to disappoint.'

'He's going to be at the festival,' she said petulantly. 'And I'm not.'

'Who is?'

'Ian.' Her eyes glittered in the moonlight. 'Ian Blackburn. He's an artist.'

'Is that who you went off with today?'

She nodded.

'I thought I saw you at Birnam Wood this morning.'

'That's ridiculous.' She held my eyes as she said it. No flinching, no flickering. 'I'm supposed to meet him at the Festival. *Please*, won't you go?'

'Lily. There's been a murder. A fairly brutal one. And some strange threats.'

She leapt down onto the roof. 'That was you? *You're* the one who fed Gran that bollocks about threats against me?' She turned around and slammed both hands down on the stone. 'You have no idea what's going on, do you?' She twisted back around. 'You know, it could be amazing tonight. A ritual knife and a ritual fight such as hasn't been seen for *centuries*.'

'Lily – where's this coming from? That knife is a lethal weapon, for Christ's sake.'

'From Corra,' she said defiantly.

'Corra Ravensbrook? You told her about the knife?' Just

last night, she'd stood in front of me and promised not to say a word to anyone.

Lily went still. 'She's brilliant.'

'*Bullshit.*' I was tired and frustrated and filled with an undercurrent of dread, and I finally snapped. 'You could roll the full moon through the holes in her logic, not to mention the evidence in her so-called scholarship, and if that's the advice she's giving you about the stage, then she's dangerous.'

I watched angry frustration rising in Lily as I spoke, her hands tightening into small fists. 'You're . . . you're . . . you're just like Gran,' she burst out.

A secret, black and midnight hag, I thought with grim hilarity.

'. . . So damned focused on facts, facts, facts, and all the possible things that could go wrong, that the beauty and power and poetry the world throws at you fly straight by. I thought – I thought you might be different. But you're so caught up in your precious Shakespeare, and your stupid stage traditions – fake exorcisms – God! How stupid was that little ritual last night? – that you can't see real magic under your nose. Wake up, Kate. Theatre is dead. Jesus, even film is dead. It's spontaneous performances by real people that matter. Happenings like the Samhuinn Festival.'

It was all I could do not to laugh out loud. She'd been spoon-fed some self-righteously radical theories about art, and she was spouting them with all the passion of adolescence. It was oddly endearing, at the same time that it was infuriating.

'I'll take Ian over you any day,' she flung at me. 'He *gets it*. Mixing up theatre and film with computer games, the internet, Twitter, music, painting, books, all rolled into one . . . He'll change the way stories are told, stretching them into new technologies to make a kind of art altogether. Something interactive. *Shared.*'

'But with his name on it, I bet,' I said sardonically.

Her eyes flashed. 'Something *real.*' She snorted with derision. 'It's what Shakespeare would be doing, if he were around today. I mean, he didn't mess around with writing, like, manuscripts or hieroglyphs, did he? He spent his life shaping the newest, coolest art form there was. Putting his stamp on it.'

She threw up her hands. 'Don't you see? You're wrecking *everything* for a whisper of dead, boring Shakespeare heard on the wind. Or maybe in your dreams. And not just wrecking it for me. For *everyone.*' She burst into tears. 'I hate you,' she cried, brushing by me and heading for the stairs.

I stared after her, seeing my fifteen-year-old self. And wondering, deep down, how much truth there was to some of her accusations.

19

Drawing in a deep breath of clean, pine-scented air, I glanced over at the hill.

Hush, if you don't want to get us both killed, Auld Callie had said in my ear on its slopes, just yesterday. And later, *Put it back.*

Put the knife back. I hadn't, and now I couldn't. I didn't even know where Lady Nairn had stashed it.

Did it matter, any more?

Lily thought it did.

Pushing those thoughts aside, I at last pulled the Aubrey from my pocket. Nearly full, the moon poured silvery light across the page. I could make out Shakespeare sparring with Macbeth in Beerbohm's *fin-de-siècle* drawing, but it was too dark to read Aubrey's cramped seventeenth-century writing. And I was shaking, with more than just cold.

Nine nights, Odin had hung on his tree, wrenching the knowledge of runes from the otherworld with a scream of agony and triumph. Runes represented secret knowledge. Hidden, arcane.

Occult.

Kate Stanley, someone had scrawled. That much, I could read, even in the moonlight.

The need to read the rest was suddenly overpowering. I rushed down the stairs, peering cautiously out into the corridor. It was clear; I hurried to my room.

Lamplight glowed on the Chinese dragons roiling on their silks. The bed, turned back, gleamed with smooth white linen and a neat swell of pillows; a fire shimmered in the fireplace. Lady Nairn's staff must have spent all day putting it to rights.

I dropped into one of the armchairs by the fire and began to read, skimming quickly over the lines I'd read before: *The Youth who was to have first taken the parte of Lady Macbeth fell sudden sicke of a Pleurisie and died.* And then I let my eye slide down to the page.

On this occasion, 'twas told me that Mr Shakspere was a man torn between two masters. Lord Salisbury would have a play to shadow forth a witch, while old Dr Dee would have him draw her sting.

I went still, barely breathing. Salisbury and Dee. Robert Cecil, Earl of Salisbury and Secretary of State. Most modern historians referred to him as Cecil; King James had called him 'my Little Beagle'. The brilliant, hunchbacked toiler in the shadows who ran the kingdom while the king played in the sun. One of England's great spymasters.

And John Dee, the greatest magus of the Elizabethan age.

188

A brilliant mathematician, but also astrologer, alchemist, conjuror of angels and demons. A man whose shadow stretched long and dark across the subject of the occult – and not only in the narrow sense of secrets. One of the foremost practitioners in England – indeed, in all Renaissance Europe – of learned magic.

I swallowed hard. What was Aubrey suggesting, naming these men as Shakespeare's masters? I read on:

Dr Dee begged Mr Shakspere to alter his Play lest, in staging curs'd Secretes learned of a Scottish Witch, he conjure powers beyond his controll. But Mr Shakspere wuld not, until there was a death, whereupon he made the changes in one houre's time.

Aubrey's tale backed Ellen Terry's, that Shakespeare had changed the play. And the Nairn family legends, too, in the matter of the Scottish witch.

I have heard it whisper'd that the Youth, Hal Berridge, dyed not of a Pleurisie but of mischief on the part of this selfsame Witch, but if so it was quieted.

I sat back, staring at the words swimming on the page in the firelight. If Aubrey was right, behind the curse was not just a death, but a possible murder. The killing of a child. One of the player's boys, probably about Lily's age.

The first Lady Macbeth.

Was it the original Lady Macbeth – the historical Elizabeth Stewart, Lady Arran, Lady Nairn's ancestress – who'd been the Scottish witch whose secrets were stolen? Lady Nairn would think so, I was certain of it. It fitted her family's legends. But then one also had to ask: was it Elizabeth Stewart's 'mischief' that killed the boy who'd first played her on the stage?

In the grate, a log collapsed, and I jumped.

What did Robert Cecil, Earl of Salisbury, have to do with this tale? His involvement was surely unlikely. On the other hand, his predecessor and teacher as spymaster, Francis Walsingham, had employed Christopher Marlowe as a spy. In earlier years, it had been Walsingham who'd centralised England's acting companies into a few closely controlled networks; there was circumstantial evidence that he'd deliberately meshed these with his network of spies. Licensed to roam the country and prowl the halls of the great, who better than travelling players to act as London's eyes and ears in distant parts of the realm? So it wasn't entirely preposterous that Cecil might reach out to Shakespeare. But why? Against whom, and for what end?

Macbeth was widely believed to be a sort of zeitgeist response to the horror of the Gunpowder Plot, in which some radical Catholic gentlemen had planned to blow up the Opening of Parliament in 1605, hoping to kill the king, the entire Royal Family, both houses of Parliament, and most of

England's top judges, lawyers, and prelates to boot. It hadn't come off – just barely. But it had sent paroxysms of fear through the English consciousness, setting off a fearsome spidering of manhunts and executions. Those horrors had burned themselves out fairly quickly – but a wary, watchful suspiciousness had lingered for years. Cecil had spent the rest of his life searching for the plot's kingpin, whom he believed had escaped justice.

Had the king's Beagle somehow tried to use *Macbeth* in his search? I shook my head. I couldn't recall anyone suggesting that the Scottish Play was, among other things, a piece of political hackwork. Political, maybe – it was popular to see all Shakespeare's work as political, in the sense of being about power: but propaganda? What was the message? Fear witches? It didn't sound very like dry, rational Cecil, bureaucrat extraordinaire.

In any case, it was Dee who was in many ways more disturbing.

What did Aubrey mean, that Dee was Shakespeare's master? Dee was an expert in fields as far-flung as navigation, geography, history, and mathematics. It didn't have to be magic for which Shakespeare owed him mastery. But it was magic that Aubrey clearly had in mind.

The magic in *Macbeth*, however, was the dark magic of witchcraft. Not Dee's cup of tea, at all. He was an intellectual, a strenuous defender of ritual or ceremonial magic as a learned and difficult process of invoking angels. There was a big difference between the intuitive, folklore-bound customs of witchcraft, or 'low' magic, and the precise, complicated ceremonies of 'high' magic. Even if *Macbeth*'s magic was a memory of some ancient pagan religion mislabelled as witchcraft, as Lady Nairn seemed to believe, why would that concern Dee?

I began to pace the room, thinking of the magic in *Macbeth*.

Double, double toil and trouble,
Fire burn and cauldron bubble.

The great cauldron scene involved witches cackling over a revolting brew of body parts. Not Dee's sort of thing at all. On the other hand, the witches weren't old village scolds, as witches on the English stage had always been before. Eerie and unearthly, they weren't human at all. They were condensations of evil whispering on an ill wind. 'Creatures of the elder world,' Shakespeare's source had written. The weird sisters. The fairies. The witch-hunters, including King James, had believed such spirits to be demons.

Maybe *Macbeth* was about demonic magic, after all.

Come to think of it, just as the witches finished stirring their grisly brew, Macbeth arrived and launched into one of his greatest speeches. *I conjure you*, it began. Rummaging about, I found my copy of the play and opened to that scene. Macbeth's words were usually taken to be metaphorical. But what if Shakespeare had meant it literally? What if Macbeth were donning conjuror's robes, casting a circle? Enacting on stage the kind of rite Dee spent his life performing for real? No stage direction specified it, but stage directions were notoriously absent from Shakespeare's plays.

Secretes learned of a Scottish witch, Aubrey had written. Legend made Elizabeth Stewart, Lady Arran, a witch, but Lady Nairn had called her ancestress a serious student of magic. In the Renaissance, that meant conjuring, not casting love charms, much less worshipping a pagan goddess. The 'Great Art' of conjuring had been thought of as an almost exclusively male pursuit. But surely not entirely: there had to have been women who'd tried their hand at it. Had Lady Arran? What if the rite Shakespeare had learned from her – if he'd learned one at all – had been high magic, not toads and newts in a stew?

I read through the speech.

I conjure you, by that which you profess,
Howe'er you come to know it, answer me.

The room felt suddenly icy. I made myself read on, the speech rising in passion and power as Macbeth worked himself up to challenge winds whipping the sea into a devouring monster, ripping out trees by their roots, hurling down churches and castles. *Even till destruction sicken*, he roared. *Answer me.*

193

He was conjuring, all right. And what he wanted was what Odin wanted: knowledge. If Macbeth's words were the remains of some magic rite, it was a rite demanding knowledge – ripping it at gale force – from demonic powers. What if the missing or altered magic in *Macbeth* wasn't witchcraft at all, but a dark version of Dr Dee's wizardry?

Dee had spent his life battling popular suspicions that he was a master of demons: that he invoked evil, not angels. All the more, after a Scottish king with a penchant for witch-hunting had ascended the English throne. Surely, he'd have disapproved of this Scottish play, seeing it, perhaps, as a reflection of himself shadowed in a dark and possibly dangerous mirror.

Pacing the room, I caught sight of my reflection in the dressing-table mirror, hands on my hips, forehead furrowed, my hair standing on end where I'd run my fingers through it. I looked like a witch myself, for heaven's sake. This was ridiculous. Last night, I'd gone to bed wondering whether Shakespeare might have recorded some long forgotten ancient rite. Tonight, I seemed to be flirting with the possibility that he was a spy and a magus. A man with two masters. And maybe a mistress.

Call me Corra Ravensbrook.

I laughed darkly at my mirror-self. Aubrey, after all, wasn't dependable as an historian. He'd been a great collector of anecdotes, but his stories – though fairly reliable as gossip – weren't trustworthy as *truth*.

All the same, my other self seemed to say, his note *did* harmonise with every other bit of evidence I'd run across: not only the Nairn family stories, but Ellen Terry's letter. She, too, had heard about the rewrite that altered the magic. Aubrey just added more details – and why not? The page was undated, but most of his diary was from the late seventeenth century. He was closer to Shakespeare than Terry by roughly two centuries.

The thought struck me: if Terry's informant had been right about the revision of the play . . . had she also been right about the survival of a manuscript?

I picked Aubrey's page up from the table where I'd left it. What did any of this have to do with Birnam Wood, and the deaths of Sir Angus and Auld Callie? At the bottom of the page, Shakespeare drove at Macbeth with his tree branch, glancing out at me with a sly, mocking smile: *Who can impress the Forrest, bid the Tree unfix his earthbound root?* It was a phrase from the same scene of conjuring. Macbeth's solution of one of the witches' riddles: that he should never be conquered until Birnam Wood came to Dunsinane.

Sir Angus had turned the phrase around: *Dunsinnan must go to Birnam Wood.* Still, he'd focused on the same subject of trees and forests and woods. Was this page what he had found? What he'd possibly been killed for? If that were the case, how did it come to be pinned to Auld Callie's dress, with my name on it? More importantly, where was it pointing?

It had to be pointing somewhere.

Whatever secrets this page was hiding, they had to have something to do with that goddamned tree. But mid-joust, Shakespeare remained stubbornly mute.

A loud, insistent knocking cut through my thoughts. Slipping the Aubrey into my copy of the play, I opened the door to find Lady Nairn, her face white with fear.

'It's Lily,' she rasped. 'She's gone.' She gripped my shoulder. 'And so is the knife.'

20

'You think she's headed to Edinburgh, for the Fire Festival?'

She nodded. 'I've called Ben. He's got people out looking for her. But I'd like you to go, too. She likes you.'

Not after tonight, I thought.

'And you think Lily took the knife?'

'She's the only other person who knows how to get in the safe.' She set the edgeless knife in my hand. 'She left this in its place. Take it. Maybe whoever wants the knife will take this in its stead.'

I doubted it. Whoever wanted it wanted the real thing: *what's a ritual knife for, but ritual?*

'*Please*,' said Lady Nairn, her heart in her eyes. 'I'm an old woman. I'd just be in the way. But you and Ben . . . you have a chance to find her.' Her voice, shaky to begin with, dropped to a whisper. 'I can't lose Lily, too.'

Ben was the last person I wanted to be anywhere near, tonight. But I had no choice. Grabbing my jacket and dropping the knife in its pocket, I took the keys she held out and hurried down to the car.

*

It was a little over an hour's drive into Edinburgh. Following directions I had from a brief, brisk conversation with Ben, I drove into the old city's confusing warren of streets, turning left as we came to the Grassmarket, a wide tree-filled, shop- and pub-lined boulevard. Up ahead, a line of sharply gabled stone buildings came to an abrupt end. I pulled up beneath the last building.

Two men detached themselves from the building's shadow, stepping quickly towards me. Ben and a shorter sandy-haired man. Ben opened my door; as I got out, pulling my jacket from the passenger seat, the other man ducked behind the wheel.

Ben led me swiftly up a stairway clinging to the side of the building, bordered on the other side by a steep grassy slope. Far overhead, atop a ragged, jutting cliff, perched the castle, shining golden in the night, never taken across a thousand years, except through treachery.

'What's the point, if you'll pardon the expression,' asked Ben, 'of slipping the real knife into the performance?'

'Authenticity, according to Lily. The question is who put that notion into her head, and just how authentic are we talking?'

Something strange happens to blades that have drunk blood, Eircheard had said. *They wake. And some of them want more.*

'You brought the stage copy?'

I patted my pocket. 'She won't want to take it.'

'She won't have a choice.'

He'd had people out canvassing the performers for Lily, but no one could recall seeing her. On the other hand, the torchbearers painted their entire faces in bold black and gold, greasing and braiding their hair into outlandish shapes or tucking it into extravagant jesters' caps. Our footsteps clattered on stone and cement, punctuating a thick ooze of worry. How far could one fifteen-year-old get, along one several-block stretch of an old city? Even with a black and gold face, she shouldn't be that hard to find.

'The way Lily told me the story, it's the Cailleach who's supposed to carry the knife,' I panted. 'My guess is that she's probably sticking close to Sybilla.'

'Hurry,' was all he said.

Halfway up the hill, we came out onto another street angling slowly upwards, left to right. Cutting across it, we ran up another stairway, steeper and narrower. Sounds drifted down from above: flutes and drums and horns, cut by laughter and the occasional shout. And singing. At one point, I thought I heard soft footsteps behind and stopped, looking back.

Below, I saw nothing but shadows moving in the wind.

The Esplanade was writhing with revellers. There were fire-breathers and fire-dancers twisting batons of flame through the darkness, and drummers dressed in green, crowned with wreaths of ivy and holly. Acrobats, jugglers, and leering devils milled about. The Winter Court stalked the fringes, cloaked in black, faces hidden beneath long-snouted wolf masks, howling at the swollen moon hanging high overhead.

In the sort of simple colour coding common in folk plays, the Summer Court was recognisable in greens and reds, all the colours of growth and harvest and fire. The Winter Court was mostly in black and grey. The Cailleach was blue, and her ice maidens white.

Where the street opened out of the parade ground, leading downward from the castle into the city, hundreds of people had lined the way, swaying and chanting: *People are returning to the ancient ways.* Lily's phrase. Into this funnel, the players were slowly pouring themselves in a chaotic procession down the hill. Between the buildings and the police barriers that kept the onlookers out of the parade, both sides of the street were packed as far as I could see. Pushing our way through the crowd down to Parliament Square, where the main show would take place, would take hours, if it could be done at all. My heart sank.

'Hurry,' said Ben again.

'How? With wings?'

'*An angel is like you, Kate, and you are like an angel.* But if you're feeling less than celestial, we could try going as wolves in wolves' clothing.'

Instead of heading towards the street, he began edging around the back of the milling crowd, between the merriment and the castle. I called to him once, in confusion, but he didn't hear. There was nothing for it but to follow.

We skimmed around the back of the Esplanade in a gigantic half-circle. In the corner on the opposite side, we came to a low wrought-iron fence in front of a white and black half-timbered house. A policeman stood in front of the gate. Seeing Ben, he opened it and stood aside, and we ducked along a short pathway and into the house.

A scullery opened into a large old-fashioned kitchen. In the middle of the room, two piles of clothing lay on a long table once painted blue. Atop each pile perched a long-snouted papier-mâché mask: the head of a wolf.

'How'd you get these?'

Ben shoved one pile towards me. 'Everything has its price. Even a place in the festival. Just ask Sybilla.' Pulling off his shirt, he started to dress in the clothes from the other pile.

We each had a long-sleeved shirt, trousers, and a cloak, all in black. Just before donning the mask, I drew Lady Nairn's unsharpened knife from my jacket pocket and tucked it into my belt beneath the cloak.

21

By the time we emerged transformed into wolves, the Esplanade had largely cleared. The Cailleach and her ice maidens had gone before we arrived. Now Eircheard and his Summer Court had gone as well, and the Winter Court, led by Jason, was well on its way. I could just see antlers in the distance. As we stepped outside, Ben leaned over to me. 'If you find her, or you run into trouble, come back here. Or to the front entrance off Ramsay Lane . . . you know where that is?'

I nodded, and my three-foot snout nearly upended me.

'That's where the car'll be,' said Ben.

'Are you planning on skipping?' I asked.

In answer, he threw back his head and howled a challenge to the night, loping into the crowd. The road was lined with torchbearers. Ben took the one side, and I took the other, scanning their faces. Behind the barrier, the crowd was twenty deep in places, swaying and chanting so that the whole street reverberated with their words: *People are returning to the ancient ways.*

Except for taking videos on their mobiles and posting them to Facebook, I thought.

I searched every black and gold face on the way down, but saw no sign of Lily.

What had she got herself into? That she was involved in Auld Callie's death I would not believe. That she'd been swept up by others whose passions were less innocent was entirely possible. Corra Ravensbrook, for one. Lily had told her about the knife, and it was Ravensbrook who seemed to have convinced her that inserting it into this festival would be a fine turn of events. Who was she? A bored housewife, Lady Nairn had scoffed, but I doubted it. Could she have some connection to Lucas Porter?

Around us, other members of the Winter Court were infiltrating the crowd from behind, as winter creeps gradually into summer, sneaking through the crowd and out into the procession from the closes, the narrow, winding alleyways that cut steeply down between buildings from the top of Castle Hill all the way to its feet.

Ahead, to my left, a wolf howled behind the crowd, and the crowd eddied and seethed, people turning in all directions, as the separation between performers and audience melted. At the edge of the scrum, I thought I saw a flip of red hair above a black and gold torchbearer's costume, and then the crowd closed around it.

I pushed my way over, and the crowd enveloped me, too. It was densely packed; I caught snatches of German, Spanish, and something that might have been Russian, along with broad Scots. Three women on stilts ducked through the close behind, their costumes the pale flowing blue and white of ice, glittering with crystals and sequins. Behind them, a puppet fifteen feet tall unfolded through the doorway: a wraith with a twisted face, its skirts of white and silver silk whirling over the crowd like a billowing veil.

A voice cold as winter spoke in my ear. 'Walk away, Kate.'

Who knew me, in this mask? Who knew my name? I twisted the wolf's head to see an old man watching me with watery blue eyes. He was gaunt and a little bent; what remained of his close-shaven hair was grey.

'Who are you?'

His dry laugh faded into a cough. 'A messenger. You're better at giving direction than taking it, aren't you?'

Suddenly, I recognised him. In the flaring darkness, his body ravaged by illness, he looked more like a figure of Death than the golden man I'd seen in pictures from his glory days in Hollywood.

'Lucas Porter,' I said, stepping towards him, but hands caught me from behind, pinning my arms at my back, holding me where I was. One of the stilt-women bumped into me. As I stumbled, my mask was lifted off and passed into the whooping crowd, bobbing from hand to hand like a trophy.

Lucas stepped close, and for a moment I'd thought he'd seen the knife at my belt and meant to take it. Instead, he slid his cheek in along mine in a sensual move that made me flinch. 'We've taken what you would not give.' His voice in my ear was harsh and rasping as a sibyl's, devoid of emotion, which somehow made the light touch of his skin against mine worse. 'Now she must die.'

'Who?' I jerked back, but the hands behind me only tightened their grip. Around us, the crowd jostled and milled, the stilt women danced, and the puppet-wraith whirled, its skirts twirling overhead like a huge parasol.

'*Begin to doubt the equivocation of the fiend that lies like truth* . . . Either Lily will die, or you will.'

He stepped back, a serpent's cold smile on his face. 'Walk away, Kate. This isn't your story.'

'It's not Lily's either.'

His eyes were dark pools of hatred. 'She was born into it.'

There was a crack and a sharp cry, and the puppeteer stumbled and fell to the ground. Fifteen feet of puppet sighed and collapsed, its silver skirts slowly settling over the crowd like the fall of a parachute. As it slipped over my face, the hands holding me let go.

By the time I worked my way free, Lucas was gone. Someone else grabbed my elbow and I spun, jerking away. It was another wolf, holding my wolf's head in its hands.

'Jesus, Kate,' said Ben's voice. 'What happened?'

'He's here,' I panted. 'Lucas.'

'You saw him?'

'He delivered a message.' It stuck in my throat. 'Either Lily will die. Or I will.'

Ben gripped my shoulder, steadying me. 'Are you all right?'

I grabbed my mask from him, settling it back on my head. 'We have to find Lily.'

We reached the main stage down in the square before St Giles' Cathedral just as the revels of the Summer Court reached their climax: red and green people gyrating around each other in squealing decadence, tumblers bouncing through the air, giants swaying on stilts, fire batons swinging flame through the night.

In the centre of the stage Sybilla sat enthroned, veiled head to toe in deep blue, almost like a burka, except that in the centre of the veil covering her face was painted a single staring white eye. In a grand gesture, she rose, slowly raising her arms skywards. From every side, horns and drums and flutes swelled into a great crescendo until with a single motion downwards, she silenced it, and with it the chatter of the crowd. For a moment there was no sound in the square save wind whipping through banners, and in the distance, the cry of a frightened child.

When she brought her hands back up, she was holding a knife.

It rippled in the firelight. I took one step closer, peering at the blade. Down its centre ran a line of runes.

Ben had seen it too. Lily had delivered the knife.

And Sybilla had accepted it? What the hell was she thinking?

Beside her, Eircheard sat wrapped in some kind of fur that made him look more than ever like a bear. Draining a flagon in noisy gulps, he tossed it away. It rang on the pavement in the silence. He pushed himself to his feet and lurched across the stage, grabbing at the knife in Sybilla's hands but coming up empty. He yelled with frustration. Around him, his court tittered with drunken laughter.

At the edge of the stage, the wolves of Winter rushed into the open space, cornering Eircheard and scattering his revellers. Through it all, Sybilla stood motionless at the centre.

As the last of the Summer Court slunk whining away, Jason strode towards Sybilla, sweeping into a great bow. As he rose, she extended the knife towards his breast. One thrust would send it piercing into his heart. I wondered whether he'd yet seen that the knife was sharp, but beneath his horned helmet, it was impossible to tell.

A deep drum began to pound out a slow beat. Sybilla offered Jason the knife, and the wolves howled in triumph. The Queen had chosen her champion.

From his corner, Eircheard bellowed with anger, and lurched over to Jason, who let him come, stepping aside at the last instant, slashing out at him as he stumbled by. A piece of Eircheard's cloak fluttered to the ground, and the crowd clattered with laughter. Eircheard turned, a puzzled look on his face, and trundled back. In another graceful arc, Jason sliced a second bit off his opponent's cloak. The crowd warmed to it, the handsome young outsider showing up the boorish old king. It was a brilliant routine, bombast versus finery, light catching and flickering on armour and silk and fur.

I heard Ben's voice in my ear. 'Watch Eircheard.'

He stood blinking and swaying, unsteady on his feet, his eyes glazed. I frowned. This wasn't an act. He was having trouble staying upright. 'He looks drunk,' I said quietly.

'Or drugged.'

Lowered his head, Eircheard went at Jason again. Another arc of the blade sliced through his cloak, and this time it caught skin. A rivulet of blood flowed down his arm and he bayed in fury.

Glancing over at the Winter King, I saw something that sent a floe of ice running down my spine. Jason's hands were large, a working man's hands that could handle a broadsword or a horse, a pick or a hoe. But the hand that held the knife had long, tapered fingers, more suited to the piano or the rapier.

Whoever was behind the Winter King's mask, it wasn't Jason.

Ben's head jerked around; he'd seen it, too.

Eircheard charged again. This time, he was tripped and fell sprawling on the pavement, subsiding into unconsciousness. The Winter King strode towards him, knife gripped in his hands, and the crowd roared with laughter.

Kill him, a woman screamed, and the Winter King raised his head, as if sniffing the bloodlust on the air. His knife rose. Pulling off the wolf mask, I began to run, but the knife was already slashing toward Eircheard's neck.

Just before the blade reached Eircheard's throat, another hand rose and parried the blow. Pulling off his mask, Ben had stepped forward. His knife was black, of some dull material that caught little light, hard to see in the night. There was a long *aaaah*, and the crowd silenced, leaning inwards.

Alone in the centre, the matte-black blade and the pattern-welded blade swayed this way and that. And then both blades flew into the air, clattering to the ground, and both men fell heavily to the pavement, rolling over and over. The Winter King dove for his knife, and as he did, Ben caught his helmet, twisting it up and away, so that it came off. The face beneath was painted entirely white, and it took me a moment to recognise him: the dark-haired man from the Esplanade.

Holding the helmet by the horns, Ben was off, scooping up the pattern-welded knife as he went, dancing about with both of them. And then he clapped the Winter King's horned helmet on his own head.

The dark-haired man charged and Ben ducked, scampering about the square, using a large statue as a shield. Drawing him, with each move, farther away from Eircheard.

Once, Ben ran behind me, using me as a shield, spinning me a couple of times so that my cloak swept outward, enveloping us both.

'Trade,' he said under his breath, thrusting the knife from the hill into my hand and plucking the stage dagger from my belt. And then he was off again, the crowd cheering him on as he led the dark-haired man in a merry chase, prancing about, juggling with the stage knife while the Winter King, no longer looking regal, lunged for it.

Across the way, Eircheard stirred. He sat up, squinting. And then I saw him recognise the antlers. With a yell, he pushed himself up and lurched across the stage, ploughing into Ben's back. There was a sickening thud and Ben went down on one knee, the knife skittering across the pavement, stopping not far from the dark-haired man's feet. Eircheard skidded after it, catching himself on his knees just in front of the Winter King. With a slow smile of victory, the man scooped up the weapon and raised it over Eircheard's head.

It had no edge and a rounded point, but it was steel. Driven hard into the chest of an unarmed man, it could still be lethal. Again, a lone woman's shrill voice filled the square: *Kill him*. This time, the crowd took it up. *Kill him, kill him*.

Within the chanting crowd, the four of us might as well have been alone on the moon.

'Strike now,' said Ben, 'and it will look like what it is. Murder. And there will be ten thousand witnesses.'

'It will look like an accident.'

'Is it worth the risk, with the wrong knife?'

The dark-haired man looked up at the blade in his hand

210

and his smile died. The crowd's chant died away and silence blanketed the square, broken only by flames crackling in the cold wind. 'You bloody fool,' he snarled, thrusting the knife hard into Eircheard, who subsided with a groan.

Someone screamed. I stepped forward. There was no blood. And then I saw the blade, lying jagged and broken on the ground. The dark-haired man had driven the knife into the stone pavement.

Throughout the fight, Sybilla had stood motionless. Now she stepped forward and gave Eircheard her hand, pulling him to a stand, and the crowd sighed in relief at the Cailleach's resurrection of the old king.

At the back of the stage, sparks spurted and a pyrotechnic display shot flames into the night. Around the edge of the square, a troupe of fire-dancers began spinning fiery batons, and the drummers pounded out a quick rising beat of anticipation.

Slowly, Sybilla reached up and unpinned her robe. The drumming grew more insistent. The blue cloak and hood fell to the ground.

Surprise stopped a cry in my throat; beside me I saw Ben do a double take. The woman beneath was not Sybilla.

She was Lily.

22

But if Lily was the Cailleach . . . if she'd been there beneath the Cailleach's blue veil all evening, where was Sybilla?

Lily held a pale hand out to the Winter King, who stepped forward and was presented to the crowd. The Cailleach's consort.

Before the crowd could cheer in approval, a single voice rose through the square: *Thou shalt not suffer a witch to live.* From near the back, a burning baton streaked straight towards the stage like an arrow, catching the edge of Lily's robe, which caught fire in a quick whoosh.

I reached the stage in two steps, tossing her to the ground, smothering the flames. Ben was not far behind.

It was over in an instant. Lily sat up. The fire had torched one side of her robe and singed her hair, but other than that she was fine. Around us, chaos erupted.

Ben turned back to the spot where the dark-haired man had stood, but he was gone. I gripped Lily's arm, as if she might also disappear. 'You're hurting me,' she whimpered.

'Who was he? The Winter King?'

She glared at me in mute fury, and I shook her. '*Lily.* He

tried to kill Eircheard. And someone's just tried to kill you. Where are Jason and Sybilla?'

'Do you have to ruin *everything*?' she wailed.

'Get her out of here,' said Ben tersely. 'And that god-damned knife, too.' And he pushed into the crowd.

Still gripping Lily, I began weaving through the crowd, but she made no move to resist.

'Where are we going?' she asked grudgingly.

'Ramsay Lane,' I said. 'Just under the castle.'

Loosed into a spontaneous dance-party on the street, the crowd made the going frustratingly slow.

A little way up, Lily motioned to a doorway opening onto one of the closes that ran down the side of the hill. 'Shortcut,' she said sullenly, 'if you want it.'

I hesitated, looking from the chaotic street to the quiet close. 'Jesus,' she said, pulling me through. 'This'll take sodding days.'

Inside, the sound of the crowd cut to a distant hum, and our pace quickened. Twenty yards in, a raucous party of drunken spectators erupted into the small space from a side door, whirling us apart as they folded us into their dance. It was a moment before I realised what they were singing:

The master, the swabber, the boatswain, and I
The gunner and his mate,

213

Loved Mall, Meg, and Marian, and Margery,
    But none of us cared for Kate.

Glimpsing Lily, I reached for her, but she was spun away. I heard light laughter and someone shoved me against the wall. There was a scream and then the crowd was running off, half uphill and half downhill, and I could not see her in the fray. 'Lily!' I shouted, turning about wildly, but in a matter of seconds, I was alone in the dark in an Edinburgh close.

   '*Lily!*' I called again. But she was gone.

The crowd had scattered in both directions, so I had no idea which way to head in pursuit. Knowing it would be futile, I tried them both. Above, the Royal Mile still surged with a dancing crowd. The lower street was mostly empty.

   My mobile buzzed. It must be Lily.

   Thank God.

   It was a text, and therefore succinct:

Lily 4 Knife. Hilltop. Midnight. Alone.

I stared at it, dread sinking through me. Up on the hill, Lucas Porter had laid out a stark choice: Lily, or me. Someone must die. But that was when they thought they had the knife.

   Now, it seemed they were willing to trade Lily for the blade.

Or was I part of the trade as well?

There only one way to find out: alone on a hilltop at midnight, with a ritual blade a thousand years old.

My call to Ben had rung twice when another text came through, from an unrecognised number. I cut off my call to Ben and pulled it up:

Contact anyone & deal off. Watching & Listening.
Car @ bottom of hill. Keys under floormat.

I looked up. The windows lining the small space all seemed curtained and dark, even opaque. But suddenly they seemed like staring eyes. Cancelling the call to Ben, I made my way quickly down the hill.

As promised, there was a car just at the end of the close, where it came out on the main road that wound down the hill towards New Town. A black Mercedes. The driver's door was unlocked and the keys under the mat. As I started the car, I found that the sat-nav was already programmed for Dunsinnan. Shaking, I pulled out into traffic.

Ben called four times on the drive north, but I didn't dare answer. *Watching &*Listening.* This car was probably bugged, and for all I knew, they were monitoring my cell calls. But I couldn't turn the phone off, in case I heard from Lily or her abductors. From that direction, though, there was silence.

What was Lucas up to? Why engineer Lily bringing the knife to Edinburgh only to pull them both back to Dunsinnan? How did the Winter King, the dark-haired man, figure into it? Where were Sybilla and Jason? *What happened to Lily?*

I looked at the knife on the leather seat beside me, gleaming now and then in the lights of the motorway. *Nothing is but what is not,* it seemed to whisper.

Other words kept playing through my head:

She must die:
She must, the saints must have her; yet a virgin,
A most unspotted lily shall she pass
To the ground, and the all the world shall mourn her.

Behind that, oddly, I heard Ben's voice: *'An angel is like you, Kate, and you are like an angel.'* Whatever had possessed him to say that, it seemed heavy with irony now.

I drove north as fast as I dared.

23

I pulled into the lay-by at the foot of Dunsinnan Hill with no more than fifteen minutes to spare before midnight. Slipping the knife from the seat, I headed quickly up the hill.

The path seemed longer and steeper, the stand of pines more ominous in the dark. My footsteps thudded softly on the grass along the field and into the heather, my breath shortening as I ran. The moon hung high overhead, dimly lighting the way. Just below the summit, I paused, my heart thudding wildly in my chest, and not just from the climb. In my hands, the knife was cold. Stupid not to have a back-up weapon, I thought suddenly. Though where I would have gotten one, I didn't know. When I handed the knife over, I'd be unarmed.

What choice did I have?

I set my shoulders and peered over the rim. The cairn seemed to have grown. Then I realised that it was not the cairn I was looking at: it was wood, stacked into a high cone. Other than that, the summit was empty.

At the base of the stacked wood, a red gleam kindled

into life. And then a breeze lifted, and the bonfire caught with a whoosh, orange and yellow flame licking upwards through the cone. From behind it, a lone figure stepped into the light. A woman with pale hair falling to the middle of her back, her face lined with the fine-china crackling of fair skin in old age. Lady Nairn, in a shimmering blue gown. In her right hand, she held a knife with an angled back and a blade that seemed to ripple in the firelight.

What was she doing here? Where was Lily?

In a low voice, she began to hum, walking in a wide circle with the knife pointing outward and down to the ground, stopping at each of the cardinal directions to cry out in words drowned out by the wind and the roar of the fire. Slowly, she walked to the centre, raising her arms to the moon. Her voice rose into a strange keening that soared into the night and seemed to wrap around the moon like a slender cord, drawing it down towards the hill.

On the far side of the summit, horns rose over the rim, branching into antlers, as if she were pulling a stag up from the deeps of the earth even as the moon dipped down. The head that followed, however, was not that of a stag, but of a man. He rose over the lip of the summit, naked and in his prime, his member erect, and strode down towards her carrying a cup, which he held high. It was his eyes I could not look away from. Fringed with feathers, they were the unwinking golden eyes of an owl.

What I had seen in Edinburgh was a play, a good-natured

performance. This was the real thing. It wasn't Lily who was the witch in the household, it was Lady Nairn.

I must have made some sound, because they both turned towards me, Lady Nairn's eyes meeting mine. *She is Artemis*, I thought, *Diana, the Lady of the Hunt, and I will be torn apart by her hounds.*

Even as that thought crossed my mind, a cry of loneliness condensed and distilled rose in waves toward the moon. To my right, a wolf leapt onto the rim of the summit, its throat arced back in a howl. To my left, others answered. And then other figures rose into view. One of them was the dark-haired man. The Winter King.

From the startled anger on Lady Nairn's face, he was as much an intruder as I was. 'Run!' she cried in a deep voice, looking straight at me.

As if blocked, somehow, from entering the bowl of the summit itself, the wolves and dark figures who stood with them began to pour around its edges, heading towards me, erupting into a cacophony of yipping and howls. I stepped back, stumbling and falling, scrambling up and away. Something nipped at me from behind, and I turned, knife in hand, as someone lunged at me. I was hit on the head, and the world went dark.

24

It was the cold I became aware of first, dimly and far away, as I slid back into consciousness. A clinging damp cold. A throbbing ache in my head. And grass prickling my cheek.

For a moment, I lay still. Hearing nothing but wind, I opened my eyes. I lay in the bowl of the hilltop, just near the rim. Thin fingers of steely light pierced a cloudy sky. This far north, in November, dawn came late. I must have been here for hours.

Lily. Her name tore through me in a silent, white explosion.

She'd disappeared after the Samhuinn Festival, and I'd come here with the knife. Where was it? Where was she?

I sat up. I seemed to be alone. Off to my left, a pile of grey ash, thinly smoking, was all that remained of the bonfire. In the grass, my hands were sticky, and a musty and metallic scent rose thickly around me. *Blood.* I looked down. I was red up to the elbows with it.

Just before blacking out, I'd slashed out with the knife. *What had I done?*

In panic, I began to wipe the blood from my hands on the

grass when I heard a shout from over the hill, and then thudding footsteps. I stumbled backwards, but there was nowhere to hide. A man rose over the rim, stopping as he saw me.

It was Ben. 'Kate – *Jesus*.' He crossed the grass in three strides. 'Where are you hurt?'

Words would not come; I just shook my head. It hadn't occurred to me to think about that. Was the blood mine?

Gently, he opened my jacket, and I saw that it, too, was covered in blood. His hands slid down my front and around my back.

'You're in one piece,' he said. Taking a bandanna from his pocket, he wet it in the dew-soaked grass and began to wipe my hands and wrists clean. 'What happened?'

Brokenly, I told him what I could remember – Lily's disappearance, coming up the hill with the knife. And now, the knife missing.

'Let me look,' he said quietly.

So I sat there, holding my aching head and once again watching him comb the hillside on my behalf. This time, though, he would not find the knife. I was certain of that.

Lily.

My pocket began to vibrate, and then to dance with a light, catchy drumming, pierced by the unmistakable scream of Mick Jagger, and the shake of maracas: the opening of 'Sympathy for the Devil'.

'Your phone, presumably,' said Ben.

I shook my head. I had never put that ringtone into it. Besides, I had switched it to vibrate last night, before coming up the hill.

Ben shoved his hand into my jacket pocket, pulled out the phone, and handed it to me.

The phone recognised the call as coming from Lily. But I had never programmed her number into my address book.

'Put it on speaker,' said Ben.

With shaking hands I answered it. 'Lily?'

'You didn't come alone.' The voice was full of reproach. I recognised it, though I'd only heard it in a snarl before. It belonged to the dark-haired man. The Winter King.

'Where is she?'

'Think of the knife as downpayment. Reference to a certain manuscript. You will find it and deliver it in two days' time. And then we release Lily.'

'*Two* – that's not enough time.'

'It's what there is.'

'And if it can't be found?'

'Ah. I think you already know. *She must die.*'

'We have to know that she's still alive and well,' said Ben.

'Still not alone,' came the reply. 'Be careful about that.' But he put Lily on the line.

'Kate?' Her voice was wobbly.

'Are you all right?'

'I want to come home.'

'We'll get you out of there as soon as we can.'

Her voice sank to a whisper. 'I'm sorry.' With that, the phone went dead.

I was still staring at it in mute anger when a siren spiralled upwards from the valley floor, piercing the quiet. Ben walked to the edge of the summit and quickly returned. 'Police, coming towards the hill,' he said.

'How would they know? Who else—' But even as I looked at him, we both knew who could send them. The people who'd taken the knife. Who'd taken Lily.

The traces of blood still on my hands seemed to burn with cold fire. Even if DI McGregor believed the manuscript-for-ransom story, she'd lock me up and look for it herself. But she wouldn't find it. And Lily would die. 'We have to go.' I started for the path, but Ben caught my elbow.

'Not that way. Unless you mean to wave and say howdy as we pass the police on the way down.'

'There is no other way.'

'This hill has other sides.'

'Have you *looked* at them?'

In answer, he strode across the shallow bowl of the summit to the southern rim. For an instant, he looked back. And then he disappeared over the edge.

Following in his wake, I saw a narrow ledge of grass just below the rim. Beyond that, a cliff sheered away into a tumble of grey rock far below. But the grassy ledge sloped down to the east, and Ben was already following it. At the end of the rock face, we found a narrow trail leading steeply down through the grass edging the western side of the cliff. 'Where the sheep goes, there go I,' said Ben with dark hilarity, plunging down the path.

It curved this way and that. In places, we slid more than walked as the path dropped a hundred feet or more. At last we neared the bottom of the cliff, turning into a wide meadow halfway down the hill. The trail dipped and rose again, and then Ben stopped so suddenly that I ran into him. Three ravens rose screeching into the air, wheeling angrily overhead.

'Don't look,' he said sharply. But I already had.

Just ahead, beneath a length of blue silk shimmering like snakeskin, someone lay sprawled in the shadow of a fall of boulders at the base of the cliff. The rocks were smeared and splattered with blood. I'd seen that gown before. It was Ellen Terry's, or a copy of it. I'd seen it last on Lady Nairn, her arms raised in wild praise to the moon.

Brushing past Ben, I stood over her for a moment. 'She was the Lady of the Hunt last night,' I said. 'I thought it was me who was going to be torn to shreds.'

I twitched aside a corner of the gown. It lifted with a light clatter, as the dried husks of a thousand beetle-backs shifted upon each other.

She lay with her head flung back, her hair cascading over rock thickly splattered and pooled with blood. Her throat had been slashed so savagely that the head had very nearly come off, and was twisted at an impossible angle. But the

224

hair was not a smooth pale blonde. It was dark gold, falling in ringlets.

Sybilla.

Beside me, Ben had gone still as the stones around us.

On my hands, the blood still lining my nails and the deep grooves in my knuckles burned like acid. I glanced down, seeing them once again as I had seen them on waking: sticky and thickly smeared with Sybilla's life. Or her death.

What had I done?

Interlude

She stood on the battlements and watched them come.

It had been a long time since Scotland had been ruled by a monarch of mettle. The young king, not quite nineteen, who rode towards her was a coward, and his mother, long imprisoned in a remote English castle, was a fool. If the countess had her way, however, that blight would soon come to an end.

Between them, she and her husband possessed all the right qualities to rule: ruthlessness, daring, intelligence, and, so far, the golden smile of the gods. Their blood-claim – the blue blood of royal Stewarts – might not be the strongest, but it was undeniably present. In her case, it was written all over her face and the bright copper of her hair. In combination with their other qualities and the possession of the crown, it would be enough.

Long ago, dark powers had pronounced that one day she would be queen, and she meant to help them, if she could. After the death of her first husband, helped along by one of her cordials when she tired of waiting for him to take her to

227

court, she had ridden south as a still-young and beautiful widow, shining with the red beauty of the royal Stewarts. Though nearly twenty years his senior, she'd intended to take the young king in hand, as Diane de Poitiers had once taken Henri II of France in hand, with almost exactly the same spread in age. She did not need the title of queen: she wanted the power.

She thought she had made her choice of second husband well: an elderly cousin of the king, old enough to leave her alone yet trusted enough to give her access to the boy. But the old man had not left her alone, lusting after her youth and beauty, and the young king, it soon became clear, though undeniably fascinated by her, reserved his deepest passions and trust for men. Deciding to cast off her second husband, she looked about for a third, a man who would rouse the king's admiration, but respond to her seductions. A man who had royal blood, and yet would need her backing to gain access to the halls of the great. A man with enough sense and sophistication to put aside petty jealousy and welcome any attentions the king might be induced to pay her, as she would welcome any attentions paid to him.

She'd found just the person she needed in the gallant and adventurous captain, now earl, who'd become her third husband. Their rise had been swift and sure. The day he had been handed the keys to Edinburgh Castle, she had swept into the storerooms that housed the wardrobe of the king's mother, Queen Mary, and shut the doors against everyone else save her old nurse. Breaking open the chests herself, she had rifled through the royal jewels and silks, furs and satins alone.

Some of the jewels she had pawned the next day; others, along with the gowns that could be recut into current fashions, she had taken for her own use. That evening, she had appeared in royal splendour high on the battlements of Edinburgh, overlooking a crowd gathering in the open space below, aware of both their wonder and their fear, but ignoring them, looking out over the city and the country which she meant to rule.

To do it, she had to rule first and foremost over the king now riding towards her, a boy who might have the colouring of the Stewarts, but not the heart. Bandy-legged and pasty-faced, he was a poor excuse for a man, never mind a king. Not that one could blame the boy, if you stopped to think about it. He'd known nothing but betrayals, assassination attempts, abductions, and rivers of blood since before he'd been born, all topped off with severe Calvinist schooling in cold castles in the years since, his boyhood alarmingly devoid of warmth in either the sense of human kindness or of weather. His mother's private secretary and possible lover – some still whispered his real father – had been slaughtered in front of her eyes by her husband while she was seven months pregnant with the boy. When he was not quite eight months old, the killer, the prince's publicly recognised father, had been strangled and his house blown up around him to disguise the murder. At the grand old age of thirteen months, James's mother was dethroned in favour of his own ascension, and he had never seen her again. A year later she was imprisoned by his 'dear cousin', the English Queen Elizabeth, with whom he nonetheless had to curry favour in hopes of one day inheriting her crown. Or, at the very least, of avoiding yet another full-scale English attempt to annex Scotland by force.

And those were just the memorable punctuation points before he'd reached the age of two. If anyone had earned the right to fear naked steel and hidden plots, it was James. All the same, it was disconcerting to watch him, a month shy of nineteen, flush like a girl at the jingle of armour, or walk in tight circles like a wandering top as he fretted over a minor slight or a major dilemma.

At least he could sit a horse.

He was sitting a horse now, in the centre of a mounted knot of his most trusted men, her husband at his right hand as she watched them approach. They looked for all the world like a cheerful party out hawking, perhaps. Bells jingling, ribbons streaming from the horses' manes, and shouts of laughter lacing the bright spring wind off the Firth of Forth as they rode. But if you knew what to look for, no doubt you could see hints of something darker. The tight hunch of the king's shoulders and his tendency to use the crop with a hard hand, for instance. A certain shrillness in his voice, perhaps. But the clearest sign was their speed. They were travelling much too fast for a party of leisure.

To be fair, this time it would not be just the king who was afraid. Most men were afraid of the Black Death, and two days ago it had broken out with a vengeance in a village to the west of Edinburgh. By yesterday afternoon, it had scaled the cliffs and entered the castle that loomed over the queen of Scottish cities. That had proved enough for the king, who had no wish to wait for the infection to roll down the hill and knock at the door of his pleasure palace of Holyroodhouse, scattering dark, foul-smelling buboes hither and yon, without respect for rank or piety.

She might have been frightened herself, had she not known that it was not yet her time to face death, black and bubo-swollen or otherwise. As plague season had approached, she had plotted with her husband to offer their newly acquired home of Dirleton Castle, a safe twenty miles east of the pestiferous city, as a refuge, where the king could find safety and a certain sophisticated beauty that enchanted him. For it was important to keep the spell of attraction strong and bright.

So she'd called in servants and laid in cartloads of food for several weeks at the approach of plague season. Hearing words of a travelling troupe of English players, she'd diverted them from the road to Edinburgh, sweetening their palms with enough money to make sure that their alternative route took in Dirleton. After a dour childhood, the king was fascinated by music, dancing, and plays.

And then Lord Henry Howard had come with a different proposition, one that twisted all her deep-woven plans to another shape entirely. A smile of satisfaction on her face, she went down to welcome the king.

Unaccountably, her husband, who had thrilled to the idea of taking the crown in the cold morning light, baulked at it amid the music and laughter of the night. With a suddenness that even the king noticed, he rose and left the great hall in the middle of the feast. She knew where to find him, on the battlements outside her aerie, looking out towards the sea.

He flinched at her touch. 'We will proceed no further in this business,' he said. 'He has honoured me of late.'

'He's a boy, and fickle. It will not last.'

'He's a boy. As you say. And frightened. And he's here in double trust, as kin and king.'

A spurt of anger and annoyance shot through her. 'I love our boys as much as you do. And yet, if I had sworn it, as you have sworn yourself to this, I'd dash their brains against the wall behind you.'

He walloped her across the cheek at that. A stinging blow, not bruising. A warning. She let the mark of his hand redden her cheek, disdaining to hold it, and pulled herself under control. The point was to persuade him, not to win a petty row. Sidling close, she began once more to paint visions in the air for him, running light fingers down his arm, lifting it high. 'He has brought the crown within our reach tonight. Put out your hand and pluck it down, before we are plucked ourselves.'

He jerked away from her.

'Another opportunity may not come.'

'*No more.*' Turning on his heel, he strode off.

She watched him go as she might watch a recalcitrant child. He'd grown to like the boy, or at least to pity him: well and fine. He would have to be schooled to see that the king, despite his liking, was still a pawn. She had worked too hard to let the chance of a crown slip away now.

A shadow detached itself from the opposite doorway and Lord Henry Howard materialised before her eyes, contempt curdling his face. 'If you cannot handle a husband, my lady, how will you control a kingdom?'

She tossed her head with impatience and distaste. 'Husbands, like horses, occasionally require to be given their heads.'

She was brushing past him when he caught her. '*Pluck down the crown, before we are plucked ourselves,*' he said in light mockery, and then his voice hardened. He pushed her backwards, pinning her against the wall. 'If I have come here on a fool's errand, I will see that both of you are plucked directly. I swear it.' Around them, the tapestries rippled and moved, and in the gap where one ended and another began, they saw the eyes. Another watcher in the night.

In an instant, Lord Henry had drawn his sword and thrust it through the cloth, but it had rung impotently against the stone as the watcher slipped sideways. Ducking out from his hiding place, the other man skittered across the room, putting the heavy oaken table between himself and Lord Henry's blade.

He was the player, she saw. The player with the half-moon brows. Come back for more of what he'd found last night, no doubt: artless, addled fool that he was. Though she felt a thrill, truth be told, at this proof of her power. For a moment, the countess remained leaning against the wall, exultation and dismay tangled in her throat. Who else had been watching in the shadows? Was the king himself lurking in a corner?

A blow thundered against the table and she pushed herself up. Unless she stopped him, Lord Henry would kill the boy, which was a waste. She'd seen him at his work earlier, prancing about in a Robin Hood play as one of the merry men. She'd found herself laughing.

Nobody was laughing now. She caught at Lord Henry, but he flung her off. Tasting blood on her lip, she pulled down a tapestry and went at him again as she had learned to stop her father's drunken men-at-arms from killing each other, whirling the heavy brocade like a net over his sword arm. The cloth wrapped around him, unbalancing him, bringing him crashing to the floor on one knee. 'Let him go,' she commanded. 'He is not your concern.'

The boy needed no further prompting. Flashing her a cheeky grin, he scampered out onto the battlements and down the stairs. No doubt he'd disappear into the hills before dawn.

Lord Henry disentangled himself from the tapestry, and rose, ramming his sword back into its scabbard in disgust. She'd expected to see rage in his eyes, but there was only coldness. 'Not my concern: then I take it he is yours. Did you rut with him last night?'

'Did you?' she shot back, still looking after the boy, the memory of his heat playing at her breasts and groin.

Lord Henry's eyes hooded. 'I would kill a man who said that.'

'You will not kill me.'

He laughed aloud at that, but it was not a sound of merriment.

'He's nothing but a poor player.'

She had expected derisive laughter. But the man went pale and deathly still, his olive skin blanching with cold anger and something she had not expected to see in his face: fear. He took a step towards her, his hands clutching like claws, and for a moment she thought he might attack her. 'What have you done?' he cried. '*Nothing but—*'

He began pacing, his hands running through his salt-and-pepper hair. 'Was he here last night?'

'That is not your concern.'

He grabbed her, shaking her with a force she had not felt since her first husband had been on a spree. '*Was he here?*'

235

She laughed in his face. 'He was. All night.'

For a moment, she thought he might squeeze the life out of her, but he put his mouth close to her ear and spoke with a low, quick urgency.

'You do not know young Robert Cecil, then. Lord Burghley's son and Walsingham's protégé.'

She went still. Burghley was Queen Elizabeth's Secretary of State and Lord High Treasurer. The quiet, conniving man who ran her kingdom. Walsingham was her master of spies. She did not know the son, but his connection to these two men made him someone worthy of caution.

'Misshapen as a changeling,' Lord Henry went on, his voice low and urgent with loathing, 'with a mind as twisted as his body. But precocious. A few years back, at his recommendation, every troupe of players in England surrendered their best actors to the queen's own company. The rest were redistributed, and many were recruited.' He'd run a long, cool finger down the line of her jaw. '*Nothing but players.* They are Elizabeth's eyes and ears at a distance. *They are spies.*'

He flung her off and backed away, and at last the scornful laughter had ripped from him. 'Within three days, Elizabeth will know everything that has passed within these walls. If she finds it to her advantage, she will pass your treason on to your king.' He'd brushed the sleeves of his doublet as if the very air of her room had soiled him. 'I must ride for England, and attempt to control the coming storm. As for you, madam, do what you will: I fear you will never be queen.' With that, he strode out the door.

'You are wrong,' she'd whispered defiantly to the empty room. 'I have seen it.'

MIRROR

You go not till I set you up a glass
Where you may see the inmost part of you.

25

Ben took the blue robe from me, laying it back down across Sybilla's face.

'*What have I done?*' I whispered.

He frowned, as if hearing me from a great distance. 'You did not do this.'

'You don't know that. *I* don't know that.' Hysteria was rising in waves.

There was a shout overhead.

'Kate, you have to go. I can't leave her, and you can't stay.' He made a move towards me and stopped, as if he could not bear to touch me. A look of blank horror filled his face. 'Listen to me: you're the only person who can save Lily right now. Go down to the house. Make sure the police aren't there. I doubt it: they have no reason to be, yet. Clean yourself up, get a change of clothes. Get money. Get whatever you need to find Lily. And then get out. Get as far away from here as you can.'

I was staring at him stupidly.

'*Go.*'

I turned and stumbled across the meadow. At its edge a

thick row of pines skated down another steep stretch of the hillside, tumbling to the road. Bracken cracked and rustled beneath my feet, small rocks tumbling and sliding around me. The wood was eerily silent.

At the bottom, the trees ended abruptly at the road. I edged forward to look up and down the pavement. The sun had not yet made its way this far down the hillside, and the road was a ravine of grey ghosts. Thinking of Sybilla rustling behind me in shimmering blue, I slipped across the road and floundered up the slope on the opposite side, towards the house. *What had I done?*

Sybilla was dead and Lily had disappeared. I had forty-eight hours to find the manuscript and ransom her.

If I did, if I found her, I might – just might – learn what had happened up on that hill last night. Learn what I had, or had not done.

Forty-eight hours.

I had to tell Lady Nairn.

The house was dark On the terrace, I looked up. There was only one light on, high in a corner tower. Lady Nairn's treasure room.

With my hand on the front door, I paused. Lady Nairn had been on the hilltop last night, her arms raised to the moon, a knife in her hand. She was a witch, a Wiccan priest-ess, that much was clear. But what other role had she played? I'd thought her a victim, when I first saw the body covered in her blue beetle-wing gown. Was it possible that she'd killed, instead? Or seen me kill? Swallowing back dread, I opened the heavy door and slipped inside.

It did not feel like a sleeping house, filled with the sense of slow breathing and dreams. It felt empty, even derelict. I felt my way up the dimly lit stairs. One floor up, just outside the hall, a vase lay smashed on the floor. The room beyond was dark save for the far corner, where faint light oozed from the door to the stairs up to the tower. Hearing nothing, I crept across the room, pausing again to listen before pattering up the steps.

At the top, the door to Lady Nairn's room was ajar. Through the crack, I saw that the chest beneath the window had been smashed, its splinters scattered across the floor. The last time I'd come, the room had been singing, the air filled with wind chimes and the quiet burble of a fountain. Now it was silent. Holding my breath, I pushed open the door.

It wasn't just the chest that was broken. Around it, the once beautiful room was a shambles. Ashes had been scattered across the floor, and the chimes ripped down and savagely bent and broken. The small bookshelf had been overturned. Some of the books smouldered on the hearth; others had been tossed into the fountain, clogging its flow. Nearby, the two armchairs had been slit. Within the circle inlaid in the tile floor, a pentacle had been drawn in what looked like blood.

Maybe it was the pentacle. Maybe it was the memory of

Lady Nairn on the hill, her arms raised to the moon. Looking around the ravaged room, I finally realised what it was: fire to the south, water to the west, chimes to the east, for air, and the window framing the hill to the north, for earth. It was a Wiccan temple. Or the ruins of one. A temple desecrated with a fury, a pointed and extreme hatred that was frightening even in its aftermath.

Through the open door, I heard the shuffle of a step on the stair below, and then silence. Whoever was out there did not want to be heard. Why? The pentacle on the floor suggested that the place was ready for some rite – missing only the celebrants. Was that who was rising up the stairs? Had the light in the tower been a lure?

The room was at the top of the tower, with only one door; the stairs were the only way out. I was trapped. Picking up a stout board torn from the chest, I slipped behind the door. Moments later, I heard a step on the threshold, and an intake of breath. I gripped the board like a bat, and the door was flung shut.

Eircheard stood facing me, knife in hand, horror spreading across his face. 'What's happened, lass? Are you all right?'

I looked down. I'd forgotten my bloodsoaked clothes. Dropping the board, I began to shake. 'It's not my blood.'

Behind him stood Lady Nairn in dark trousers and a thin sweater, her face drawn. 'Where's Lily?'

'It's not hers, either.'

'*Where is she?*'

I took a deep breath. 'We found her last night at the festival. But she was taken again. From me, Lady Nairn. It's why I came back up the hill last night . . . I'm sorry.'

As I spoke, she raised a hand to her mouth, stifling a cry. Now she turned away. As quickly as I could, I recounted all that had happened from seeing Lucas up through the phone call from Lily's captors.

'Who are they?' demanded Lady Nairn.

'I don't know. I saw Lucas at the festival. But he told me to walk away. On the hill last night, I saw the Winter King. It was his voice, on the phone.'

'The bastard who first drugged and then tried to kill me?' asked Eircheard.

I nodded. 'I don't know who he is. None of this makes sense.'

'What do they want?' Lady Nairn snapped.

'They took the knife. Now they want the manuscript of *Macbeth*.'

She wheeled about the room. 'How do they even know about it?'

'I don't know. They gave me forty-eight hours—'

She stopped at the window that had once sung with chimes, fingering a shard of mother-of-pearl and crystal from the sill. 'The mirror, the knife, and now the manuscript,' she murmured.

'The mirror?'

245

She turned and surveyed the room. 'This . . . this isn't just hatred for me and my religion. Though it's both of those things.' She shook her head. 'It also covers a theft. Whoever did this also took the mirror.'

Dim and spotted with age within its heavy silver frame, the mirror she'd kept in here had once belonged to the King's Men; it was said to have been used as a prop in the first performance of *Macbeth*.

'I've been wrong, Kate,' she said, her face grim. 'It isn't sabotage we're dealing with.'

'They're stealing your finest treasures,' I said bleakly. *Including Lily.*

She shook her head impatiently. 'They're gathering tools.' She crossed her arms, her eyes dropping to my jacket. 'Whose blood is it?'

'Sybilla's. She – she's dead,' I faltered.

'Dead how?'

'Her throat was cut.'

Eircheard snorted with outrage, while Lady Nairn cried out, putting a hand down on the sill to steady herself. Briefly, her eyes met his. 'Then they've consecrated it – the knife,' she said. 'And probably the mirror as well.'

'*Consecrated?*'

'To make holy.' She exhaled in sardonic disgust. 'In Wiccan practice, we mostly consecrate with light, usually moonlight.'

'So you are one, then. A witch.'

'I prefer the term priestess.'

I didn't care what term she used: why hadn't she told me?

'There are older, darker rites, though,' she went on, 'still whispered about in corners, that use other forces. The most powerful – and the most dangerous – is blood.'

Rubbing her forehead, she stood staring at the pentacle smeared on the white floor. 'Like I said, this isn't sabotage. It's a hijacking. It isn't just Lucas trying to ruin my show. He . . . and others, maybe . . . are taking it for their own. To work the magic . . . Black magic,' she added. 'Blood sacrifice.'

26

Nausea rippled around me as I thought of Sybilla sprawled on the rocks, Ben's bleak face staring down at her body. 'Sybilla was killed in a rite of black magic?'

'In preparation for one,' said Lady Nairn.

'*Preparation?*' My voice was hoarse. 'That was *rehearsal?*'

'It was a rite of consecration. Not the Great Rite itself, whatever that's intended to be.'

'What were you doing up there?'

'Our Samhuinn rite. A ceremony of celebration and thanksgiving.'

Staring at my hands, I began to shake. 'I woke covered in blood. And missing hours . . .' My voice dropped to a whisper. 'I might have done it.' I looked up. 'I might have killed Sybilla. Or helped to.'

Eircheard took both my hands, his face solemn. 'You've got blood on you, maybe. But not killing.'

I twisted to look at Lady Nairn. 'Did you see it? Did you see what happened?'

Her jaw twitched. 'No.'

'Then you don't know,' I said, pulling away from

Eircheard in despair. '*You can't.*' From the way my head felt, I was pretty sure I'd had a concussion. It would explain the amnesia and the headache, but not the action. What had I done in the hours that I'd lost?

'You saw something horrible, there's no doubt about that,' said Lady Nairn. 'No one deserves that kind of death.' She shook her head slightly. 'You said that Lily's captors wanted the manuscript. Did they ask you to deliver it?'

'Yes.'

'Then I'm afraid there's another possibility, Kate. They consecrated the knife with blood. They may also have consecrated you.'

I went still, the air slicing against my skin suddenly sharp as a million small knives. 'For what?'

'Blood sacrifice, lass, requires a death,' said Eircheard.

She must die, Lucas had intoned. Lily would die, he'd said. Or I would.

I looked down. Did the blood on my hands mark me as killer or as victim?

Lily had been taken on my watch, her hand literally slipping from mine in that wild, dancing crowd in the Edinburgh close. She was my responsibility. Furthermore, if I'd killed Sybilla, or participated in any way . . . if I'd just *been* there . . . saving Lily was the best shot at redemption I'd ever be likely to manage.

249

And her captors were the only route I had towards finding out what I'd done.

Whatever the cost, I had to find Lily.

Lady Nairn was looking out the window, one toe tapping against the floor. 'Forty-eight hours, you said?'

I nodded.

Again, her eyes sought out Eircheard, who'd begun to pick up the pieces of the smashed chest and stack them carefully against one wall. 'Even the timing fits,' she said. 'In two nights, the moon will be full.'

'Aye,' said Eircheard. His eyes were bloodshot and bleary; a livid bruise was darkening across one cheek. 'There's to be a total eclipse, as well.'

'Rare enough to begin with. Even rarer, on the Samhuinn moon. The Blood Moon,' Lady Nairn said softly. She folded her arms. 'They'll need the cauldron, too.'

Having neatly stacked the remains of the chest, Eircheard righted the bookshelf and began filling it with whatever books he could find that weren't sodden or singed. 'This mess maybe sprang, in part, from frustration at not finding it.'

'The great silver bowl?' I asked. 'It's downstairs. I saw it as I came up.' Hard to miss a gleaming vat of silver three feet wide and two high, really.

'That's a copy,' said Lady Nairn. 'They'll need the original, and that's in the vault. Though I suppose I ought to check that as well.'

'It'll be the manuscript they'll be wanting most of all,' said Eircheard.

'They need to know what to do, don't they?' I said. 'The earlier version of the play . . . it's supposed to lay out a real magical rite.'

Gathering up bits of shattered wind chime, Lady Nairn sighed. 'It may be more than a general description they're after, Kate. In witchcraft, at least the way I practise it day to day, spells are intuitive and improvised. Lived in the moment. Power, whatever there is, inheres in the witch, as a vessel of the goddess.'

She smoothed her hair back from her face. 'But other practices are different. In ceremonial magic, precision matters: spells depend upon using exactly the right tools in the right way at precisely the right time. Most of all, ceremonial magic requires the right words said in the right order, with the right pronunciation.' She turned to look at me. 'In witchcraft, as I said, power inheres in the witch. The speaker, the spell-maker. But in ceremonial magic, power inheres in the language of the spell, in the words spoken.

'Most Great Rites, whether white or black magic, are at least in part ceremonial. So you see, to get it right—'

'They want the manuscript as a script for murder,' I said. *They meant to use Shakespeare to shape murder.* In the last few minutes, Lady Nairn seemed to have grown smaller, somehow, and harder. As if Lily's disappearance had burned away everything but a single cold, ruthless purpose. 'The lone bright spot is that they don't yet have everything they need. And we must make sure they never get it. We need to rescue Lily, Kate, so we have to find the manuscript. *But we must also see that they never get hold of it.*'

Eircheard was watching me. 'Why are they assuming you can find it in the first place, in that kind of time?'

In my mind's eye, I saw my name scrawled on a blood-stained page: *Kate Stanley.* 'Come with me,' I said, heading down the stairs.

Lady Nairn and Eircheard hurried in my wake.

Up in my room, I put Aubrey's notes in Lady Nairn's hand. As she read, Eircheard looking over her shoulder, I grabbed some jeans, a black turtleneck, and black Skechers and went into the bathroom to change. I looked longingly at the shower, but didn't dare take the time, settling for scrubbing my face and arms in the sink.

Walking back out, I set out on the desk Lady Nairn's other evidence: the photocopied entry in the household account book, dated 1589, and the letter from Ellen Terry to her mysterious Superman, dated 1911.

Lady Nairn had set the Aubrey down. 'Where did you get this?'

'Ben found it on Auld Callie.'

She looked up sharply. 'It was left there on purpose? For you to find it?'

'I can only assume so. Could it be what Sir Angus found?' I asked.

'Possibly.' Her eyes were shining. 'It backs the family legends.'

I nodded. 'It also links Shakespeare to Dee. To conjuring – to ceremonial magic – as much as to witchcraft.' Quickly, I told her what I'd worked out the night before, on the subject of Macbeth conjuring for the sake of knowledge.

'I'm no expert on Dee,' she said with a frown. 'If that's the direction things are going, we'll have to consult Joanna Black, down in London.'

I'd heard of Joanna – had been told I ought to meet her for years, actually. She, too, had left academia for practice. But where my study had been Renaissance drama, chiefly Shakespeare, hers had been Renaissance magic. She had a D.Phil. from Oxford in the History of Religion and Science. I'd headed into the public world of theatre; she'd headed into the reclusive world of magic and the exclusive world of occult collectors. I knew where her shop was, but that was about it: I'd never met her.

'I've never met her in person myself,' said Lady Nairn. 'But she's quite lovely on the phone and in email, and that's all we'd need.'

'Bollocks!' said Eircheard, looking up from the desk. 'What matters right now isn't who made Shakespeare change the sodding play, or why. What matters is where it got to, so we know where Kate needs to go. And Dee's got bog-all to do with that. The last-known whereabouts of anything useful have to do with Ellen Terry's *Monsieur Superbe Homme*. Who is he, do you suppose?'

Lady Nairn shook her head.

'Look,' I said, skimming through Terry's letter with one finger to point at the last line: *As it is, I am hoping that you can glimpse the Forest through the Trees.*

'And then here,' I said, sliding over to the Aubrey, to Beerbohm's cartoon of Shakespeare brandishing a leafy branch at Macbeth, with its caption of a loosely scribbled line from *Macbeth: Who can impress the Forrest, bid the Tree unfix his earthbound root?*

'It's got to have something to do with that goddamn tree,' I said.

'*Superbe Homme,*' murmured Eircheard. '*Sous* pear bum. Under the pear-shaped arse.'

'Focus,' I said shortly. 'Both Terry and Beerbohm yammering on about forests and trees can't be a coincidence. Especially in light of Sir Angus's last words. *Dunsinnan must go to Birnam Wood.*'

'That isn't what he said,' grumbled Eircheard.

'What?'

'Birnam Wood. That isn't what he said.'

Lady Nairn rolled her eyes. 'He'd just had a stroke. It was what he meant.'

Eircheard looked at me. 'What he said was "Dunsinnan

must go to the Birnam Tree". Not "the wood". And if you're wanting to put a really fine point on it, it wasnae Birnam he said, either. Birble, or burble, or bourbon or something.'

'Birbam,' said Lady Nairn curtly. '"Dunsinnan must go to the Birbam Tree".'

'Pear bum, bare bum,' Eircheard chanted under his breath, back to puzzling out Ellen Terry's correspondent. 'Beer bum, burr bum.'

'Will you be quiet?' snapped Lady Nairn.

'No,' I said suddenly. 'Say it again.'

'Beer bum, burr bum?'

I felt a flicker of excitement. 'Did he say "go to *the* Birbam Tree"?'

'No. Just "to Birbam Tree".'

'You're a *superbe homme* yourself,' I said, kissing him on the cheek. 'It's not Birnam, and it's not Birbam.' I pointed to the drawing. 'It's *Beerbohm*.'

'The cartoonist?' asked Eircheard. 'Max Beerbohm?'

'Beerbohm, yes. Max, no. His older half brother, Herbert.'

Lady Nairn's eyes lit up. 'Herbert Beerbohm *Tree*.'

'*Tree*?' hooted Eircheard.

'One of the great Shakespearean actors and theatre impresarios of the late Victorian and Edwardian eras,' I said. 'His family name was Beerbohm, but when Herbert went on the stage he felt it didn't sound English enough, so he translated the last syllable, *bohm* or *baum*, from the German to get Tree. As it happens, one of his greatest roles was Macbeth.'

'*Monsieur Superbe Homme*,' said Eircheard with satisfaction.

I smiled. 'A cross-language pun of sorts. At a guess, the name "Beerbohm" is pronounced something between "pear bum" and "bare bum" in French. He's supposed to have been superb, too. Tall and handsome. Witty. Gallant. He started RADA – the Royal Academy of Dramatic Arts, and was knighted. Also *superbe* in the French sense: splendid, magnificent, proud. Though apparently not arrogant . . .'

'But dead, I take it,' said Eircheard.

'Quite.'

'So how was Sir Angus going to go to him? Do we know where he's buried?'

'I don't.'

'Where he lived?'

'No – yes.' I stood up and sat down again. '*Yes*. Lady Nairn, was Sir Angus a fan of *Phantom of the Opera*?'

'Angus hated musicals,' she said. 'Fairly sniffy about them, actually. He preferred Verdi and Wagner. But after his stroke, I found two tickets to *Phantom* in his wallet. I assumed he meant to take Lily.'

I stood still in the centre of the room, adrenaline surging through me. 'He wasn't going to Birnam Wood. Or the Birnam Tree. He was going to Beerbohm Tree. And Tree lived at the theatre. *His* theatre. The theatre he built and ran. Her Majesty's Theatre, in London.'

'Oh good Lord,' said Lady Nairn.

'What?' asked Eircheard. '*What?*'

'Where *Phantom*'s been playing for nearly three decades,' I said.

I turned to Lady Nairn. 'Do you have anything of Tree's in your collection?'

She was skimming out of the room when the sound of sirens floated through the window.

Coming back to the desk, Lady Nairn slid the papers back into the folder, which she stuffed into a tote and handed to me along with the tight bundle of my blood-soaked clothes. 'Time to go, Kate.'

27

'My place,' said Eircheard. 'We'll burn those clothes in the forge, and get you on your way for London.'

Lady Nairn led us swiftly to a back stairway. At the bottom, we came to a small postern door opening onto a walled garden. The trees of the surrounding pine wood marched right up to the garden wall. Lady Nairn unlocked the small, stout oak door that led through it.

'I have something of Tree's you should see,' she said with quiet urgency. 'I'll be ten minutes behind you. If I'm longer than that, don't wait. Now go.'

As two police cars rolled up the gravel drive, Eircheard and I slipped south through the trees. After a while, we turned back westward, Eircheard's rolling gait giving our footsteps a kind of jazz syncopation; other than our footsteps, the woods were quiet. High wispy clouds raced across sky. Past the turning off to the hill, we cut back to the road. Edging through the dry bracken, Eircheard found a place dappled with dark shade and beckoned me forwards. We quickly crossed the lane and entered the woods on the opposite side.

Five minutes later, we walked into the smithy. I prowled about, feeling exposed, until Eircheard said, 'Make yourself useful,' and showed me how to work the bellows as he stoked up the fire. The fire blazed up from red to orange and yellow that paled into white. He had just fed my bloody jacket into the flames when Lady Nairn scurried in, her cheeks pink and her breath coming in short gasps. 'McGregor,' she gasped. 'On a mission. Headed this way and looking for Kate.'

Eircheard thrust the rest of my clothes into the fire, and Lady Nairn grabbed my hand, pulling me back outside. As we ran across the field towards the woods at the side of his house, I heard the clang of a hammer on metal. Eircheard was forging. We ducked into the trees, and a car turned into the drive behind us.

Crouching beneath some dying ferns, we watched the police car pull to a stop, its doors flashing in the sun as they opened. DI McGregor and her sergeant got out and went into the forge. Eircheard's hammer beats never paused.

'Kate—'

I shook my head impatiently. 'I need to hear what McGregor has to say.'

'Eircheard will tell us. I need to tell you who's behind all this.' My eyes locked on hers. As she caught her breath and the pink in her cheeks subsided, she looked ashen. I let her draw me deeper into the trees, into a clearing where pale light and the odd birdcall drifted down through lacy branches whose last clinging leaves were dry as paper. I blinked, realising where we were: back in the stone circle. In the morning sun, the standing stones looked squat and sleepy. Stones that had seemed to loom taller than I in the darkness rose only to my shoulders; half of them had tipped and fallen. Even so, it was a place of brooding power. Asleep, not drained or dead.

We crouched in the shadow of one of three big stones fallen together, where I could still see the smithy and the car.

'I'm sure Lucas is involved. He has to be. But with him, or behind him, is someone far worse.' She swallowed. 'It's my niece, Kate. My sister's child. Her name is Carrie Douglas.

'I'd rather face Lucas, any day. His hatred may be thick, but it's standard flesh-and-blood wickedness. Jealousy and greed: things you can understand in a visceral way. But Carrie—' She paused. 'Her evil is uncanny. Fey.'

She ran a hand over her mouth. 'After my sister died, when Carrie was twelve, Angus and I took her in – my sister had never identified the father. We gave her a home, and did our best to love her, but she was . . . cruel. Not in the normal small ways of children still learning to be civilised. She enjoyed causing pain, and her eyes always looked as if she were seeing more than she ought to be. Frankly, she frightened me. And she'd frightened her mother, though my sister was too loyal to say so. But she was bright and curious, especially about the craft.'

'Witchcraft?'

'It's in her blood. In our family, it's a tradition passed down from mother to daughter. It's in her name, too: Carrie's short for Cerridwen . . . a Welsh triple goddess famed for cauldron magic. But her mother was dead, and I would not teach her.' She sniffed. 'Walling her out was not, I've thought since, the right response. She went off and found other masters.

'On her seventeenth birthday, I found her on the hilltop with my daughter. There was a cauldron. In it was a dead adder and the head of Elizabeth's pet cat.'

I grimaced.

'Next to it, Elizabeth was bound and naked. Carrie had . . . cut her.' She put a hand out to the stone, as if she needed steadying, though we were both sitting down. 'She likes to mark things – and people – with the old Pictish symbol of a cauldron. A large circle with two tiny circles on either side, a line running through the centre of all three.' With one finger, she traced the design on the rock:

'It's a cauldron seen from above, hanging from a bar over a fire, with the two lugs or handles on each side.' Her eyes narrowed as she looked out towards the smithy. 'She'd carved it right over Elizabeth's pubic area. Elizabeth was ten.'

She gave a little shake, pulling herself loose from the memory and turning her attention to me. 'Angus wouldn't prosecute her. More because he did not want to drag our daughter through the consequences, than out of any family loyalty. But he banished her from our house and our lives then and there . . . this was almost thirty years ago.'

'And you think she's back?'

'I've just spoken to Ben, Kate. He saw a symbol carved into Sybilla's belly.' My stomach tightened with revulsion. 'A large circle with two small circles on either side. It seems to have been scratched into Auld Callie's shoulder as well. McGregor asked me about it. I told her I had no idea what it meant.'

'Jesus.'

'It makes sense, of a kind, of Callie's murder, even before they needed blood for ritual consecration,' Lady Nairn said bleakly. 'She could identify Carrie, you see.'

'Does Lily know any of this?'

Her face clouded. 'No. I've never told her about either Lucas or Carrie. I probably should have, especially when she got so taken with Corra Ravensbrook. All that stuff about Dunsinnan in *Ancient Pictland*—'

'You think it may have come from Carrie?'

'She's not a bored housewife.' Her lips twisted in disgust. 'The Scottish counterpart of Cerridwen is a crane-goddess named Corra. And "Douglas" is Gaelic for "Dark Water".'

'Ravensbrook,' I murmured. 'So Corra Ravensbrook *is* Carrie Douglas.'

She nodded. 'I started to tell Lily, more than once. But somehow it always seemed like taking a hammer to her innocence.'

And what's happened to her innocence now? I thought. 'What's Carrie after?' I asked aloud. 'I mean – Macbeth works his magic to gain knowledge. But the ability to play the stock market or manipulate Vegas—' I shook my head. 'It seems too mundane, anticlimactic even, for someone who'd . . .'

'Hang Auld Callie and carve up Sybilla?' Lady Nairn said softly.

'Yes.'

'Don't be distracted, Kate, by Aubrey or Dee or even Macbeth himself. Ellen Terry's source, my family's legends, and now Aubrey all say that what Shakespeare altered – what's missing – isn't something to do with Macbeth conjuring. It has to do with the witches' magic . . . *What is it you do?* Macbeth cries as he enters. And the witches answer as one—'

My voice slid through the words along with hers: '*A deed without a name.*'

'That's the rite that's missing,' said Lady Nairn. 'That's what Carrie wants.'

'But it's not missing. The witches are there, dancing around a cauldron.'

'Oh, there's cauldron magic present, but it's the stuff of nursery rhymes. Or nursery nightmares. And if Macbeth could see and hear what they're doing: *why ask?*'

She had twisted her hands together. 'Celtic myth is scattered with cauldron magic, Kate. Cauldrons of plenty and prophecy, mostly. But the goddess Cerridwen's cauldron is also, quite specifically, about poetry. Shorthand for inspiration of all kinds. For genius. The charismatic ability to conjure up shared dreams so bright and so strong that they move people to action. No amount of hard work or study or card-counting can buy you that. Nothing can *buy* it. It's a flash of fire from the gods that you are given, or you are not.' Her eyes met mine. 'But if there was some promise of manipulating such a flash of power? Of directing or luring the thunderbolt of the gods to land where you wished? That, I think, someone like Carrie might well kill for.'

Lily had boasted that her beau would reshape storytelling, as Shakespeare once had. I pushed that thought away. 'What promise?' I asked shortly. 'This is the twenty-first century. What *promise* could Carrie convince herself of?'

Lady Nairn drew in a deep breath. 'There are those who say that the play itself is proof. More specifically, the playwright.'

'Shakespeare?'

Her famous turquoise eyes, holding mine, seemed fathomless. 'Some say he was able to record such a rite because he witnessed it, Kate. And having witnessed it . . . that he benefitted from it.'

I jumped to my feet, my breath coming in short bursts as if I'd been running. 'Are you suggesting that Shakespeare's genius came from a rite of magic? *That's absurd.*'

Lady Nairn rose beside me. 'Is it? He was a poor boy, a glover's son, from a provincial backwater. He left behind no record of education. No records at all, really, save that he sired three children and then disappeared for seven years, after which he showed up in London, his pen flowing with astonishing brilliance.'

'It's extraordinary, I'll give you that. But to explain the inexplicable by totting it up to a moment of hocus-pocus—'

She was as calm and cool as I was exasperated. 'Did what you saw last night look like hocus-pocus?'

I was silent, remembering the sweep of moonlight and starlight on the hill, the strange rise of the keening voice. And the horned man, with the eyes of an owl. 'Who was he?' I asked tightly. 'The horned man?'

'Eircheard.'

'No.' It was not Eircheard I had seen. It wasn't possible. I'd seen a younger, fitter man who'd had no limp.

But Lady Nairn was adamant. 'He's been a member of my coven for a number of years, Kate. After Angus died, he stepped into the role of priest. I had a driver collect him after the festival and drive him back here directly. He was – worse for wear, let's say – but he was here. Just before you saw him, he'd called down the god . . . why? Who did you see?'

I stared at her, feeling the world sway beneath me. The very air playing over that hill seemed to make me see things that weren't there. I didn't want to think about that. 'You meant to work magic with this production as well, didn't you?'

A couple of leaves had stuck in her hair. She looked like a dryad.

She smiled. '*There are more things in heaven and earth, Horatio, than are dreamt of in your philosophy,*' she said lightly. 'What you or I can or can't believe, Kate, doesn't matter. It's what Carrie believes that matters just now. However he came by it, it seems that Shakespeare wrote a dark and terrible rite of cauldron magic into *Macbeth*, and later withdrew it. If Carrie believes, as I think she does, that she can use it to manipulate divine inspiration, then if she gets hold of it, she will perform it.'

Beyond the wood, the hammering stopped. Presently Eircheard emerged with the two detectives, walking around to the back of the smithy. While McGregor stood talking to Eircheard, the sergeant peeked into the bedroom and opened the back of the van, apparently with Eircheard's permission.

Silently, I drew forward to the edge of the wood. Their voices floated thinly across the field. 'What makes you think Kate was up there?' asked Eircheard.

McGregor's smile was cold. 'Fingerprints tentatively matching those in her room are all over a car at the base of the hill. And there's blood in the boot. A lot of it.'

Bile rose in my throat. Had Sybilla been in the car as I drove? Already dead – or even worse, still alive? Had I driven her to her death?

'Give her up,' McGregor said silkily, 'and I'll go lightly on you.'

'Kind of you,' said Eircheard, his hands in his pockets. 'But I don't have her to give.'

McGregor sniffed, surveying the smithy and the heap of scrap metal behind it. 'Be careful, Mr Kinross. A knife like some that you've made seems to have been involved in two homicides.' She turned back to him. 'I know your history. If you had anything to do with either of them, I'll see to it that you never see the light of day again.'

There was a stiff moment of silence. 'Good day,' said McGregor. And then she turned on her heel, her mouth still curved in a serpent's smile, and left, her sergeant trotting alongside.

Eircheard watched her go and then went back around and into the smithy. As the police car pulled out, he began hammering again.

It's what Carrie believes that matters just now. Whatever other madness was twisting the world, that at least made terrible sense. If she believed she could draw down divine inspiration by a rite of black magic, she'd perform it. And that would mean more death.

It seemed like an age, though it was probably only a few minutes, before the hammering ceased again and Eircheard came back around the building. Opening the door to the van, he leaned against the vehicle's side. He was holding the bag with the folder full of papers. Lady Nairn pressed something into my hand. I looked down. It was an iPod. 'When you have time, just pop it off Hold and push Play.'

'Lady Nairn—' I faltered. 'Forty-eight hours isn't much time.'

She put a hand on my shoulder. 'Find Lily,' she said. 'But Carrie can't be allowed to have that manuscript.'

'How—'

She shook her head. 'I'll do everything in my power to help you.'

'Get the police in on this, too,' I said. 'The more people looking for her, the better.'

'No,' she said vehemently. 'That woman will crucify you, given half a chance, and get Lily killed. There's no good that will come of going to the police, I'm afraid. If anyone can find her, Kate, you will.' She passed her hand over my head in benediction. 'Blessed be,' she said, and smiled. 'It's the witches' farewell.'

I turned and walked towards Eircheard. 'Into the van with you, then,' he said. 'Dunsinnan must go to Beerbohm Tree.'

I glanced back as I slid into the passenger seat. Under the eaves of the beech trees, Lady Nairn looked like a small shadow that had lost its body. The next time I looked, she had melted into the woods.

28

Shorn fields and autumnal woods slipped by in a blur. In the hedgerows, the hawthorns were bright with berries. I seemed to be staring out at the world through a veil of shadow. 'What did McGregor have to say?' I asked after a while.

'If you heard her outside, you got the gist of it. She wants your bonnie hide, and she's willing to knock other heads together to get it. Mine especially.'

'I gathered.'

'Bit of a chequered past.' He leaned back comfortably against the seat, one hand spread over the steering wheel, the other fidgeting with a small twisted bit of iron, the size of a large marble. 'Did some time a while back, for robbery.' He shrugged. 'Feedin' a habit. But there was a brawl afterwards, and another bloke got killed. With a knife. I didn't do it, but I was present. McGregor'll make hay out of that, given half a chance.'

My stomach turned over. 'Eircheard – you can't do this. Get me to the railway station in Perth,' I said. 'I'll be fine from there.'

'Do you have any idea how many surveillance cameras there are in those stations? McGregor'll have you before you reach Edinburgh, never mind London. No. I'll drive.'

'If she finds me with you, she'll have you, too.'

'Then we'll just have to make sure she doesn't find us, won't we?' He drove as if he were at the wheel of a Ferrari on the Autobahn, so fast that the battered van shook; even so he looked relaxed, as if he had all the time in the world. He slowed up only for speed cameras, whose locations he seemed to know by some sixth sense.

'It's not all for you, lassie,' he said with a wry smile. 'Though it's true I've taken a liking for your smile. But don't be taking the sins of the world on your shoulders. I owe the Nairns a great deal . . . met Lady Nairn in prison. She's a chaplain with the pagan prison ministry, did you know? Saw something in me that I couldn't. Or wouldn't. To this day, I can't tell you what. But she latched on and wouldn't let go.' He shrugged. 'I suppose I'd always been something of a pagan. But talking to her, the cycles of things just began tae make some sense. Afterwards, she and Sir Angus helped me apprentice to a blacksmith. And then they gave me a hand, setting up my own forge.

'That was when Lily was no more than a wee mite.' He shook his head. 'So you see, I'd be hard pressed to forgive any bastard as harmed a hair on her head.

'But it's not all for her, or for them, either.' His mouth twisted. 'Bloody eejit down in Edinburgh tried to kill me.

271

I'm no saint, Kate. I did my time. Wouldn't mind seeing that he does his.' The van careened along the shores of a shimmering blue lake. 'So you've had my story. What about yours? What did Lady Nairn come running to say to you?'

I told Eircheard what Lady Nairn had told me, watching his face go taut with disgust at Carrie's history. 'I knew of her,' he said. 'But not about the cutting.'

'How could she think that – that what she did to Sybilla and to Auld Callie would in any way contribute to a flowering of genius?'

I thought of Shakespeare, of the ease with which bright and dark worlds flew from his pen, bubbles blown carelessly on a breeze. What made his genius so luminous was partly his range: his moods stretching from silly to tragic, sometimes spinning from one to the other on a dime, his characters ranging from innocent girls to aged kings, from rollicking drunkards to ferocious queens, from sly and cynical bastards to hot-tempered youths chasing dreams of heroism. He gathered as his raw material all the fundamental experiences of being human, from birth to death, and all our passions in between: love and lust, hatred and hilarity, greed, jealousy, wrath and murderous revenge.

But there were other great writers who had done all these things. What set Shakespeare apart, for me, even from other greats, was his generosity: his invitation, even insistence, for others to join him in the act of imagining. His words had the power to conjure up bright worlds: but Shakespeare did not claim that power all for himself. Far from it: he scattered it like petals or glittering confetti. Unlike Shaw or O'Neill, who'd left stage directions that ran to entire pages, or the Beckett police, who insisted on licensing productions to ensure that they adhered to the master's vision, Shakespeare did not specify much about interpretation or setting or action, about political or moral message, or the lack thereof. His reticence made his works wonderfully elastic. It also made them demanding – sometimes maddeningly so, for directors and actors who had to figure out at every turn why these words and no others needed to said right here and now. But Shakespeare was also demanding of his audiences: yes, you could almost hear him say, you are sitting in a fairly barren wooden theatre. But dream yourselves to France. To a seacoast in Bohemia. To a magic-haunted island in a tempest-tossed sea. *I dare you.*

And for four hundred years, in every corner of the earth, people had taken his dare and sailed into imagined worlds – together. For the art that Shakespeare had shaped was communal, shared in a way that books and even films never are. It was a singular gift: the infinite and unceasing invitation to crowds to come together with half-cocked brows of scepticism, a fair dash of rowdiness, and most of all, sheer delight, and collectively imagine worlds into being.

'To suggest that all this had its source in some lightning bolt that struck while watching a rite on a Scottish hill,' I said, 'strikes me as not only preposterous but insulting to whatever forces of creation produced him.'

Eircheard had remained mostly quiet through my rant, a little smile playing on his face from time to time. 'Only if you're insisting on a narrow definition of magic,' he replied. 'As narrow, in some ways, as the sniffy productions that drive you mad.'

I bit my lip. 'Lady Nairn gave me Crowley's definition: "the science and art of causing change to occur in conformity with will."'

'Ah well, there's a nice double meaning there, for a man named Will.' He gave me a sly sideways grin. 'Never liked Crowley much, myself, or his definition, either. He equates magic with change. Willed change, but change, all the same. I'd put it a wee bit differently. "Making," for instance. Did you know that poets used to be called "makers" in Old English?'

'So did the Greeks,' I said, feeling suddenly exhausted. 'The word "poet" comes from their word for *to make*.'

'Well there you are, then.' He turned the bit of iron in his hand. 'Whatever you want to call it, some people seem to be able to tap into it strongly. Shakespeare, Michelangelo, Beethoven. But it isn't the moment of tapping – even if you could pinpoint it – that's important for any of them, or for any of us, if you see what I mean. It's the unfurling, the blossoming. Do you count conception, now, as the single miraculous moment of a life? Or are the nine months of

274

growing curved in the dark, the bursting out into light, and, after that, the long unfolding of a life in the world, all equally miraculous?'

'By that light,' I said quietly, 'all life is magic.'

A gruff rumbling of assent rose from him. 'Creation, I think, is the word I'd use. But yes, that's the deepest magic. Making whole shared worlds, like Shakespeare – maybe that's one of the highest forms. Very nearly divine in its power. But some of the most profound magic is fairly simple. Cooking, I'd say, and gardening, or farming. Rearing children. But you can also find it in making cabinets or clocks or quilts.'

'Or swords?'

'Definitely swords.' He grinned. 'As for being annoyed about a rite glimpsed on a hill – well, ritual is just a way of celebrating certain snapshot moments. Turning points. Making you really see them, focus on them. Not making them *happen*.' He shrugged. ''Course, that's just my opinion, and I'm not a scholar or anything. Just an ex-con who enjoys banging on steel.' He stretched and shifted in the seat. 'What did Shakespeare think about magic, now?'

I shook my head. 'It's hard to pin him down.'

'Try.'

It was no longer a question that was merely academic. Two lives might hang on it. One of them mine.

I stared out the window, at the fields of Scotland rolling by. 'His plays are laced with it, from first to last.' In my

275

mind, I went over the great conjuring scenes, from the *Henry VI* plays right at the beginning of his career, around about 1590, through to *The Tempest*, near the end, twenty-odd years later. 'He was definitely a cynic about the capacity of politicians and prelates to use witch hunts for their own ends. And I'd say he was a sceptic,' I added slowly, 'about the ability of humans – either witches or conjurors – to control supernatural forces just by casting a circle, waving a wand about, and uttering a few odd words. But, you know, in the few actual scenes of conjuration he wrote, the demons or spirits always come. Within the world of the play at hand, they're real. They make prophecies and promises that always turn out to be true, though often in some tricky way – Macbeth says that the dark powers lie like truth. But you might just as well say that they tell the truth like a lie, I suppose.

'Oddly enough, if anything, there's more magic, more deeply wound into his plots, in his final works than his first efforts. Prospero, in *The Tempest*, is the real thing: a white wizard, imagined, I've always thought, with some affection. Very possibly a fictional version of John Dee, though it's also popular to see him as Shakespeare himself: poet as magician. Earlier, he was less reverent. In the first part of *Henry IV*, written in the mid 1590s – during Shakespeare's first great flowering of genius,' I said, giving Eircheard a little jab, 'the Welsh leader Owen Glendower is another Dee figure, but he's a proud, prickly, and somewhat empty boaster. *I can call spirits from the vasty deep*, he claims, but he's undercut by the equally proud and prickly Hotspur, who cares for swords more than spells and who shoots back, *Why, so can I, or so can any man: but will they come when you do call for them?*

'And then there's *Midsummer Night's Dream.*'

'Full of fairies, eh?'

'English fairies, not Scottish. Flower imps, mostly. Cobweb, Moth, and Mustardseed. But there's a shadow of Scottish witchcraft; already, almost a decade before King James forced Scottish notions of witchcraft down English throats. In Titania, Queen of the Fairies.'

'Up here,' mused Eircheard, 'the Queen of Fairies is also the Queen of Witches.'

'Exactly. And Titania's great comic scene has her kissing a weaver named Bottom, magically given an ass's head.'

'One way to kiss ass,' said Eircheard with a shrug.

Sybilla's voice hung between us: *Titania waked, and straightway loved an ass.*

'It's a parody of the Black Mass that so enthralled King James and the Continental witch-hunters,' I said after a moment, 'but which the English more or less scorned. The central rite of that mass was supposed to consist of the witch kissing the devil's bottom.' I shook my head. 'Talk about generosity of spirit. Shakespeare took a belief that was being used to torture and kill thousands and made of it one of the great comic scenes in all of drama.'

'While up here we were saddled with King Jamie lighting fools the way to dusty death, burning them at the stake,' said Eircheard. 'Jesus.'

'Far as I can tell, Shakespeare had no respect for witch-hunters, and he suspected most conjurors as either con men or fools. But he believed in spirits and demons, and maybe fairies and ghosts. One of his earliest plays shows it best. *Henry VI, Part Two*. Wretched title, that: all it does is slot the play into others that were written later. Its first title was *The First Part of the Contention of the Two Famous Houses of York and Lancaster.*'

'That's a blooming mouthful.'

'More accurate, though: it was the first history play he wrote, right around 1590. One of the plays that made his name. In it, a duchess is wild for her husband to pluck the crown from the king's head and don it himself. Her husband's enemies lure her into consulting a conjuror, to see whether what she wishes will come to pass, and when she does, they use it to disgrace and banish her, and ruin him. As far as they're concerned, she's shown up as a silly woman, and the conjuror as part quack, part political hack. But the thing is, the conjuration, which Shakespeare specifies should be staged as the casting of a circle, pulls up a real demon. Real, at least, in the world of the play. The audience can see him, and he utters prophecies that work out to be true through the whole series of his Wars of the Roses Plays. It seems to work out like that a lot: in Shakespeare, humans can call spirits from the vasty deep, but they can't control them. It's pretty much the other way around.'

Maybe Lady Nairn was right, I thought suddenly. Maybe Macbeth is a dupe. Led to believe in his furious passion that he's conjuring, when all along it's the witches around him who are invoking the spirits. I shook my head. If there was anything that Dee would have liked less than a play that made a conjuror the master of demons, it was a play that made a conjuror their dupe. Their puppet.

'A duchess who wants her husband to take the crown, and who's willing to listen to evil spirits,' mused Eircheard. 'She sounds a lot like Lady Macbeth.'

'She does, doesn't she? I've always thought she was a practice run. That she stayed with him, gestating in some dark corner of his soul, until he knew what to do with her.'

'If Lady M is Lady Nairn's ancestor, you think this duchess is, too? You think she's another fictional version of the Scottish witch?'

'I don't know.' *But Elizabeth Stewart, Lady Arran, was rumoured to have lusted after the crown. I knew that.* 'I don't know how he could have known her story: she fell from power in the mid-1580s, for heaven's sake. What would have kept him drawn to her for so long? And what would have made it spill out in *Macbeth* when it did?'

'So what was he thinking when he wrote *Macbeth*? In between the early scepticism and the late acceptance?'

I pulled out the page from Aubrey and read it once again:

Dr Dee begged Mr Shakspere to alter his Play lest, in staging curs'd Secretes learned of a Scottish Witch, he conjure powers beyond his controll. But Mr Shakspere wuld not, until there was a death, whereupon he made the changes in one houre's time

What had William Shakespeare, laughing sceptic that he was, made of the magic he was jotting down, and the request to remove it? Had he been parroting it for fun, and found that he scared people, like Orson Welles reading *War of the Worlds* over the radio? There were tales of productions of Marlowe's great conjuring play, *Dr Faustus*, emptying theatres when audiences thought they saw one too many devils appear on the stage at the magician's call. Had Shakespeare been playing with something a lot of people around him thought was fire – even if he didn't – and found that the real-world consequences were too great?

Or, had he been experimenting with magic himself? He was 'a man torn between two masters,' Aubrey had written. And one of those was John Dee. Had Shakespeare played the sorcerer's apprentice behind his master's back?

The only way to find out was to find the manuscript.

And to hope that the finding – or failure to find it – did not result in either Lily's death or mine.

I pulled my knees up to chest, as if I might squeeze this whirl of thoughts and the terrible possibilities that danced around them out of my body altogether.

29

'Are you going to do something with that?' asked Eircheard, stealing a glance at my hands.

I looked down, and realised I was still clutching the iPod Lady Nairn had given me. I flicked off the Hold button, and it glowed into life. I pushed Play.

The screen went black, and then the high wavering chords of Bach's Toccata and Fugue in D minor swelled into life, spilling into their grand downward swoop. Gradually the black screen lightened to swirling silver clouds which cut to a title in white curlicued letters: *Macbeth, by William Shakespeare.*

Beneath that, in roman numerals, was a date: MCMXVI. 1916.

'What?' asked Eircheard.

But I shook my head in stunned silence. The tiny screen oscillated light and dark as camera closed in on the jack-booted star in a dark tunic. His dark wavy hair was long, and his moustache very nearly longer. His eyes grew impossibly wide, his face twisted in triumph, as he killed an enemy with a flourishing sword thrust.

'That's him,' I said. 'Beerbohm Tree. As Macbeth.' I held it up on the steering wheel so that Eircheard could steal a glance.

'Looks like an underbudget haunted house video,' he said doubtfully.

'In some quarters, this alone would be enough to kill for.'

'You're joking.' He looked over at me. 'Jesus. You're not, are you?'

I shook my head. 'It's Tree's *Macbeth* of 1916. One of the great lost films from the silent era. From any era, I suppose. One of the great lost productions of Shakespeare.'

And the Nairns possessed it in a digital copy.

Dunsinnan must go to Beerbohm Tree. Had Sir Angus seen something in this film?

The set was monumental Hollywood, an odd combination of medieval Scotland and Mycenaean Greece. As the film went on, thick black blood spilled across the stage, and the white flickering eyes of the actors grew wider and wider with horror.

I fast forwarded, watching the actors rush about like Keystone Kops until the screen cut to black again. Gradually, light rose, though the scene remained dimmer, and a little fuzzy. Up to this point, Tree's costume of high black boots and a black tunic criss-crossed with a wide black leather belt looked more Prussian than medieval Scottish, maybe more Hell's Angels than either. Now, though, Tree walked in wearing chain mail, a long dark cloak, and a winged silver helmet somewhere between Viking and proto-*Lord of the Rings*. And he was no longer in a castle, either Scottish or Ancient Greek. Instead, he looked entirely out of place in a cosy panelled room with a small graceful fireplace set a little left of centre on the back wall. Or a room that might have been cosy, at any rate, if three witches had not been cackling in glee over a cauldron hanging over the fire.

It was the room, though, rather than the witches or the bloody-minded warrior that sent prickles running up and down my skin. 'I know this room,' I said. 'I've been there.' It was Tree's private retreat, tucked up under the dome at the very top of Her Majesty's Theatre. The Dome Room, it was called. It was rented out as rehearsal space. I'd spent hours up there a few years back, running through *Othello*.

The camera cut from the witches to Tree's startled eyes, and then to a black title-screen with fancy lettering in white:

How now, you secret, black and midnight hags:
What is't you do?

The witches cavorted with evil delight.

A deed without a name.

The camera cut to a close-up of the bubbling cauldron, and then pulled back to reveal the entire wall beside the fireplace, before cutting across to Macbeth again, swelling with pride. Advancing slowly toward the camera, he raised his arms.

I conjure you, howe'er you come to know it:
Answer me.

The witches recoiled, as if in terror, but Macbeth kept advancing. The camera pulled back to reveal the entire wall beside the fireplace. In the panelling to the right, a rectangle of darkness had appeared, the smoke of hell billowing from its depths.

I hit Pause. In 1916, I thought, that recess in the wall wasn't just a trick of light. There was a cupboard there. A cubbyhole in the panelling.

But there wasn't. Not in the room I knew. I rewound to an earlier shot of the wall. I was right: there was no door visible. Not so much as a crack.

'What's happening?' asked Eircheard.

I let the film roll on. Macbeth – Tree – strode to the Hellmouth. Plunging in his hand, he plucked from the darkness a book – Odin pulling wisdom from the underworld. With a flourish, he opened it and began to pronounce a spell.

Though you untie the winds,
Though trees blow down and castles topple,
Though palaces and pyramids do slope . . .

The Shakespeare had been drastically cut for the title frames, but its power was still recognisable. Film-maker and actor alike had no doubt intended viewers to focus on the concentrated fury on Tree's face as he commandeered the forces of the hell. But it was the book that captivated me. It looked old, a leather-bound tome with one word just visible on the spine: *Dee*.

I let the iPod slip onto the seat beside me and began rifling through the folder for Ellen Terry's letter. On the seat, Bach's Fugue in D Minor sounded tinny and distant through the headphones. Skimming through the letter, I came to the sentence I wanted: *I think the book queer enough, but it is the letter inside that you will find most curious.*

In 1911, she'd sent Beerbohm Tree – *Monsieur Superbe Homme* – a book to do with Macbeth . . . on the eve of his theatrical premiere. By 1916, he could have spliced into his film an older version of the conjuring scene. One that had him reading from a volume by Dee.

A volume he had pulled from a hidden cupboard in the wall of his theatre.

'So the room's still there?' asked Eircheard.

'Yes.' Whether or not the book was, though, was another question.

An image of Lily floated up in my mind, as I had last seen her: wrapped in the blue Cailleach's veil, her hand slipping from mine in the dark Edinburgh close. Lily rising in fury in the hall, red hair gleaming in the firelight. The image flickered and shifted, to the ghostly sight of her lying bound on the hillside, a thin red line across her neck. And a symbol of one large circle and two small ones, carved into flesh.

Forty-eight hours.

'Drive faster,' I whispered.

30

The sky condensed to sodden grey wool as we slipped down out of Scotland and into the steep hills and fells of north-western England. We stopped once, for sandwiches, at a service area somewhere outside Preston, in Lancashire.

Lily's parents had died on the motorway outside Preston. The chicken and bacon sandwich went tasteless in my mouth, though I knew it wasn't.

Soon after we got back on the road, the shimmying of the van lulled me into fitful sleep. When I woke, London had swallowed us, and the afternoon was thickening towards early nightfall. The thought of driving in London soured my stomach at the best of times, but Eircheard drove like a glee-ful madman through streets clogged with the evening rush and spattered with rain. We parked at a multi-storey car park near Leicester Square, and I slipped a flashlight from Eircheard's glove compartment into my bag, along with the iPod and the folder full of precious papers. Huddling together under a single lopsided umbrella, we hurried up a dank, narrow street. Stepping into Haymarket, lined with grand buildings, was like walking into a completely different city. Just down the street sat Her Majesty's Theatre, lit like a dowager in diamonds, its blue-grey square dome in the French baroque style as imposing and intricate as a Marie Antoinette coiffure.

I pointed at the dome. 'That's it. The room we want is just under the cupola.'

'And just how do we plan to get there?' asked Eircheard.

'Same way that Sir Angus meant to, for starters. We buy our way in.'

We bought two tickets for the Dress Circle, as close to the exits as possible, and headed up the stairs. It wasn't long before the house lights went down and the iconic white mask of the Phantom began to glow from the covers of programmes scattered through the audience. I wove my way through cluckings of disapproval back out to the plush corridor, followed by Eircheard. When the lone usher disappeared, leading another late soul into the Phantom's lair, I veered to the end of the corridor and pulled back a curtain to reveal a nondescript door.

'Fingers crossed,' I said under my breath. I pulled the whole door upwards and turned the knob slightly, and the locked clicked open – a quirk long known by everyone who knew someone in the cast of *Phantom*, which was pretty much everyone in the theatrical world.

We found ourselves in an entirely different place from the gilt and red plush of the front of the house. As the entire theatre hushed, leaning towards the stage, we wound into the labyrinth of corridors behind. I closed my eyes, trying to remember my way around. Rattling up to the top floor in a tiny pale blue elevator, we hurried down a narrow hall with threadbare red carpet and peach walls punctuated by white doors, all closed.

Up a few steps here, around a corner, I paused by an old radiator. Behind it, a large barrel key hung on a wall from a tassel. Down one more short corridor and up a half flight of steps we came to a wide landing before an immense arched door whose medieval look was faux, but whose studded oak solidity was not. 𝔚𝔈𝔏𝔆𝔒𝔐𝔈, it read, in Old English letters.

I inserted the key into the lock.

The door opened, exhaling the scent of rehearsal rooms: dust; old sweat; wax for the linoleum. And dreams. One wall of the outer room was lined in mirrors, like a dance studio. On the other, high windows looked over Haymarket. From beams criss-crossing the dome overhead hung massive circular iron chandeliers – the kind that burned real church candles, though their sockets were empty and drear.

As Eircheard slipped in behind me, I shut the door and locked it from the inside, leaving the key in the lock. And then I switched on the flashlight.

'Jesus,' he said. 'Could ye get more cliché for a Phantom's lair?'

'He lives in the dungeons,' I said absently. 'This is more like Quasimodo's tower. Though old Sir Herbert would be put out by both comparisons. He's supposed to have given fab dinner parties here. Lived here, as much as he could. Didn't much care for the niceties – or the narrowness – of Victorian home life, apparently.'

I'd spent long wonderful hours here away from home, too, rehearsing *Othello*.

A wide archway led through to a more intimate room, panelled in warm Jacobean squares and filled with an oval table probably built for the room. Beyond was an offset stone fireplace.

'That's it,' said Eircheard quietly.

I nodded. 'The room in the film. Which means that that part of the film didn't belong to the original, which was shot on location in Hollywood.'

'You think it was shot later?'

'Or earlier. The costume he's wearing in this room looks like the costume from his *Macbeth*, which premiered here. In 1911. The same year that Ellen Terry wrote Monsieur Superbe Homme.'

I slid past the table to the opposite wall. The door in the wall, if there really was one, should be on the right of the fireplace. But even close up, I could not see it, or even its seams, much less a latch.

I stood back, biting my lip. Had it, after all, been a trick of light? The magic of film? Slipping the iPod from my pocket, I brought up the cauldron scene. Just before the cupboard opened, the camera lingered in close-up on the cauldron.

I went to the fireplace. There was no obvious chain or lever from which to hang a cauldron, now. But it wouldn't be a working fireplace any more, in any case. Not in a theatre. I leaned in and looked up. A small slice of sky was visible far above.

I ran a hand up the stones. Nothing. I felt around all four sides . . . wait, one stone jutted out. It was loose. Carefully, I prised it out. Behind it, folded up, was a lever. I pulled it down. At its end was a hook.

A thunderous knocking exploded on the door behind us. 'Desmond, you sodding wanker,' said a deep voice. 'It's my turn to use the roof.' He tried a few more times, and then he went grumbling away.

I turned back to the film. The witches bent around the cauldron, stirring it. Something had been *in* it. Weighting it down. My heart in my mouth, I pulled the lever even further, putting some force into it.

There was a pop, and several panels in the wall next to me pushed outwards and over the wall in a sort of sliding wooden door. Behind was a cupboard full of shelves, bowed and bent with books, their titles obscured beneath a duvet of dust a century thick.

I hovered above it, loath to disturb it. Finally, I ran a finger across the spines, and glimmers of tarnished gilt appeared in partial words.

Secretor– and *–catrix* and *Daemono–* They were, at a guess, some of the oldest printed grimoires. And a few, even older, in manuscript.

This time I swept my palm across the books, dust

cascading to the floor. The titles leapt out: *Secreta Secretorum*. Aristotle, read one. *Picatrix*, said another. And *Daemonologie. King James I and VI.* Weyer, *De praestigiis daemonum*. And Bacon, *The Mirror of Alchimy*.

'You think Tree was a wizard?' asked Eircheard.

'Doesn't fit the general picture of the man,' I said. There was no way of knowing if he *used* these books. But he was certainly a connoisseur of magical books. I wondered, fleetingly, if the owner of the building had any idea what was hidden back here. From the thickness of the dust, he did not.

It would be the project of a lifetime to work through these books, figure out just what was here. With regret, my hand passed over rare volumes that even the British Museum and the Bodleian might well not possess. Occult esoterica was one subject in which private, hidden libraries were still better stocked than the great repository libraries, which had gotten a late start on officially banned books.

There were books claiming to be by Roger Bacon, Aristotle and Agrippa, Hermes Trismegistus, Solomon, and Trithemius. But nothing so short and sweet as Dee.

At last I came up with what I was looking for: *The Monas Hieroglyphica.* Dee's treatise on symbolic language, in which he devised a single sign, or sigil, supposed to contain all knowledge within it. The monas was a curious stick figure, like a little man wearing a horned hat. Heart in mouth, I opened it and riffled through the pages.

No letter.

Damn. Setting it back on the shelf, I skimmed on down through the shelves. There. At the bottom. A thin book, almost a pamphlet. 'DEE' was stamped lengthwise in gold on the narrow spine. I looked closer.

DEE & The Theatre, it read.

I pulled it out and opened it. On the flyleaf was a neat inscription: *Herbert Beerbohm Tree, 1911.* The year he had opened *Macbeth.* The year that Ellen Terry had sent him a present.

I flicked through the pages. It was not a printed book. It was, for the most part, a notebook full of geometrical drawings. Bound in front of that, however, was a letter. In an italic hand. I skimmed down to the signature. Arthur Dee. John Dee's eldest son and favourite child. Heart in mouth, I moved up to the beginning.

My dear Sir Robert:

Apologies for the tardiness with which this will no doubt find you, but news must take a while to travel to Moscow and back. I am apprised that you are interested in ferreting out certain books and papers once in my father's library. You possess, I know, a number of them already, and admiring your esteem for books and for learning, as I do, I cannot think of better hands to protect them.

Those which you propose to find, however, are of a different nature. You may discover, after perusing them,

that it is you who needs protection, rather than the books.
My father, at any rate, felt so.

The moon flitted through a cloud, sending a shadow over the lines. I looked up at the windows, but saw nothing.

> *You ask, in particular, after any with connexions to a*
> *witch my father called Medea. This was the Lady*
> *Elizabeth Stewart, sometime countess of Arran, and also*
> *of Lennox and March.*

There was a small ping somewhere in my abdomen. Lady Nairn was right. Her ancestress *was* mixed up in this, somehow. With a nickname of Medea, for heaven's sake. Possibly the most infamous worker of cauldron magic in Renaissance myth.

Another woman with a penchant for carving the life out of people.

> *My father possessed, at one time, two manuscripts*
> *concerning this quondam countess. One, a work as wicked*
> *as it was ancient. The other, borrowing wholecloth from the*
> *first, was a sly piece meant to shadow her forth on the*
> *stage . . .*

Was he talking about *Macbeth?* If so, the letter backed Aubrey, and Shakespeare had stolen the Lady Arran's magic:

294

but not just that. He'd also stolen her person, and he'd set both on the stage. Had she killed, in response? Had she murdered the boy who played her? If so: *why*? Why Hal Berridge, and not Shakespeare? Did it have to do with his scrying? Or with the rite of magic? 'Aubrey says that Dee begged Shakespeare to alter the play,' I said, thinking aloud. 'So Dee must have seen the early version. *Maybe he kept it.*'

Eircheard whistled. 'Does his son say?'

I skimmed through the letter, my finger coming to rest on a sentence that I could not read aloud.

Looking over my shoulder, Eircheard read it. '*Deeming that their pages might tarnish even the noonday sun, my father buried these and other works of darkness where they belonged, in the dark at the bottom of his garden.*'

For a moment, we both stared at silence at the book shaking a little in my hand. Buried in Dee's garden. Where the hell was that? Mortlake. I'd always thought it the perfect home for a wizard: *Dead Lake. Lake of the Dead.*

But it was little more than a word to me. Somewhere west on the Thames, on the way to Hampton Court, I knew, but couldn't get much more precise than that. In Dee's day, it had been a quiet village, well out in the country, but the chances that his garden on the Thames had remained undisturbed in the booming centuries since was virtually non-existent.

What if Dee's works of darkness had been destroyed long ago?

I pushed that thought aside. They had to exist.

'We need someone who knows about Dee.' In London, as Lady Nairn had pointed out, that meant one person: Joanna Black, of Joanna Black Books and Esoterica, in Covent Garden. The problem was that Joanna was elusive. I'd been told I must meet her, and I'd been to her shop once or twice, the public part of it at any rate. But I had never laid eyes on her. It was said that somewhere in the back was a small door that opened onto a labyrinth that only the wealthy and well-connected could penetrate. Beyond that lay inner rooms that not even money would open: where only serious students of Dee's Great Art were granted entry.

I knew only one person who might gain me quick access to Joanna. Without waiting to read the rest of the letter, I texted Lady Nairn.

I had just pushed *send* when I heard a small click and whirled around. The key was turning in the lock.

31

Switching off the flashlight, I stood in the moonlit darkness, watching as the key continued to turn. I looked quickly around the room. The only other way out was the fire escape, a wide wooden ladder that led up to one of the high windows. Eircheard was looking at it in dismay. We had no time to wait. Slipping the book into my bag, I dashed up the ladder.

The window opened with a groan. Outside, a peaked roof sloped steeply to the left. The rear of the building stretched away, long and narrow, into the distance. Slick with rain, it would be treacherous going for me. It might well be impossible for Eircheard.

I turned and ran back down the ladder, pulling Eircheard with me to the door. When it opened inward, we'd have to hope its angle would hide us while the open window drew the picklock forward. With luck, we'd have just long enough to slip around the door and out before the intruder turned around.

The key clattered to the floor, and the door slowly pushed open. A man stepped inside and stopped. He was dressed all in black, down to gloves; the long barrel of a pistol with a silencer extended from his right hand. In the darkness, I couldn't see his face. A gust of wind sent rain clattering through the window, and he looked sharply up at it.

He was halfway across the room when I moved out from behind the door. At a small squeak in the linoleum he spun, and I found myself gazing down the barrel of the silencer. The face above it belonged to the Winter King. The dark-haired man.

'Put it down, Kate,' he said.

Beside me, I felt Eircheard flinch. 'You're the pile of shite from the festival,' he grunted.

'This time, the reach of my arm is longer,' said the dark-haired man. The high whine of a bullet whizzed past my ear, thudding into the oak door behind me. 'Step forward to the table and set the book down,' he said.

'Not worth dying for,' said Eircheard, giving me a nod.

Slipping the book from the bag, which I handed back to Eircheard, I did as I was told, rage pressing around me. As I set the book down, he motioned me away again with the gun, and I walked stiffly back to the door. Stepping forward, he flipped the front cover open, revealing the letter, and then he scooped the book under his arm.

'Step outside,' he said, 'and close the door.' Presently we heard him approach the door from the inside, and the key fumbled in the lock. If he locked us out, he'd escape out the fire exit and disappear into London without a trace. 'He can't get away with that letter,' I said. 'He can't.'

Eircheard moved back three steps and hurled himself like a battering ram against the door, which flew open, knocking our stalker halfway back across the room. Both gun and book skidded away from him. The gun slid somewhere under the table, amid a welter of chair legs. But it was the book he went after and came up with.

He also came up with a knife. I thought of Sybilla on the rocks, and my insides turned to water.

He backed up the ladder, holding us both at bay with the blade, and ducked out onto the roof.

'Go,' said Eircheard tightly. 'I'll be hobbling a bit behind ye, but I'll be there. With some firepower, too, if I can reach the bloody gun.'

I raced up the ladder and into the night.

Overhead, the clouds were washed a dull and dirty pink, reflecting the city's lights. Crouched low, the dark-haired man was running down the spine of the roof. Some way up, he half-slid, half-ran down the slope to the left, and I followed, mostly on my rear. At the bottom, a low access door hung open. A narrow ladder disappeared into the darkness within. Somewhere below, footsteps pattered downwards.

And music twined upwards. A sweet, romantic duet: the first act of *Phantom*, crooning to its climax.

I stepped onto the ladder, feeling my way as fast as I dared, suddenly aware of vast space beneath me. I'd gone maybe twenty steps when I heard Eircheard's voice above. *'Kate?'*

'Heading down,' I said.

Somewhere below I heard a chuckle that might as well have come from the Phantom. I picked up my speed. A couple of storeys down, I at last came to the fly floor, the narrow ledge to the side of the stage and high above it, used by stagehands to pull the ropes controlling stage equipment and scenery. But the dark-haired man had disappeared up ahead into an intricate netting of ropes and pulleys and weights, though I could hear snatches of teasing laughter. I stilled for a moment, trying to hear him through the billowing music, pinpointing his whereabouts. Eircheard landed with a heavy step beside me.

Then we saw him, weaving back among the ropes towards the catwalk that crossed from stage left to stage right, along the back wall. I began to run. Up ahead, he reached the catwalk even as the music swelling up from below darkened and picked up speed, cascading into heavy minor chords.

His voice cutting through the music, Eircheard bellowed at the fleeing man to stop, but he only quickened his pace. I saw a kick of dust hit the wall in front of him and he skidded to a stop. I glanced back. Eircheard had taken a shot, and was prepared to take another. Turning, the dark-haired man crossed his arms, waiting.

I reached the end of the catwalk and started across

towards him. When I was ten feet from him, he said, 'Me or the book, Kate. Not both.' Around us the Phantom's manic laughter cascaded through the space. And before I knew what was happening, the dark-haired man tossed the book into the air, sending it tumbling in a high arc back over my head. I had no choice. I turned and raced back in the direction of its fall, catching it just before it plummeted over the rail to the stage below. Below, people in the wings began glancing up. I turned back to the dark-haired man. At the other end of the catwalk, three stagehands appeared, starting out towards us.

'*Go*,' screamed the Phantom, and the dark-haired man loosed a coil of rope over the balcony. As the gigantic chandelier that had been cinched to the ceiling all through the first act now swooped down across the theatre at the Phantom's command, swaying over the stage, the dark-haired man stepped over the side of the catwalk's balcony and, gripping the rope, slid three storeys down to the stage, landing with a reverberating thud and running off stage right. Already rising into their end-of-the-act applause and escape to the bars, the audience gasped, and here and there a woman shrieked. Moments later, the stage door opened and the dark-haired man pushed his way out and melted into the crowd.

On the far side of the catwalk, the stagehands, looking none too pleased, set out in my direction. I didn't wait, fleeing back to the other side.

'Jesus,' said Eircheard as I reached him. 'Do you think he thinks he can fly?'

'He damn near can, apparently,' I said. 'Just now, it might be helpful if we could too.'

Eircheard was already wiping down the gun. 'I don't fancy being caught with this, now that he's gone,' he said, sliding it behind some ropes. 'God only knows what it's done.' We took off back across the fly floor. Coming to the narrow stairs, we pounded down them.

Why? I kept thinking. *Why take the book at gunpoint, and then throw it back?*

At stage level we darted through a gathering crowd of actors staring up at the now empty catwalk and out another door leading to the house. As we funnelled our way up the aisle toward the exit, I searched every face in the crowd for the dark-haired man, but he'd vanished.

In my pocket, my phone, set to vibrate, began to buzz. It was a message of two words: *Joanna waiting.*

32

Outside the theatre, we darted across Haymarket at the first break in traffic, heading back up the narrow lane we'd come down. On a rainy November night, it seemed more like an alley.

Twice, the ring of footsteps on the pavement gave me pause, but once it was a woman in high heels, head down against the damp, and then an older gentleman who might have been a banker; both of them turned off into the parking garage. Clutching Dee's book, I felt exposed, as if every window, every shadowed doorway and corner held prying eyes.

Eircheard could move surprisingly fast with his odd rolling gait; I had to trot to keep up with him. Passing along the back of the National Gallery and the National Portrait Gallery, we emerged into Charing Cross Road, still bustling with crowds looking for pubs or restaurants or bookshops open late. One block up, we turned into a small pedestrian street lined with bow windows and hung with carved and gilded signs; it looked as if it hadn't changed much since Victoria sat on the throne. 'Cecil Court,' I said. The heart of bibliophile London. Five doors up was a simple sign in black and white: *Joanna Black Books and Esoterica.*

The window was filled with small white lights; inside, the shop looked dark. Eircheard pushed open the door and we hurried inside to the shimmering of small silver bells. It was warm, after the chill damp outside, and fragrant with a spicy incense. The high ceiling was painted a deep midnight blue, and small lights like stars seemed to float and spin like fireflies overhead. Momentarily, I had the impression of standing on a windy hill on a moonless night.

But the horizon was made of tall shelves of books, each dimly lit so that you could read its titles without the light ruining the overall effect of the room. Up ahead, behind a carved wooden ledge, sat a man with long, lank hair and a top hat. At the sound of the chimes, he looked up. His right ear, I saw, was oddly folded over, a quirk he accentuated with a pierced earring of dangling silver in the shape of a pentangle. His eyes were ringed with smoky black eyeliner. 'Kate Stanley?' he asked, leaning forward intently, as if murmuring a secret password. When I nodded, he rose, unfolding a body as lank as his hair. The fingernails on his right hand were long and slightly pointed ovals. His handshake, though, was firm. 'Joanna is expecting you. She'll be right out. Make yourselves at home,' he said with a sweep of his arm.

In the centre of the room, on a round marble-topped table, gleamed a wide silvery cauldron. On its front, in raised relief, was the figure of horned man sitting cross-legged, a serpent in one raised arm. Below, the space from tabletop to floor had been glassed in, making a cylindrical terrarium. Inside this, on a freeform tree made of antlers, a boa was coiling in slow gleaming spirals. Off to one side, a black cat with emerald eyes sat on a long velvet sofa watching the snake.

'Meet Medea,' said the man behind the desk.

'The cat or the snake?'

'The cat is Lilith. She will introduce herself, if she pleases.'

She swished her tail, but did not look away from the snake.

I was too wound up to do anything but wander restlessly. The bookshelves bore titles like *Divinatory Arts*, *Shamanism*, and *Goddess Spirituality*. But books were only part of what the shop had to offer. An open hutch was stacked with candles of all colours – 'virgin beeswax,' read a placard, 'touched only by a solitary candlemaker in Sussex, a hedge-witch.' There were ritual soaps and bath crystals for various kinds of cleansings; goblets of blown glass, pewter, and carved wood; blown eggs of various sizes and colours; wands – 'blanks, to be personalised by the owner'; and blank books bound in tooled leather and marbled paper, to be used as Books of Shadows – a witch's or coven's private diary/collection of spells. The tiny drawers of an antique spice cabinet held herbs – 'organically grown, picked at the full

305

moon in Dorset' – as well as spices I'd never heard of and aromatic resins and gums: frankincense, myrrh, aloe, and bright red dragonsblood.

'Look at these,' said Eircheard. Hands behind his back, he was bending over a bow-fronted Victorian display case. On its upper shelf lay a varied collection of knives with handles of black bog oak; beneath that was a shelf of smaller white-handled knives. 'Some of them are beauties,' he said gruffly.

'Quite a compliment, from a master swordsmith,' said a woman's low voice with some amusement.

We both straightened to see a slight woman, about my height, with long curly black hair and wide dark eyes barely hatched with laugh lines, standing in a doorway behind one of the tall bookshelves, which had hinged outwards from the wall. She wore a low-cut tunic of some rich tribal material that showcased her necklace, an intricate Afghan collar of silver mesh set with lapis. Heavy silver bracelets clinked on her wrists. Something in her stance and her wary amusement reminded me, a little, of a younger version of my old mentor at Harvard, Roz Howard.

'Joanna Black,' she said, stepping forward to shake hands. 'Lady Nairn has been singing both your praises. What can I do for you?'

My grip on the book under my arm tightened. 'John Dee's garden,' I said anxiously. 'Where is it?'

She raised one brow. 'Mortlake. About seven miles west.

306

Halfway to Heathrow, more or less. Right on Mortlake High Street. Only, I'm afraid the question ought properly to be past tense. It's under concrete, I'm afraid. A block of flats called the John Dee House. Used to be Council Housing. It's been privatised, but it's still 1960's ugly.'

Lily. A lump rose in my throat. If the play lay entombed beneath a block of flats, it was unreachable. If it had been moved – well, I had no trail to follow.

She looked from me to Eircheard and back. 'From what Lady Nairn said, you're not just looking to spend some quiet hours in an Elizabethan garden.'

Having lost the last string through the labyrinth, I had nothing to lose. I held out the book. 'We're looking for some of Dee's papers. Not his plants.'

She ran a finger along the spine, its gilt lettering winking up at us. *DEE & the Theatre.*

'Come with me,' she said, turning back through the door behind the shelves. We hurried after her down a long passageway, passing half-glimpsed rooms and other corridors as we turned this way and that, going up five steps, turning, and then down three again before coming to a stair that took us up two storeys to a landing with a heavy arched door, ajar. Pushing it open, she ushered us inside.

Candlelight played on panelled walls, and two deep windows lined with old-fashioned shutters overlooked the street below. Beside the fireplace stood a tall grey stone covered with Celtic knots; on the mantel was a carved African mask.

A long empty library table was surrounded by several high-backed chairs upholstered in deep green brocade. Unlike the rooms below, this room was spare, a setting for displaying rare treasures.

Pulling a red velvet cradle such as archival libraries use from her desk, Joanna set the book down on the table. One finger on the cover, she looked at me. I reached across and opened it. Her breath caught in her throat, the tip of her tongue between her teeth, as she saw the letter.

'Read it,' I said.

As she did, her fingers twining in the mesh of her necklace, I let my mind play back through Arthur Dee's words. How had he put it? *A sly piece meant to shadow Lady Arran forth on the stage?* Surely that was *Macbeth*, borrowing from an earlier manuscript of dark rites. Lady Arran and her husband eerily echoed the Macbeths, from their ambitious scheming, their interest in witchcraft, right down to their deaths. Lady Arran had died miserably, according to some Scottish chronicler. Fading out in misery, as Lady Macbeth does. And her husband had been ambushed, his head struck off and raised on a pole.

If the play was indeed *Macbeth* – then it *did* contain a rite of black magic. Surely that was the implication of the younger Dee's letters – of bits copied wholesale into the play from a work of wickedness so dark it had frightened even Dee.

Dee senior had called Lady Arran Medea – a sorceress

308

who had a habit of carving up ageing kings, on the promise of making them young again: a promise she did not always feel bound to keep. She was also said to have poisoned her husband's mistress, and to have killed her own children, feeding them to their father in revenge for his desertion. What had possessed Dee to liken Lady Arran to Medea? Was her magic, like Medea's, bloody cauldron magic? Aubrey, for one, implied that she had blood on her hands.

What would Carrie Douglas, carver of cauldrons, make of that?

And what was her relation to the Winter King?

Joanna looked up as she finished the first page. 'Do you know what you have?'

'Some idea,' I said.

She rose, pacing before the fireplace. 'The manuscripts – you're after the missing rite in *Macbeth*, aren't you?'

I hesitated, but I needed her help. After a moment, I nodded.

'Do you think that's wise?'

'Probably not.'

Beside me, Eircheard snorted. '*Wise!* It's about as daft as things get. But we're after it nevertheless. Can you be of any help, madam, other than telling us that they're buried under a building?'

'Not yet,' she said. Lifting the page, she glanced at me, the question in her eyes. I nodded, and she turned it over.

Eircheard and I drew in around her, so that we all read it together.

> The manuscripts, should you find them, are yours. There is one object, however, that I would reserve for myself. I am not at all certain it is there to be found: the Howards wanted it, and I do not know whether my father kept it from their grasp.

The Howards! One of the most powerful and ruthless families of Renaissance England. I'd met up with them before, clashing with Shakespeare on another subject. And here they were, pursuing Dee – in a matter that I hoped also included Shakespeare.

> It is a mirror.
>
> Many years before I was born, when Lady Arran was almost still a child herself, she presented herself to my father in Antwerp, asking to be taught in his Art. When he refused on account of her tender years and her sex, she flew into a fury. That night, she stole the mirror, knowing that he set great store by it, and fled away.
>
> Years later, it was returned, from an unexpected quarter, along with another treasure, this one hers: a manuscript of words so evil that my father himself quaked to read them, and indeed would not until urged to it by his angels. I never learned how he came by them, but with these gifts,

310

Mr Shakspeare established himself as one of my father's scholars.

There it was: Shakespeare, Dee, and Lady Arran in a triumvirate linked by the study of magic and an evil manuscript. And also a mirror.

Could that be Lady Nairn's mirror, which had once belonged to the King's Men? The one stolen from her tower? My breath caught in my throat as I hurried on:

An honour which he rather trampled in the muck than burnished bright, not only in word, but most appallingly in deed. In later years, he asked to borrow the mirror back, along with the boy who was then my father's scryer, for use in a play before the king. My father was reluctant, but the boy was talented – he had foreseen the Powder Plot – and the request came from a quarter impossible to refuse. When he understood, however, that the boy was not to play a scryer, but to be prinked and powder'd as a queen, and a witch queen at that, he grew fiery with rage and demanded to read the play.

Dee's boy had been set to play a part . . . the part of a queen. *Had he played Lady Macbeth? Had Hal Berridge, the boy who died, been John Dee's scryer?*

'A boy?' asked Joanna in some consternation. 'His scryer was a boy?'

311

I nodded, and she began drumming her fingers on the table. 'All Dee's scryers were grown men. But there is an ancient tradition – one that Dee certainly knew – that boys were better: the purer the vessel, the clearer the sight. Which put youth and virginity at a premium. And we don't know *who* he was using in 1606, around the time of *Macbeth*: the diaries of his last years are lost.'

'We do know,' I said quietly, pulling out the page from Aubrey and handing it to her.

While she read Aubrey, I went back to Arthur Dee.

It was worse than his worst imaginings.

I was not surprised about the boy. I had warned my father against him: neither virgin nor even chaste, he was a Ganymede who corrupted the house, but my father was besotted with his powers, with his clarity of sight.

The poet, however, was another and more dangerous matter. For he was ever a sly watcher in corners . . .

Shakespeare? Was he the poet? A sly watcher in corners? What had he seen in Dee's household?

. . . and it was not just the mirror that he borrowed, but a rite that out-Medea'd Medea, stolen in part from my father's translation of the witch's manuscript. Father warned the poet against such folly. Mr Shakspeare, tho', would not listen until the boy was dead.

So Aubrey's sources on that tale were solid, at least as far as the boy's death. And surely Arthur Dee was at least implying that the death was not accidental.

You will know the mirror by its black surface, and by a posie around its edge:

> *Nothing is but what is.*

Eircheard started.

'You recognise the saying?' asked Joanna.

'Young Dee got it wrong,' said Eircheard. 'Left off a word. *Nothing is but what is* Not.'

'It's a round,' I said quietly. 'Carved around the perimeter of a circle. The first three letters of the first word and the last word overlap.'

'An infinite circle linking being with not being, life with death,' said Joanna, a smile of satisfaction slipping across her face. 'Powerful magic.'

'It's from *Macbeth*,' I said. Whatever else this mirror was, it wasn't the one stolen from Lady Nairn, which was silvered glass. It might be spotted with age, but it had never been black.

Rising, Joanna switched off the light, leaving the room in candlelight. From a drawer in her desk she pulled out a hard circular case; inside lay a black velvet bag. From this, she withdrew a disk of glimmering darkness, laying it on the table.

'Polished obsidian,' she said.

I bent over it. Within its surface swam a world of shadows.

'Is this it?' I asked. 'Dee's mirror?'

'God, no,' she said with a laugh. 'But it's a fine copy.'

'And the original?' asked Eircheard. 'Are you going to tell us it's under cement out in Mortlake?'

'No,' said Joanna. 'As I said, I can't tell you about the manuscripts, or the rite that's in them, either. More's the pity, believe me. They'd fetch an astronomical price at auction. But I can take you to the mirror.' She looked at her watch.

I put both hands on the table and rose. '*Where?*'

'Just up the road,' she said with a mischievous smile. 'At the British Museum. Open late tonight. If we hurry, we can just get there before closing.' She ran a finger lightly across the surface of her mirror. 'I've been trying to get the curator to open the bloody case and let me examine that mirror in person for three years. I think you may just have delivered the key.' Deftly, she slipped her own mirror back into its bag, and then into the case. 'But I'd have to call and tell him at least part of what you've found.'

'Call,' I said hoarsely.

As she made her call, I sat staring at the mirror case, my mind spinning. The manuscripts were out of my reach. But whoever had taken Lily also wanted the mirror: *Blade, Mirror, Cauldron* . . . On the score of the mirror, as of the knife, they were surely resting quietly.

Lady Nairn's mirror had supposedly belonged to the King's Men. But this one, if Arthur Dee were right, had not only passed through the hands of Dee, Lady Arran, and Shakespeare, *it had been the original mirror in Macbeth*. If so, it was this mirror, not Lady Nairn's, which Carrie and her friends would want – no, *need* for their ritual. Which made it the key to more than just a case in a museum, I hoped tightly. It might be the key to Lily's release.

If I could not take the manuscript to ransom Lily, I would take the mirror.

Across the room, Joanna had reached the curator. She had her back to us, staring out the window at the shops along the street below as she spoke to him in quick, clipped tones. Before I could think about it, I opened the case, slipped out the velvet bag with the mirror, and dropped it into my bag.

Eircheard stared at me in open-mouthed astonishment.

'I mean to play bait-and-switch. I'll need your help.'

'At the British fucking Museum?' he hissed. 'Are you mad?'

'Just gallus, I hope,' I shot back. 'Don't you think a piece of black stone is worth Lily's life?'

He shut his mouth in a tight line, his fist closing around the smooth bit of iron he'd been toying with all day. 'Do you trust her, about the manuscripts?' he whispered. 'Or do you think she's having us on, meaning to go after them herself later?'

'She's a respected antiquities dealer. Not a position you can reach or keep if you scoop finds from your clients or their friends. In any case, do we have a choice?' I pointed at the bit of iron in his fist. 'Hand that over.'

He let it slide from his hand to mine, and I set it inside the case. At least it wouldn't feel entirely empty. I shot Eircheard a bleak smile. 'Besides, at the moment, I'm the one who's not trustworthy.'

'Tonight,' Joanna said firmly into the phone. 'Yes, that's brilliant, thanks.' Ending the call, she came back with a smile. I felt a momentary pang: she was going out of her way to help us, and I was stealing her mirror. A stone for a life, I told myself. It had to be done.

In five minutes, we'd put on our coats and were hurrying north up St Martin's Lane, towards Bloomsbury. The rain had stopped, but the air was still damp and the streets slick and gleaming.

33

'You think he'll really let us see it?' I asked, as we wound through Seven Dials, ringed with restaurants and pubs, jazz spilling through a briefly opened door and bouncing along the wet pavement at our feet. 'Why?'

'Because up to now, there's been no proof that it's actually Dee's mirror. Though the Museum so far has gone out of its way not to say so in public, seeing as it's touted among the cognoscenti as one of its great British objects.'

'But it might not be?'

'Walpole said it was Dee's.'

'*Castle of Otranto* Walpole?' I squeaked. 'The inventor of Gothic fiction?'

'Good old Horace,' she replied with a smile. 'He of the creaking doors in the night, the distant scream, the bats fluttering about the moonlit tower. All the great clichés of ghost stories and horror films. Yes, that Horace. He gave us Dee's magic mirror, too. Unfortunately, there's suspicion in some quarters that his tale about the mirror's history might be as fantastic as his fiction. Not quite fair, really. He was a true collector, a connoisseur of esoteric art and occult

317

objects. And the provenance he gave the mirror winds plausibly back through eccentric aristocrats to a man who patronised both Dee and his son.'

'Arthur?' I asked. In the bag on my shoulder, the weight of the stolen mirror seemed to grow heavier.

'Arthur. Physician to the Czar of Russia. Son of an English wizard. And most importantly, at least tonight, correspondent of Sir Robert Cotton – maybe the most important collector of ancient books and manuscripts in Britain's history.'

For a while we walked in silence, our footsteps ringing on the pavement.

'Right now, the mirror has pride of place in the Enlightenment Gallery, under the aegis of Owen Knight, Head of European collections. A curator who's half Welsh and wholly fascinated by Dee. Steeped in British history. But there's a struggle brewing behind the scenes between Owen and his counterpart in charge of the Americas. Because the mirror may or may not be Dee's. But it is most certainly Aztec.'

'*Aztec?*' I exclaimed.

'An attribute of the god Tezcatlipoca. Dark twin and eternal rival of the better-known Queztalcoatl. The mirror is supposed to have been fixed to his leg after a sea monster bit off his foot in a titanic battle at the dawn of creation. The Aztecs believed the mirror worked two ways. Priests could see in it visions of whatever the god cared to show them –

things near or far, past, or present, or yet to come. But the god also used it as a window through which to gaze out on the world he had helped to create, watching the people he sometimes chose, on a whim, to destroy. Lord of the Smoking Mirror, his name means. God of Poetry and Jokes, he was. Sounds bright and beautiful, doesn't it?' Her eyes twinkled with mischief. 'But he was also the god of Night and Mockery, of Disease and Sorcery and Death. The Enemy, he was called by those who worshipped him. The Trickster. The Spanish missionaries had another name for him: the Aztec Lucifer.'

'How did such a thing fall into Dee's hands?' asked Eircheard, rolling along on the other side of Joanna.

She shrugged. 'Nobody knows. It's not like it's the only one. Tezcatlipoca was a major god, and most of his statues had these mirrors attached to them. The Conquistadors hacked up the statues as evil idols, but trinkets like these mirrors tended to be slipped out of the carnage by the foot soldiers when the priests weren't looking. A number of them were floating about Europe in the sixteenth century. Dee made several extended visits to the Continent, where he had rock-star status as an intellectual, though he was shamefully ignored at home. It's not implausible that at some point he picked one up from a Spaniard in the Low Countries. He was in Antwerp, for instance, in 1563, in search of rare manuscripts.

'We know he had one. The question has always been, is it

319

this one? Your letter – assuming it's genuine – offers proof. And since Owen's locked in a territorial battle over the thing, he'll probably kiss your feet, never mind letting you hold the damn mirror. You'd think it was one of his own balls, the way he protects it.'

We turned a corner and the museum soared into sight, its colonnade and grand sculptured pediment glowing gold in the darkness. Behind its high wrought-iron fence it looked like an immense beast, a hoarder of knowledge. Late on a rainy autumn night, its grand stairway was eerily deserted. We followed Joanna up the steps, our footfalls echoing in the night.

We ran up the steps and in through the dim echoing entry hall, into the blinding white space of the Great Court, mostly empty. It was dizzying, like walking through a hard, cold, echoing egg, turned inside out. In the centre was a circular tower, the old Reading Room of the British Library before it had moved to its new digs farther north a decade earlier.

Joanna marched us towards a grand pedimented door-way leading off the court to the right. Inside was a long narrow gallery, dark after the brightness of the court. I stood blinking in the entryway for a few moments until my eyes adjusted to the dimness, aware only of the room stretching far into the distance on both left and right.

'Enlightenment Hall,' said Joanna. 'A tribute to the seek-ers of knowledge. Displayed in their fashion.' Which meant lots of classical statuary, apparently, and display cases packed chock-a-block like curio cabinets with objects gathered by abstract ideas – *Justice, Geography, Religion, Magic* – rather than by the time or place of their making.

We turned left, past a lion-headed Egyptian goddess in black stone – Sekhmet, Goddess of Chaos and Destruction, noted Joanna – and stopped at a case that held magical objects of all kinds. The antithesis, I thought, of the Enlightenment and its proud rationality. In one corner was a small black disc of polished stone, about a quarter inch thick. It had a handle with a hole drilled through it.

'Tezcatlipoca's foot,' said Joanna.

'That's it?' asked Eircheard, clearly unimpressed.

Nothing was visible around its rim.

Joanna pulled out her phone to call the curator, and, casting a baleful glance at me, Eircheard limped off for the men's room. But I stood entranced by the dark mirror. A blank bit of darkness. It seemed preposterously small to hang a human life upon.

Its reflections were dim shadows. It was like the night sky, except that the more I stared into it, the more light seemed to recede from the surface, almost as if I were pouring into it. Clouds skidded across it, growing and dissolving. Barely discernable, without stars in the distance.

And then I saw a shadowy reflection. The face of a man over my shoulder. With dark hair and pale, wolfish eyes. The Winter King. Then I saw the gleam of a knife.

I whirled, my heart knocking against my ribs. But I was alone in the gallery, save for one shadowy figure at the far end: too far off to have cast the reflection.

'Kate?' It was Joanna. 'Are you all right?'

Dumbly, I nodded.

'Owen's waiting for us at the restaurant.'

34

We crossed back through the court to the stairs at the base of the reading room. Wide steps spiralled up around it to the museum's upper level, where a chic postmodern restaurant was tucked in behind the reading room, prickling with the muted clink of cutlery. The few patrons left looked to be an even mix of obvious tourists and well-heeled Britons. It was an airy space, the steel netting overhead now dark.

A man with a shock of dark gold hair and a finely cut suit rose as we approached, and Joanna introduced Owen Knight, Curator of European Collections. He gave Joanna a cool kiss on the cheek, his smile faintly lascivious. 'I took the liberty of ordering already, as the kitchen was closing. I hope you like calamari.'

There was a mound of them on a plate in the centre of the table. I realised I was ravenous.

'How are things with Gloria?' Joanna asked.

He leaned back in his chair, grimacing. 'Greedy Gloria.' He had a soft 'r' that sounded more like a 'w'.

'Gloria Moreno,' explained Joanna. 'Curator of the Americas. She has an interest in Dee's mirror.'

'If she'd put it like that, I'd be ecstatic,' he grumbled. 'But she won't admit it's Dee's. Says it belongs in her rooms as indisputably Aztec.'

As they talked, Eircheard and I ate, content to listen to their sparring.

'No one *knows*, actually, if it's Dee's mirror at all,' said Joanna.

Owen coloured a little. 'It's Dee's.'

'But you can't prove it.' Joanna leaned forward. 'Yet.'

He went still. 'What have you got?'

'A letter from Arthur Dee,' she said. '*You will know the mirror by—*' She stopped with a sweet smile.

'By what?' Sweat had sprung up on his upper lip.

Joanna leaned back. 'Hard to tell from the display. It will have to come out of its case.'

He sat back. 'Impossible. You know that.'

Joanna set her drink down on the table. 'Pity. As Ms Stanley's adviser, I've told her that the best price will come via select auction among occult collectors. As I've said, this might mean it could disappear from view for centuries. Such a secretive set.' She rose.

'Wait.' He ran a hand through his hair. 'Come back to my office.'

She unfurled a wide smile. 'With pleasure.'

I took one more calamari for the road, and then we clattered down the stairs and back into the Enlightenment Gallery, this time turning right, away from the mirror. At

324

the lower end of the gallery, we passed into another, smaller room, turned left into a long hallway of offices and study rooms, and then right.

The office had high ceilings and two windows that looked out over a narrow side yard cluttered with a few cars. Beyond that, a black iron railing fenced off the tree-lined street that ran along the eastern side of the museum. A large desk and a long table cluttered with papers and bits of statuary faced each other across the room. Every available surface seemed to be filled with body parts in cold, beautiful stone. Most of them female. The lioness-head torn from another statue of Sekhmet, goddess of chaos, pestilence, and bloodlust. A white marble foot. A single, impossibly perfect breast. *Did Owen fancy himself Pygmalion? Or Dr Frankenstein?*

He sat on the edge of the table, arms crossed. 'What have you got?'

Joanna put both hands on the table and displayed her prodigious memory, quoting a sentence she'd seen only once before. *'You will know the mirror by its black surface, and by a posie around its edge.'*

'You'll have to do better than that,' said Owen, retrieving a piece of paper from his desk and laying it on the table. 'Second enquiry in as many weeks, as it happens, about lettering around the perimeter.'

The page was a photocopy of a daguerreotype. A man with Victorian sideburns in a kilt and an immense tam-o'-shanter with a cockade and a tall pheasant plume. He stood

325

holding a dark circular mirror like a trophy. At the bottom was scrawled a date: *May 10, 1849.*

I started and then stopped myself, hoping Owen hadn't seen it.

He was staring at the photo. 'Nothing for years, and then two enquiries in two weeks. Odd, don't you think?' He looked up. 'Unfortunately, unhelpful. It was ground down at some point. Nothing legible left.'

'No marks at all?' asked Eircheard.

'Nothing useful unless you know what it says.'

'But we do,' said Joanna.

Owen's fists clenched involuntarily, his voice tightening. 'What?'

'It comes out of the case, first.'

We had to wait, he said, none too graciously, until the museum emptied of patrons for the night.

'I'll need some help,' said Owen, looking pointedly at me.

Beyond him, Joanna gave a slight shake of her head. *No.*

'I'll do it,' said Eircheard.

We hung our jackets in his closet, and I set my bag with Dee's book on the floor. And then we sat on the floor in the dark, out of sight from the windows, watching the moonlight slip over the walls.

I thought of the black velvet bag inside my bag. I had no idea how I'd manage the switch. But Eircheard was a clown. No doubt he'd improvise some distraction when the time came.

Half an hour ticked slowly away before Owen rose and beckoned to Eircheard, and the two of them disappeared into the hall, the door closing quietly behind them.

Through the windows, the lights of London bounced off the clouds, giving the sky a strange pinkish glow. The wind rattled against the panes in gusts that sent leaves whirling about.

'He's not telling all he knows,' I said.

'Neither are we,' said Joanna. 'Particularly you. That picture startled you.' She went to the desk and picked it up.

'It's the date: the day New Yorkers rioted over *Macbeth*.' I laughed at the look on her face. 'Sounds absurd now, but it remains one of the worst riots in US history. Twenty thousand people in the streets, and New York's National Guard firing into the crowds. A lot of people died.'

'Over Shakespeare?' Joanna's voice cracked.

'*Macbeth* was the trigger. Class warfare was the chronic rumbling that fuelled it. That, and the sheer delight that some of the big street gangs had in fighting. But it was sparked by a personal and stylistic clash between two actors: an American named Edwin Forrest, and a Brit named William Charles Macready. Brawn vs. elegance. In their sensibilities, it was a little like a contest between John Wayne and Laurence Olivier.'

She held the photo before us. 'Bound to be one of them, don't you think?'

'Let's find out which.' Taking the page from her, I went

to Owen's desk. His computer was on; the screensaver was a finely painted Renaissance portrait floating around against a black background. A disappointed looking man with long nose and dark, reproaching eyes under a black skullcap, a long white pointed beard flowing over a compact Elizabethan ruff. He might have been scowling. It was hard to tell beneath the beard and moustache.

'John Dee,' Joanna said softly. 'Still the archetype for our ideas of what a wizard should look like.'

We were in London, so I googled Macready first. It wasn't him. Just to make sure, I typed in Forrest's name. The picture was different, but the man was the same.

Where had he come from? Who else had known to ask about a posie?

The keyboard was under my hands. I pulled up Owen's email and glanced at the subject lines. 'Look what we've got here.'

Dee's mirror.

The email was brief. *Could you tell me whether John Dee's mirror has any lettering engraved around the perimeter? I attach a photo that might feature this mirror. If you have further information, or would like to know more about the photo, please contact me at this email address or the cell number below.*

The signature was an automatic one: Professor Jamie Clifton, Department of English, College of Mount Saint Vincent, New York.

I pushed print, and the printer hummed into life. As I was picking the page up from the printer tray, the computer cut out, and the lights in the room flared once and died.

35

I went to the window. As far as I could tell, the whole museum had gone dark, though the buildings across the street still had power. The room, however, was not entirely black. Light from the street lights, from the ambient light of London, drifted through the windows.

Eircheard and Owen should have been back by now, surely. I listened at the door, but heard only silence. I folded the copy of the photograph and the email together and shoved them in the pocked of my jeans. 'I'm going after them,' I said.

Joanna did not care to sit alone in the darkness, so we slipped out of the office together. With one hand on the wall, I turned right, counting three more doors before the corridor turned left. Up ahead, a faint light spilled into the corridor from the galleries leading off to the right, more like paler darkness in a shade of grey, rather than actual light, like the mysterious light in Rembrandt's gloomier paintings. I sped up, heading for it. Behind me, Joanna kept up.

I paused at the wide doorway leading into the Enlightenment Hall. The pink glow of London's lights washed in through the high windows up along the gallery, bright enough to cast faint shadows of the trees and branches swaying outside, so that the whole hall seemed to be moving, dancing around the space amid lashing branches. The movement of the trees made the statutes – Cupid, Pan, Hermes, Sekhmet – look as if they were moving, swaying to some silent music.

'I don't hear anything,' said Joanna.

'That's the problem,' I whispered back. 'We should hear *something*.'

'What have you dragged me into?' Joanna said with more than a hint of accusation.

'Sorry, but we have to find Eircheard.'

Keeping to the deep shadows in the narrow lane between the long wall of books and a line of exhibit cases, we crept forward across the room. As we came to the wide open space in the centre, where the grand doors led out to the Great Court, we stopped.

The court seemed to be empty, save for the white lion-legged vase. More disturbing, we heard and saw nothing in the northern end of the gallery, where Eircheard and Owen should be.

We darted across the open space, sliding back into the shadows between the books and the exhibits until they came to an end, guarded by Sekhmet, sitting stiffly upright on her black throne.

'Kate.' Joanna was pointing. Something was draped across

the goddess's lap. A man's tweed jacket. She stepped out and picked it up. Beyond I saw something flicker on the floor. A crystal ball. And beyond that a thick circle of wax lay on the floor, broken in two. I looked up at the case.

It was gaping open.

I drew forward, filling with dread. The mirror and its case were gone. And at its foot a body lay in a heap. Owen, with a bullet hole between wide-open eyes. I looked around for Eircheard, but saw no one else.

The glass of the case, though, was smeared with some-thing. *Blood.* On the floor at my feet was a small pool of it; a trail of smaller droplets led straight on through the gallery. My stomach twisted in a sudden twinge of fear.

Coming up behind me, Joanna made a small squeak. At a quick motion from me, she went silent. I stood, hands on hips, thinking. We'd heard nothing, though this was an echoing space. That meant a gun with a silencer. Such as our stalker at the theatre had possessed. But it couldn't be that one.

Pulling Joanna forward, I followed the trail of blood.

At the end of the gallery, it led into a grand echoing stair-well, dimly lit somewhere far above. Beyond lay a smaller gallery, muffled in almost total darkness. A small spattering of drops crossed into the dark.

My eyes adjusted. Two more cases were open.

A cry rose from depths of the museum, rising in waves of agony and anger, and cut to silence. It entered the small gallery from both ends and seemed to wind through space, bouncing off walls and cases.

Eircheard.

I turned back, peering out into the Great Court. It looked and felt like the ghost of some ancient snowstorm, pale and ethereal and cold. It was entirely silent, as if that cry, and perhaps all other sound, had never been. Against the far wall, faint in the distance, I thought I saw a trail of dark petals dropped haphazardly across the floor. Blood?

Somewhere above, we heard the clatter of hard shoes on marble, the spat of radio static, and a man's voice barking orders. Security.

The mirror, I thought, suddenly afraid. It was the one remaining thread, fragile as it was, that led somewhere through the darkness towards Lily. Pulling Joanna forward across the court, I ducked into a postcard shop, roped closed, as the security guard passed at a trot.

The trail of blood by the wall curved around the Reading Room, following it around to the front, stopping at the double doors facing the museum's main entrance. One of them was ever so slightly ajar. Fear coiling around me, I pushed it open.

It was darker here than in the Great Court, but not so dark as in the galleries. High rounded windows circled the space three floors up, before the ceiling bent inward in a dome I knew to be blue and gold, the blue of robins' eggs and the Virgin Mary, though now it looked nearly black.

'A temple of knowledge,' my Aunt Helen had said. She'd brought me to study here for a week the moment she heard the British Library had been slated to be moved. The wheel of learning where Virginia Woolf and Karl Marx and Charles Dickens had toiled. With the departure of the national library up to new digs by King's Cross, the space had been divided like a cathedral, the front third an empty, echoing nave where unhallowed tourists were allowed to wander. Separating the profane from the sacred, a long curved line of desks swept across the room. Beyond lay the museum's private library.

'*Eircheard?*'

In answer, I heard nothing but a steady, slow drip.

Up ahead, there was a gate through the black granite-topped information desk, like the little gate in an altar rail. Beyond curved a line of low shelves. Above these flickered two points of light. Candles.

In a library? The candles stood atop the line of shelves, as if on some high altar.

With mounting dread, I crossed the room and stepped through the gate. Just inside, a stench of sewer thickened the air, and I stopped again, so suddenly that Joanna bumped into me. A little way off to the left, two white pillar candles stood six feet apart on the shelf. Between them, a black velvet shroud veiled a body. Just beyond it, a wide-eyed face leered at us, fangs bared.

I stepped back, hearing someone gasp, and the candles guttered.

My heart thudding against my ribs, I realised that the face was a human skull inlaid in wide stripes of black and turquoise stones, its eye sockets filled with large gleaming grey discs. Without lips, its teeth looked like bared fangs.

'The mask of Tezcatlipoca,' whimpered Joanna. *The Lord of the Smoking Mirror.*

Dee's mirror. I glanced along the body, but the black mirror was nowhere to be seen. Beneath the closest candle, though, lay a stone knife, its blade a pale milky green.

Stepping forward, I lifted a corner of the shroud. Beneath lay a man with ginger hair. *Eircheard.* His face, which had so quickly come to seem dear, was contorted beneath his red beard, his eyes wide and staring. He was dead.

I reached out and brushed his eyelids closed; he was still warm. A sound scraped in my throat, and I gripped the edge of the counter to stay upright. What had they done to him?

I gave the shroud a small tug, and velvet slid to the floor with a small whisper that made the candle flames dance.

They'd stretched him naked on his back, his body arched over arms bound beneath him. Blood had pooled and thickened on the shelf top, dripping in slow, steady drops. Just below his ribcage, a wide slash gaped across his abdomen like an obscene mouth. Above that, a mark had been carved into his skin: a circle flanked by two smaller circles, all cut with a horizontal line. Carrie's mark.

She'd killed him to consecrate the mirror.

For a moment, everything went black before my eyes, and my ears filled with a thunderous rushing as fury spread through me. I looked wildly around the room.

'*Carrie!*' I heard myself cry. '*Cerridwen Douglas!*'

My voice echoed around the dome and died away. A rasping voice scraped through the darkness to my left. '*Nothing is but what is not.*' I spun towards it, but the light of the candles did not penetrate deep enough into the shadows.

From the other side came another voice. '*She shall be queen hereafter.*' And then laughter sputtered down from above. I looked up. Ringing the room were two catwalk galleries lined with bookshelves, the upper one lit faintly by light drifting in through the high arched windows. A dark figure stood there, spread-eagled at the balcony as if embracing the night. Three more words echoed through the dome. '*She must die.*'

At the back of the room, the double doors flew open. Joanna grabbed me and dove for the ground, pulling us under the information desk, clamping a hand over my mouth as several pairs of footsteps strode forward across the floor.

Interlude

Summer, 1590
Shoreditch, north of London

For the first time, Dr Dee walked into the building that he had helped old Burbage, the famous actor's father, design: The Theatre, in the fields of Shoreditch, north of London. At least, it had been set among fields when it was built – almost fifteen years ago, that was, now. In the intervening span, though, a hotch-potch of vaguely and not-so-vaguely disreputable taverns, brothels, and tenements had sprung up around it until it seemed to be pretty much an extension of the city.

It would be interesting, he supposed, to see his design at work. He'd drawn it partly from the inns and great halls that players had long been accustomed to playing in, as Burbage had insisted, and partly from drawings of old Roman theatres. Less well known, he had also drawn on a different tradition of performance entirely – which, were the truth to be known, was the reason Burbage had come to him in the first place.

The crowd streaming in around him was boisterously jovial. By the time he reached his seat, he'd been propositioned at least three and possibly four times by ladies of questionable virtue – the last of them wearing a concoction of orange feathers on her head that would surely annoy whoever had the misfortune to sit behind her. In fastidious black scholar's gown and skullcap, Dr Dee found her plumage alarming enough seen briefly from the front.

He had come to see the first public performance of young Master Shakespeare's new play, *The First Part of the True Contention Betwixt the Two Famous Houses of York and Lancaster*. An extravagant title on the part of a little-known upstart, though possibly the most prodigal thing about it was the promise implied by the word 'first'. What, after all, had a mere player, a glover's son from provincial Warwickshire to say about the mighty ones of the kingdom?

On the other hand, Master Shakespeare had the backing, it seemed, of the Earl of Derby's charming scamp of a younger son, the Honourable William Stanley, with whom he was much of an age, though their stations in life could hardly be more different. Dr Dee bit his lip, considering. If anyone could tell the Lancastrian side of the 'contention' in question, a long and bloody dynastic war that had lasted generations, it would surely be the Stanleys, who'd acquired their earldom by decisively backing the correct side in the last battle, setting the crown on the queen's grandfather's head.

It was not, however, the politics or the history of a war of roses – the Lancastrian red against the Yorkist white – that had captured Dr Dee's curiosity. In general, he cared little about what young men more prone to revels and riots than to

338

study might say about matters best left to the wise. But this play, he had heard, strayed into territory altogether more dangerous, and more dear to his heart. Mr Shakespeare had dared to conjure a demon on the stage.

He was not the only one who'd heard the whispers. Most of the mob, he reckoned, seemed to be there for the same reason that he was – to watch the magic – though more out of prurience, to be sure, than a learned and professional attachment to the subject. Stuffed to its rafters, though the day was hot and sticky and the sky threatened to dump rain, the whole place was abuzz with wonder and a deep thrill of fear: would the play – *could* the play – raise something more in its circle than a stage demon? Would the spirits of hell know the difference between a proper conjuror and a player-conjuror? Would they care, even if they knew?

Dr Dee did not, as he had feared, have to sit through wearisome hours of warriors' bombast before arriving at the magic. It appeared – or at least the dark promise of it did – almost as soon as the characters began speaking and the crowd's chatter subsided. Young as he was, Mr Shakespeare, thought Dr Dee, knew how to stick bums to seats.

A short time later, however, when the magic itself arrived, Dr Dee was no longer so sure about that. On stage, two Jesuit priests, a witch, and a fool of a duchess gathered in the company of a conjuror. Somewhere, someone began rippling a thunder sheet, the sound of it so low at first that it was felt more than heard. The conjuror began to move, casting a circle around himself using words and motions and even props that lifted every tiny hair on Dr Dee's body. Up on the stage, the man gathered speed and force, and around him the rumbling of thunder rose. A deep voice roared *Adsum!* – 'I come,' in Latin – and a demon appeared growling on the stage. A player, of course, but his entrance was unsettling.

'Asnath!' shrieked the player-witch, naming the spirit. As her cry died away, there came a great crackling of sound that no thunder sheet could ever make. With a sudden stench of sulphur, lightning hit the flagpole rising from the building's tallest turret. The banner that hung there burst into bright fire even as the skies opened up in a downpour that drowned the flames.

As one, the audience rose, the seated to their feet, and the standing to their toes, and a long ooooh spiralled around the stage. Behind the player-demon, a shadow loomed skyward. Dr Dee, a tall man, pushed himself up to stand on the bench and pointed a long finger at the stage. *Void*, he bellowed in a voice that might quell the waves.

On the point of dissolving into trampling chaos, the crowd suddenly stilled. Even the actors froze, and the rain blew over as quickly as it had started: until the only movement was the trembling of the old wizard's arm. He stepped down from the bench and walked solemnly down the aisle, people parting a way for him. Down the stairs he went, and back into the street.

In the theatre, a tucket of trumpets broke out at Burbage's insistence, and the play went on, fighting to be heard over a great murmuring among the audience. Heading back towards the city on foot, Dr Dee did not notice, the world having closed into a dark tunnel around him.

He did not, like most of those in the crowd, ask what had happened up on the stage. He knew what had happened. What he wanted to know was how the boy had done it. How had he learned what he'd put on the stage?

He had first come to Dr Dee's attention last December in the company of Derby's son, at one of the lowest points in his life, returning after several years on the Continent to find his precious library in his home out at Mortlake ransacked: four thousand books – the collection of a lifetime – gone, the precious glassware in his alchemical laboratory smashed or taken, the two globes Mercator had made especially for him stolen, even the shelving stripped from the walls. Into this mess had walked Master Stanley with Master Shakespeare, a mirror under one arm and a manuscript under the other.

Master Shakespeare, Derby's son had explained, after introducing them, had recently returned from Scotland, where he had come into the possession of certain objects Dr Dee might welcome. As the boy set the round mirror of polished black stone in his hands, Dr Dee had looked up sharply. This, too, had been stolen from his library: but not this library, and not recently. He had last seen it in Antwerp

341

twenty-five years or so before, in the hands of a young witch with red hair and a Scottish accent.

Without a word, the lad had laid atop the mirror a manuscript. It was old, in an antique form of Welsh that even Dr Dee found difficult to read. So far as he could make out, it concerned a Welsh witch who lived in a lake and wove strong spells with the aid of a cauldron.

Exactly how he'd come by either mirror or manuscript, Mr Shakespeare remained coy. Dr Dee, however, let the question slide, as collectors often must, he told himself. He was intrigued. He was enthralled. And he was happy to start his library anew with two such rare finds at its heart. He had welcomed Mr Shakespeare to visit when he pleased and make use of his library how he might.

That had all been well and good. The books trickled back, and with them intellectuals from all corners of the kingdom. His home once again became a gathering place for scholars of all sorts, hashing out questions of all kinds. How many ships could the Emperor of Cathay command? What was the proper title and style of the Emperor of Russia? How did geese navigate their migrations? Was there such a thing as an unbreakable cipher? And what was the hierarchy of Hell?

It was the last question that a small coterie of his best and brightest students – the most daring thinkers of the kingdom – pursued, among others. His scholars of the night, they called themselves. It was among these, William Stanley and his protégé included, that he'd shared a summary of his deep studies of Mr Shakespeare's manuscript.

Not even among this select group, however, had Dr Dee shared the information that he intended to attempt one of the rites described in the manuscript. Cleaned up, of course, polished into something acceptably Christian. He had shared that, in fact, with no one save Arthur, his eldest son, ten years old, who was currently serving as his scryer. It had taken three days to prepare the room and the properties, and one more to fast and bathe, to make the two of them ready. A month or so ago, this had been. They had retired at nightfall to his innermost study, beyond the double sliding doors, with the black mirror and a candle, and they had set to work.

How someone else came to be there, he still could not understand. Surely he had seen that the room was empty before they started. He could not quite remember, but it was force of habit: how could he have failed on this occasion? But it seemed equally odd to suppose that someone could have entered after they had begun, without their knowledge. He had purposely left a creak in the doors for just such an eventuality, but no sound had disturbed either him or his son.

But someone *had* been there. A shadowy presence he became aware of as they finished the rite: not knowing how long he had been there, or what he had seen. Not knowing, indeed, who he was, though he and Arthur had both given chase through the maze of his library and out into the street.

In the rite, they had been equally disappointed. It had promised clarity of both sight and thought, but neither he nor his son had noticed a change. Dr Dee had long been resigned to the fact that he would never see the spirits for himself, save on the rarest of occasions, and then only dimly. But for Arthur, this blindness to the spirit world was still a raw hurt that the boy strove to heal, and the failure of this ceremony had seemed a hard blow. It had, however, been a private disappointment.

Until this afternoon, when he saw it, mimicked and even parodied, lifted on the common stage. How had the player known, unless he had been the watcher in the shadows? Knowledge, though, was for sale the width and breadth of the kingdom. The watcher need not have been the boy himself, Dr Dee thought.

Except that there had been one or two details in the casting of the circle that not even a glimpse of Dr Dee's private ceremony could explain. Details available only in a singular manuscript in a crabbed and antique form of Welsh that he would not believe the young man had at his command. And if he had acquired these details neither from Dr Dee nor from the strange manuscript, *where had he got them?*

And the only answer Dr Dee could light upon was the possibility of having glimpsed, in some other place, a different version of the rite than his own.

Mr Shakespeare has recently returned to us from Scotland, Mr Stanley had said, upon introducing them. Words that now haunted Dr Dee. Where in Scotland, and when? With whom? *And to what effect?*

At the start of the afternoon, the player's unprecedented rise in poetic power and popularity had seemed no more than a curiosity. Now, there suddenly seemed to hang around his reputation a faint stench of sulphur such as Dr Dee had scented on the air in the playhouse.

His fine black gown bespattered with mud and grime, the old wizard reached the Thames without much awareness of having walked right through the city. Treading heavily down some stairs and into a waiting barge, he bespoke a row upriver to Mortlake.

Leaning back in his seat, the cool pull and slip of the water rushing by his ears, Dr Dee shuddered. Young Master Shakespeare had written what he should not, he was sure of that. How he'd come to know it perhaps not even heaven knew.

CAULDRON

Double, double toil and trouble,
Fire burn and cauldron bubble.

36

Huddled in Joanna's arms beneath the desk, I twisted to look back up at the high balcony. The mocking figure was gone.

Below that lay Eircheard. As the footsteps moved steadily towards us, I made him a silent promise. *I will kill her. I will find Lily, and then Carrie will die.*

Near the little gate, the footsteps slowed. Stepping through, two pair of shiny black shoes stopped, so close to us that I could have reached out and plucked at their trousers. Overhead, radio static scratched the darkness. Security guards, then.

'*Jesus,*' said a male voice. Further back, a third person spun away, and I heard the sound of heaving. Then another sound cut through it. Somewhere at the back of the room, a door creaked.

'Bastard's still here,' growled the closest guard. 'Hey!' shouted the second. 'Stop!' They took off running, the third stumbling after.

Joanna and I wasted no time. Scooting out from under the desk, we ran in the opposite direction, sprinting through the main doors into the Great Court, our footsteps ringing against the marble floor as we turned back towards the Enlightenment Gallery. Behind us, someone shouted, pattering down the stairs curving around the Reading Room.

We didn't look back. Skidding through the gallery, we crouched behind an exhibit case as scattered footsteps ran into the room after us, stopping just inside the door. There was a slight jangling of keys, and another burst from a radio. Guards, again.

What had happened, back there in the library? What door had opened? There must be an emergency exit, presumably out to the Great Court level we were on. But there were also doors, somewhere, that led down into the warren of rooms beneath the Reading Room – the old stacks of the British Library. Where had the killers gone? Was there a floor between us, or had they too, headed back this way? How many of them were there?

And how many guards?

Somehow, we had to avoid all of them and get out of the museum before the police arrived.

Whoever had killed Owen had taken the mirror. Would they, as we had done, go looking for more information? In his office? Jesus, his office. *I'd left Dee's book, my bag with all our other papers, my jacket – everything – in Owen's office.*

Flashlight beams sliced through the darkness. There was a fifty–fifty chance that our pursuers would go left instead of right. If they glimpsed the open case, that chance went up to a certainty . . . and once they saw the trail of blood, they'd surely follow it as fast as we had. It would give us a chance.

Fishing in my pockets, I found a pound coin and lobbed it high. It clattered down somewhere in the distance, and the lights instantly swept that way, catching on the open case. As the guards stepped down towards it, Joanna and I sped in the other direction. As we reached the staff corridor, I caught her hand, stopping her. After the gallery, the window-less corridor was utterly dark. I did my best to still my breath, listening for sounds up ahead.

Behind us, the museum had become a tangle of echoing shouts and footsteps, but ahead, I heard nothing. Guiding ourselves with hands on the wall, we plunged into the void. The corridor seemed to have stretched to a mile or more, so that it took for ever to come to the turn leading right and begin counting the doors. At the fourth, we stopped and I put my ear up to it. Had anyone else got here first? Hearing nothing, I flung it open.

The room was empty, but one of the windows had been opened wide, so that gusts of chill autumn air swirled around the room, moaning lightly in the corners, A handful of leaves scraped and swirled across the floor.

Grabbing a war club from a shelf, I yanked open the closet. No one was there, but our jackets still hung inside. On the floor sat the bag with Dee's book and the folder from Lady Nairn. I looked in the bag. Everything was still there.

Gathering our things, we went to the open window. Whoever had been here had gone through it, but it was still our best bet for getting out unseen. I leaned out. The night air was tangled with sirens, but I saw no sign of a person.

Climbing out, I let myself drop to the ground. Joanna dropped beside me. We were in a narrow gravelled and tree-lined side yard – essentially a private roadway used as an employee parking lot, separated from the public street by a wrought-iron fence. Joanna pointed off to the left. Twenty yards up stood a narrow gabled guardhouse the size of a telephone booth. Beyond that a gate opened onto the street. We edged forward.

The gate clanked in the wind. Drawing up to the guard-house, I glanced inside. The guard was slumped back, a bullet hole between his eyes. He'd died the same way that Owen had.

At the bottom of the road, a siren screamed along Great Russell Street heading for the Museum's front entrance. In the other direction, it looked as if there weren't another cross street for a half a mile. Row houses, many of them converted to hotels, lined the road on both sides. Lights began to flick on in their windows.

Taking my hand, Joanna darted through the gate and across the street, dragging me up a little way to a spot where the row houses ended and a brick wall, twelve feet high and covered in ivy, began. She began to climb. Slinging the bag over my shoulder, I followed. The brick was old, scarred and pitted from centuries of urban air, and made for easy climbing. We were up and over, landing in a spiky pile of conkers, just as a siren veered around into the road behind us and a car squealed to a stop.

We stood in a garden fronting two houses set back from the street; between them and the last row house, a path led back into shadows. Joanna pulled me towards it.

The path led back to a narrow tree-studded garden stretching left and right the length of the entire block, surrounded by buildings on all sides. Around us, dogs were beginning to bark, and more lights winked on.

Eircheard. I felt bile crawling upwards again, and swallowed hard against it. I needed to think.

Beside me, Joanna was trembling, her face taut with horror. 'The mask of Tezcatlipoca, the knife. Even the cut. It's how Aztec priests sacrificed: cutting just under the ribcage and up through the diaphragm to reach the heart.'

Tezcatlipoca, I thought. *God of Mocking Laughter. God of Night and Sorcery and Death. The Aztec Lucifer. Lord of the Smoking Mirror.*

'Jesus, Kate, that was an Aztec sacrifice. Owen was right, that woman is insane—' Her voice was rising toward hysteria.

'Listen to me.' I took her by both shoulders. 'It wasn't Aztec. But it was a sacrifice.'

'Not—'

'The mirror was missing. If Eircheard's killers had really

353

been Aztec devotees, they'd have taken all three objects. Not just the mirror.' *And they wouldn't have quoted Macbeth.*

'Why the mirror?'

'It was being consecrated. With blood.'

Her eyes widened. 'But the only reason for that—'

'Is to work black magic.'

Joanna took a step back. 'You *knew* how dangerous this was, and you still involved me?' she asked thickly. 'Without warning?'

In my pocket, my phone drummed to life. 'Sympathy for the Devil' again. *Lily.*

It was a picture message. A photo of Lily, bound as I'd seen her in my dream on the hill, except this time, she was also blindfolded. Beneath the photo were two words: *24 hours.* 'What's going on?' demanded Joanna.

I shook her off, frowning at the phone. The manuscript they'd asked for looked to be untraceable, and they'd taken the mirror. What else did they want? What was I supposed to do now?

How had they known? I wondered suddenly. How had they known to come to the Museum? To go after Dee's mirror? Possibly, they'd followed Eircheard and me. Or had they somehow bugged one of us? I stared at the phone in my hand – the phone whose ringtone they'd reprogrammed. What else had they done to it?

It gleamed in my hand, a mocking and treacherous magic mirror of an all too modern variety. Suddenly I wanted nothing more than to throw it as far as I could, to drown it in some fathomless deep, but it might as well have been chained to my bones: it was the one frail link I had to Lily.

I began to shake.

Think.

They'd taken the mirror. But they hadn't yet given up on the manuscript.

Which meant I couldn't, either. But what other leads did I have?

Owen's snide voice slid through my mind: *You'll have to do better than that . . . Second enquiry in as many weeks about lettering around the perimeter.* He'd held out the old photograph. A page that I'd shoved into my pocket, just after the lights had gone out.

I fished it out.

Holding the dark mirror, Macbeth glared out at me beneath his preposterous hat. Edwin Forrest, on the day of the riot he'd helped to instigate, or at least had done nothing to quell.

Forrest.

As Joanna stared open-mouthed, I crouched down, setting the bag on the ground and scrabbling through the folder to pull out Ellen Terry's letter and Aubrey's diary. *I am hoping that you can glimpse the Forest through the Trees,* wrote Terry. And at the bottom of Aubrey's page, Max Beerbohm had quoted *Macbeth*: *Who can impress the Forrest, bid the Tree unfix his earthbound root?*

355

Both of their 'trees' referred to Beerbohm Tree. Did both of their 'forests' also point to a man? Either Max Beerbohm had misspelled 'forest', or he'd spelled 'Forrest' correctly. Was Terry's 'forest' – with one 'r' – also a reference back to the American actor? And if so, what did her reference mean?

Her letter said nothing of the mirror. But it did speak of the manuscript. And the 'poor soul' who believed herself the guardian of its whereabouts was 'a fellow denizen of the drama whose personal tale is as tragic as any role she might encharacter on the stage'. *Was she someone who'd known Forrest? Who'd been caught up in the gunfire and screaming and blood of the riot?*

I slid the email from behind the photo. The photocopied photo – or maybe scanned was a better term – had been emailed by Professor Jamie Clifton of New York, who'd somehow known to ask about the posie around the mirror. How? What did the original photograph reveal that the copy did not?

It was a thin filament to follow through a dark labyrinth. But it was all I had. I phoned Lady Nairn to tell her what I knew and what I needed: a meeting with a man and a daguerreotype in New York.

37

'*Eircheard?*' Lady Nairn exclaimed with a strangled cry when I told her he was dead. 'They killed Eircheard?'

I spared her the details for the time being; I didn't trust my voice to deliver them without quivering, in any case. Instead, I told her what little I knew about Jamie Clifton. 'I need to make sure the man's there, before I get on a plane.' I rubbed my temple as if I might squeeze out a coherent plan. 'He'll be expecting news from Owen Knight, the curator he'd contacted at the museum. Let's set up a meeting between Clifton and Knight for tomorrow morning, early. With the implication of passing on news about the photo and its mirror that will leave the professor panting.'

'Will Mr Knight go along with this?'

'He's dead. And since Carrie and company killed him, I like to think he won't mind us taking his name in vain.'

'And you'd like me to arrange it?'

'Not you. Ben.' His very name tasted bitter with guilt and sadness.

'Would you like to speak to him?'

Yes, some part of me cried in silence. *More than anything.* But I couldn't: not with Sybilla's blood on my hands. Aloud, I said, 'No. But you need to.'

'Leave it to me, then,' said Lady Nairn, suddenly all brisk business. 'In the meantime, head for Farnborough. I'll have a plane waiting. As soon as we confirm that Professor Clifton's at home, you can take off.'

'And if he isn't?'

'We'll cross that bridge when we come to it.'

I felt suddenly drained. 'Carrie's killed for both the knife and the mirror, Lady Nairn. She'll come after the cauldron too – within the next twenty-four hours, if Lily's captors aren't lying about their timing.'

'Let them,' she said darkly. 'They shan't have it. Now go and hail a taxi.'

As I hung up, Joanna glared down at me, hands on hips, her earlier hysteria condensed to anger. Her long dark hair lifted a little in the wind; moonlight glinted on the silver mesh around her neck, rising and falling with each breath. 'The knife, the mirror, and the cauldron? Plus three dead bodies, one of them a sick ritual killing? *What insanity have you pulled me into?*'

I had the time neither to answer in detail nor to babysit her. 'Kidnapping and murder. I'm sorry,' I said, shoving the papers and the phone into the bag. 'But a fifteen-year-old girl's life hangs in the balance. Your client's granddaughter.'

'Lily? Lady Nairn's Lily?'

'You know her?'

'Not personally, but I know a bit about Lady Nairn and her family.'

'I'm trying to get her back. So was Eircheard.' I rose. 'The manuscript of an early version of *Macbeth* is her ransom.'

'Jesus, Kate. So you really do think it still exists?'

'Someone thinks it does. Strongly enough to kill in anticipation of delivery. As you saw. I have twenty-four hours remaining, more or less, in which to find it.'

'And if you don't?'

'Lily dies. Or maybe I do. They're being cagey on that subject.'

'You think someone means to perform the missing rite from Macbeth?'

'You saw what happened to Eircheard. Do you think they'll flinch at witchcraft?' If Carrie could rip out a man's heart just to prep a tool, what was she capable of in the grand rite itself?

'They'll call it witchcraft, won't they?' She took a step toward me, her hands balling into fists. 'Everyone will. They have to be stopped.'

I lifted the bag to my shoulder. 'That's what I'm doing. Or trying to.' I sighed. 'You should go. Now.'

She touched my arm. 'I can help.'

'*No.*' My breath came out close to a sob. 'I let Eircheard help.'

'You didn't kill him, Kate.'

'I let him come with me when I shouldn't have. I let him get killed.'

She clasped my arm just above the elbow. 'I've spent my life working to restore respect to the pagan way of life. To witchcraft and ceremonial magic. These people – they're beyond the fringe. They're psychopaths hiding behind a sick fantasy of paganism. They don't represent who we are. But the instant this story hits the news, everything I and a lot of others have worked for . . . it will crumble like so much dust. In two days, they'll have destroyed a lifetime of labour. The only way I can see to right that particular wrong, at least partially, is for a witch to be part of stopping them.'

'I won't have your blood on my hands.'

'My blood, my hands,' she said quietly. 'You want to save a girl, Kate. I want to save an entire religion.'

Who was I to argue with that?

'Who's there?' called a voice off to the left, and footsteps headed towards us.

'Come on,' said Joanna. Cutting to the right, she wound around trees and bushes until we came to another narrow path between buildings, fronted by another high wall, this one with a door in it. It opened onto a road one street over from the museum. *Head straight into thick of things*, I heard Ben's voice say in my head. *It's what innocent people do.* So I turned right, back towards Great

Russell Street, Joanna at my side. On the kerb, we stood blinking in the whirl of headlights and sirens. In a lull, we crossed the street and hailed a cab heading west.

38

We stopped at Joanna's flat in Chelsea just long enough to retrieve her passport; I waited in the cab. Just as she was returning, Lady Nairn called back. 'Board the plane,' she said, 'the professor's at home and waiting – from what I gather, probably standing on a ladder beneath a clock, speeding the hands around.'

While Ben had arranged the meeting, she'd looked up Clifton on the college website. A scholar of drama and theatre history, she said. His dissertation had been about Edwin Forrest and the growth of celebrity culture in nineteenth-century America. He was currently at work on a book about the Astor Place Riot. The *Macbeth* riot, whose date was scrawled beneath the photograph. 'Which makes his home address intriguing,' she added.

'Where's that?'

'Astor Place.'

Around me, the world flushed cold and then hot.

'It would appear that the professor's interest is not only professional, it's personal,' said Lady Nairn. 'Bordering on the obsessive, I'd say, but living in a house called

Dunsinnan, that might be the pot calling the kettle black . . . Did I mention that Clifton's invited the curator round to his condo for breakfast? Seven-thirty?'

'That's brilliant, Lady Nairn. Joanna Black will be with me.'

'*Find Lily*,' she said, as she hung up.

The taxi drove right up to the plane, where a sleepy customs official was waiting. All he wanted was a flash of valid passports. And then we were up into the plane and on our way. During take-off, I sat looking at the photograph of Forrest. 'Tell me what you know about him,' said Joanna.

'Not much. He was one of the great tragedians of the nineteenth-century American stage. Maybe the greatest. A man's man. Worked his way up from nothing, which endeared him to the masses. He played heroes, and Americans loved him: he was all noble strength and innocence. The British thought him uncouth and extravagant, which he was.'

'Macbeth doesn't quite fit, does it? Was it a sort of side speciality?'

She was right. 'I don't think it was considered his greatest role. But it was dear to his heart. His parents had emigrated from Scotland. For all I know, he considered it his birthright. He certainly considered it a vehicle for competing with Macready.

'They started out as friends. But when Forrest got a cold reception in Britain, he blamed Macready. Took to following the older man about, watching his performances, or scheduling his own to conflict with them. In Edinburgh, once, he stood up in an otherwise rapt theatre and hissed at Macready during some tense moment in the middle of *Hamlet*. Everyone saw and heard him. He might as well have called his rival out in a duel – and other men would have settled the score at dawn, in a barrage of pistol fire. But Forrest and Macready fought their battles by proxy, on the stage.'

'And let other people do the dying, apparently,' said Joanna. She ran a finger over the date: 10 May, 1849. 'Why date the photo with a day of infamy?'

I shook my head. The play's curse was beginning to seem more real than I liked to admit. What had been Forrest's role in the riot? And what about the mirror? Was it Dee's mirror, in Forrest's hand? Was it the same mirror the museum had? Or used to have?

Those who'd taken it would need a scryer, just as Dee had. The purer the seer, Joanna had said, the clearer the sight. Lily had been learning to scry, I thought suddenly. What if they'd taken her as a seer? Hal Berridge had not survived the experience of scrying in that mirror.

Eircheard had not survived its theft. I rubbed my temples, trying to press away the prick of tears. Whatever Clifton knew, I prayed it would be useful. I had twenty-four hours, and the flight to New York would eat seven of them. Fourteen, if I had to fly back.

'*She must die.*' Shakespeare's words ran through my mind like some imp of the perverse.

Did they point at Lily? Or me?

I'd promised Eircheard I would save her.

Twenty-four hours.

As the plane levelled out, I moved to a sofa, laying out the evidence on the coffee table and walking Joanna through it. She'd risked her life, coming along. She might as well know what and who we were up against.

'So you think it'll be a cauldron rite?' she asked, peering up over her glasses.

'Lady Nairn's convinced of it.'

'Makes sense of Arthur Dee's Medea comment.'

'Makes sense of a hell of a lot more than that.' I told her about Carrie – Cerridwen – Douglas and her penchant for carving people with the Pictish cauldron symbol.

Joanna's eyes crinkled with revulsion.

'Lady Nairn thinks she's become a writer. Maybe you've heard of her: Corra Ravensbrook.'

'Ravensbrook?' She took off her glasses and ran a hand through her dark hair. 'I'm sorry to say so, but in that case, the cutting and the killing both make more sense than I'd care to admit. I won't stock her books. She sends parents frantic. Not that I usually pay much attention to parents' whining – but they have a point about Ravensbrook. Teenagers who are easily led have gone, well, badly astray under her influence. I imagine the police have a file on her. But she's very clever. She never quite comes out and says

kill. On the other hand, she preaches the beauty of folding death into life, and life into death. And she brings ancient rites of sacrifice alive quite uncannily. She talks about the bog bodies, for instance, with ghastly relish.'

'Bog bodies?'

'Ancient bodies, many of them victims of violent death, who've been discovered ritually buried in peat bogs, mostly in Britain, Ireland, and north-western Europe. They're decent evidence for fairly regular human sacrifice among both the Iron-Age Celts and Germanic tribes, though the scientists keep insisting they might be the victims of capital punishment. Hard to see how so many young children and older women were thought to have committed crimes meriting execution, though.

'Ravensbrook, as I recall, is especially taken with the Kayhausen Boy, who was found in a peat bog in northern Germany with his feet tied together, his hands bound behind his back; another length of cloth was wrapped around his neck and passed lengthwise around his body through his groin. The ghoulish woman rabbits on for what seems like pages about how similar that binding is to the binding a lot of modern covens use in their initiation rites.'

It was how Sybilla had been tied. How I'd seen Lily tied. I pulled up the picture of Lily on my phone and set it down before Joanna. 'Like that?'

She leaned forward to look. 'Jesus. Is that Lily?'

I nodded. 'You think it's some kind of initiation?'

'Are you joking? Ravensbrook scorns modern covens as namby-pamby pablum. Not exactly the opiate of the masses – "the watered-down wine of starry-eyed fools" was how she put it, once.' Her mouth pursed in distaste. 'She has not made herself warmly welcome among the pagan community.'

If Lady Nairn was right, it wasn't initiation Carrie was after. It was inspiration. Genius. *The thunderbolt of the gods*, Lady Nairn had called it. Carrie would kill for it, she'd said. I ran my tongue around dry lips. She *had* killed for it. Eircheard had been carved into an Aztec sacrifice, Auld Callie hanged and pierced like Odin, and Sybilla bound like an Iron-Age bog body, before having her throat slit. *Why?* What was this leading up to?

Across from me, Joanna suddenly looked up from the Dee book. 'Do you know what this is?' she asked in a strangled voice, smoothing it open. Beneath her hand, the pages were strewn with diagrams in blotted ink, as if drawn in a hurry: circles and triangles, separate and apart, some of them fitted together in octagons and even more elaborate structures. They made no sense to me.

'Plans,' she said. 'For the Theatre, with a capital "T". Burbage's Theatre, 1576.'

'The round wooden O,' I murmured. The first sole-purpose theatre built in Europe since the fall of Rome, the Theatre had been the home of Shakespeare's company, in the fields of Shoreditch. Twenty-odd years later, when they'd had trouble with the landlord, they'd sneaked in and pulled it down, board by board, on a single cold winter's night at the end of 1598. Quietly shipping it in pieces across the Thames, they'd rebuilt it in Southwark, on the southern bank of the river, and renamed it the Globe. *Dee* had designed it?

'The magical community has long suspected so,' said Joanna, tracing one of the circles with her finger. 'But I don't know about "sole-purpose". I've seen these same diagrams elsewhere among his papers, I'd swear it.'

'Where?'

Her gaze was faintly challenging. 'In notes showing how to cast circles of power.'

The darkness and cold outside the plane seemed to press inward. 'For making magic?'

'For invoking demons. Or angels,' she added with a small smile. 'Depending on your point of view.'

I pushed back from the table and rose, unable to sit still. 'What are you saying? That the Theatre – the foundational structure of English drama – was designed as a place to work magic?'

'To invoke spirits.' Her eyes were shining with excitement as she held up the book. 'This is proof, Kate. Proof positive.'

There wasn't much room on the plane, but I paced wildly through what there was of it. Had Shakespeare known? *One of my father's scholars*, Arthur Dee had said. True, men had sought out John Dee in pursuit of all kinds of knowledge. His library had been one of the finest all Britain, bettering even the queen's on certain topics, and far outstripping anything Oxford or Cambridge had to offer. But according to Arthur, Shakespeare had bought his way into Dee's coterie and his collection of books with a strange mirror and an even stranger manuscript. Begging the question, a scholar of what?

I conjure you, by that which you profess . . . answer me. What was it that Shakespeare had professed? I came to a stop before Joanna, my voice cracking. 'The Theatre was built for conjuring?'

'Conjuring and performing were closely linked, at least in some minds, in the Renaissance. You must know that.'

'Raising spirits in a circle,' I said. It was what conjurors did. It was also what companies of players did. Shakespeare said as much, near the end, in one of his finest speeches, given to his great magician, Prospero, after he literally conjures up a bit of theatre:

> *Our revels now are ended. These our actors,*
> *As I foretold you, were all spirits, and*
> *Are melted into air, into thin air:*
> *And, like the baseless fabric of this vision,*
> *The cloud-capped towers, the gorgeous palaces,*
> *The solemn temples, the great globe itself,*
> *Yea, all which it inherit, shall dissolve*
> *And, like this insubstantial pageant faded,*
> *Leave not a rack behind.*

Had Shakespeare meant the globe, as in the earth, or had he meant the Globe, the theatre in which the actor playing Prospero would have pronounced the words? Or both? And if he'd meant both: just how closely did he link theatre and magic, in his own mind?

I exhaled sharply. 'Of course he also made "raising spirits in a circle" refer to sex.'

Joanna rolled her eyes. 'He made *everything* refer to sex. The man had the libido of a lovesick seventeen-year-old boy crossed with a bull, permanently. That doesn't mean he couldn't be serious about a subject on occasion, as well.'

I dropped back onto the couch. 'What was the point of conjuring? What was Dee looking for, when he invoked his angels?'

Joanna stretched, crossing her hands behind her head. 'He spent decades at it, Kate. Not fair, really, to demand a single burning focus.' She leaned forward, her dark eyes gleaming, a thrill running through her voice. 'But ultimately, he was searching for the lost language of God. A tongue that carried such force that one could say *fiat lux* – let there be light – and light would appear. Dee and other Renaissance magi believed that the languages they knew and spoke and studied were descended from that divine original, but that they'd dwindled in power, though there were still flashes of it left in certain combinations of sounds. Especially in Latin, Greek, and Hebrew rites of magic, closely guarded as precious and dangerous secrets.'

Her reading glasses dangled like a pendulum from one hand. 'It's not entirely far-fetched, you know. There *are* certain phrases, in every language, that don't merely describe the world, but make things happen.'

I nodded. 'Speech-act theory. One of the few corners of literary theory I could make sense of, once upon a time.'

She leaned back. 'The doctorate that got away?'

'I like to think that I was the one doing the escaping.' I'd left the ivory tower for the theatre with all the eagerness of an eloping bride; the only regret I had about it was the lasting rift it had opened between me and Roz Howard, my academic mentor. Whom Joanna was reminding me of, more and more.

'Quite. Well, then you know that in what's called performative language, uttering phrases like *I do* at a wedding, or *I promise* and *I bet* bring certain states of affairs into being.'

I bit my lip. 'Words with the force to change the world.'

'In Shakespeare's England, the phrase *I conjure* was widely thought to have such force.'

If the point of conjuring was a search for the language of God, language that could create worlds with words, it was tied even more closely to theatre than I'd thought.

'I've always thought that's one reason the Puritan preachers hated theatre so,' said Joanna softly. 'They ranted on about loose morals and whore-mongering and people being lured away from church. But idol-worship was one of their most serious charges, and beneath that, I think, lurked a

371

recognition of theatre's power. They saw in it the same thing that Dee and Shakespeare saw: the shadow of the language of God.' Her voice gathered into dark intensity. 'And I think it scared the shit out of them.'

She leaned back over the book. 'And they weren't the only ones worried. In conjuring, circles of power are cast for one reason: protection. They keep the demons at bay. Often, there's a triangle off to the side: that's meant as a kind of unbreakable holding-cell for whatever spirits should arise.' She pointed at the diagrams, full of circles and triangles. 'Maybe the Theatre was designed to raise spirits in safety.'

Maybe. 'If so, it wouldn't have worked for *Macbeth*. Not for the premiere, anyway, which took place at Hampton Court, in the rectangle of the Great Hall.'

'Maybe that's why it was so dangerous,' said Joanna.

For a moment we stared at each other unspeaking, the only sound the drone of the plane.

Modern theatres, for the most part, were no longer built in the round, on Dee's plan. They hadn't been, since the Restoration. Could that be why the play had grown a reputation for being cursed?

Good grief, what line of thought was I allowing myself to be drawn down? I stood up quickly, as if I might shake off all this talk of magic like a dog shaking off water.

'It makes the play a catch-22,' said Joanna. 'Play it to the hilt, capture the essence of the conjuring, and even without the exact rite, you'll half-wake forces beyond most people's control, without any safe place to contain them. Fail, though, and you invoke Macbeth's curse.'

I frowned.

'End of the cauldron scene,' said Joanna. *I will be satisfied*, the king screams when the witches warn him off pursuing more knowledge. *Deny me this, and an eternal curse fall on you!* So you see, in the hands of the untrained, either the magic half-works, in a terribly dangerous way, or it doesn't, and the production pulls a curse down on its own head.'

'If you believe in magic,' I said.

'If it exists,' said Joanna, 'it doesn't matter a toss whether you believe it or not.'

Lady Nairn had said something very similar. 'No,' I said. 'What matters is what Carrie believes.'

'If she's Corra Ravensbrook, she believes in magic. Death magic.'

I pulled my knees up to my chest and buried my head in them. Dee had spent years and most of his treasure invoking angels, trying to rediscover the language that could bring force to a statement like 'let there be light': *fiat lux*.

Now, someone was out there grasping towards something much darker. '*Fiat mors*,' I whispered. 'Let there be death.'

Was that what she wanted? And meant to have, via some ancient rite of cauldron magic?

It was a power she'd already grasped. Images and sounds slipped through my head. Auld Callie in the tree, the rope creaking against the oak. The blue gown pattering down across Sybilla's body, tied and bloody. My own hands, smeared with her blood. Killer, or consecrated victim? For all I knew, she'd foisted some of the killing off on me.

And Eircheard. Rollicking, irreverent, kind Eircheard, his face twisted in agony, his heart, for Christ's sake, torn beating from his chest. *The bitch had torn out his heart.*

And now she was toying with Lily.

If she'd been present, I think I might have torn her limb from limb like a Maenad. If I'd been on the ground, I might have run screaming into the night sea, or crowds, or wide empty fields spreading under the moon. Somewhere large enough to hold the grief and anger pent-up within me. In the tin can of a plane, all that passion had nowhere to go but tears. I wrapped my arms tighter and tighter around my knees, trying to hold it in, but the sobs welled up and out all the same.

Beside me, Joanna gathered me in her arms and let me cry.

Somewhere over the Atlantic, I slept. I woke in darkness to Joanna's gentle shaking. We'd arrived at Teterboro Airport, on the New Jersey side of the Hudson. It was three in the morning, local time. The meeting wasn't till seven-thirty, but I saw no point in waiting: I had no hours to waste.

I glanced in a mirror. My eyes were bleary, still rimmed with red, but nothing that someone who didn't know me might not chalk up to being awake at a preposterous hour. I ran cold water over a couple of wash cloths and brought them with me, to cool down my face. It was the best I could do.

'You think he'll just invite us in at this hour?' asked Joanna.

'I don't intend to give him a choice.'

A limo was waiting at the foot of the stairs. We drove through suburban New Jersey, into the glazed glare of the Lincoln tunnel, and up into the cement canyons of midtown Manhattan. Past the Empire State Building, past the darkness of Union Square, down towards the Village and left into Astor Place, where the cab drew up to a graceful Romanesque building in terracotta brick, its windows soaring up six storeys to curve in semicircular arches. Up ahead, a few giggling tourists were spinning the famed Cube statue on its axis, but at half past three the open space – not quite a plaza, though it seemed to aim in that direction – was otherwise mostly quiet.

In the lobby, the doorman was hunched over a computer screen, watching a third-rate horror film, judging by the soundtrack. Hearing that we were old friends of Clifton's, he glanced up with heavy-lidded eyes. 'The professor's expectin' ya?'

I gave him a wide, giggly smile. 'With shots of tequila.'

He waved us on with a smirk.

I phoned Clifton from right outside his door. 'God, this better be good,' said a luxuriant voice into my ear.

'Come to your door and you tell me.' Reaching into my bag, I pulled the mirror I'd taken from Joanna from its black velvet wrapping and held it up before the peephole.

Behind me, Joanna stirred. 'Is that mine?' she whispered. I nodded.

'This will drain its power,' she hissed.

'I'm sorry,' I mouthed. 'I owe you.' If I had to lie naked in a field with the disc of cold black stone lying on my belly at every full moon for a year to recharge it, I would. Meanwhile, if it could help show the way to the manuscript and Lily, it would be magic mirror enough.

A few moments later, I heard an intake of breath over the phone. In the door, bolts turned in their locks.

39

The door opened on a willowy woman with short dark hair tousled with sleep. She wore a silk robe of multicoloured stripes that made me think of Joseph and his Technicolor dreamcoat. In one hand she held the phone on which she'd been talking to me. I stood in the hall, blinking in surprise. Jamie Clifton was a woman.

The promise, dangled before her, of learning more about the mirror whisked us inside, where we perched on an uncomfortably low but doubtless very cool leather sofa, while Jamie padded around the kitchen, making coffee. The condo was a model of sleek urban chic, a loft-like space with high ceilings, exposed brick walls, and a lot of gleaming steel and granite. Almost one entire wall was a window overlooking the plaza below. The glass coffee table before us, though, was piled with papers to grade, and the kitchen island was scattered with takeout cartons, which cluttered the image.

'How'd you know about the lettering around the rim?' asked Joanna, as Jamie set mugs of coffee down in front of us. 'There's nothing visible in the photo you sent Owen.'

'He showed you?' she shrilled in annoyance. 'Asshole.'
Sinking cross-legged into an armchair in a cloud of striped
silk, she breathed in the steam rising from her mug. 'Explain
to me again why I should help you?'

She could play coy all she wanted, but she'd let us in at a
ridiculous hour of the morning. She was interested. I leaned
back against the sofa. 'Because you'd like to know what it
spells.'

'You've seen it?' There was an eager catch in her voice.

I smiled. *Knowledge, the oldest temptation.*

She disappeared down a hall and came back with a hinged
frame, folded closed. 'The photo I sent . . . it was only half
the picture. Not quite above-board, maybe, but I wanted to
give the Brits a reason to take my inquiry seriously, without
giving the game away. The image you've seen – it's freakin'
gorgeous, of course, but it's the companion shot that's really
fabulous. Taken at the same sitting. They're both by
Matthew Brady, the civil war photographer. He had a studio
in New York before he went down to Washington. Did you
know that? He did society portraits. Very solemn, most of
them. But he convinced some of his clients who were actors
to experiment with emotion and action.'

She'd hardly taken a breath since she started, her words
tumbling out in a quick staccato patter. Opening the frame
with a flourish, she set it down on the table before us. On
the left was the photo she'd sent Owen. On the right was
another, again showing Forrest in the same kilt and plumed

bonnet. But this pose was more akin to a still from a silent film than to the Victorian solemnity of the other portrait. A woman, turned away from the camera, faced him, holding the mirror as he leaned back in exaggerated horror. What he saw in the mirror remained unseen. But in the woman's hand, a few letters were visible around the rim of the disc: NGISBU.

They were the letters from the middle of Arthur Dee's identifying phrase, NOTHING IS BUT WHAT IS NOT, minus the first five letters of 'nothing' and everything after the 'u' in 'but'. I glanced up at Joanna.

'It's Dee's,' she confirmed.

Jamie looked from me to Joanna and back. 'No shit? You can tell? Just like that?'

My voice raspy in my throat, I quoted Arthur Dee: '*You will know the mirror by its black surface, and by a posie around its edge: Nothing is but what is . . . not,*' I added. 'It's the mirror that originally played *Macbeth.*'

'The mirror that originated the curse,' said Joanna.

'Well then it came into play on the tenth of May, 1849.' Jamie shook her head. 'He had it the day of the riot. Did you know that? *Forrest carried it the day of the riot.*'

'But it was Macready who was acting at the Opera House, wasn't it? Forrest's fans were on the outside, throwing stones.'

Jamie shrugged. 'Some say he *was* there.' She walked to the window. '*There,*' she snorted. '*Here.* It was here. This

379

building rose from the ashes of the Astor Place Opera House . . . Imagine twenty thousand people down there, throwing paving stones and oil-soaked torches. And then cavalry and infantry marching in behind, squeezing them ever closer in to the building, filled with a standing room only crowd.'

Her voice seemed to people the night with the cries of men and the screams of horses, the roaring of flame and echoing volleys of gunfire. 'Who knows where Forrest was? He might have been in the crowd, or even in the building. Probably idle speculation. But the suspicion was there.'

I tried to keep my mind on the photos. 'Who's the woman?' I asked.

'I don't know,' said Jamie. 'At first I thought she might be his wife, Catherine. She was an actress herself, you know. But this can't have been her. They'd already parted, by the riot. Sad story, that. Forrest could be a real bastard. With regard to his wife, he became a character out of one of his plays. Henry VIII, maybe. Or even worse, Othello.'

The person Ellen Terry had her story from had been a woman, *a fellow denizen of the drama*, she'd written, *whose personal tale is as tragic as any role she might encharacter on the stage.*

'What happened?' asked Joanna.

'Catherine Sinclair was beautiful and vivacious, the daughter of actors, and Edwin swept her off her feet when she was very young and he was already an international star.

380

For twelve years, they had a blissfully happy marriage – as happy as one can be, at any rate, that endures the death of every child born into it. She bore four children to full term, but none of them lived more than a week.'

'Jesus,' said Joanna.

'In the spring of 1848, he took Catherine on tour with him. One afternoon he returned unexpectedly to their hotel room and found her in what he regarded as a compromising attitude with another actor, a known ladies' man. Then, in the early months of 1849, he went snooping among Catherine's things and found a letter from the same man. A ridiculous letter, really. Completely over the top in declaring its passion for her – and no proof that she returned it. But that was it for Forrest. He decided his wife was a fallen woman, and he was a wronged man. There was one bitter fight that went on all night, apparently, and then six icy weeks of silence. And then he threw her out.

'Beyond all understanding, she seems to have still loved him. She jumped through all kinds of hoops for him, and signed some really humiliating letters that he dictated. It wasn't until he tried to cut her off without enough money to live a respectable life that she began to fight back. In an era both phobic of publicity and fascinated by it, any sensible person would have settled matters out of court, for his own pride, even if he couldn't muster the tiniest crumb of sympathy for a woman he'd adored for twelve years. But Edwin had become a vengeful god. He forced Catherine into court for a divorce trial and accused her, in open court, of adultery with numerous men. It became one of the sensations of nineteenth-century America.'

Had Ellen Terry's 'poor soul' who regarded herself as the guardian of a *Macbeth* manuscript been Catherine Forrest? *I am hoping that you can glimpse the Forest through the Trees,* she'd written to Herbert Beerbohm Tree.

'What happened to her?' I asked, gripping the edge of the sofa.

'Remarkable woman, actually,' said Jamie. 'After the divorce, she went west to run theatres in gold-rush California: San Francisco, Sacramento, the gold camps. Toured Australia, then London, and then travelled through Scotland on her own. Her parents were Scottish by birth. Same as Forrest's.'

'She went to Scotland?' I asked. 'You're sure?' *Sir Angus had believed that Terry's informant was the dark fairy of Dunsinnan legend.*

'Twice, that I know of,' said Jamie. 'Can't pinpoint the date of the first trip, but the second was 1889. She saw Ellen Terry's *Macbeth.*'

Plucking the frame from the table, I examined it, but there was nothing to be seen that we hadn't seen already. At the back, both sides were sealed with brown paper. Picking it up, I walked into the kitchen, found a knife, and slit one side open.

'What are you doing?' cried Jamie. 'They're in the original frame. It's half of what makes it valuable.'

'Not so valuable as a life,' I said, lifting the photo out. It was the photo with the date. There was no other inscription. No mark of any kind. I slit open the other side of the frame.

The back of this photo, by contrast, had more than a few markings. It had been used as letter paper for a note written from Hell's Delight, California, in 1855:

Mr Forrest,

Not for your sake, but for posterity's, I must beg you to read one further missive from me.

When you were in Edinburgh last, a curious opportunity came my way regarding Macbeth, the very play that you and Mr Macready had chosen to make your battleground. I acquired a curiosity I intended as a surprise for you, but never delivered.

Tho' wonderful, it was a dark gift that I trembled to look on. More than once, I have wondered whether its presence, even in secret, may have poisoned our love, as I believe the mirror did.

You will find it beneath our sweet fountain on the hill. Or, if you do not, it is at least safe, under the watchful eye of heaven.

Farewell,

Mrs Edwin Forrest

At the last sentence, Jamie rose in excitement. 'The Fountain-hill. Fonthill. The castle on the Hudson that Edwin built for Catherine.'

'Does it still exist?' I asked.

Jamie laughed. 'It does. He sold it, in 1855, to some nuns.'

'Under the watchful eye of heaven,' said Joanna.

'They ran a school in what's now Central Park. After they moved north, it became the College of Mount Saint Vincent . . . where I'm on the faculty. The building's just called the Castle now. It's where I teach.'

'I have no time to wait for bells to ring. We have to go now!' I fairly shouted at her.

I could see, though, that there would be no hesitation. It took Jamie no more than five minutes to throw on jeans, a sweater, and a jacket. Downstairs, we stepped out into the cold darkness of early morning. I looked at my watch as we slid into the car. It was a quarter past four.

40

We headed west through Greenwich Village, winding through tree-lined streets that sprouted at odd angles. At the tail end of a cold night at the edge of winter, the streets that refused to sleep looked either sad or seedy, even in Manhattan: the haunt of garbage trucks and revels gone on too long. At the drive lining the island's west side, we turned north.

Fonthill, Jamie told us as we drove, had been named in homage to Fonthill Abbey, in England.

'A church?' asked Joanna.

Jamie laughed. 'Sounds like it, but no. It was a preposterously grand home erected by one of the wealthiest Brits of the eighteenth century. Inherited money from Jamaican sugar – slavery, in other words. Damn near bankrupted himself, though, building Fonthill.' She shook her head. 'He was one strange dude, was William Beckford. Wrote a weird gothic novel called *Vathek*, about demons and human sacrifice and the unbridled need to know everything. He said it was a response to some things that happened to him at Fonthill one Christmas. So maybe it shouldn't be too surprising that the

Forrest's little Fonthill is at least as much in line with the occult as with the church.'

'Do you think the Forrests knew that?' I asked.

'Don't know if Edwin did. But Catherine almost certainly knew. Ran with a Bohemian crowd, when occult investigations were all the rage. She was into Spiritualism later. Trying to contact her dead babies. And she seems to have forged a psychological link with Lady Macbeth. Did a lot of research on Elizabeth Stewart, at any rate.'

Elizabeth Stewart, the original Lady Macbeth.

I pulled my jacket tighter around me. Off to the right, the city's skyscrapers clawed upwards into the sky and then subsided again. The George Washington bridge swooped off left to New Jersey. Trees lurched up and swallowed the road. In the darkness it seemed as if we were gliding through some primordial forest, in a world made only of road, trees, and the shimmering waters of the Hudson.

The parkway crossed a small, ordinary bridge as it emptied into the Bronx, and the city slipped into view, battling back the trees. After a while, we shot past a long low stone wall edging tall trees to a traffic light, where we turned in. 'Welcome to the College of Mount Saint Vincent,' said Jamie. We wound back to a gatehouse, where a guard looked up sleepily from his book, saw Jamie, and waved us on.

The road carved through trees, between brick buildings, mostly dark, and back to a wide expanse of lawn out of which rose a small knoll topped by a castle. A toy castle, next to Windsor or Caernarvon or Edinburgh. But for all that, a castle: octagonal towers of rough-hewn grey stone huddling together, raising battlements like fists into the night.

'*Our sweet fountain on its hill*,' said Jamie. 'Fonthill.'

The driver stopped the car at a tall pointed archway filled with double doors, and we got out. Wind whistled around the building. Jamie avoided the steps up to the great door, darting off into the darkness to the right. Skirting some rhododendrons, we came to a steep stairway leading down. In the wall, half above ground, was a door. Unlocking it, Jamie beckoned us inside.

I found myself in a bare hallway smelling of earth and damp, though the walls were a utilitarian white. We went up some stairs and down a hall to find ourselves in a domed octagonal room on the ground floor, lit only by the moonlight drifting down through a skylight far overhead at the dome's apex. A dark wooden balcony ringed the room at the level of the second storey. At ground level, dark rounded archways led into other rooms. This central room, though, was bare of furniture save for a few stiff armchairs against the wall. At our feet, a cross was inlaid in green and burgundy tile on the floor.

'When he first saw the cross,' Jamie said, 'Forrest said he thought it looked like he'd built the place for the Roman Catholics. And then he sold it to the nuns before he could ever live here. A little ironic. Especially since the cross with equal arms is Greek, not Roman.'

'Not just Greek,' Joanna said softly. 'Celtic. Babylonian. Pre-Columbian American. Inside a circle, it's one of the oldest symbols of all.'

'The oculus,' said Jamie. She was staring down at a thick quartz-like slab of translucent glass set into the middle of the cross, where the arms intersected. 'Early renewable energy: it's supposed to light the basement with the sunlight from the skylight overhead.'

'*Oculus* is Latin for "eye",' said Joanna with a sharp glance at me.

'*Under the watchful eye of heaven*,' I murmured, glancing from the skylight to the floor. I knelt down. It fitted tightly into the floor. There seemed no way of prising it loose. I sat back on my heels, thinking. And then I rose and hurried back downstairs. The others followed.

At the end of the dank white basement hall was a thick metal door. On the other side, the building morphed into a cave. It was lined with furnaces that probably hummed all day, but at night the room was silent and cold, colder than the night outside.

'Carved right into bedrock,' said Jamie.

The eye in the ceiling lit the room with a faint greenish glow. A little off to the side, what I'd taken at first for a table wasn't: it was an immense slab of bedrock like a bier. The entire room seemed to have been chipped out of rock. If

Catherine Forrest had hidden something at Fonthill, *under the watchful eye of heaven* . . . you'd think it would be here. But where? There seemed no way of hiding anything underneath the eye.

I trotted back up the stairs, glancing morosely at the eye, and then turning to take in the whole of the room. On the walls were four carvings in shallow bas relief. Joanna was standing before one of them. 'Strange art,' she murmured. It showed Macbeth staring horrified at hands curled like claws, dripping with gore. In the background, Lady Macbeth disappeared through a doorway, a dagger in each hand. In gilt letters beneath was picked out a quotation from Shakespeare:

What hands are here? Ha! They pluck out mine eyes.
Will all great Neptune's ocean wash this blood
Clean from my hand?

I moved to the next scene. It was Othello the Moor, eyes starting from his head, his hands around Iago's neck; Iago's face, twisted away, wore a cruel smile. In the background, a young woman walked alone in a walled garden, a handkerchief on the ground, her maid bending to pick it up.

O, beware, my lord, of jealousy;
It is the green-eyed monster which doth mock
The meat it feeds on.

I looked back at Macbeth. His face had the same features as Othello, though not the same expression.

'It's Forrest,' said Jamie. 'They're all portraits. His favourite roles,' she added.

'They're all eyes,' said Joanna. 'Hamlet's across the way, attacking his mother in her bedroom, turning her eyes into her black and spotted soul.'

The fourth scene wasn't a tragedy. It was from *Twelfth Night* – one of the great comedies. Dressed as a boy, the young heroine Viola faced the gaunt and priggish hauteur of the steward Malvolio, pointing at a ring lying on the ground between them. Malvolio's whole body seemed to be pointing – long finger, long nose . . . he had even extended a leg with pointed toe at the offending ring. But what seemed suddenly strangest was that he wasn't a portrait of Forrest – neither in body type nor in facial features.

'Three for Forrest,' said Jamie. 'One for Catherine. That's pretty much how their marriage seemed to work, even when it *did* work.'

'So it isn't him?'

'Not Forrest, no. At least, not *Edwin* Forrest.' She pointed at Viola. 'But that's Catherine as Viola. A role she never played on stage, though she maintained it was her favourite.'

It was everybody's favourite. Viola was one of the greatest roles ever written for a woman, full of sexual passion for both a man and a woman, romance, hilarity, and music. Longing and fear, too. I looked at Mrs Forrest's face. She was beautiful. Fragile somehow, with high cheekbones and small pursed lips.

But it was the gilt inscription beneath the scene that caught me. Not poetry, as the others were, but prose, all run together on one line:

If it be worth stooping for, there it lies, in your eye; if not, be it his that finds it.

Malvolio's words to Viola, or Catherine's to her husband?

I looked down at the oculus, the eye in the floor. *If it be worth stooping for, there it lies, in your eye.* I turned back. The ring was very nearly life-sized, in deeper relief than the rest of the carving.

I put a finger into the ring. Nothing happened. I pushed, and faintly, I heard a grinding noise and an exhalation of breath long held. I turned to see the oculus lowering and sliding under the floor.

Would it still be there – whatever Catherine had found? Was she right? Was it – could it be – a version of Macbeth? Whatever she'd found, she'd thought it evil.

Crossing to the hole in the floor, I dropped to my knees. The green stone had moved down, leaving an open space between the floor and the ceiling of the basement below. Sitting on the ledge in a coat of dust a century and a half thick lay a small packet tied in faded ribbon, addressed with two words in a woman's hand:

To Edwin.

With shaking fingers, I pulled it out, dust cascading down through the open hole onto the stone and into the basement below. The ribbon crumbled as I touched it, but the wax seal was intact, pressed with what might have been a signet ring. Two trees. One for Catherine, and one for Edwin. A fine and private forest.

I broke it open. Scrawled on the inside of the cover sheet was a letter in handwriting I'd seen before. I glanced at the signature to be sure. *Catherine.* I handed it to Jamie.

Inside was another sealed packet, the paper darker and finer, its seal already broken. It had no address.

I heard a small squeak behind me. '*Be it his who finds it,*' said a deep voice.

I turned to look. A man was standing just inside the room with one arm around Joanna's neck, clamped over her mouth. With his other hand, he had a gun to her head. He was gaunt, his hair white and close shaven.

Lucas Porter.

41

'Hold it up,' he demanded. 'Where I can see it.'

I did as he asked, my eye on the cold hard lines of the gun.

He skimmed the page, his lips moving as he read. Caught in the crook of his arm, her face wide with fear and fury beside him, Joanna's eyes flickered. She was reading along.

Reading what?

'Next,' snapped Lucas, and I shifted the pages.

'*Ha!*' he burst out, and then his voice fell to rhythmic chanting echoing around the room.

Double, double toil and trouble,
Fire burn and cauldron bubble.

'Then it's the *Macbeth* manuscript?' Without realising what I was doing, I stepped forward.

His grip on Joanna tightened. 'Get back,' he growled.

Joanna's brow pinched, and ever so slightly she shook her head. I stepped back.

'Stay there,' he ordered, and went back to reading. 'The

393

key lines are there,' he crowed after a few seconds. 'The heart of the witches' ceremony.' His voice cracked in exultation. 'The collection of parts, around it in the First Folio, that's rubbish. Ghoulish nursery rhymes, not to mention cliché. But *double, double* . . . that's different. What, for instance, do you suppose that it means? What's the double toil?'

'Can't you just let me see it?' I pleaded.

'Maybe in another life. *What's the double toil?*'

'Nobody knows,' I said shortly. It was the truth, but it was also the answer he was looking for, I surmised. He wanted to talk, it seemed. I wanted him gone, and the rest of us safe. Mostly, I wanted the damned manuscript I held in my hands. A *Macbeth* manuscript, for Christ's sake.

Tightening his grip on Joanna, he laughed drily. 'Sex and death, Kate. The two great rites of passage. Death and birth. Or at least conception. They're very powerful moments. Make them simultaneous, for one man, and you create a whirlwind of energy, a dark vortex, allowing a spirit to drain like Odin, into the underworld, while making a channel through which it can veer back directly.'

'What are you talking about?' I was watching him for an opening, the least moment of dropping his guard.

'The deed without a name, Kate. Putting a man back into the womb.'

'*What?* How?'

'That's the great mystery, isn't it?' he chortled. He was *enjoying* this, the sick bastard. 'But I've worked it out, with a little help from Shakespeare and Ovid. Did Janet tell you that I used to beat her and her bearded fool of a husband at auction from time to time? Once, I scooped a copy of Arthur Golding's translation of Ovid out from under them. *The Metamorphoses.*'

Possibly Shakespeare's favourite book. He'd mined it for plots and subplots, for themes and vocabulary and phrasing. Golding's Ovid was laced through Shakespeare.

'It wasn't the Ovid I cared about,' said Lucas, 'so much as a single note in the margin next to the story of Medea. *A deede without a name.* In a hand that looks like Shakespeare's.'

'How do you know what that looks like? All we have is six signatures, for Christ's sake. And those are all different.'

'It's his phrase, and his hand. I had it confirmed. Which suggests that the missing and unnamed deed, you see, was based on the rite next to that notation. The witch Medea slitting an old man's throat to pour his blood into a cauldron, from which he springs forth young again.'

'That's not what happens,' I said. 'She puts in an old ram and pulls out a lamb: but it's pretty clear she's pulled a bait and switch. What makes the old man young again is the liquor she brews up, poured back into his empty veins.'

'It's a mythic substitution, and a sexual myth at that: an old man's life poured into a cauldron, from which he comes out young again. The old man dies, to be born again.' His eyes glittered, his voice dropping to a half chant. 'The blade for the death, the cauldron for the birth.'

395

'And the mirror?'

He shrugged. 'So much crossing rips a wide passage between the living and the dead, and those with the gift of sight, or the power of calling, can summon other spirits through the void. Especially at Samhuinn, when the veil between life and death is thin to begin with.'

His voice was eerily calm. Coupled with images of Sybilla and Eircheard dead, his serenity suddenly seemed obscene. 'You don't have the cauldron,' I said hotly.

'Too literal, Kate,' he sniggered. 'A quirk that got Macbeth into trouble. The cauldron is a vessel, but not one of silver or bronze. A woman. And we've had her all along.'

Lily? 'Where?' I cried hoarsely. 'Where is she?'

'Back where it all began.' He smiled at my confusion. 'Fifty years ago, Janet Douglas walked out on me. Destroyed the film that was to be my magnum opus. *Macbeth*.'

'There were other actresses.'

'Not like her. She denied me her body, and my children her bloodline.' His mouth twisted. 'Did she tell you? She's a direct scion, mother to daughter, of Elizabeth Stewart, the countess of Arran. And of John Dee, as well. I dreamed of her. Of my seed mingled with a bloodline of great power. I plucked her from nothing, when I discovered that. Catherine Sinclair was another of Stewart's offspring, did you know that? No doubt why Forrest wanted her.'

Beside me, Jamie stirred.

'Everything else I did with Janet was dry rehearsal for *Macbeth*. And then she left, on the eve of filming. I swore then that one day I'd take what she'd denied me, and now I am . . . Taking Lily is a grand revenge, you have to admit. Worthy of Dante or Dumas.'

'It's insane,' I whispered.

'Cold, logical, perfectly rational, I assure you. If the magic works, I die and return, my blood mingled with hers. If not, then I take my revenge and go out with a marvellous bang.' His laughter sputtered around the room.

I'd been so focused on Lily, I'd ignored the other half of his rite. 'It requires a death,' I said.

'We all owe one. In my case, quite soon. I am dying of pancreatic cancer. So I have nothing to lose. And everything to die for.'

I stared at him in disbelief. 'You mean to die—'

'Just as I come. The great death and the little death converging.' He was leaning into Joanna, as if he were imagining it already. Joanna closed her eyes.

'And how will you do that? Will your heart to stop?'

'That wouldn't contribute much to my grand revenge, would it?' he said softly. 'No: I'll get Lily to kill me. And I'll get the whole thing on film. Do you see the beauty of it? Lady Nairn will find losing Lily to prison in some ways worse than losing her to death . . . Now fold up those papers and set them on the floor.'

I did as he asked, as slowly as I could. Somehow, I had to

keep him talking. 'I was bringing the manuscript to you. Why go to the bother of stealing it?'

'I didn't want you to succeed.' He laughed at my surprise. 'Carrie Douglas is almost as single-minded as I am. Not quite, or she'd be standing here in my place. But if she gets hold of that, she'll use it. And I have no intention of scrapping my script for anyone else's, not even Shakespeare's. Now turn and walk to the wall, please.' He nodded at Jamie, too. 'Both of you.'

I had to pull her along with me. Knowing we were fast running out of time.

'On the other hand,' he went on, 'if I have the manuscript, Carrie will do exactly as I please, in order to get it. For the length of one ceremony, at any rate. But that's all that matters. They'll have other chances. I won't.'

He sighed. 'She's made things difficult. You, now, you'd be easy to control. With Lily, for starters. But I can also tell you what you want to know . . . *Guilty or Not Guilty?*'

Of course. He'd been there. 'Anybody can tell me,' I said bitterly. 'Can you make me believe it?'

He eyes were wide in the darkness. 'I filmed Sybilla's death.'

I started and stilled. *He'd made snuff films before. He was planning to direct his own death, for God's sake. Why shouldn't he have filmed Sybilla's?*

'I don't want you to think me ungenerous,' he said. 'Ask me one question.'

Guilty or Not Guilty? I thought of my hands on the hill, smeared with dark blood, and the revulsion on Ben's face, as he looked up at me from Sybilla's body. I thought of Lily.

'Where is she?' I asked quickly. 'Where's Lily?'

He laughed aloud. 'Altruistic to the last. Optimistic, too. Admirable, but also delusional, in this case . . . Like I said, she's where it began. On an island in a boiling lake. Now, say goodnight to the light, Kate.'

Next to me, Jamie let out a sob.

I'd turned my head slightly, so I could just see him. The instant he pulled the gun from Joanna's head, I dove, pulling Jamie with me, hurtling as hard as I could into Lucas. A shot boomed through the space, and all four of us crashed to the floor.

Interlude

October, 1606
Mortlake, west of London

Dr Dee lowered himself carefully into the high-backed green brocade chair at his writing table in his inner sanctum. Just shy of eighty and twisted with rheumatism, it was no longer such an easy thing merely to sit down. He massaged his fingers, kneading enough looseness into them to hold a quill, at least for a while.

Though the afternoon was chill, he had the window open to the garden. He could no longer hear the songbirds well, but he liked watching them among the autumn leaves blushing red as the robin's breast. His eyes, at least, weren't failing. Not yet. For a man of his scholarly bent, that was a great comfort; at times, it even had the lift of joy.

Not at all times, however. His reading, yesterday, of Master Shakespeare's new play had seemed to dim, for a moment, all the brightness and colour of the world. He dipped his quill in ink and set it to the page. And then he pulled it off again, tickling his nose with the bit of feather he'd left at the end. What to say to the impudent poet, and how best to say it?

Somehow, he had to make him see reason. Because this time, it wasn't books or sums or even reputations at risk. This time, lives hung in the balance.

What Robert Cecil, Lord Salisbury's hold over Shakespeare was he did not know, though he knew it extended deep into his past, to his boyhood in Warwickshire. In all likelihood, that meant Catholic plotting against the old queen: that part of the country clung stubbornly, obdurately and most imprudently to the old religion. Dr Dee sighed and shook his head. Poor man. He'd probably breathed easier since the queen's death three years earlier. The new king, just down from Scotland, could have no grudge against a player from the provinces. Far from it, His Majesty adored players and playing, and in short order had adopted Shakespeare's company as his own: the King's Men.

And then had come the Powder Plot, almost a year ago now, hatched among men Shakespeare had surely known, or at least known of, in his youth. Salisbury's old leash, whatever it was, had probably tightened to a stranglehold.

It was Salisbury, Dee knew, who had demanded this infernal play from Shakespeare's pen. Not just a play about king-killing, nor even 'just' a play about witches: but a play that would shadow Elizabeth Stewart and her husband, the quondam Earl of Arran, on the stage. Favourites of the king in his youth. They had fallen from grace twenty years ago now, however, fleeing into exile in the remote mountain fastnesses of Scotland, no doubt hunching over peat fires among the wild clansmen of the north, conspiring their return to the glittering courts of the south.

So why this story, why now? Especially since their plotted return had not come to pass. A decade earlier, the earl, stripped of his title, returned to the status merely of 'Captain', had been ambushed by his enemies as he rode through some hills, his head raised high on a pole and carried off in triumph, thus fulfilling a prophecy that his head should be higher than any of those around him. The lady had died the year before that, swollen mightily and thus fulfilling a prophecy of her own: that she might be the greatest woman in Scotland. Some said she had died in child-bed, others said of the dropsy. Neither story was true, if Dee's source was to be believed: she'd been caught by a witch-hunting mob and torn to pieces.

He'd kept tabs on her from afar since the day she had arrived at his doorstep in Antwerp, her hair bright as flame, her eyes dark and sly. She was a mink, he thought: a strange slippery cross between serpent and cat, with tiny, sharp teeth and a streak of cruelty beneath her red beauty. And she had the sight that had eluded him all his days.

It was why, in the end, he had refused to teach her. He'd dreamed of Viviane or Nimue as some of the old manuscripts called her: Merlin's Lady of the Lake, who'd sat as demurely at her master's feet as Elizabeth was then sitting at his – until she'd learned all that Merlin could teach. At that moment, she'd raised herself up like a hooded snake and struck the hand that fed her, locking Merlin away in an enchanted palace of dreams, asleep in some still-hidden hollow in the Welsh hills. Dee had wakened in a cold sweat that night, unable to return to sleep until he could dismiss her.

Lady Elizabeth's response to his refusal – the theft of his mirror, the burning of a manuscript – only confirmed to him that his choice had been wise, and that he had, indeed, made a narrow escape. He had kept a watch on her from afar ever since, aware of her growing power. Regretting only that in the wake of his refusal, she had gone back to the Highlands and found other masters. Or mistresses, to be more accurate.

That Salisbury – and his father – would have set their own watch on her made sense, after she'd made herself and her third husband powers to be reckoned with behind a king whom they'd rightly predicted might one day rule England as well as Scotland. But still, Dee could not fathom why it should matter now, with both of them long dead.

Still less could he fathom why the Howards should care, particularly Henry Howard, the king's dark spirit. His evil genius, whom the king had elevated from Lord Henry to the Earl of Northampton.

It all seemed to revolve around the face that his scryer,

Hal Berridge, had seen in the mirror. Who was she? Salisbury thought her a woman at court, and set the boy to look for her. Northampton appeared to fear that she was someone whose identity might come home to roost, unpleasantly, in a Howard nest.

The upshot was that the boy's life was in danger, and Mr Shakespeare's play was making things worse. Dr Dee dipped his quill in ink once more.

Salisbury has commanded, and you have obeyed. Northampton will not command, he will kill. If you choose to put yourself in the Howards' way, so be it, but I beg you: find some way to leave the boy out of it. He is a talented child, almost as talented, in his way, as you once were. If he should die in other men's quarrels, merely because he once looked into a mirror for me, I will bear the burden of his death on my soul: but I will not bear it alone.

He again lifted the quill, absentmindedly drawing marks on the tip of his nose. He had set down part of his worries, but only a part. The others were somehow more formless and shifting. Truth be told, Dr Dee suspected that the boy had seen the red-headed witch. The Lady Elizabeth Stewart. If that was the case, one must then ask *when?* Had he looked into the past, the present, or the future? Surely the past: she had been dead eleven years.

But it was the present that worried him. Or perhaps *presence* was a better word. For if Dr Dee were honest with himself, he would have to admit that he sensed her presence. A peculiar malevolence that had its own spiky, sweet scent.

And that he thought he understood. For in his new play of *Macbeth,* Mr Shakespeare had done it again: had lifted a magical rite onto the stage. *Her* magical rite, drawn from her manuscript. But not entirely. Not only had Mr Shakespeare filled in a certain detail that Dr Dee had left out of the translation, but the playwright had filled in details that were not in the *original* manuscript. Perhaps they sprang from his imagination. But Dr Dee worried that they sprang from memory.

What had he seen, in his long-ago travels in Scotland? Dee had done some digging. He'd discovered another player who could remember a journey north out of Edinburgh, to Perth and beyond, in the company of Mr Shakespeare. The fellow had remembered, too, playing at a castle called Dunsinnan which figured in the new play. They had been there, he said, at All Hallow's Eve, and seen the heathen fires burning on the hills. Gave him quite a turn, it did, just thinking of it now, the old actor had said.

What sort of a turn had it given his companion?

If anything would call the witch back, even from the dead, it was the blasphemy of parading both her magic and her person on the public stage. If she were dead: for he would swear he could feel her. Once more, Dr Dee set his pen to the page, scratching his final warning with a flourish: 'Beware lest, like the Hydra hidden in the Lernaean spring, this serpent is scorch't, and not dead.'

A DEED WITHOUT A NAME

How now, you secret, black and midnight hags!
What is it you do?

42

The gun clattered across the tile; I went scrambling after it. Behind me, I heard Joanna cry out and a confused welter of footsteps. I reached the gun and swept it back up, looking for Lucas. He was gone and so was Joanna. From the corridor, I heard footsteps pattering up the stairs.

Jamie was crouched by the wall, trembling. 'Hide,' I said, and left her there. In the corridor, an arched doorway opened on to a turret tower occupied entirely by a spiral staircase. At the bottom, I stood listening. The footsteps had stopped. I crept upward. Joanna stood on the first landing.

'Did he have it?' I asked quietly.

Seeing me, she put one finger to her lips.

'*Did he have the goddamned manuscript?*'

She nodded impatiently, again motioning me to silence. Around us, the building was silent.

We were stepping into the second floor corridor when we both heard the scrape of a door directly overhead. Two more flights up, near the top, a shutter banged loose in the wind. Running up, I found that it was more like a small door, leading onto the roof of the adjoining tower. The roof was empty. I stole to the edge, peering over. An easy drop of one storey below was the roof of yet another tower, also empty.

From far below, another shot exploded through the night, the sound ricocheting around the building. *Jamie.* I'd left her alone and terrified. We pounded back downstairs.

In the octagonal hall, the arched double doors leading outside gaped open, bathing the room in moonlight. Jamie was nowhere to be seen. On the floor by the open oculus lay a single sheet of paper, pale in the silvery light. *Dearest*, it began. It was the cover page I'd handed Jamie.

I picked it up and strode across the hall to glance in each of the adjoining rooms. They, too, were empty.

'*Kate*,' cried Joanna from just outside the arched doors, in a tone of urgency that made me run across the room to her side. 'He's leaving,' she said, pulling me down the stairs at a trot. 'The bastard's leaving.'

She pointed off to the right. The castle sat alone on a hill overlooking the Hudson. The closest buildings were several hundred yards off; even so, lights were winking on around us. In the distance, a siren rose into a wail. In the moving shadows under the trees, it was impossible to see clearly, but I thought I saw a man hurrying down the slope towards the river. 'Two of them,' said Joanna.

We ran down the hill in their wake, in and out of the shadows. At the bottom was a narrow private lane. On the other side, a fence overgrown with a thicket of brambles and spindly trees bordered a deep railway cutting. I glanced up and down the fence. Nothing.

'Two?' I whispered. 'He's got Jamie hostage?'

She shook her head, her eyes gleaming wide in the moonlight. 'Didn't look like it.' She pointed. Off to the left the gate to an old wooden bridge hung open. It led across the tracks to a small spit of land ending in a narrow rocky beach. Beyond, three-quarters of a mile wide, spread the dark murmuring waters of the river. A private dock jutted into water. Around it, a number of small boats bobbed up and down.

No – one of them was moving more purposefully than the others, in a steady line away from the dock. The wind veered around, and I heard the whine of an outboard motor. I could just see the hunched shape of someone at the tiller. Around the dock, the other boats began to bunch up and drift away from the dock, slipping into the river's current.

Lucas had cut them all loose.

Behind us, sirens spiralled towards the castle. We broke into a run.

The last of the remaining boats bumped around the dock's upriver corner just as we clattered out to the edge. I caught its line just as the river spun it clear, plucking at it, pulling it out towards deep currents. It took both of us to haul it back.

'How much do you know about Jamie?' Joanna asked as she stepped in the boat.

413

'Just what Lady Nairn told us: professor of theatre, obsessed with *Macbeth*—'

'Are you sure that's her name?'

I looked back, my eyes meeting Joanna's. 'Who else . . . you think she might be *Carrie*?'

'I think we have to consider it.'

The motor sputtered and caught, and we headed out into the open water. Low in the west, the nearly full moon laid a rippling path of gold on the water. Well north of it, the other boat was a small moving speck of darkness on the face of the river. Their boat was more powerful than ours. As ours bucked and strained against the current, theirs pulled steadily ahead, making for the opposite shore.

'How much did you see, back there? Of the manuscript?'

Joanna shook her head. 'Not a lot. His arm kept getting in the way. The first page – that was in John Dee's hand. A letter, I think. After that came the play. There's a death, Kate. The witches brew isn't about body parts. It's about a body.'

Staring balefully at high line of cliffs, I leaned forward over the gunwale as if I might move the boat faster by sheer force of will. We were still little more than halfway across, though, when the other boat beached among some boulders and headlights flashed once in the trees along the shore. The boat, now empty, bobbed back out into the current.

The cliffs loomed tall and threatening as we neared. By the time we reached the shore, though, both boat and car were gone. In my pocket, my phone began to drum. I knew what it would be before I answered. Another photo of Lily, this time with a different message: *12 hours.*

This time, it seemed a cry of triumph.

Back where it all began, Lucas had said, when I'd asked where he'd taken her. What would that mean, for him? The only person who might know was Lady Nairn.

On the phone, her voice sounded as if it were drifting in from the stars. 'An island on a remote loch. Taken up mostly by a ruined castle. It was the first place he took me alone. I danced for him, under the moon.'

I thought of Lily spinning under the moon, on the lawn of Dunsinnan House. 'What loch, Lady Nairn. *Where?*'

'I never knew its name. Up in the Highlands, somewhere. It was a long time ago, and I wasn't driving. I was staring at a man I thought was a great artist, giddy with love, or what I thought was love—'

'*He's got Lily, Lady Nairn. He's got the manuscript.*'

She stopped short. 'We drove out of Inverness . . . What does he want?'

'To take from her what he couldn't have from you.'

'I'll meet you in Inverness,' said Lady Nairn.

Joanna had arranged for a driver while we were still on the river. All the same, it took him half an hour to reach us; by the time we clambered in the back seat, dawn was silvering the eastern shore. 'Where to?' he asked.

415

Back where it all began. The Boiling Lake.

'Teterboro,' I said. Teterboro and then Inverness. And from there, apparently, into the realm of fairy tales. In Scotland, that was not a comforting notion.

A little while later, the plane Lady Nairn had hired for us took off as an orange sun rose over the towers of Manhattan, glowering with the fires of Apocalypse.

43

On the plane, I switched on the computer and pulled a map of the Highlands off the net. The white land mass was thickly speckled with blue water like some mad marbled egg.

'It'll have to be close to Inverness,' said Joanna. 'That'll cut it down some.'

'Not enough,' I said bleakly. By the time we land we'd have no more than a few hours before the beginning of the eclipse.

'What about your other evidence?' asked Joanna. 'Does anybody else mention a lake?'

I shook my head. Only the Nairn's dark fairy. And then I remembered the page I'd skimmed up off the floor at Fonthill. I pulled it, partly crumpled, from my pocket.

It was the letter from Catherine Forrest to Edwin that I'd handed to Jamie.

Dearest, it began:

While you have been gone these long weary weeks, I have had an adventure of my own – and what an adventure!

417

And the best part is, there is a surprise for you at the end of it!!

A distant cousin had contacted her father, it seemed, requesting a visit from Catherine, whom she was close to settling on as her heir, and specifying that she must travel alone. In a private note to Catherine, she'd intimated that she wished to pass on a great treasure.

It was the first stirring of interest in the world that Catherine had felt since losing her fourth child. She'd taken passage on a ship up to Inverness.

Joanna drew close. 'Go on.'

At the dock, Catherine had been met by an immense black carriage and six driven by a coachman in old-fashioned livery and a top hat. No sooner had she settled inside than a whip had cracked, and the carriage had thundered along the sea, turning inland to wind up through pine forest and out into moorland, rumbling along the edge of a loch.

Some way out, castle walls rose from the water with the suddenness of Excalibur thrusting upwards from the depths. The loch was so still that there seemed two castles, one shimmering in the black mirror of the water, and another rearing its broken teeth into the sky.

The track ended at the loch's edge, but the horses plunged into the water without breaking stride, and for a moment she thought they would drown. But a shallow causeway lay just beneath the surface, and the carriage pulled up under wide arches and into a courtyard on a small island. The coachman had leapt down and helped her out, where, to her surprise, he had whipped off his cloak and hat and turned butler, escorting her inside.

As he led her upstairs, she saw that the place was half derelict, its rooms empty but for echoes. High up in one tower, however, one large room was furnished in modern comfort.

Her hostess was an old woman in the black crepe of mourning, but she held out two hands to Catherine in greeting, and her smile was warm. 'Welcome,' she'd said. 'To my home in the Boiling Lake.'

'That's it,' I said to Joanna. 'It's not only the beginning of Lady Nairn's story, but of Catherine Forrest's, too.'

After supper, the old lady had at last shown Catherine her treasure.

I could not take my eyes from it. The instant I saw it, I had to have it for you, though the price she named was staggering. She would use it, she said, to restore the castle to its former glory.

She told me that the pages had passed down for generations, mother to daughter, from the original owner, a countess reputed to be a witch and known, once, as the Lady of the Lake. A woman, furthermore, whom Shakespeare had known. Whom he had shadowed forth in the character of Lady Macbeth.

     'My ancestress,' she said. She sat back, eyeing me in appraisal. 'Yours, as well.'

     'Is that why you have chosen me?' I asked.

     'I did not choose you,' she said. 'I saw you.'

I sat back. 'It's Elizabeth Stewart's home, this Boiling Lake.'

Joanna swallowed hard. 'What do you know about Elizabeth Stewart that puts her in the vicinity of Inverness?'

I frowned. Her *Macbeth* years had been spent far to the south, near the king in Edinburgh and Stirling, or at castles close by. But she was a Highlander by birth. Daughter of the Earl of Atholl.

Joanna shook her head. 'I know Blair Castle, seat of the earls and dukes of Atholl. Even in the nineteenth century, you'd have gone by train to Dunkeld, I reckon, and then north in a carriage. There's no way that south from Inverness would've been anyone's first choice of routes. And it couldn't possibly have been a single day's journey, in a carriage.'

At the computer, I typed in the words 'Elizabeth Stewart Arran', and up popped an entry in *The Oxford Dictionary of National Biography*.

'It's her first husband,' said Joanna, pointing at the screen. Another Highland lord, and a great clan chief: Hugh Fraser, fifth Lord Lovat.

I skimmed down through the entry. After their fall from power, she and her third husband had withdrawn from the glittering world of the court, where many people wanted them dead, to her dower lands in the wilds of Inverness-shire.

'How about Lovat's castle?' asked Joanna.

But Beaufort Castle was not on a loch.

'It's near a river,' said Joanna hopefully 'Do you think that counts?'

I shook my head. 'Catherine was clear. Walls rising sheer from the water. Besides, according to this article, Beaufort wasn't built until the late nineteenth century. Too late. And its predecessor was destroyed just after the Battle of Culloden, in 1746: too early.'

Trying not to watch the time ticking away in the lower right hand corner, I looked back at the biographical entry. The sources weren't much help.

'Not much out there on Lady Arran,' said Joanna.

'We don't need books about *her*,' I said slowly. 'We need books about the Frasers. And clan histories were popular in the nineteenth century.' I pulled forward to the keyboard and started typing. 'It means they're out of copyright. It means there's a good chance they'll be searchable on Google books. The largest library on the planet, in digital – and searchable – form.'

It didn't take long to find her, scattered in venomous mention across a number of Fraser histories. 'The Lady Jezebel.' 'An ambitious, avaricious, and ill-natured woman.' A whore who consorted with witches.

And yet, in fear for her life, she'd gone back to these people who despised her.

It was a measure, I supposed, of the depth of the hatred she faced farther south, and the thickness of clan loyalties in the north. The Frasers might revile her, but she was the mother of their chief. So long as she lived among them, they'd allow no one else to kill her.

The details of her exile among them, however, seemed wrapped in a forbidding wall of silence. I'd have to sift through the histories one by one, wading through their thick Victorian prose from beginning to end.

The first turned up nothing. As did the second. The third wasn't really Victorian: a nineteenth century edition of an obscure seventeenth-century manuscript called the *Polichronicon*, or the Wardlaw manuscript.

In the lower right corner of the screen, the time sped on.

Six hours into the flight, I sat up. Tucked away in a passage that mentioned neither her nor her husband by name – and thus slipped beneath the radar of word searches – I read that 'the great, though not good lady' and her husband had whiled away their time in exile by hunting.

Being under continuall feare, their residence was in the Isle of Lochbruyach, a fort remoat from any roade . . .

Lochbruyach.

'Loch Bruiach, in the Kiltarlity Hills,' read a terse footnote.

With shaking fingers, I entered it into Google maps, and a Loch Bruicheach popped up, south-west of Inverness.

'Think that's the one?' asked Joanna.

'There's no island.'

'There has to be.' She toggled over to the satellite view, which showed a tiny white speck in the water.

I looked at the clock. We'd have one chance to find Lily. Did I trust it to a speck seen by satellite on a loch with a not-quite-right name? And why had people called it the Boiling Lake?

Out of curiosity, I searched 'Loch Bruiach Place-Name'.

'Look at this,' I said softly. '"Bruiach" comes from an old Gaelic word *Brutach*, meaning "boiling or raging one". It is, quite literally, the Boiling Lake.'

'That's it, then,' said Joanna.

I looked back at the map. It was still remote from any road.

'I'll arrange for a Range Rover,' said Joanna. 'How are you at back-country driving?'

The last hour, perversely, was the hardest. There was nothing further I could do, save pace back and forth in the aisle.

'Think of something else,' said Joanna.

'Like what?'

'Dee, for starters. And Shakespeare.'

I stopped in front of her.

'You saw the manuscript, didn't you? Back at Fonthill.

What did it say?'

'The first page was a letter. *The witch is not dead*, it read. *I can feel her presence. She is near. She is the red-haired woman my boy saw in the mirror, I know it. You, of all people, should know the danger that imports, and not for the king alone.'*

'Whose letter?'

'It was Dee's handwriting. I did not see to whom he'd addressed it.'

'You think it was Shakespeare?'

'Do you think it wasn't?'

We called Lady Nairn as we were landing, but there was no answer. It was long since dark; the full moon had risen huge in the east. 'Call the police,' I said, as we drove out of the airport in the Range Rover, heading west along the sea.

'Lady Nairn didn't—'

'She's not thinking straight,' I said. 'Call the goddamned police.'

Joanna put in a call. 'I need to report a kidnapping,' she said.

As she began to go through the details, I heard her voice harden. 'No, no relation. No, she hasn't been reported missing. At the Samhuinn Festival in Edinburgh, I understand . . . She's being held, we think, on an island in a loch. Loch Bruiach . . . Heard a threat of rape against her. In New York . . .'

She hung up pale and shaking. 'Bastards. Clearly think

424

I'm a nutter. But they promised to send a constable round to check the place.'

Prickles crept over me. I hoped to God he'd be discreet.

No police, the voice on my phone had said.

'Drive like the bloody wind,' said Joanna.

We drove briefly through the glare of city lights, and then back out into country darkness. It had snowed that morning, and was supposed to snow again that night; the slush on the road squealed against the car's tyres. We left the sea, turning inland through snowy fields and then climbing into hills. The road narrowed, its curves tightening. Traffic, sparse to begin with, thinned and disappeared, until we were the only car I'd seen for miles.

The shrill of Joanna's phone made us both jump; she answered in half a ring and hung up with a sour look. 'The police have checked. There's no one there.' She gave me a sideways look. 'And there's been no one there, apparently, for over a century.'

'They're wrong,' I said, tightening my grip on the steering wheel. 'They have to be.'

Soon afterwards, we left the pavement altogether for deeply rutted track. A forest closed around us, glowing an eerie blue and silver in the moonlight, and the track veered steeply downwards, I thought of Catherine hurtling along in the black carriage. Hushed with the anticipation of snow, the world was utterly silent save for the grind and slip of the car.

Just beyond the edge of the forest, we came to a stop at a fence. Tracks in the snow looked as if another car had stopped here recently. I stepped out, shivering in a wind sharp with the needling tang of pines. Beyond the gate, open moorland rolled down and away, stark and strangely beautiful, about as blasted as a heath could get. No loch was visible, only the moor bound in the far distance by ancient, worn hills. The moon hung in the south-eastern sky like an immense luminous pearl, but clouds were thickening in the west, fingers of darkness upon darkness.

There were no buildings and no lights. Save for a single set of tracks leading out, and the same track coming back, there was no evidence that humans had ever walked here at all. Had ever existed, for that matter – as if not only my species, but our history had been obliterated. Or had not yet occurred.

Back to the beginning.

If Lucas and Jamie were here, there was no sign of them. Either we had somehow passed them, or there was another way in.

The track wound down into a shallow fold between two slopes. Half an hour later, we curved to the right and struggled back up a slope. Beyond, the loch suddenly appeared, dark, cold and menacing, lapping at our feet with greedy little slaps. Close to the opposite shore, a castle rose from the water. Wind ruffled the loch's surface, however, so there

426

was no reflection: no second castle in a dark mirror. And no sound, either, save the slap of the wavelets and the moaning of the wind.

And then a wolf's howl rose into the night, in a place where no wolves should be. I glanced over at the moon. A sliver at its edge had darkened to orange. The eclipse was beginning. I looked back at the island and caught a spark of light. Flame flickered and grew. Someone had set one of the turrets ablaze.

'They're starting,' I said. I pulled out my phone. No service. Joanna had none, either. I put the car key in her hand. 'Go back to the road. Drive if you have to . . . find somewhere with a signal. Call the police again and drag them here if you have to tell them you've witnessed murder yourself.'

'Where are you going?'

'To find Lily.'

I took off around the loch at a run.

44

The path skimmed the edge of the lake. Bent low, my feet slipping in icy mud, I ran until the cold air scoured my lungs and it hurt to breathe. On the island, the fire licked upward into the night. The shore curved in towards the island, and I came to a stop in a dark stand of trees opposite the main entry.

The place was ruinous, some of the towers half crumbled away, but I recognised it all the same. It was Fonthill, writ large. Or rather, Fonthill was this place writ small and drawn from memory. Catherine Forrest had shown her husband the castle all right . . . she had designed for him a copy, remembered rather than exact.

Behind me, another howl rose through the night. On the hill at Dunsinnan, wolves had heralded the attack that scattered Lady Nairn's rite and left Sybilla dead. I had no wish to wait and see what would emerge from the trees. I waded into the loch, hoping the shallow causeway Catherine had described was still there. The water was icy, and ten feet in, I could no longer feel my feet. I had to move slowly. But the water came no higher than my knees.

A stone drive sloped up from the water's edge, leading through the archway into a small courtyard. Icy snow crunched underfoot, the sound of my footsteps loud in the silence as I made my way through stones fallen from the surrounding towers. The shape of the castle's main doorway echoed the arch in the wall behind. The doors themselves were missing.

Around the main hall clustered battlemented towers of various heights, their walls pierced with windows like staring eyes. The hall was a great octagon; if it had once been domed, like Fonthill's, the dome had long since disappeared. It was open to the sky. For a moment, I stood in the shadow of some fallen stones in the courtyard, listening. The only sound was the crackling of the fire, and the skittering of leaves across the ground. Easing the safety catch off the pistol, I stepped inside.

Around the floor stretched a circle of candles such as Lily had once danced within, except that these were enclosed by hurricane glasses. Even so, their small flames bent and fluttered in the wind. But there was no dancer here; the hall was empty. Directly across, a large window framed the moon, its disc being devoured by a deep orange shadow. The floor was paved with stone, not tile, but just as at Fonthill, there was a central stone different from all the others. An eye.

Stepping into the circle, I walked forward through the room. Cut into an octagonal stone in the centre of the floor was a small circular groove with an irregular protrusion. In it – the groove clearly made for it – lay a handled disc of polished black stone. It was not, as at Fonthill, a translucent eye. It was a mirror.

Dee's mirror.

In its surface shone a small reflection of the dying moon.

Off to the side, I heard a small noise and turned. In a doorway stood Lily, a blue silk gown rippling around her, her eyes wide with terror. Behind her, stood a hooded and cloaked figure with arms around her neck, a knife at her throat.

'Drop your weapon,' someone said, and I whirled towards the voice.

In another doorway stood Lady Nairn. She wore her own clothes, but she too had a keeper with a knife at her throat.

'*Drop*,' said another whisper.

Lily and Lady Nairn were both being used as shields; I had little chance of rescuing either of them by force, and none of freeing them both. Carefully I set the gun down on the floor, cursing my own stupidity.

A shadow flittered over me and I looked up. Another gown of blue silk floated down towards me like wings. Blue silk shimmering with beetle's wings.

'*Put it on.*'

Pulling it from the air, I wrapped it around me.

A deep, slow drumbeat boomed through the space. A high voice rose, twining up to the sky. As if drawn by it, from every door drifted figures cowled in black, their faces invisible. In their right hands, each one held a knife.

'Let her go,' said a voice behind me. I turned. In the doorway to the courtyard stood Lucas. *'Lily is mine.'* He stepped forward to the edge of the circle, flinging away one of the hurricane glasses, which shattered, and picking up the candle within.

'Enter two kings, old and young,' said the figure holding Lily. *'Double, double toil and trouble* . . . Not one king and the double deeds of sex and death, but two kings, young and old. Shall we guess which of them ravishes the maiden?'

'I don't need to guess,' said Lucas. 'I have the manuscript.' He raised the candle's flame near its edge. 'As it happens, the answer is neither. Which is why we're not following the script. Not this time. Let her go.'

Behind him, a shadow detached itself from the rocks strewn across the courtyard and slipped silently up the steps.

The figure gripping Lily did not move.

'She is mine,' said Lucas, touching flame to the paper.

In a flash of silver, steel slashed across his abdomen. A deep scream burst from him as he pitched forward onto his knees, and the burning pages fell to the ground. The shadow darted from behind, smothering the flames.

On his knees, Lucas was holding his entrails in his hands, blood welling through his fingers. The figure turned, and the knife flicked out again, slashing his throat.

431

Stepping back from the blood spilling across the stones, the figure loosed the cloak and let it fall away, revealing a woman clad in another blue gown. She turned back towards the circle and I saw her face.

Joanna.

Still holding the knife, she raised bloody arms to the moon. In a deep voice, she called aloud to the darkness: '*Nothing is but what is not.*'

45

'Meet my niece,' said Lady Nairn in a voice of loathing. 'Cerridwen Douglas.'

Joanna? Joanna, not Jamie, was Carrie. Jamie was probably dead in a corner at Fonthill, while I'd brought Joanna with me every step of the way. Discussed every piece of evidence with her, shared everything I knew. Spilled my sorrow and my fury to her. Wept in her arms, for Christ's sake.

Left her to call for help . . .

In a wash of despair, I realised no help would come. There would be no police. There had probably never been any police – just one of her followers on the other end of the phone, someone who'd driven out to the gate and made believable tracks in the snow.

Why? The only reason to do that was to lure me on.

Which meant she still needed me.

Double, double toil and trouble, Lucas had said. *One spirit draining into death, another rising into life, at the same time.*

What role did she mean to hand me? Victim, or killer?

Another voice slipped out from memory. My own, facing

Eircheard's body. *I will kill her. I will find Lily, and then Carrie will die.*

Around me, the candles guttered in a gust of wind. I stepped forward, heart knocking against my ribs. 'You have the manuscript. You have me. Let Lily go.'

Joanna – Carrie – looked up from the manuscript. 'When we are finished with her.'

'That was the deal. I bring the manuscript, you release her.'

'And we will. When you are finished with your role, and she with hers.'

'What role?' My throat was dry.

'Have you not guessed?' She folded the pages and slipped them into a pocket. *'Thou shalt be queen hereafter.* Hecate, Queen of Witches. Not the cackling fool added by some later hack. The triple goddess: maiden, mother, crone. There, and not there, as Ellen Terry put it, in the three witches. A girl to gaze, a mother to mate, and a crone to kill.'

I frowned. *What are these, so withered and so wild in their attire*, Shakespeare had made Banquo say: *You should be women, and yet your beards forbid me to interpret that you are so.*

'Come on, Kate,' Joanna chided.

Not Joanna, I told myself. *Carrie.*

'You of all people should know better than to trust what one character says . . . in any case, there's a stage direction here that disputes Banquo's observation as illusion.'

All was illusion, nought was truth.

'In any case, without Lily, we have no maiden. No one to see . . . Lucas was right about one spirit draining into death, and another rising into life.' She lifted her voice to a ritual cry. 'The old king is dying. The new king must take his queen.'

The drumming rolled out again, and the wordless song rose once more into the night. The figure behind Lily pushed her forward into the centre of the circle. 'Dance,' he commanded.

The instant she was clear of him, a man hurtled down from above, landing like a cat in the centre of the circle, pulling Lily close and hauling her to the door, sweeping the room with a gun. The cowled figures who'd begun to close on him pulled back.

All but one. Lady Nairn had pulled loose from her captor, wresting the knife from his hand.

'Let her go,' said Ben.

It was only then that I realised he was talking about me.

In the confusion, a man had come up behind me. Now his arm snaked around me, pulling me back into the corridor from which Lily had emerged, using me as a shield for both himself and Carrie. As he dragged me into a spiral stairwell, I twisted and writhed, catching a glimpse of his face.

He was the dark-haired man. The Winter King.

I slammed his arm against the wall, and he dropped his knife, but before I could reach it, Carrie tossed him hers, which he brought up against my throat. Beneath the blood clotting the blade I saw runes, and a pattern of blue-grey whorls.

Nothing is but what is not.

I caught one last glimpse of Ben's face before I was dragged backwards up the stairs.

46

Up and up we wound, the blade cold against my throat, the stone wall on one side hot to the touch. It was the tower adjoining the stair turret that was burning. We passed floors opening onto rooms that were empty, and others that were missing floors. On the fifth floor, all that remained of the corridor was a narrow ledge. I was pushed across it at knife-point and shoved into a high vaulted room holding a table, two high-backed chairs and an unnecessary fire glowing in the grate. Two crumbling windows looked over the loch and the dark orange moon; wind moaned through the room.

'Strip,' said my captor.

One spirit must die, another must rise.

'No.' I slid around the table, backing against the far wall.

Tossing the furniture aside, he strode towards me, the blade gleaming dully in his hand

'*Ian.*' Carrie stood in the doorway. 'She must be a vessel of the goddess. She must consent.' At the sound of her voice, he stopped, panting a little, his body still poised to spring.

'*Consent!*' I burst out. I was watching the knife in his

hand. Somehow, I had to get it away from him. 'You think I'll consent to a rape?'

Carrie looked at me coldly. 'If you consent, it will not be rape.'

Ian, I thought, backing into the alcove made by one of the windows. It was the name of the man Lily had talked about with shining eyes. *This* was her beau? The Winter King? 'Have you touched her?' I asked, my voice thick with disgust.

His mouth curled in a faint leer. 'Nothing that she did not want. And not as much as she wanted.'

With scryers, Joanna had said, virginity was at a premium. *The purer the vessel, the clearer the sight.* Which meant he was toying with me. 'She's fifteen,' I said shortly. 'She doesn't know what she wants. And I'll bet she didn't know what you were up to, either, or she wouldn't have let you anywhere near her. She probably still doesn't know.'

'Do *you* know what you want?' He gazed at me with the calculating eyes of a cat, the knife weaving in the air as he spoke. 'It took two months to stack the tower next door for the bonfire. Nine sacred woods, three storeys high. It will collapse eventually, and bring down this whole tower and everything in it as well, in a cataclysm of fire. You'll want to be gone by then, if you want to survive. But to get out, you have to get past me. For a price.' His voice lowered to a dark caress. 'So what is it you want, Kate? How badly do you want to live?'

I glanced out the window. Five storeys down, the wind

whipped the loch to an angry froth. The boiling lake, I thought. And the burning tower. *Double, double toil and trouble, fire burn and cauldron bubble.* I knew how cold the water was. How deep was it?

'You'll die,' said Ian. 'I'm offering you life.'

'It's not life that she wants,' said Carrie, walking forward with another offer. In one hand, she held what looked like a necklace with a rectangular silver pendant and some papers. The manuscript. In the other, she, too, held a knife. The one I'd knocked from Ian on the stairs. 'I can tell you what you want to know. Shakespeare's past, or your own.'

I stilled, hearing my voice, wailing on the hill. *What have I done?*

She'd known. She'd known the entire time she'd held me on the plane, holding me like a mother holding a child. I realised that betrayal with the force of being slammed into a wall of cold stone. 'Even if I were in the market,' I said through clenched teeth, 'what reason would I have to trust any word from your mouth?'

The pendant she was dangling was a flashdrive. 'Lucas's raw footage,' she said. 'He filmed Sybilla's death. Auld Callie's and Eircheard's, as well.' She dropped it on the table, tossing the knife down next to it, and spreading out the papers. 'The fruit of the knowledge of good or of evil. Of innocence or guilt.'

Looking at that small silver rectangle, listening to Carrie's voice, other certainties began to drop into place, pieces of a puzzle floating of their own accord into a picture that made appalling sense. Carrie may have masterminded much of the killing, but she'd been with me when Eircheard died. The hand that held the blade had not been hers. And even bound and on his back, Eircheard could have swatted Lucas aside like a gnat. I looked at Ian, rage making the very air around him seem to ripple, like the quivering of heat around a mirage. 'That was you, wasn't it? *You* killed Eircheard.' I could feel my hands pumping into fists. I'd promised Eircheard as he lay dead in the library that I'd kill Carrie, but that was when I thought she'd wielded the knife. It had been Ian, though, now standing before me with the killing blade in his hand, a mocking leer on his face.

Lunging for one of the chairs, I shoved it into Ian and darted towards the table, reaching for Carrie's knife. I almost had it when Ian caught me, dragging me to the floor and pinning me down with both hands.

I must have knocked his knife away with the chair, I realised, even as his hands clamped in a chokehold around my neck.

He leaned in as if for a kiss. '*Put out the light, and then put out the light.*'

Othello's words, while killing Desdemona. The opposite of the language of God. Not *fiat lux*, 'Let there be light,' but *fiat mors.* Let there be death.

'You're beautiful when you're angry, Kate. Not smart, maybe, but beautiful. Wild cat, wild Kate.' His face began

440

to go dark. Around the edges of things, lights began to glow like fiery haloes. It wasn't my death that he wanted, though. Not yet anyway. It was darkness. If I lost consciousness, I realised, he'd do what he wished to my body and count it consent, when I didn't fight back.

In one last burst of strength, I hurled him off, rolling away, scrabbling for the blade that I knew had to be on the floor somewhere. Even as he pulled me back towards him by the feet, I saw a glint of steel, and my hand closed around the black hilt. *Nothing is but what is not.*

I slashed out at him, and the blade caught his arm, trailing a bright line of blood. He flinched, and I scrambled to my feet, keeping the knife before me as Ben had once taught me. *In a knife fight*, he'd said with unusual seriousness, *the only defence worth having is an offence.*

'Ian!' Carrie cried, and once again I saw her knife soaring through the air toward his hand. I couldn't let him catch it. As he reached for it, I launched myself into him, hitting him square in the chest with the full weight of my body, unbalancing us both, so that we crashed to the floor. With a thud, my knife drove into his belly up to the hilt.

The other knife clattered harmlessly to the ground, and a wild, deep cry split the room. For a moment he gripped me hard. Then he jerked away. I stumbled to my feet, the knife in my hand rippling red in the firelight.

Pushing himself up, Ian gripped his belly, blood welling through his fingers.

A loud rumble filled the room, and the floor lurched. Grabbing at the windowsill to stay upright, I dropped the blade. Ian staggered into the table. For a moment, there was silence. Then the wall behind him disappeared, collapsing in a sheet of flame. The floor rippled and bucked, dropping him to his knees, and the room began to tilt. Across the room, Carrie stepped back into the doorway, clinging to the doorframe. In the centre, Ian was still gripping the table. Another jolt, and the floor heaved again, tilting further. Before I could reach it, the knife slid away from me, heading towards Ian. Bellowing with rage, he scooped it up and threw it. I ducked, and it sailed threw the window into the night, plummeting down to the lake.

Ian began throwing everything he could lay his hands on. Papers, pens, books. There was a glint, and the flash-drive on its chain snaked through the air. I reached for it, and it brushed my fingers. It clattered against the stone, but before I could grab it, it slid down the outside of the wall and disappeared.

Inside, the floor lurched a third time, and disintegrated. With one last wail of fury, Ian slid backwards into the flames, his cry lost in the roar of the fire. Where he'd stood, loose pages of manuscript floated on the heated air like slow butterflies, bursting one by one into flame.

47

From the doorway opposite, a wail rose from Carrie. 'What have you done?'

The heat in the room was intense; the cold wind sweeping over my back was all that made it bearable.

'Did you not think the spirit of Shakespeare worth calling forth from the deeps?' Carrie went on.

'That's what all this killing was for? To conjure *Shakespeare?*'

'Not the man,' she said with contempt. 'The spirit who possessed him. The man was dross, merely. Do you know what Dee wrote?' She held out a page from the manuscript. *You are a servant of the great, no more, a bit player who glimpsed the Great Rite not once, but twice: both times, uninvited, from the shadows, and both times, stole its fire for yourself.* She looked up, her eyes full of contempt. 'Fire and power that was meant for me and mine: for Arran's daughter. For Dee's son. And it lit, instead, on the poor clay of a glover's son.' A narrow strip of floor along one wall was all that remained of the room. She began advancing across it.

'You seriously mean to suggest that spying on some magical rite explains Shakespeare's genius?'

'I would have called it forth again. Made it light upon my son.'

Ian was her son?

'He was an artist,' she said. 'A visionary. A conduit of power.'

It was what Lily had said. A genius, she'd called him. *He will change the way stories are told . . . make a new kind of art altogether.*

'He was a killer,' I said aloud.

'An artist in flesh and blood,' said Carrie. 'A man who would shape the world by the force of his will. I thought you might have the imagination to help.'

'*You thought I would help?*' I thought of Auld Callie, strung up in the tree. Of Eircheard, his body slashed in the darkness in the British Museum, his heart torn out. Of Sybilla with her throat cut, and Ben's face looking down on her.

'You are no better than your petty-minded poet. *Shakespeare.*' She spat the name. 'He took a gift of great power, the shadow of the language of God, and did what with it? Wasted it. Exhaled it on the public stage, grabbing at pennies here and there in exchange for doling out cheap delight to the grubby masses.' Her voice rose in contempt. 'He could have shaped kingdoms and crowns. He could have seized wisdom from the deeps of time.'

'He *did* shape kingdoms and crowns,' I said quietly. 'Not

444

the everyday England of Elizabeth and James. Kingdoms of the mind. He made new and bright worlds from nothing but words. The shadow of the language of God: your words. It wasn't angels or demons Shakespeare chose to conjure. It was people: audiences.

'He offered humans a brush with the divine. And he harmed no one, doing it . . . *An it harm none, do what ye will.* Isn't that the one rule of witchcraft?'

'A rule made by those afraid of its old powers. But to celebrate life, you must also celebrate death. To create life, you must create death.'

'You don't create anything. You destroy only. But you can't even do that, not with words alone. You can only make it happen by finding someone to do it for you: a terrible shadow of Shakespeare's weird sisters getting Macbeth to do their dirty work by whispering on the wind.'

I shook my head. 'But you are also Macbeth. Your magic, your power, it's nothing but a sham. An illusion. You are no better than Shakespeare's bloody king, lured into acting as the robotic arm of evil.'

She laughed aloud. '*Watch* . . .' She began to raise her arms, her voice a low throbbing chant. 'I conjure you—' The wind buffeted through the window, tearing her words away, so that I heard them only in snatches.

Though you untie the winds . . .
. . . trees blown down . . .

Though castles topple . . .
Even till destruction sicken . . .

Outside, the storm slammed into the castle with a fury, buffeting the walls like some hammer of the gods, churning the water below into high waves clawing at the stone. Whipped to frenzy, the fire rushed upwards in a thundering whirlwind of sparks and shooting flame.

'*Answer Me!*' cried Carrie, and in a sudden gesture of triumph, she brought her arms down to her sides.

Behind her, the corridor imploded in a deafening roar. For a split second the fire darkened to glimmering red embers and then it billowed back, exploding skywards, almost, it seemed, in the shape of a raging man. With a wild shriek of triumph, Carrie turned, the blue gown floating out around her like wings, and walked into the flames.

The heat rolling off the fire was intense. I slid down the outer side of the window, dangling from the sill, letting the tower wall shield me from the worst of it. For a moment, I hung there, fighting to cling to the damp stone, though it was heating up by the second.

No one would imagine I had survived that last cataclysm. I barely believed it myself. And if they had . . . what then? Between the storm and the fire, there was no way to reach me by land or air or water. *Fire burn or cauldron bubble*. I had a choice of deaths: water or fire.

From far away, I heard the wail of sirens, weak as the mewling of newborn kittens.

Even if I did survive, clinging to the stone till the fire died, what then?

What part I had played in Sybilla's death I did not know, and never would: everyone else who had been there was now dead, and the flashdrive with its footage had been swallowed up in the fire. All that remained was a trail of evidence that said, beyond the shadow of doubt, that I had been there.

Whatever I had or had not done to Sybilla, I had killed Ian. He had been cruel, a killer, and very likely insane, but it was still a death. Blood on my hands.

Around me, the wall began to steam, and I realised, as if from a distance, that my fingers were blistering where they dug into crannies in the stone.

In the sky, a sliver of white appeared at the edge of the moon as the shadow began to slide off. Somewhere, I heard singing, a lone voice, rising like silver in the night, joined a few moments later by another. As suddenly as it had hit, the wind now subsided. Below, the angry waves were subsiding, the water cold and dark beneath a surface of red and gold. Out over the loch, snow began to fall in flakes large and slow as drifting feathers.

Suddenly, I was aware of nothing but empty exhaustion. It was not physical: I could have clung to that wall for a while yet. But for what?

I let go.

It seemed to me that a cool silvery light rose around me, wrapping about me like a cool slip of silk. For a moment, I thought, it buoyed me up. Then I felt a shock of cold. And dark water closed over my head.

48

Darkness and cold swirled around me, smooth as glass, as if I'd fallen into the dark mirror. The next thing I remember is the shock of hands, a rushing, and air scraping across my body. I coughed and retched, and a face swam into view above me, ringed with the glow of the fire.

Dark, wet hair and green eyes. The planes of his face chiselled with damp and fire.

Ben.

'Kate,' he said, his face very close to mine as he wiped wet hair from my eyes, wrapping his body around mine so that warmth flowed from him to me.

We seemed to be on a rocky shore. The singing had stopped, and the silvery light was gone. The moon laid a long glittering path of gold across the dark water. From the other direction, red and blue lights flashed over the water. Emergency vehicles, I thought. *Police.*

Behind Ben, other faces peered down at me. Lady Nairn, full of concern, and Lily, her face pale with relief and something I would not recognise till later: pride.

'How did you find me?' I asked Ben.

'*I can call spirits from the vasty deep,*' he said lightly, his mouth tipping into a smile.

I frowned. 'How?'

'Lily told me where to dive.'

Just beyond him, she'd bent to pick up something among the rocks. A silvery rectangle dangling from a chain. 'I saw you,' she said, looking back with a smile. 'In the loch.'

But that's not possible, I thought, slipping back into unconsciousness.

Interlude

4 November, 1606
Hampton Court Palace

Not long after the boy Hal Berridge had come to Mortlake to serve as his father's scryer, Arthur Dee had walked in on the boy kissing his younger brother Rowland – a particularly deep and passionate kiss. He'd reviled the boy as a catamite ever since, a Ganymede corrupting his little brother. He spat vile terms at the boy, aiming hidden kicks and blows his way, whenever he could. Not only because of the allure he had for Rowland, but because Arthur found himself also gazing at the boy, tingling when he walked by. Deep down, he knew it was not entirely the issue of sex that rattled him, however, no matter how startling he found the attraction. It was jealousy, and not of his body. Of his sight. With the possible exception of Edward Kelley, Hal Berridge was the best seer his father had ever employed.

Though his father had been crestfallen, Arthur, for one, had breathed more than one sigh of relief when the boy left Mortlake for Hampton Court at the invitation of Lord Salisbury. Then, on the eve of the play in which Berridge was to star as a queen, Arthur discovered that Rowland had made an assignation with him at the palace. Telling himself that he was protecting his little brother's reputation, Arthur had got Rowland stupendously drunk, left him snoring in the music room, and then gone downriver himself to keep the appointment.

The exact spot turned out to be deep in a deserted wing of the oldest part of the palace. Arthur had arrived early to find the otherwise empty room warmed by a fire of apple logs scented with lavender. He had laid Rowland's cloak on the floor and retired behind the door to wait.

The boy's blue velvet skirts whispered sweetly against the flagged floor as he entered the room. Arthur stepped swiftly behind him, closing and latching the door. The creature had turned, and Arthur had enjoyed the flash of fear on the boy's face.

'Arthur—'

'Don't foul my name in your mouth,' he said, and lunged.

Berridge managed to duck, and Arthur's elbow hit his jaw with a glancing blow. The boy kept his feet, barely. As Arthur came back at him, he pulled a knife which slid across Arthur's arm, trailing a bright line of blood. A scratch, really, no more, but it made him shout with rage.

He aimed another blow at Berridge's head, and this time connected with more force. Winding a fist into the long hair of the boy's wig, he dragged him across the floor. When the wig did not come off, Arthur stopped and, with his other hand, tore at the gown, which ripped down to the waist.

As if Berridge had suddenly turned to a serpent in his hands, Arthur stepped back, his eyes widening, his breath seizing. 'But you are not – you are not a boy,' he stammered.

Naked from the waist up, the person in front of him was a woman. A beautiful woman with long red hair. 'Would your father have taught me, in this shape?' she charged.

Arthur's mouth opened and closed. 'And Rowland—'

'Has known almost since the beginning,' she said.

He blinked, still trying to process her transformation, and she stepped close and took his hand in hers. With a smile, she slid his hand up to her breast.

Suddenly all the longing that he had bottled up inside, twisted and questioned and tried to press out of himself for over a year tumbled forth. An instant later, his arms locked around her, and she let him pull her down onto the cloak spread over the floor, where they mounted one another with a wild, rutting urgency.

Some time later, she lay atop him, her head in the small of his shoulder as the dark explosion of climax drained away. Hearing a sound, he opened his eyes to see an old man he did not know lunging at them, a knife in his hands. Arthur rolled, flinging Berridge – or whoever she was – away.

Stumbling with the force of his drive, the other man ran past them but turned quickly, leaping at them again.

How the knife – the one she'd cut him with, still marked

with his blood, and with strange characters running down the blade – came into Arthur's hand, he didn't know. And what happened next happened so quickly that he could never quite remember it: as their attacker darted around him, clearly headed for her, Arthur's hand flicked out and slit his throat.

The other man dropped to the floor, blood welling and spurting into pools on the flagstone. Arthur heard the knife clatter to the floor as well, and stood staring at his hand in horror.

Moments later, the Berridge who was not a boy propelled him out the door, saying he must save himself, and that she would clean up as necessary. And she'd added a strange request: send Mr Shakespeare.

January, 1607
Castle Bruiach, Scotland

Well wrapped in furs on a still and moonless night, she sat alone in an open window high in a tower, staring down at the dark ice of the loch. Once, her mother had ruled this castle. Just that morning, however, after a quick but decisive seduction of the young lord who now had charge of it, she had become the new lady of the lake. The way she sat, one hand resting protectively on her still-flat belly, might have made her new husband proud, thinking he had tilled his field well. Inside her, though, another man's child was already growing, a fact she had not found fit to share with her new lord.

The night before, in a sudden bitter cold, the loch had frozen, its surface smooth as black glass. Still uncluttered by snow or the tramping of men, it glimmered faintly in the starlight. Letting her breathing slow and her body relax, she stared at its surface without really seeing it, and after a while, pictures began to form in her mind. At first, they were memories, though she saw the scenes with a detached clarity, not, as she'd first seen them, from within her body, but floating somewhere overhead.

She had always looked young and boyish, so it was easy to bind her breasts and dress like a boy five years younger than her true age. She had refused, however, to cut the bright hair that had always seemed, somehow, to be an extension of her soul, some part of herself more intrinsic than other, less unique features. So she acquired a wig and a large cap, and she experimented with various substances until she found one that could slick her long hair down inside them. And then she travelled south all the way to London.

West of London, to be exact. To a place called Mortlake. From a boiling lake, she thought with dark satisfaction, to a lake of the dead. There, she presented herself to the English wizard Dr Dee, in order to steal the learning out of which he had cheated her mother.

Her mother had been dead for nearly a decade, but the

girl had forgiven neither the wizard nor the thief for their part in making her mother's life a disappointment. Though she had met neither man, the whole of her young life had been one long exercise in reviling them. Neither man, in fact, had any reason to know of her existence, though the thief, Mr Shakespeare, had been present – as an illicit observer – at the hour of her making. During a Great Rite, her mother had told her, at the top of Dunsinnan Hill, in the light of a Samhuinn fire. Later that night, he had stolen away the mirror and the manuscript whose loss had made her mother howl at the moon. She had been born, the girl sometimes thought, with the express purpose of retrieving those two lost treasures. She had gone to London to hold true to that purpose.

Dr Dee sensed her power at once and took her in. He had been in the dark, when it came to the spirit world, since his last scryer of real talent, Edward Kelley, had got himself killed in Bohemia. So he welcomed this new boy Hal Berridge with open arms and trembling delight, giving thanks to a gracious heaven. In the guise of a boy, she toiled for him dutifully, and he repaid her efforts, unveiling, layer by layer, all the deep learning of his long life. More than her mother could ever have dreamed.

She spent all her spare hours in the maze of his library in that rambling set of conjoined cottages on the banks of the Thames. It took her almost a year to find her mother's manuscript in his most closely guarded hiding place, behind the moveable stone in the fireplace of his innermost study. She could not read the original, but she could and did read the translation, making her own copy sentence by sentence in the moments she could finagle alone with it. By the time she finished, she had engraved its tales of the goddess Corra – also called Cerridwen, Dee had noted – and her rites word for word, into her memory.

It would not, however, be enough. For always, Dr Dee taught her, learned magi left some crucial detail out of their written records of magical rites, lest they fall into the hands of the uninitiated. It was why apprenticeship was so crucial, and why Dee's refusal to teach her mother had rankled so.

Dr Dee as good as told her that he'd remained silent on some key aspect of what she sought: the deed without a name. In all probability, the writer of the original manuscript had done the same. If she meant, as she did, to reenact the rite whose secrets had gone to the grave with her mother, then she would have to milk that knowledge from a witness. And she knew the identity of only one.

A man who had stolen, according to her mother, not only the mirror and the manuscript, but also something more precious: a thunderbolt from the gods. The first two, she intended to take back. The third she intended to avenge.

And then vengeance landed in her lap. First, in the face of a red-headed woman she had seen in the mirror. The face of a woman with a knife. Dr Dee, she knew, suspected that it was the face of her mother. It was not, but it was useful, nevertheless, in a way she had not dreamed. It took her, willy-nilly, to court, where she found herself lodged in Hampton Court Palace.

And then, in a strange chain of events, it had prompted the misshapen Earl of Salisbury to call for a play from Mr Shakespeare. An early draft had been sent out to Mortlake, which had brought the old wizard back to court in a quavering rage. At first, when she'd realised that it shadowed her mother, she'd thought she had yet another reason to wreak revenge on Mr Shakespeare. And then she'd realised that it also conjured up something else: the memory she had been seeking, of a rite seen long ago on a hill in Scotland. A deed without a name. A deed Mr Shakespeare had remembered, it seemed, without the guile of a wizard, recording it in full.

After that, she laid her plans well. The suggestion that she might be given a role in the play came from her, though it reached Salisbury's ears through a circuitous route. The play was to be offered before the king amid the celebrations around the anniversary of the Powder Plot. The Samhuinn moon fell just before the appointed day: and she appointed that night for her revenge.

She'd found the empty wing of the palace and chosen the room with care, arranging an assignation there with Rowland Dee. Some time before, she'd gone fishing for Mr

Shakespeare's eyes; feeling them fall upon her, she'd done her best to keep them there. She'd sent a message to him, as well, begging his company.

And then she'd seen what she'd seen in that mirror, the moment it passed her by in that last rehearsal.

Dressed in her queen's costume, her real hair cascading around her in coppery waves, she left the rehearsal in the Great Hall, heading back to the buttery that served as a green room. She knew exactly where they kept the mirror in its chest. It was the work of a moment to pick the lock and take it, and then to slip back out, unseen by the rest of the company riveted by Burbage in full-blown rant.

She made her way through the palace's web of corridors to the old deserted wing, but from there her deep-laid plans went awry. First, Arthur Dee had appeared instead of Rowland. And then the old man who'd been tailing her had died, instead of Mr Shakespeare.

She'd sent Arthur quickly away, telling him to send the playwright back.

As soon as he was in the corridor, she latched the door behind him, and set about the work she needed to do. She had just drawn the blue gown over the body, stripped naked and bound, when she heard a tap at the door.

Mr Shakespeare, at last. 'You are late,' she said as he took in the form of the body draped in blue on the floor. 'That was meant to be you.'

He looked up with horrified eyes. 'And if I cry murder?'

She held his eyes coolly. 'They will arrest the killer. Arthur Dee.'

He would not consign his old master's eldest son to the executioner, and they both knew it.

She had quoted his words to his face, enjoying it: '*Look like the innocent flower, but be the serpent under it.*'

As Arthur had recently done with her, she now enjoyed watching him realise who she was. 'The Lernaean Hydra,' he murmured. 'Lady Elizabeth Stewart's child.'

In exchange for her silence and her disappearance, they agreed upon a trade: he had brought, as requested, a folded wad of pages excised from the first version of his new play – a version that he said was now obsolete, after he'd spent the last few hours revising.

He insisted, however, that she leave behind the mirror. She looked at it, briefly, with regret, for it was beautiful, and a thing of power. But she did not need it. There would be another, more powerful, where she was going. So she opened her fingers and let the dark circle drop, rolling into the folds of the blue gown.

After that, they had both exited through a high window, leaving the door latched behind them. The way he had come, he thought, was being watched. In the garden below, they parted. She turned one last time before fading into the dark, a smile playing at the corners of her mouth. *The queen, my lord, is dead. And I shall be queen hereafter.*

*

In the tower window, the memories went dark. And then another picture arose, not a memory, though whether it belonged to past or future, she could not tell: the face of a red-headed woman with a knife.

And in the background, the tower in which she sat, in flames.

EPILOGUE

The following day, the remains of a body, blackened beyond recognition, were pulled from the smoking ruins of the castle. It proved to be Ian Blackburn. Though a police forensic team searched the ruins with a fine sieve, no trace of Carrie Douglas was ever found.

Their followers at Castle Bruiach were charged with the Scottish version of accessory murder in the death of Lucas Porter. A lot about the deaths of Sir Angus, Auld Callie, Sybilla, and Eircheard, however, would never be explained, because everyone who knew the details was either missing or dead.

At the hospital, they told me I'd recently had a pretty serious concussion. It explained my amnesia on the hilltop, along with the headache and sluggishness I'd wakened with. But not, I fretted, what I'd done. Or hadn't.

It was Lucas's flashdrive, in the end, that did that. He'd documented, in cold detail, three murders. On a sullen grey afternoon at police headquarters in Perth, DI Sheena McGregor summoned Lady Nairn, Ben, and me to view the film if we wished. 'Wish' seemed a very odd choice of words: I would not wish that sight on anyone. But I needed to see with my waking eyes what I had done, or not done. So I sat with my hands tightly clasped in my lap, watching myself dip in and out of consciousness in the background as Carrie held Sybilla down, and Ian raised the ritual blade. The cry from Sybilla as it struck was hair-raising even on a small screen. At the moment of its happening, it had roused me from my stupor. I'd stumbled to Sybilla's side as if drunk, trying to stop the blood, to pour it back into her body with my hands. As Carrie laughed, Ian had back-handed me so that I spun away, sliding once more to the ground, unconscious.

That was all I needed to see. I walked out of the room before the camera pulled away from me. I could not bear to see Ben either looking at me, his face a careful blank, or looking studiously away. And I had no wish to watch Eircheard die.

There are some things that, once known, cannot be un-known. Cannot be forgotten or erased.

I walked out of the building to find Lily sitting on a bench outside the door. She looked pale and very young, her face pinched with grief inside the bright halo of her hair.

'It's my fault,' she said, swallowing back tears. 'It's all my fault.'

I sat down beside her. 'You're not responsible for what Carrie and Ian did, Lily.'

'I thought he was brilliant. I thought he was cool. I thought he *liked* me. I'm an *idiot*,' she wailed.

'He used you, sweetheart. So did Carrie.'

'I went along with him,' she said, her voice ragged with self-loathing. 'I lied to you: it *was* me on the hill, that first day you were at Dunsinnan. I thought we were rehearsing a secret initiation rite. And I was with Ian the next morning, after they killed Auld Callie. I didn't know, but I should have. And then I went with him, after the fire festival. I thought it was a lark. And they almost killed you. And Eircheard – Eircheard is dead.' She bit her lip, looking away as her voice dropping to a whisper. 'I miss him.'

'So do I.'

'I'm sorry.' Her face crumpled and sobs racked through her. I put my arm around her, and let her cry. She'd been naïve, not evil, but she would have a hard time forgiving herself. It was one of the worst sins of evil, I reflected. Twisting naïveté and innocence to its own use.

Holding Lily, I sat lost in my own thoughts. That she'd been on the hill explained part of what I'd seen, but not everything: the image of her neck thickly smeared with blood was still vivid in my mind. Surely what I'd seen had been half-dream, twining around reality, twisting its shape.

It took time to sort out everything we'd found, and some things that we'd lost.

The manuscript we'd found at Fonthill had vanished in

the flames at Loch Bruiach. What little I'd heard about it came from Carrie and Lucas. Tantalising as their hints had been, I could not trust a word of it – even, at times, the basic identification of a letter by John Dee, presumably to Shakespeare, and a manuscript of *Macbeth*. No one else would likely want to trust even the fact of the finding. I knew the sort of media storm that Shakespeare manuscripts stirred up. It was easier to wonder about what I'd nearly seen – and rue its passing – in quiet, and let others blather publically about just what Catherine Forrest may have found.

The mirror proved to be Dee's and went back to the British Museum – its exact fit into the groove in the floor of Castle Bruiach noted, though no one knew quite what to do with that information. Marks on the side were consistent with the lettering identified by Arthur Dee – but they were also consistent, noted the lab, with random lettering.

It went on rotating display, half the year in the Enlightenment Gallery, half the year in the Mexican room, attached to a statue of Tezcatlipoca, at the foot. Museum staff noted that every once in a while, in either place, some-one would be found in front of it, shaking in terror, claiming to have seen visions of blood and fire. The guards avoided looking at it.

Lady Nairn's mirror was found in a ritual room deep inside the maze at Joanna Black Books, surrounded by black and purple candles, half burned away. Nearby lay a knife with traces of Auld Callie's blood. The only prints on the handle were Joanna's. Or Carrie's, I should say.

The loch, which had so easily cast me back out, kept close and secret hold of the knife from the hill, which remains unrecovered.

The owner of Her Majesty's Theatre was discreetly informed of the cache of magical books in the dome room; what he did with most of them remained still more discreet. Dee's book with Arthur's letter inside, however, he donated to the British Library, where scholars began to squawk over just what the phrase 'one of my father's scholars' implied. No one was as certain as Joanna had been that the diagrams had anything to do with the Globe.

Aubrey's diary went to join the bulk of his papers at Oxford University's Bodleian Library, on permanent loan from Lady Nairn.

Plans for a private production of *Macbeth* using objects from her collection were scrapped. Instead, Lady Nairn opted for the first public exhibition of the Nairn collection, to open at the National Museum of Scotland, in Edinburgh, later travelling down to the British Museum. As part of it, she decided to include screenings of Herbert Beerbohm Tree's lost film of *Macbeth*.

She still wanted a production of the play to run in tandem with the exhibition, but thankfully she did not ask me to direct it. Instead, she asked me to direct as its counterpart, light balancing darkness, the comedy that told another story of witchcraft: *Midsummer Night's Dream*. To that, I happily said yes.

Both Carrie and Ian died intestate; under Scottish law, this made Lady Nairn the sole heir of them both, as aunt and 'sibling of a grandparent', respectively. So Lady Nairn found herself in possession of a Covent Garden bookshop and a fine collection of rare occult esoterica, including a black, staring cat named Lilith and an unimpressed snake named Medea, as well as the royalties of Corra Ravensbrook's book, which became an instant bestseller when news of the murders broke.

Jason Pierce surfaced in Australia. Two hours before the Samhuinn Fire Festival was to start, he'd received a call from someone purporting to be with the festival organisers, offering him an out via his understudy. Jason had never once rehearsed the role of the Winter King and had had enough of Scottish gloom. He'd been so relieved that he'd jumped into his car and headed straight for London and then the surfing beaches of home.

Jamie Clifton turned up alive at Fonthill. After hearing shots, she had pulled herself, terrified and quaking, into an adjoining room, huddling beneath a desk. At her suggestion, the College of Mount Saint Vincent, which had no archival library, loaned the letter from Catherine to Edwin Forrest to the New York Public Library for the Performing Arts, where it could be properly housed and studied. Jamie began a biography of Catherine Sinclair.

Eircheard had been mentoring a young man in Perth, trying to keep him out of the sort of trouble that had landed Eircheard in prison. The fires of the forge had barely gone cold when Lady Nairn offered the youth the use of the smithy; he had moved in the next day. He had a long way to go before he could touch Eircheard's mastery in the making of swords, but he had nothing but time on his hands. That, and determination, and a chance to do something with his life. To become a maker, as Eircheard might have said. Eircheard, said Lady Nairn, would have found that legacy enough.

The morning of Auld Callie's death, Effie Summers had been found on her knees in Dunkeld Cathedral. Thereafter, she'd endured several days of police attention as a prime suspect in that murder. She attributed the revelation of her innocence to divine intervention. Much to Effie's surprise, Lady Nairn agreed. 'Of course,' Lady Nairn told me brightly over the phone, 'our opinions as to the identity of the deity doing the intervening differ markedly. But it did not occur to Effie to ask.' When the cathedral's regular minister returned to work, the Reverend Mr Gosson took his fire and brimstone to another post, and Effie followed him.

Sheena McGregor was promoted to Detective Chief Inspector. Lily went back to school.

In the spring, Lily called to invite me back to Dunsinnan, her voice both shy and excited. She was to be initiated into her grandmother's coven at Beltane: May Day. The other great festival of the Celtic year, the celebration of life and light, as Samhuinn was the celebration of death and darkness. Lily wanted me to present her to the coven.

'It's unusual for an outsider to do the presenting,' said Lady Nairn, after Lily had ceded her the phone and danced away. 'But it's not entirely unheard of. It does complicate things a wee bit, though. There are parts of the rite, you understand, that you may not witness. I must ask you to honour that rule.'

I laughed. 'I won't hide in a bush and watch.'

'There are no bushes,' said Lady Nairn. 'It will be on the hilltop.'

I took a deep breath. If it had been anyone other than Lily, I would have said no in an instant. I was not ready to go back. As it was, it took all my willpower to hold my voice steady. 'I won't go up the hill alone, then.'

'Good girl. Though in this case, it'll be more a question of heading down it, on cue.' Lady Nairn sighed. 'I would have waited, you know. It's customary to require initiates to be at least eighteen. But she has seen the darkest side of the craft, and I've judged it more important to balance that darkness with a vision of the light than to hold to arbitrary considerations of age.'

Balance. It was something I managed, in a fragile way, most days. But I still had to fight for it more nights than I cared to admit, when the smell of blood rose thickly around me.

'How's Ben?'

The question startled me. 'We aren't in touch.' *There are some things that, once seen, cannot be forgotten. Once known, cannot be un-known.* He would never be able to look at me without seeing Sybilla's blood on my hands.

'Never is a very long time,' said Lady Nairn, as if I'd spoken aloud. 'It will become bearable, in time. If you let it.'

I'd said something similar once, to Lily. 'How do you know?' I asked, my voice ragged in my throat.

'I've seen it,' she said simply.

So, on a blustery day at the end of April, I took the train north once more, this time all the way to Perth, where Lady Nairn and Lily picked me up at the station and drove me back to Dunsinnan House.

On a table just inside the door, the silver cauldron was filled with yellow daffodils and bright purple thistles. Up on the bed in the room of pale blue silk and dragons, a dress the colour of peacocks was laid out on my bed. Beside it lay a folder. 'Open it,' said Lily.

Inside was a single scorched page. It seemed to be a letter from a woman writing to an unborn daughter, telling a tale about a death that was not intended and a boy who was not a boy.

'Hal Berridge?' I asked, looking up sharply at Lady Nairn.

'So it would seem.'

The writer went on to claim for the yet-to-be-born girl heritage from Elizabeth Stewart, Lady Arran, and the English wizard John Dee.

'What will you do with this?' I asked.

'Keep it,' she said. 'Keep it quiet. But we thought you had earned the right to know.'

She and Lily soon excused themselves. Lily, however, hung back at the door, her fingers twisting on the doorknob. '*Look like the innocent flower,*' she said bleakly, '*but be the serpent under it.* I've been the serpent, more than the lily.'

'Not necessarily a bad thing: the snake is an old symbol of wisdom, you know. Female wisdom.'

'That's what Gran says.' She smiled wanly. 'From a time when the goddess ruled in harmony with the god, before men set him above her, crushing her serpent beneath his feet. But I've been anything but wise . . . I'm sorry, Kate. Though I don't think I can ever say it properly. Or enough.'

'It's not what you say that will make it have meaning. It's what you do. How you live your life.'

She took a deep breath and straightened. 'Right then. I suppose I'd better go and get on with it. Thank you. Again.' With the brief flash of a grin, she disappeared.

A maid brought dinner to my room on a tray, but I wasn't hungry. I stood at the window for a long time, watching the setting sun light the hill to gold which deepened to pink and purple shadows, draining to grey as the sky fired to liquid sapphire and finally went black. At last I stirred, and began to dress. This far north, dawn would come so early that it was pointless to go to bed. I was to leave early in the morning, directly after the ceremony, to make it back for a rehearsal in London in the afternoon. I could sleep on the train.

At three o'clock in the morning, Lily tapped on my door. She wore a dress of white with a long pointed bodice and tight sleeves that Guinevere would have envied. On her head was a wreath of creamy rowan blossoms that frothed with a heady sweet scent as she moved. In her dress, she might have walked out of a painting or poem by Rossetti, or Millais, or Burne-Jones. But the red hair curling loosely around her was Botticelli's Aphrodite.

Outside, a full moon was spearing itself on the trees to the west. In silence, we walked up the lane to the woods surrounding the stone circle, and I waited while Lily went in to greet her goddess alone.

She came back, her face alight with excitement, and we walked around the hill to the path that led up its northern slope. As we trudged upward, dawn began to silver the eastern sky. We crested the summit and this time I saw two bonfires piled side by side, framing a doorway opening to the east. On the narrow path running between them, someone hunched low, twirling a small stick inside a hole carved in another. A small red glow sprang to life, nursed to a tiny flame. Just as the sun crested the hill's eastern rim, the new fire was divided in two and fed into each stack of wood.

As the sun rose and the fire caught, a man stepped out of the darkness, silhouetted against the growing light. Tall. With curly hair and a way of standing that that I would have known anywhere.

Ben.

Yellow and orange flames licked upwards, crackling, through the bonfires, and he held out a hand to Lily. She took him with her left hand, drawing me forward with her right, and the three of us walked between the fires. Just on the other side, we stopped.

A white candle in her hand, the wreath of pale blossoms around her head, Lily looked like St Lucy. *Lux, lucis*, I thought. The Bride, the Maiden, the personification of Light. Which was, come to think of it, exactly who St Lucy was: another aspect of the goddess that, like Mary, Christianity had taken in and hidden in plain sight, beneath the veil of sainthood.

In the centre of the summit, a circle was marked out with candles, as yet unlit; inside waited a small knot of people. At their feet gleamed the cauldron. Lady Nairn, her hair pale above a shimmering blue gown, raised her arms and called Lily forward. *Lilidh Gruoch MacPhee. Do you enter this circle of your own accord?*

I do, said Lily, dropping our hands and walking forward. As she crossed into the circle there was, ever so slightly, a nod from Lady Nairn. A sign of thanks, a sign of dismissal. Together, Ben and I turned and walked back through the fires.

473

Beside me, I could feel his nearness, though we did not touch. At the edge of the summit, I paused briefly, watching the sun unroll across the wide, sleeping valley below, bird-song rising like lace into air that smelled clean and new. Something brushed my hand. I looked down. Ben's hand, taking mine.

In silence, we headed down the hill. At the bottom, as promised, Lady Nairn's driver was waiting with her Range Rover. Ben opened the door for me, and I slid into the back seat, swallowing back sadness as his fingers slipped from mine.

'*I can call spirits from the vasty deep,*' he said quietly. The phrase from the loch. Glancing up, I saw calm on his face, and the ghost of a smile.

This time, I had a clear enough head to respond. '*But will they come when you do call for them?*' I said, returning his smile.

'Goodbye, Kate.'

For a while, I thought, as the car pulled out from under the shadow of the hill and into the sun. It was not time. Not yet. But it no longer seemed impossible that at some point, one of us would call, and the other would come.

I could see it.

AUTHOR'S NOTE

Macbeth opens with eerie, unearthly condensations of evil adrift on a dark wind, whispering words that gnaw at a good man's mind, propelling him into horrific violence. Belief in such terrifying supernatural malevolence was rife during Shakespeare's lifetime, but on the Renaissance English stage, witches tended to be comic evil: village scolds or cackling hags dealing in grotesque potions. As different from the norm of its day as Stephen King's bone-chilling evil in *The Shining* is from the Disney witches of *Sleeping Beauty, Snow White,* and *The Little Mermaid, Macbeth* is one of the first great horror stories in modern literature.

What makes the 'Scottish Play' different from other tales of terror is that its evil does not stay put in the story. It leaches from the stage, spilling into real life with catastrophic consequences for productions and people – or at least, it has been fervently thought to do so for at least a century. The story of a curse on the play, the theatrical taboos around quoting or naming it, and the ritual for exorcising its evil are long-standing traditions still current among many actors the world over.

The fact that the story of the curse began with a hoax is not very well known, even among Shakespearean scholars. As Kate notes, however, the fin-de-siècle *bon vivant*, wit, and caricaturist Max Beerbohm does seem to have concocted the story of Hal Berridge's death in 1898, at a mischief-provoking moment of boredom with his day (or rather, night) job: reviewing Shakespeare on the stage.

Beerbohm attributed his fib to the seventeenth-century antiquary John Aubrey, and Aubrey, happy magpie that he was, is manna from heaven for a novelist with a need to uncover lost documents and seed trails of evidence. An inveterate gossip with the inclinations of a scholar and the organisational skills of a distracted adolescent, Aubrey recorded historical fact, hearsay, and ludicrous gossip with equal relish, sometimes twining them in the same paragraph, if not the same sentence. His notes are a scattered and incomplete mess. If anyone might have written a long-lost, secretly surviving page recording strange and suggestive tales about Shakespeare and Dee, it was Aubrey. He made notes on both men, after all, within living memory of their deeds, recording details and vignettes preserved nowhere else. And he was a relation of Dee, who was his grandfather's cousin and 'intimate acquaintance'.

So this novel began, in part, with a 'what if?': *What if Max Beerbohm really did find the tale of Hal Berridge in an Aubrey manuscript? What if Aubrey had told the truth? What if the curse of Macbeth extended all the way back to the beginning?* What then? What might be the source of *Macbeth*'s admittedly strange power to frighten both audiences and actors?

This set me to wondering about the magic in *Macbeth*. As first published in 1623 in the First Folio – the first edition of Shakespeare's collected works – the play is uneven in its sinister vision. In addition to the three spectral Weird Sisters, the Witch Queen Hecate arrives to sing and dance with all the chortling glee that English audiences expected from stage witches: think of Walt Disney and Stephen King competing for the soul of a single film. So sharp is the chasm between Hecate and the Weird Sisters that scholars have long suspected that Hecate – who makes no necessary contribution to the play's action – is a late intrusion.

The general scholarly consensus is that someone other than Shakespeare revised the original *Macbeth* at some point before publication, bringing it more into line with what audiences would happily pay to see, namely evil that was more amusing than horrifying. To do so, the reviser turned to *The Witch*, by Thomas Middleton, which also has a witch-character named Hecate. The reviser lifted some silly songs from Middleton's newer play into Shakespeare's old play, and wrote in a new version of Hecate (very different from Middleton's) in order to explain the sudden burst of song and dance amid the gloom. It's the sort of light-fingered patchwork that was then part and parcel of the quick-turnaround mill of the theatre.

As time went on, this alteration was intensified. By the time *Macbeth* reappeared on the Restoration stage in 1666, the witches had grown in number from three to an entire Ziegfeld chorus of hags, some of them zooming about overhead on wires. Even while noting that they were 'a strange perfection in a tragedy', the diarist Samuel Pepys thought the witches' song-and-dance bits, or 'divertissements' as he called them, the best part of the play. Interest in 'authentic' Shakespeare revived across the nineteenth century, and major productions gradually pared the play back to the text in the First Folio . . . but that is the earliest version of *Macbeth* that survives. What did the witches and their magic look like in Shakespeare's original?

Many scholars and directors happily pluck out Hecate and her songs and leave it at that. It's possible, however, that the alterations were more extensive. For starters, the play's central scene of witchcraft, the cauldron scene – Act Four, scene one – is an odd cobbling of grotesque cauldron magic and the learned magic of conjuring demonic spirits. Furthermore, there are other scenes that appear out of order and garbled. Finally, *Macbeth* is remarkably short: one of Shakespeare's shortest plays in any genre, and easily the shortest of his tragedies. Of the four great tragedies he wrote in the first five years of King James's reign, the others – *Othello*, *King Lear*, and *Antony and Cleopatra* – are all longer by roughly a thousand lines or more. *Hamlet* – written at the end of Queen Elizabeth's reign – is nearly twice as long. What, if anything, has gone missing from *Macbeth*?

It is impossible to say, but intriguing to wonder about: and in the wide space of that wonder, this novel was born.

In this novel, the key objects of blade, mirror, and cauldron are all real, or based on real objects. With two exceptions, the places where I've set major scenes are all real places with links to the historical King Macbeth, famous productions and actors of Shakespeare's play, or historical people whose lives Shakespeare may have used in shaping his play. I have altered them, in some cases, to suit the fiction, however. The myths are real – as myths – and the magical traditions and ideas of both the 'black' and 'white' variety have been put forward, historically, as real magic, though not necessarily tied specifically to *Macbeth*. Save for Carrie's final attempt to invoke a demonic spirit, however, the specific rites of black magic concocted by Lucas, Ian, and Carrie are my own inventions. For the most part, the historical characters are fantasias on fact. The modern characters are all fictional.

Samhuinn is the Scottish Gaelic name for the ancient pagan Celtic festival better known in some circles by its Irish name of *Samhain*, and certainly widely known across the world by its Christian-co-opted descendant of All Hallow's Eve or Halloween. It is one of the two great fire festivals of the old

479

Celtic year once celebrated across the British Isles and Ireland – and much of western Europe, for that matter. The other is Beltane, or May Day. Whereas Beltane celebrates fertility, sex and new birth, Spring and Summer, and the return of light, Samhuinn celebrates – or at least acknowledges – death and the dead, Autumn and Winter, and darkness. In the Scottish Highlands, Samhuinn was celebrated into the early twentieth-century with bonfires on hilltops. Various folk traditions suggest that once upon a very long time ago, the celebration may have included sacrifice, possibly human sacrifice.

Edinburgh's Samhuinn Fire Festival, run by the Beltane Fire Society, is a spectacular yearly celebration of this ancient holiday. I have tried to be as accurate as possible to the carnival spirit of actual performances, which change every year, though the basic story of the Cailleach and the two battling kings remains the same. I have had to alter some practices, however, in order to slot my characters into main roles. In particular, Lily is too young to be involved, and I doubt that the BFS would ever cast a film star like Jason Pierce in a lead role in exchange for money. I hope the Society's members will forgive me those lapses as minor technicalities and enjoy the festival's fictional appearance in a thriller.

Whether or not Shakespeare ever travelled to Scotland is unknown. In fact, we know nothing at all of his whereabouts between the christening of his twins Hamnet and

480

Judith in Stratford-upon-Avon, on 2 February, 1585, and 1592, when he had made enough of a name for – and by some lights, a nuisance of – himself on the London stage to be attacked by Robert Greene in his *Groatworth of Wit* as an 'upstart crow', a 'Shake-scene' stealing other men's thunder. However, the Scottish geography in *Macbeth* is surprisingly accurate – I had no idea just how accurate, in fact, until I started to research this book. That he might have been in Scotland is as much a possibility as him being anywhere else; companies of English players travelled north of the border with some frequency.

In 1583, Queen Elizabeth's spymaster, Sir Francis Walsingham, forced a reorganisation of England's theatrical companies by cherry-picking the best actors from each for a new company called the Queen's Men. Why he did so is unclear: he was not a known patron or enthusiast of theatre, nor were players part of his day-to-day concerns as a secretary of state. (Regulating the players was part of the Lord Chamberlain's duties.) Walsingham's motives may well have included weaving actors into his network of spies. Roving players, after all, offered perfect cover for watchful eyes and ears inside the far-flung houses of the great. At the very least, as scholars Scott McMillin and Sally-Beth MacLean have argued in *The Queen's Men and Their Plays*, from this point on, Elizabeth's spymaster used government licensing of travelling acting troupes to give the impression of a vast network of watchfulness. Later, Walsingham certainly used some playwrights, most famously Christopher Marlowe, and possibly Thomas Kyd, as spies. It is my imagining that the young Shakespeare might also, willingly or unwillingly, have been among his 'intelligencers'. It does seem likely, however, that any player caught in the dubious circumstances into which I set Mr Shakespeare at Dirleton would have found himself suspected as a spy.

In the autumn of 1589, the Queen's Men were sent north to Edinburgh to join in the celebration of King James's impending marriage to Princess Anne of Denmark. The celebrations had to be postponed after storms drove the princess's fleet back from Scottish shores, all the way to Scandinavia, and the impatient king took ship in pursuit. (Eventually, those storms were blamed on witches, resulting in one of the worst witch-hunts in Scottish history, spearheaded by King James himself, but that is another story.) That same year, civic records show that a company of English players acted in Perth, about ten miles distant from Dunsinnan and within striking distance of Dunkeld and Birnam Wood. I am not the first to wonder whether a 25-year-old actor named William Shakespeare could have been among them. The Dunsinnan House account book, however, is a fictional document.

Shakespeare's main source for *Macbeth* was Raphael Holinshed's *Chronicles of England, Scotland, and Ireland*. He did not rely solely on the history of King Macbeth, however, but pieced together a story using dramatic episodes from the lives of other kings. In particular, he had to fish about for the story of Lady Macbeth because the historical Lady Macbeth, whose name was Gruoch (Lily's middle name), is little more than a blank. It is usual to see Shakespeare spinning her tale from the brief mention of another nobleman's revenge-urging wife. Some scholars, however, have also noted the uncanny resemblance that her story bears to the near-contemporary history of Elizabeth Stewart, countess of Arran.

This lady was, as stated in the novel, the daughter of John Stewart, fourth Earl of Atholl. The date of her birth is unknown, though it must have been after May, 1547, when her parents married, and before 1 April, 1557, when her father remarried, following her mother's death. She was married herself on 24 December, 1567, which would make her only thirteen by the birth year of 1554 sometimes proposed for her (without, so far as I can tell, any basis in fact); I have chosen to push her birth to an early point in her parents' marriage, mostly to allow for a fictional meeting with John Dee at a time when he was in Antwerp in 1563.

She went through three husbands: Hugh Fraser, fifth Lord Lovat, who died suddenly and some thought suspiciously in 1577; the king's elderly great-uncle Robert Stewart, successively Earl of Lennox and then Earl of March, whom she married in 1579 and divorced in 1581, on grounds of impotence while pregnant with her third husband's child; and the swashbuckling Captain James Stewart, for a time Earl of Arran, whom she married two months after her divorce from March was final. She did have royal, if also bastard, blood in her veins, as one of her maternal great-grandmothers was an illegitimate daughter of Scotland's King James IV. A Highlander both by birth and by her first marriage, she was said to frequent 'the oracles of the Highlands' and possibly to be a witch herself. She was also said to lust after the crown.

She appears to have been both fashionable and sensuous, with a French-inflected sophistication of style, speech, and sexual morality that bewitched the king but made his Calvinist ministers come close to spitting with rage. The story of her breaking open Queen Mary's chests of gowns and jewels as soon as her husband was given the keys to Edinburgh Castle was recorded by the English ambassador to Scotland.

For a while in the early 1580s, she and her third husband were two of King James's most trusted courtiers, people he sought out for both policy and play. So quick and decisive was their rise to power that they aroused envy and fear on the part of almost everyone else around the king. After they fell from grace in late 1585, they took refuge, just as Kate discovers, with her eldest son by her first marriage, Simon Fraser, sixth Lord Lovat, in the lands of Clan Fraser, south and west of Inverness, where they were said to live on a remote isle in Loch Bruiach. It is a place that is still surprisingly remote, a distillation of the stark beauty of the Highlands.

The earl's end mimics Macbeth's – though perhaps it was the other way around: as Kate says, in 1596 he was ambushed by enemies who cut off his head and flaunted it on the tip of a lance. With enemies like that, their long sojourn on a remote island becomes understandable.

Lady Arran's end is somewhat mysterious and at least metaphorically off-stage, just like Lady Macbeth's. She was first reported dead in childbed in 1590. Elsewhere, she was said to have died 'miserably' in 1595 up in the Highlands; perhaps that misery was a euphemism for the suicidal end that Shakespeare suggests for Lady Macbeth. Yet another, later, tradition has her die swollen to marvellous size, thus fulfilling a prophecy that she should be the greatest woman in all Scotland. The possibility that she was attacked as a witch is my own addition to history.

How Shakespeare came across her story is also unknown, though a handful of English players working in London as he rose to fame had a fair amount of experience working in Scotland, and might have told him her tale. Among these was the king's favourite English actor during his tenure in Scotland, Lawrence Fletcher, another of the original members of the King's Men. It seems equally possible, however, that if Shakespeare went up to Scotland in his youth, he might have learned of her – or seen her – for himself, and possibly even acted before her.

The Arrans are known to have entertained James with a sumptuous feast and a play of Robin Hood when the king spent twelve days at their newly acquired castle of Dirleton, beginning on 1 May, 1585 – as it happens, the old Celtic festival of Beltane. The king was not coming to celebrate either May Day or Beltane, however, but to escape a fierce outbreak of plague in Edinburgh. The earl is said to have fallen deathly ill after the banquet – perhaps he left abruptly in the middle. While the festivities at that castle are historical, Shakespeare's appearance there is of my making.

John Dee was one of the foremost intellectuals in England during Shakespeare's lifetime, though he was shown more respect on the Continent. His interests, whether focused on mathematics or magic, were both theoretical and practical.

He was in Antwerp in early 1563, copying an exceedingly rare manuscript of the *Steganographia* by Johannes Trithemius: a work nominally about using angels and demons to convey secret messages at a distance. In reality, it is a book about codes, in code. Dee knew that about the first two books; the code of the third book is not known to have been broken until the late twentieth century, and was generally believed to be about demonic magic, as it claimed to be. Whether or not Dee possessed the secret of the third book is unknown. It is this manuscript that I have imagined him accepting the young Lady Elizabeth Stewart's help in copying.

Most of Dee's life is traceable through letters and diaries, including a spiritual diary that covers in detail many of his attempts to invoke angels. No diaries survive, however, from 1601 to his death in 1608 or 1609, the period that covers the discovery of the Gunpowder Plot and the writing of *Macbeth*. This may be because he had stopped keeping a diary; on the other hand, his diary may have been destroyed.

Dee was not adept at seeing spirits in his mirrors and crystal balls himself; he almost always used a seer or scryer. His eldest son Arthur tried to fill this role for a time during his boyhood, but apparently with no more success than his father had. For many years, Dee's most trusted scryer was a man named Edward Kelley – who seems, at this distance in time, to have been at least half con man, a fact that makes it very difficult to understand Dee. Kelley and Dee parted ways on the Continent, however, before Dee returned to England in 1589.

Beyond the close of Dee's surviving diary in 1601, we know very little about his scryers or his dealings with the spirit world. Persistent rumours repeated through the nineteenth century, however, said that he – or one of his scryers – foretold the Gunpowder Plot by seeing it in a mirror. Linking his scryer and his black mirror to the boy-actor Hal Berridge and the mirror in *Macbeth* is my fiction.

That Dee's papers are fragmentary should not, perhaps, be surprising. What's astonishing is that any of them survived. The first editor of his spiritual diary, published in 1659, claimed that Sir Robert Cotton, the collector of a library perhaps even greater than Dee's, dug up a number of

Dee's manuscript diaries from his garden. Others were discovered in a hidden compartment in an old chest and partly used up by a cook looking for scrap paper to line her pie tins before her master realised what she was using.

Dee invoked angels into mirrors and 'show stones' or crystal balls. The black obsidian mirror stolen by the witches in this book is a real object, and its history as given is pretty accurate: it was once a ritual object belonging to the Aztec god Tezcatlipoca. Dee is thought to have acquired it during his travels on the Continent, when he would have had easier opportunity to come into contact with Spanish culture, including precious objects plundered from the New World, than he would have had at home, at least after Queen Elizabeth's Protestant reign set England and Spain at odds.

That is, if Dee acquired it at all. The attribution to Dee comes from Horace Walpole's eighteenth-century identification, which is based on hearsay and does not clearly trace the mirror's passage back through time to Dee. Walpole's claim, however, is certainly seductive and has long been accepted as the likely truth. The mirror is on display – as Dee's – in the British Museum's Enlightenment Gallery.

The other mirror – Lady Nairn's mirror claiming to be a prop used by the King's Men – is a figment of my imagination. So far as I know no known prop certainly belonging to that company has survived.

Lady Nairn's silver cauldron – and the cauldron in Joanna's shop, for that matter – are both based on the huge Gundestrup Cauldron, in the National Museum of Denmark, in Copenhagen: the most glorious silver object of Iron-Age Celtic Europe. Probably made in the first century BC, it shows, among other scenes, a horned man sitting cross-legged and holding a serpent, and another man being thrown into a cauldron: possibly a scene of human sacrifice.

The cauldron symbol that Carrie uses is a real Pictish symbol found on stone carvings in Scotland.

The knife that Kate finds is no particular real knife, but a variant on the *seax*, a single-edged style of blade used by Anglo-Saxons, Vikings, and Scots – both men and women – throughout the pagan period. Several knives and swords of similar date have been found with runic inscriptions, some of which appear to have been magical.

In Wiccan tradition, a black-handled knife or *athame* is part of the ritual equipment used by each individual witch. *Athames* are not used for cutting, which is actually taboo: they are used for directing energy. White-handled knives, or *bolines*, are used when cutting, carving or whittling is necessary. Carrie and Ian's willingness to use their knives not only for cutting but for killing sets them far beyond the bounds of any acceptable behaviour in Wiccan practice.

The making of pattern-welded blades is an ancient and exacting art. There are still a few swordsmiths in Scotland

and elsewhere, however, forging blades that men like the real Macbeth would probably love to have wielded.

Dunsinnan Hill is a real place with the remains of an Iron Age hill fort at its top. Medieval Scottish chronicles say that Macbeth refortified it with great difficulty, and apparently with great irritation to his followers. It has been excavated twice, in the early and mid nineteenth century. The trenches from those excavations still pock the summit, which has fine views of Strathmore and the Highlands to the north. Lower down the hill, a modern and still active quarry has significantly gnawed away the western side of the hill, though the summit with its fort is protected.

There are more legends and stories about this hill than I could include in this novel. The nineteenth-century excavations, for instance, found evidence of collapsed souterrains – or stone-lined underground chambers of unknown – but possibly ritual – significance. One of them is said to have held three skeletons: a man, a woman, and a child with a battered skull. Other tales say that the hill was once the hiding place of the real Stone of Scone or Stone of Destiny.

At the western foot of the hill is a small wood that hides the Bandirran Stone Circle. There is a cottage or bothy roughly where I put Eircheard's smithy. So far as I know, it has never been used as a forge.

In contrast to the hill and the stone circle, Dunsinnan House is a castle of my making; a farmhouse stands in roughly the spot where I situated it. There is an actual Dunsinnan House – which I discovered after I had already built my fictional one – but it is in a different place and has nothing to do with the building in this novel.

The Birnam Oak and its two companion sycamores are all that remain of the primordial virgin forest that once blanketed much of the lower Highlands. They do seem, as Kate muses, *creatures from an elder world*.

The island in Loch Bruiach is a crannog: a man-made islet probably first constructed in the Neolithic or Iron Age periods. There is no castle on it, and I have my doubts whether it could support such a heavy stone structure, other than in fiction. However, if the Fraser chronicles are to be believed, it must once have sported a suitable home for a dowager Lady Lovat. I based my castle on three buildings: the ruined Castle Urquhart on the shores of nearby Loch Ness, the rebuilt castle of Eilean Donan, on Scotland's western shores, and Fonthill, in Riverdale, New York.

The current incarnation of Her Majesty's Theatre was built for Sir Herbert Beerbohm Tree; it opened its doors in 1897. It is the fourth theatre to stand on the same site on Haymarket, which has been part of London's theatrical world since the Restoration. Since 1986, it has been running *Phantom of the Opera*. Beerbohm Tree's dome room is a real place, currently rented out as rehearsal space, though both the secret cupboard and its cache of occult books are my invention. With the exception of *DEE and the Theatre*, the titles of the books in that cupboard, however, are real – and each of those volumes potentially quite valuable.

Joanna Black Books and Esoterica is obviously a fictional shop, but Cecil Court, the street in which it stands, is one of my favourites in all of London. Joanna's shop is a composite of actual occult bookshops elsewhere in London, descriptions of John Dee's library as it once existed out in Mortlake, and other details from my imagination. The name 'Joanna Black', is a female and anglicised version of John Dee: Joanna being a feminine form of John, and Dee coming from the Welsh *du*, meaning 'black'.

In New York, Jamie Clifton's condo is in a real building that now stands on the spot of the Astor Place Opera House: ground zero of the 1849 riot. A large Starbucks on the ground floor gives the public access to at least a portion of the building.

Up in Riverdale, Edwin Forrest laid the cornerstone of Fonthill Castle in 1848 as a token of love for his wife Catherine, but by the time it was finished, the couple had split in a scandalous divorce. The oculus and the cross in the floor of the central octagonal hall are remarkable design features. I have added, however, the Shakespearean scenes sculpted on the walls, as well as the secret hiding place in the floor. The name – and certain design elements – were indeed borrowed by the Forrests from William Beckford's Fonthill

Abbey in England. The castle is now the Admissions Building of Mount Saint Vincent College.

As Kate notes, the saga of Edwin Forrest and Catherine Sinclair reads like a Shakespearean tragedy; his behaviour towards his once adored wife seems as irrational, unjust and toweringly egotistical as Othello's. Forrest at least opted to end the marriage in divorce rather than his wife's death. On the other hand, his cruelty to her remained implacable. He never seems to have experienced even the small surge of repentance and grace that Shakespeare granted to Othello. Catherine Forrest, after losing four children and then the husband that she loved, took back her maiden name of Catherine Norton Sinclair and went west to make her own way in the theatre, leaving a lasting mark of sophistication on the dramatic tastes of gold-rush California. After touring Australia and then England, she retired to New York where she quietly lived out the remainder of her days, first with a sister and then with a nephew. She never remarried. I know of no record that she returned to London to see Ellen Terry in *Macbeth* in 1889, though she lived long enough to have done so. Her earlier journey to Loch Bruiach and acquisition of a *Macbeth* manuscript are fictional.

By all accounts, Ellen Terry's Lady Macbeth was one of the finest in history. John Singer Sargent's monumental 1890 painting of her in her blue beetle-wing costume is one of the treasures of the Tate Britain. The original gown is housed in

Terry's cottage of Smallhythe Place, in Kent, now run by the National Trust. She was a friend and colleague of Sir Herbert Beerbohm Tree, but her letter to Monsieur Superbe Homme is my forgery.

Beerbohm Tree's 1916 film of *Macbeth* is one of the great lost productions both of Shakespeare and of silent-era Hollywood. A few still photographs survive: it is from these that I took the descriptions of set and costume.

ACKNOWLEDGEMENTS

This book owes more than usual to the heroic ministrations of Brian Tart, my editor and publisher at Dutton, his assistant Jessica Horvath, and my agent Noah Lukeman. Together, they nursed and prodded it – and me – through a writer's block of cursed proportion; all that is good about this book owes its existence to them. Thanks, too, to David Shelley, Thalia Proctor, and Sphere for their patience and speed.

I had the great good fortune to have advice and help from numerous experts while researching places, people, and practices for this book. I would like to give special thanks to Wiccan priestesses Ashleen O'Gaea and Carol Garr, along with their covens, for their openness and generosity.

In Scotland, Helen Bradburn, Cailleach of the 2008 Samhuinn Fire Festival in Edinburgh, gave me invaluable insight into the workings of that spectacular celebration. Colin Campbell, a photographer with a fine eye for the Scottish landscape, along with his wife Linda and dog Cal, got me out to Loch Bruiach on a silent, snowy November afternoon. Jamie and Karen Sinclair gave me the great gift of a family paper on the history of the real King Macbeth, as well as the loan of their collection of books on Dunsinnan and its environs while I was in the area, traipsing up and down the hill. Inspector Paddy Buckley-Jones of the Tayside Police kindly enlightened me on some details of police procedure; any irregularities in police behaviour in this book are my fault, not his.

In London, Chris Green, House Manager, Paul Rotchell, Assistant Manager, and John Fitzsimmons, Theatre Manager, all ensured that I learned what I needed to know about Her Majesty's Theatre; Chris gave me a much appreciated tour of Sir Herbert Beerbohm Tree's dome room. Jamie de Courcey served as my eyes and ears at the British Museum at times when I could not drop in myself; Dr Silke Ackermann, Curator of the British Museum's European Department, helped with the workings of the museum and its collections, John Dee's mirror in particular. Christina Oakley Harrington and her staff at Treadwell's Bookshop identified useful books on various occult subjects.

In New York, Sister Carol Finegan, Director of Institutional Research, gave me a long and detailed tour of Fonthill Castle, now the Admissions Building of Mount Saint Vincent College, in Riverdale.

On the academic front, Professor Dan Donoghue of Harvard University's English Department undertook to translate some Shakespeare into Anglo-Saxon poetry, and then transliterate it into runes. Chris Tabraham, Principal Historian for Historic Scotland, helped me with details of Edinburgh Castle and its environs as they would have been in the sixteenth and early seventeenth centuries. Stuart Ivinson, Library Assistant at the Royal Armouries in Leeds, provided much needed research on Anglo-Saxon and Norse knives and swords, and John Oliver, Curator (Fiction) of the BFI National Archive at the British Film Institute enlightened me on material aspects of silent-era films.

Others who helped with various angles of research are: Ilana Addis, Martin Brueckner, Brian Schuyler, Bill Fetzer, John Alexander, Eric Baker, Bill Kapfer, René Andersen, Lauren Galit, David Ira Goldstein, Nick Saunders, Louise Park, Bill Carrell, Laura Fulginiti, Sandy and Brian Stearns, Jill Jorden Spitz, Stephanie Innes, Pamela Treadwell-Rubin, and Assistant Chief Kathleen Robinson and Susan M. Shankles, Crime Laboratory Superintendent, both of the Tucson Police Department.

Charlotte Lowe and Ellen Grounds both read parts of the manuscript and gave encouraging feedback. Dave Grounds has a special and much appreciated talent for listening to me wander through tangled thickets of plot and then cutting straight through the chaos with sensible suggestions. My mother, Melinda Carrell, and Kristen Poole remain two of my most trusted readers.

Without my husband, John Helenbolt, this book would never have seen the light of day. He and our son Will give me day-to-day proof that the world is indeed full of strange and wonderful magic.